Monstrous Affections
by David Nickle

ChiZine Publications

FIRST EDITION, SECOND PRINTING

Montrous Affections © 2009 by David Nickle
"The Geniality of Monsters" © 2009 by Michael Rowe
Jacket artwork © 2009 by Erik Mohr
All Rights Reserved.

LIBRARY AND ARCHIVES CANADA CATALOGUING IN PUBLICATION

Nickle, David, 1964-
Monstrous affections / David Nickle ; editors: Brett Alexander Savory &
Sandra Kasturi ; graphic designer/cover artist: Erik Mohr.

ISBN 978-0-9812978-1-1 (bound).--ISBN 978-0-9812978-3-5 (pbk.)

I. Savory, Brett Alexander, 1973- II. Kasturi, Sandra, 1966- III. Title.

PS8577.I33M65 2009   C813'.54   C2009-903945-1

CHIZINE PUBLICATIONS
Toronto, Canada
www.chizinepub.com
info@chizinepub.com

Edited by Sandra Kasturi
Copyedited and proofread by Brett Alexander Savory

To Karen Fernandez, whose affection is never monstrous and always essential.

Table of Contents

The Geniality of Monsters
by Michael Rowe

It's a truism that horror cannot exist separate from comfort, safety, and love. It is impossible to experience horror—which is a destination, not a departure point—without first experiencing the security of a place, literal or conceptual, from which the ground will fall away, revealing a vast, awful blackness of terrible possibility; a cold lightless country of sharp teeth and claws. An eternally rediscovered country where pain is the default national condition, and terror is the gross national product.

The stories in *Monstrous Affections* are indeed horror stories by any objective standard, and they are superlative horror stories—the work of a scrupulous and demanding writer who would wrestle the Devil himself for a the perfect word. Within these pages you will meet a variety of monsters, including a Cyclops, a family of mutants with a terrible gift for love, and yet another family with harsh ideas about generational hierarchies and the price of defiance. But they are also first-rate short stories of high literary quality. No less an authority than Peter Straub has written of the entirely *ersatz* classification system that keeps certain stories, and certain writers, outside the velvet ropes of the self-perpetuating bookish elite no matter how excellent, how transcendent, the writing is.

There is writing of that calibre among the short stories in *Monstrous Affections*.

The term "Canadian gothic" is an overused one, and it has come to mean many things to many people—readers, critics, academics, and students—over the course of the development of Canadian literature as a self-conscious literary school. It's not often applied to horror fiction, largely because of unfortunately persistent literary prejudices and stereotypes. But I would say that, first and foremost, the Canadian gothic literary canon is where I would place the speculative fiction work of David Nickle.

The majority of his work is set unapologetically in Canada, his homeland. For a speculative fiction writer, that has traditionally been a challenge due to a perception that American editors and readers will not take horror fiction seriously with a Canadian setting.

On the other hand, this is one of the areas where, among horror writers who are also serious literary writers, the men are separated from the boys (and indeed the women from the girls— to wit, the blood-ruby short fiction of International Horror Guild Award-winner Gemma Files). Nickle's vision of Canada will be a revelation to any reader who might be expecting the round-edged, inoffensive, long-suffering Canada of legend. His literary road trip along the moonlit country roads of the various small towns that dot the farmland outside the cities (especially the town of Fenlan, his particular corner of the dark universe) will be, simultaneously, immediately recognizable to anyone who is familiar with small towns, and dreadfully disorienting in the way a dream gone terribly wrong is disorienting, especially when you try to wake up, and realize you can't. I dislike clichéd terms like "national treasure," but David Nickle is a succinct answer to the endless gripe about why Canada hasn't produced more horror stars.

He knows the undertaste of familial relationships—for instance, in "The Sloan Men," the time-honoured rite-of-supplication of meeting your true love's mother for the first time—and how they can be pushed to the literal edge of madness. He understands, as in "Polyphemus' Cave," exactly what love and loyalty cost, and that sometimes all it takes is a little nudge to the brink of darkness to turn the process of growth into a scarlet, blood-soaked scream.

But mostly, he understands that horror really can't exist separate from comfort, safety, and love—or friendship. My personal favourite in this collection is "The Webley," a story marked by a singular absence of the supernatural or the paranormal. The monsters in

"The Webley" live in the most spectral realm of existence extant, the human mind. It's a story that contains an essential quality of heartbreak and poisoned nostalgia that will haunt you, and follow you like the sound of breathing in a dark room. Breathing you know isn't your own. His monsters can, on occasion, be quite genial. But make no mistake; they are monsters in every sense of the word.

What to say of David Nickle personally? How to separate the dancer from the dance? If we must, here's a sketch: He's a good and loyal friend. He's fiercely intelligent and kind. He's a gentleman around women (and around men too, for that matter) and he can hold his liquor. He's affable about giving rides home from conventions to friends without cars. He's dry, funny as hell, and generous to a fault. Also, he's not bad looking, to be honest.

OK, enough?

Having been his editor over the course of three original horror fiction anthologies, I can say without reservation that he is one of the most professional authors I've ever worked with. He's a courageous writer who isn't afraid to step outside his comfort zone in the service of his fiction, and a deadly serious one when it comes to pushing himself and his material through however many drafts it takes till the story is as close to perfect as he feels it can be, a fact I see amply reiterated in this first, stellar collection of his best short stories.

This closed book is—or was—that comfortable place I spoke of earlier, the aforementioned place of comfort, safety and love, the border between safety and a world tilted into chaos. The act of opening the covers has set horrible, efficient machinery into motion. And you are solely responsible for what you have released into the world by starting it up. When you close your eyes tonight, your dreams will serve as a subterranean passageway for any of the monsters, which had previously been safely contained within the pages of this book, to tunnel their way out into the world.

Your world. Our world. *My* world.

Thank you *so* very much for that, my dear. It isn't as if we don't all have nightmares of our own to contend with, without you dreaming your own into existence—with David Nickle, the author of this collection, as your medium.

The Farmhouse, Toronto
Summer 2009

The Sloan Men

Mrs. Sloan had only three fingers on her left hand, but when she drummed them against the countertop, the tiny polished bones at the end of the fourth and fifth stumps clattered like fingernails. If Judith hadn't been looking, she wouldn't have noticed anything strange about Mrs. Sloan's hand.

"Tell me how you met Herman," said Mrs. Sloan. She turned away from Judith as she spoke, to look out the kitchen window where Herman and his father were getting into Mr. Sloan's black pickup truck. Seeing Herman and Mr. Sloan together was a welcome distraction for Judith. She was afraid Herman's stepmother would catch her staring at the hand. Judith didn't know how she would explain that with any grace: *Things are off to a bad enough start as it is.*

Outside, Herman wiped his sleeve across his pale, hairless scalp and, seeing Judith watching from the window, turned the gesture into an exaggerated wave. He grinned wetly through the late afternoon sun. Judith felt a little grin of her own growing and waved back, fingers waggling an infantile bye-bye. *Hurry home*, she mouthed through the glass. Herman stared back blandly, not understanding.

"Did you meet him at school?"

Judith flinched. The drumming had stopped, and when she looked, Mrs. Sloan was leaning against the counter with her mutilated hand hidden in the crook of crossed arms. Judith hadn't even seen the woman move.

"No," Judith finally answered. "Herman doesn't go to school. Neither do I."

Mrs. Sloan smiled. She had obviously been a beautiful woman in her youth—in most ways she still was. Mrs. Sloan's hair was auburn and it played over her eyes mysteriously, like a movie star's. She had cheekbones that Judith's ex-boss Talia would have called sculpted, and the only signs of her age were the tiny crow's feet at her eyes and harsh little lines at the corners of her mouth.

"I didn't mean to imply anything," said Mrs. Sloan. "Sometimes he goes to school, sometimes museums, sometimes just shopping plazas. That's Herman."

Judith expected Mrs. Sloan's smile to turn into a laugh, underscoring the low mockery she had directed towards Herman since he and Judith had arrived that morning. But the woman kept quiet, and the smile dissolved over her straight white teeth. She regarded Judith thoughtfully.

"I'd thought it might be school because you don't seem that old," said Mrs. Sloan. "Of course I don't usually have an opportunity to meet Herman's lady friends, so I suppose I really can't say."

"I met Herman on a tour. I was on vacation in Portugal, I went there with a girl I used to work with, and when we were in Lisbon—"

"—Herman appeared on the same tour as you. Did your girlfriend join you on that outing, or were you alone?"

"Stacey got food poisoning." *As I was about to say.* "It was a rotten day, humid and muggy." Judith wanted to tell the story the way she'd told it to her own family and friends, countless times. It had its own rhythm; her fateful meeting with Herman Sloan in the roped-off scriptorium of the monastery outside Lisbon, dinner that night in a vast, empty restaurant deserted in the off-season. In the face of Mrs. Sloan, though, the rhythm of that telling was somehow lost. Judith told it as best she could.

"So we kept in touch," she finished lamely.

Mrs. Sloan nodded slowly and didn't say anything for a moment. Try as she might, Judith couldn't read the woman, and she had always prided herself on being able to see through most people at least half way. That she couldn't see into this person at all was particularly irksome, because of who she was—a potential *in-law*, for God's sake. Judith's mother had advised her, "Look at the parents if you want to see what kind of man the love of your life will be in thirty years. See if you can love them with all their faults, all their habits. Because that's how things'll be . . ."

Judith realized again that she wanted very much for things to be just fine with Herman thirty years down the line. But if this afternoon were any indication . . .

Herman had been uneasy about the two of them going to Fenlan to meet his parents at all. But, as Judith explained, it was a necessary step. She knew it, even if Herman didn't—as soon as they turned off the highway he shut his eyes and wouldn't open them until Judith pulled into the driveway.

Mr. Sloan met them and Herman seemed to relax then, opening his eyes and blinking in the sunlight. Judith relaxed too, seeing the two of them together. They were definitely father and son, sharing features and mannerisms like images in a mirror. Mr. Sloan took Judith up in a big, damp hug the moment she stepped out of the car. The gesture surprised her at first and she tried to pull away, but Mr. Sloan's unstoppable grin had finally put her at ease.

"You *are* very lovely," said Mrs. Sloan finally. "That's to be expected, though. Tell me what you do for a living. Are you still working now that you've met Herman?"

Judith wanted to snap something clever at the presumption, but she stopped herself. "I'm working. Not at the same job, but in another salon. I do people's hair, and I'm learning manicure."

Mrs. Sloan seemed surprised. "Really? I'm impressed."

Now Judith was sure Mrs. Sloan was making fun, and a sluice of anger passed too close to the surface. "I work hard," she said hotly. "It may not seem—"

Mrs. Sloan silenced her with shushing motions. "Don't take it the wrong way," she said. "It's only that when I met Herman's father, I think I stopped working the very next day."

"Those must have been different times."

"They weren't *that* different." Mrs. Sloan's smile was narrow and ugly. "Perhaps Herman's father just needed different things."

"Well, I'm still working."

"So you say." Mrs. Sloan got up from the kitchen stool. "Come to the living room, dear. I've something to show you."

The shift in tone was too sudden, and it took Judith a second to realize she'd even been bidden. Mrs. Sloan half-turned at the kitchen door, and beckoned with her five-fingered hand.

"Judith," she said, "you've come this far already. You might as well finish the journey."

The living room was distastefully bare. The walls needed paint and there was a large brown stain on the carpet that Mrs. Sloan hadn't even bothered to cover up. She sat down on the sofa and Judith joined her.

"I wanted you to see the family album. I think—" Mrs. Sloan reached under the coffee table and lifted out a heavy black-bound volume "—I don't know, but I hope . . . you'll find this interesting."

Mrs. Sloan's face lost some of its hardness as she spoke. She finished with a faltering smile.

"I'm sure I will," said Judith. This was a good development, more like what she had hoped the visit would become. Family albums and welcoming hugs and funny stories about what Herman was like when he was two. She snuggled back against the tattered cushions and looked down at the album. "This must go back generations."

Mrs. Sloan still hadn't opened it. "Not really," she said. "As far as I know, the Sloans never mastered photography on their own. All of the pictures in here are mine."

"May I . . . ?" Judith put out her hands, and with a shrug Mrs. Sloan handed the album over.

"I should warn you—" began Mrs. Sloan.

Judith barely listened. She opened the album to the first page.

And shut it, almost as quickly. She felt her face flush, with shock and anger. She looked at Mrs. Sloan, expecting to see that cruel, nasty smile back again. But Mrs. Sloan wasn't smiling.

"I was about to say," said Mrs. Sloan, reaching over and taking the album back, "that I should warn you, this isn't an ordinary family album."

"I—" Judith couldn't form a sentence she was so angry. No

wonder Herman hadn't wanted her to meet his family.

"I took that photograph almost a year after I cut off my fingers," said Mrs. Sloan. "Photography became a small rebellion for me, not nearly so visible as the mutilation. Herman's father still doesn't know about it, even though I keep the book out here in full view. Sloan men don't open books much.

"But we do, don't we, Judith?"

Mrs. Sloan opened the album again, and pointed at the Polaroid on the first page. Judith wanted to look away, but found that she couldn't.

"Herman's father brought the three of them home early, before I'd woken up—I don't know where he found them. Maybe he just called, and they were the ones who answered."

"They" were three women. The oldest couldn't have been more than twenty-five. Mrs. Sloan had caught them naked and asleep, along with what looked like Herman's father. One woman had her head cradled near Mr. Sloan's groin; another was cuddled in the white folds of his armpit, her wet hair fanning like seaweed across his shoulder; the third lay curled in a foetal position off his wide flank. Something dark was smeared across her face.

"And no, they weren't prostitutes," said Mrs. Sloan. "I had occasion to talk to one of them on her way out; she was a newlywed, she and her husband had come up for a weekend at the family cottage. She was, she supposed, going back to him."

"That's sick," gasped Judith, and meant it. She truly felt ill. "Why would you take something like that?"

"Because," replied Mrs. Sloan, her voice growing sharp again, "I found that I could. Mr. Sloan was distracted, as you can see, and at that instant I found some of the will that he had kept from me since we met."

"Sick," Judith whispered. "Herman was right. We shouldn't have come."

When Mrs. Sloan closed the album this time, she put it back underneath the coffee table. She patted Judith's arm with her mutilated hand and smiled. "No, no, dear. I'm happy you're here—happier than you can know."

Judith wanted nothing more at that moment than to get up, grab her suitcase, throw it in the car and leave. But of course she couldn't. Herman wasn't back yet, and she couldn't think of leaving without him.

"If Herman's father was doing all these things, why didn't you just divorce him?"

"If that photograph offends you, why don't you just get up and leave, right now?"

"Herman—"

"Herman wouldn't like it," Mrs. Sloan finished for her. "That's it, isn't it?" Judith nodded.

"He's got you too," continued Mrs. Sloan, "just like his father got me. But maybe it's not too late for you."

"I love Herman. He never did anything like . . . like that."

"Of course you love him. And I love Mr. Sloan—desperately, passionately, over all reason." The corner of Mrs. Sloan's mouth perked up in a small, bitter grin.

"Would you like to hear how we met?"

Judith wasn't sure she would, but she nodded anyway. "Sure."

"I was living in Toronto with a friend at the time, had been for several years. As I recall, she was more than a friend—we were lovers." Mrs. Sloan paused, obviously waiting for a reaction. Judith sat mute, her expression purposefully blank.

Mrs. Sloan went on: "In our circle of friends, such relationships were quite fragile. Usually they would last no longer than a few weeks. It was, so far as we knew anyway, a minor miracle that we'd managed to stay together for as long as we had." Mrs. Sloan gave a bitter laugh. "We were very proud."

"How did you meet Herman's father?"

"On a train," she said quickly. "A subway train. He didn't even speak to me. I just felt his touch. I began packing my things that night. I can't even remember what I told her. My friend."

"It can't have been like that."

Judith started to get up, but Mrs. Sloan grabbed her, two fingers and a thumb closing like a trap around her forearm. Judith fell back down on the sofa. "Let go!"

Mrs. Sloan held tight. With her other hand she took hold of Judith's face and pulled it around to face her.

"Don't argue with me," she hissed, her eyes desperately intent. "You're wasting time. They'll be back soon, and when they are, we won't be able to do anything.

"We'll be under their spell again!"

Something in her tone caught Judith, and instead of breaking away, of running to the car and waiting inside with the doors locked until Herman got back—instead of slapping Mrs. Sloan, as she was half-inclined to do—Judith sat still.

"Then tell me what you mean," she said, slowly and deliberately.

Mrs. Sloan let go, and Judith watched as relief flooded across her features. "We'll have to open the album again," she said. "That's the only way I can tell it."

The pictures were placed in the order they'd been taken. The first few were close-ups of different parts of Mr. Sloan's anatomy, always taken while he slept. They could have been pictures of Herman, and Judith saw nothing strange about them until Mrs. Sloan began pointing out the discrepancies: "Those ridges around his nipples are made of something like fingernails," she said of one, and "the whole ear isn't any bigger than a nickel," she said, pointing to another grainy Polaroid. "His teeth are barely nubs on his gums, and his navel . . . look, it's a *slit*. I measured it after I took this, and it was nearly eight inches long. Sometimes it grows longer, and I've seen it shrink to less than an inch on cold days."

"I'd never noticed before," murmured Judith, although as Mrs. Sloan pointed to more features she began to remember other things about Herman: the thick black hairs that only grew between his fingers, his black triangular toenails that never needed cutting . . .

and where were his fingernails? Judith shivered with the realization.

Mrs. Sloan turned the page.

"Did you ever once stop to wonder what you saw in such a creature?" she asked Judith.

"Never," Judith replied, wonderingly.

"Look," said Mrs. Sloan, pointing at the next spread. "I took these pictures in June of 1982."

At first they looked like nature pictures, blue-tinged photographs of some of the land around the Sloans' house. But as Judith squinted she could make out a small figure wearing a heavy green overcoat. Its head was a little white pinprick in the middle of a farmer's field. "Mr. Sloan," she said, pointing.

Mrs. Sloan nodded. "He walks off in that direction every weekend. I followed him that day."

"Followed him where?"

"About a mile and a half to the north of here," said Mrs. Sloan, "there's an old farm property. The Sloans must own the land—that's the only explanation I can think of—although I've never been able to find the deed. Here—" she pointed at a photograph of an ancient set of fieldstone foundations, choked with weeds "—that's where he stopped."

The next photograph in the series showed a tiny black rectangle in the middle of the ruins. Looking more closely, Judith could tell that it was an opening into the dark of a root cellar. Mr. Sloan was bent over it, peering inside. Judith turned the page, but there were no photographs after that.

"When he went inside, I found I couldn't take any more pictures," said Mrs. Sloan. "I can't explain why, but I felt a compelling terror, unlike anything I've ever felt in Mr. Sloan's presence. I ran back to the house, all the way. It was as though I were being pushed."

That's weird. Judith was about to say it aloud, but stopped herself—in the face of Mrs. Sloan's photo album, everything was weird. To comment on the fact seemed redundant.

"I can't explain why I fled, but I have a theory." Mrs. Sloan set the volume aside and stood. She walked over to the window, spread the blinds an inch, and checked the driveway as she spoke. "Herman and his father aren't human. That much we can say for certain—they are monsters, deformed in ways that even radiation, even thalidomide couldn't account for. They are physically repulsive; their intellects are no more developed than that of a child of four. They are weak and amoral."

Mrs. Sloan turned, leaning against the glass. "Yet here we are, you and I. Without objective evidence—" she gestured with her good hand towards the open photo album "—we can't even see them for what they are. If they were any nearer, or perhaps simply not distracted, we wouldn't even be able to have this conversation. Tonight, we'll go willingly to their beds." At that, Mrs. Sloan visibly shuddered. "If that's where they want us."

Judith felt the urge to go to the car again, and again she suppressed it. Mrs. Sloan held her gaze like a cobra.

"It all suggests a power. I think it suggests talismanic power." Here Mrs. Sloan paused, looking expectantly at Judith.

Judith wasn't sure what "talismanic" meant, but she thought she knew what Mrs. Sloan was driving at. "You think the source of their power is in that cellar?"

"Good." Mrs. Sloan nodded slowly. "Yes, Judith, that's what I think. I've tried over and over to get close to that place, but I've never been able to even step inside those foundations. It's a place of power, and it protects itself."

Judith looked down at the photographs. She felt cold in the pit of her stomach. "So you want me to go there with you, is that it?"

Mrs. Sloan took one last look out the window then came back and sat down. She smiled with an awkward warmth. "Only once since I came here have I felt as strong as I do today. That day, I chopped these off with the wood-axe—" she held up her three-fingered hand and waggled the stumps "—thinking that, seeing me mutilated, Herman's father would lose interest and let me go. I was stupid; it only made him angry, and I was . . . punished. But I didn't know then what I know today. And," she added after a brief pause, "today you are here."

The Sloan men had not said where they were going when they left in the pickup truck, so it was impossible to tell how much time the two women had. Mrs. Sloan found a flashlight, an axe and a shovel in the garage, and they set out immediately along a narrow path that snaked through the trees at the back of the yard. There were at least two hours of daylight left, and Judith was glad. She wouldn't want to be trekking back through these woods after dark.

In point of fact, she was barely sure she wanted to be in these woods in daylight. Mrs. Sloan moved through the underbrush like a crazy woman, not even bothering to move branches out of her way. But Judith was slower, perhaps more doubtful.

Why was she doing this? Because of some grainy photographs in a family album? Because of what might as well have been a ghost story, told by a woman who had by her own admission chopped off two of her own fingers? Truth be told, Judith couldn't be sure she was going anywhere but crazy following Mrs. Sloan through the wilderness.

Finally, it was the memories that kept her moving. As Judith walked, they manifested with all the vividness of new experience.

The scriptorium near Lisbon was deserted—the tour group had moved on, maybe up the big wooden staircase behind the podium, maybe down the black wrought-iron spiral staircase. Judith couldn't tell; the touch on the back of her neck seemed to be interfering. It penetrated, through skin and muscle and bone, to the juicy centre of her spine. She turned around and the wet thing behind pulled her to the floor. She did not resist.

"Hurry up!" Mrs. Sloan was well ahead, near the top of a ridge of rock in the centre of a large clearing. Blinking, Judith apologized and moved on.

Judith was fired from her job at Joseph's only a week after she returned from Portugal. It seemed she had been late every morning, and when she explained to her boss that she was in love, it only made things worse. Talia flew into a rage, and Judith was afraid that she would hit her. Herman waited outside in the mall.

Mrs. Sloan helped Judith clamber up the smooth rock face. When she got to the top, Mrs. Sloan took her in her arms. Only then did Judith realize how badly she was shaking.

"What is it?" Mrs. Sloan pulled back and studied Judith's face with real concern.

"I'm . . . remembering," said Judith.

"What do you remember?"

Judith felt ill again, and she almost didn't say.

"Judith!" Mrs. Sloan shook her. "This could be important!"

"All right!" Judith shook her off. She didn't want to be touched, not by anyone.

"The night before last, I brought Herman home to meet my parents. I thought it had gone well . . . until now."

"What do you remember?" Mrs. Sloan emphasized every syllable.

"My father wouldn't shake Herman's hand when he came in the door. My mother . . . she turned white as a ghost. She backed up into the kitchen, and I think she knocked over some pots or something, because I heard clanging. My father asked my mother if she was all right. All she said was no. Over and over again."

"What did your father do?"

"He excused himself, went to check on my mother. He left us alone in the vestibule, it must have been for less than a minute. And I . . ." Judith paused, then willed herself to finish. "I started . . . rubbing myself against Herman. All over. He didn't even make a move. But I couldn't stop myself. I don't even remember wanting to stop. My parents had to pull me away, both of them." Judith felt like crying.

"My father actually hit me. He said I made him sick. Then he called me . . . a little whore."

Mrs. Sloan made a sympathetic noise. "It's not far to the ruins," she said softly. "We'd better go, before they get back."

*

It felt like an hour had passed before they emerged from the forest and looked down on the ruins that Judith had seen in the Polaroids. In the setting sun, they seemed almost mythic—like Stonehenge, or the Aztec temples Judith had toured once on a trip to Cancun. The stones here had obviously once been the foundation of a farmhouse. Judith could make out the outline of what would have been a woodshed extending off the nearest side, and another tumble of stonework in the distance was surely the remains of a barn—but now they were something else entirely. Judith didn't want to go any closer. If she turned back now, she might make it home before dark.

"Do you feel it?" Mrs. Sloan gripped the axe-handle with white knuckles. Judith must have been holding the shovel almost as tightly. Although it was quite warm outside, her teeth began to chatter.

"If either of us had come alone, we wouldn't be able to stand it," said Mrs. Sloan, her voice trembling. "We'd better keep moving."

Judith followed Herman's stepmother down the rocky slope to the ruins. Her breaths grew shorter the closer they got. She used the shovel as a walking stick until they reached level ground, then held it up in both hands, like a weapon.

They stopped again at the edge of the foundation. The door to the root cellar lay maybe thirty feet beyond. It was made of sturdy, fresh-painted wood, in sharp contrast to the overgrown wreckage around it, and it was embedded in the ground at an angle. Tall, thick weeds sprouting galaxies of tiny white flowers grew in a dense cluster on top of the mound. They waved rhythmically back and forth, as though in a breeze.

But it was wrong, thought Judith. There was no breeze, the air was still. She looked back on their trail and confirmed it—the tree branches weren't even rustling.

"I know," said Mrs. Sloan, her voice flat. "I see it too. They're moving on their own."

Without another word, Mrs. Sloan stepped across the stone boundary. Judith followed, and together they approached the shifting mound.

As they drew closer, Judith half-expected the weeds to attack, to shoot forward and grapple their legs, or to lash across their eyes and throats with prickly venom.

In fact, the stalks didn't even register the two women's presence as they stepped up to the mound. Still, Judith held the shovel ready as Mrs. Sloan smashed the padlock on the root cellar door. She pried it away with a painful-sounding rending.

"Help me lift this," said Mrs. Sloan.

The door was heavy, and earth had clotted along its top, but with only a little difficulty they managed to heave it open. A thick, milky smell wafted up from the darkness.

Mrs. Sloan switched on the flashlight and aimed it down. Judith peered along its beam—it caught nothing but dust motes, and the uncertain-looking steps of a wooden ladder.

"Don't worry, Judith," breathed Mrs. Sloan, "I'll go first." Setting the flashlight on the ground for a moment, she turned around and set a foot on one of the upper rungs. She climbed down a few steps, then picked up the flashlight and gave Judith a little smile.

"You can pass down the axe and shovel when I get to the bottom," she said, and then her head was below the ground. Judith swallowed with a dry click and shut her eyes.

"All right," Mrs. Sloan finally called, her voice improbably small. "It's too far down here for you to pass the tools to me by hand. I'll stand back—drop them both through the hole then come down yourself."

Judith did as she was told. At the bottom of the darkness she could make out a flickering of light, just bright enough for her to see where the axe and shovel fell. They were very tiny at the bottom of the hole. Holding her breath, Judith mounted the top rung of the ladder and began her own descent.

Despite its depth, the root cellar was warm. And the smell was overpowering. Judith took only a moment to identify it. It was Herman's smell, but magnified a thousandfold—and exuding from the very walls of this place.

Mrs. Sloan had thoroughly explored the area at the base of the ladder by the time Judith reached her.

"The walls are earthen, shorn up with bare timber," she said, shining the light along the nearest wall to illustrate. "The ceiling here tapers up along the length of the ladder—I'd guess we're nearly forty feet underground."

Judith picked up the shovel, trying not to imagine the weight of the earth above them.

"There's another chamber, through that tunnel." Mrs. Sloan swung the flashlight beam down and to their right. The light extended into a dark hole in the wall, not more than five feet in diameter and rimmed with fieldstone. "That's where the smell is strongest."

Mrs. Sloan stooped and grabbed the axe in her good hand. Still bent over, she approached the hole and shone the light inside.

"The end's still farther than the flashlight beam will carry," she called over her shoulder. "I think that's where we'll have to go."

Judith noticed then that the tremor was gone from Mrs. Sloan's voice. Far from sounding frightened, Herman's mother actually seemed excited. It wasn't hard to see why—this day might finish with the spell broken, with their freedom assured. Why wouldn't she be excited?

But Judith couldn't shake her own sense of foreboding so easily. She wondered where Herman was now, what he would be thinking. And what was Judith thinking, on the verge of her freedom? Judith couldn't put it to words, but the thought twisted through her stomach and made her stop in the dark chamber behind Mrs. Sloan. *A little whore*, her father had called her. Then he'd hit her, hard enough to bring up a swelling. Right in front of Herman, like he wasn't even there! Judith clenched her jaw around a rage that was maddeningly faceless.

"I'm not a whore," she whispered through her teeth.

Mrs. Sloan disappeared into the hole, and it was only when the chamber was dark that Judith followed.

The tunnel widened as they went, its walls changing from wood-shorn earth to fieldstone and finally to actual rock. Within sixty feet the tunnel ended, and Mrs. Sloan began to laugh. Judith felt ill—the smell was so strong she could barely breath. Even as she stepped into the second chamber of the root cellar, the last thing she wanted to do was laugh.

"Roots!" gasped Mrs. Sloan, her voice shrill and echoing in the dark. "Of course there would be—" she broke into another fit of giggles "—roots, here in the root cellar!" The light jagged across the cellar's surfaces as Mrs. Sloan slipped to the floor and fell into another fit of laughter.

Judith bent down and pried the flashlight from Mrs. Sloan's hand—she made a face as she brushed the scratchy tips of the two bare finger-bones. She swept the beam slowly across the ceiling.

It was a living thing. Pulsing intestinal ropes drooped from huge bulbs and broad orange phalluses clotted with earth and juices thick as semen. Between them, fingerlike tree roots bent and groped in knotted black lines. One actually penetrated a bulb, as though to feed on the sticky yellow water inside. Silvery droplets formed like beading mercury on the surface of an ample, purple sac directly above the chamber's centre.

Mrs. Sloan's laughter began to slow. "Oh my," she finally chuckled, sniffing loudly, "I don't know what came over me."

"This is the place." Judith had intended it as a question, but it came out as a statement of fact. This *was* the place. She could feel Herman, his father, God knew how many others like them—all of them here, an indisputable presence.

Mrs. Sloan stood, using the axe-handle as a support. "It is," she agreed. "We'd better get to work on it."

Mrs. Sloan hefted the axe in both hands and swung it around her shoulders. Judith stood back and watched as the blade bit into one of the drooping ropes, not quite severing it but sending a spray of green sap down on Mrs. Sloan's shoulders. She pulled the axe out and swung again. This time the tube broke. Its two ends twitched like live electrical wires; its sap spewed like bile. Droplets struck Judith, and where they touched skin they burned like vinegar.

"Doesn't it feel better?" shouted Mrs. Sloan, grinning fiercely at Judith through the wash of slime on her face. "Don't you feel *free*? Put down the flashlight, girl, pick up the shovel! There's work to be done!"

Judith set the flashlight down on its end, so that it illuminated the roots in a wide yellow circle. She hefted the shovel and, picking the nearest bulb, swung it up with all her strength. The yellow juices sprayed out in an umbrella over Judith, soaking her. She began to laugh.

It does feel better, she thought. *A lot better*. Judith swung the shovel up again and again. The blade cut through tubes, burst bulbs, lodged in the thick round carrot-roots deep enough so Judith could pry them apart with only a savage little twist of her shoulders. The mess of her destruction was *everywhere*. She could taste it every time she grinned.

After a time, she noticed that Mrs. Sloan had stopped and was leaning on the axe-handle, watching her. Judith yanked the shovel from a root. Brown milk splattered across her back.

"What are you stopping for?" she asked. "There's still more to cut!"

Mrs. Sloan smiled in the dimming light—the flashlight, miraculously enough, was still working, but its light now had to fight its way through several layers of ooze.

"I was just watching you, dear," she said softly.

Judith turned her ankle impatiently. The chamber was suddenly very quiet. "Come on," said Judith. "We can't stop until we're finished."

"Of course." Mrs. Sloan stood straight and swung the axe up again. It crunched into a wooden root very near the ceiling, and Mrs. Sloan pried it loose. "I think that we're very nearly done, though. At least, that's the feeling I get."

Judith didn't smile—she suddenly felt very cold inside.

"No, we're not," she said in a low voice, "we're not done for a long time yet. Keep working."

Mrs. Sloan had been right, though. There were only a half-dozen intact roots on the cellar ceiling, and it took less than a minute for the two women to cut them down. When they stopped, the mess was up to their ankles and neither felt like laughing. Judith shivered, the juices at once burning and chilling against her skin.

"Let's get out of this place," said Mrs. Sloan. "There's dry clothes back at the house."

The flashlight died at the base of the ladder, its beam flickering out like a dampened candle flame. It didn't matter, though. The sky was a square of deepening purple above them, and while they might finish the walk back in the dark they came out of the root cellar in time to bask in at least a sliver of the remaining daylight. The weeds atop the mound were still as the first evening stars emerged and the line of orange to the west sucked itself back over the treetops.

Mrs. Sloan talked all the way back, her continual chatter almost but not quite drowning out Judith's recollections. She mostly talked about what she would do with her new freedom: first, she'd take the pickup and drive it back to the city where she would sell it. She would take the money, get a place to live and start looking for a job. As they crested the ridge of bedrock, Mrs. Sloan asked Judith if there was much call for three-fingered manicurists in the finer Toronto salons, then laughed in such a girlish way that Judith wondered if she weren't walking with someone other than Mrs. Sloan.

"What are you going to do, now that you're free?" asked Mrs. Sloan.

"I don't know," Judith replied honestly.

The black pickup was parked near the end of the driveway. Its headlights were on, but when they checked, the cab was empty.

"They may be inside," Mrs. Sloan whispered. "You were right, Judith. We're not done yet."

Mrs. Sloan led Judith to the kitchen door around the side of the house. It wasn't locked, and together they stepped into the kitchen. The only light came from the half-open refrigerator door. Judith wrinkled her nose. A carton of milk lay on its side, and milk dripped from the countertop to a huge puddle on the floor. Cutlery was strewn everywhere.

Coming from somewhere in the house, Judith thought she recognized Herman's voice. It was soft, barely a whimper. It sounded as though it were coming from the living room.

 Mrs. Sloan heard it too. She hefted the axe in her good hand and motioned to Judith to follow as she stepped silently around the spilled milk. She clutched the doorknob to the living room in a three-fingered grip, and stepped out of the kitchen.

Herman and his father were on the couch, and they were in bad shape. Both were bathed in a viscous sweat, and they had bloated so much that several of the buttons on Herman's shirt had popped and Mr. Sloan's eyes were swollen shut.

And where were their noses?

Judith shuddered. Their noses had apparently receded into their skulls. Halting breaths passed through chaffed-red slits with a wet buzzing sound.

Herman looked at Judith. She rested the shovel's blade against the carpet. His eyes were moist, as though he'd been crying.

"You bastard," whispered Mrs. Sloan. "You took away my life. Nobody can do that, but you did. You took away everything."

Mr. Sloan quivered, like gelatin dropped from a mould.

"You made me touch you . . ." Mrs. Sloan stepped closer ". . . *worship* you . . . you made me lick up after you, swallow your filthy, inhuman taste . . . And you made me *like* it!"

She was shaking almost as much as Mr. Sloan, and her voice grew into a shrill, angry shout. Mr. Sloan's arms came up to his face, and a high, keening whistle rose up. Beside him, Herman sobbed. He did not stop looking at Judith.

Oh, Herman, Judith thought, her stomach turning. Herman was sick, sicker than Judith had imagined. Had he always been this bad? Judith couldn't believe that. Air whistled like a plea through Herman's reddened nostrils.

"Well, no more!" Mrs. Sloan raised the axe over her head so that it jangled against the lighting fixture in the ceiling. *"No more!"*

Judith lifted up the shovel then, and swung with all her strength. The flat of the blade smashed against the back of Mrs. Sloan's skull.

Herman's sobbing stretched into a wail, and Judith swung the shovel once more. Mrs. Sloan dropped the axe beside her and crumpled to the carpeted floor.

The telephone in Judith's parents' home rang three times before the answering machine Judith had bought them for Christmas switched on. Judith's mother began to speak, in a timed, halting monotone: "Allan ... and ... I are ... not ..."

Judith smoothed her hair behind her ears, fingers tapping impatiently at her elbow until the message finished. She nearly hung up when the tone sounded, but she shut her eyes and forced herself to go through with it.

"Hi, Mom. Hi, Dad." Her voice was small, and it trembled. "It's me. I know you're pretty mad at me, and I just wanted to call and say I was sorry. I know that what we did—what Herman and I did, mostly me—I know it was wrong. I know it was sick, okay? Dad, you were right about that. But I'm not going to do that stuff anymore. I've got control of my life, and ... of my body. God, that sounds like some kind of feminist garbage, doesn't it? *Control of my body.* But it's true." With her foot, Judith swung the kitchen door shut. The gurgling from upstairs grew quieter.

"Oh, by the way, I'm up at Herman's parents' place now. It's about three hours north of you guys, outside a town called Fenlan. You should see it up here, it's beautiful. I'm going to stay here for awhile, but don't worry, Herman and I will have separate bedrooms." She smiled. "We're going to save ourselves."

Judith turned around so that the telephone cord wrapped her body, and she leaned against the stove.

"Mom," she continued, "do you remember what you told me about love? I do. You told me there were two stages. There was the in-love feeling, the one that you get when you meet a guy, he's really cute and everything, and you just don't want to be away from him. And then that goes away, and remember what you said? 'You'd better still love him after that,' you told me. 'Even though he's not so cute, even though maybe he's getting a little pot belly, even though he stops sending you flowers, you'd better still love him like there's no tomorrow.' Well Mom, guess what?"

The answering machine beeped again and the line disconnected.

"I do," finished Judith.

Janie and the Wind

The eaves of Mr. Swayze's island lodge rattled like soup bones loose in a bin. There was a wind up—a wind roaring across the bay that shook the eaves—a wind that'd knock you down where you stood, if you hadn't a grip on something solid. It'd knock you down like Janie'd been knocked down herself not long past; except Janie'd have been able to get up right away if it were just the wind, and not her husband Ernie who'd done it to her.

Ernie had hit her bad, worse than usual. And Janie didn't know why, which also wasn't usual.

She was looking at the stem of a birch tree, cut short for the leg of Mr. Swayze's coffee table, and past it to the big front window—which ought to be boarded up, the way the sky was rolling and darkening beyond it. She was on the floor, and her chest hurt and when she tried to swallow her neck felt like a needle was in it, and her head was in some stickiness that Janie figured was some of her own blood.

Why'd Ernie hit her like that?

It wasn't like she'd been up to anything, after all. She was just looking through one of Mr. Swayze's little story magazines, the ones that he sometimes wrote for. Her reading was getting better, improving each year, and the magazine had pictures at the front of each story, which gave her a good clue what ones she'd enjoy. Janie'd found one with a pretty girl and what looked like a horse but it had a long, corkscrew horn coming out of its head, which reminded her of something—

—and then her husband Ernie'd showed up.

He was supposed to be out fishing. That's what he spent the days at, for the entire week they were at Mr. Swayze's lodge on Georgian Bay.

Sky had been clear when Ernie stepped inside. Janie hadn't heard the boat, but she was getting going in her story so she maybe wasn't too attentive. The door rattled closed, and Ernie cleared his throat.

"Hi," said Janie. She placed her magazine down on her page. Ernie stepped out of the doorway, and scratched at his neck. Sunlight made the hair there glow like copper.

"You hold still now, Janie," he said.

Janie did like she was told—but it puzzled her. Ernie would only say that, in the way he just said it, when she got to one of her spells and was set to do herself some harm.

"I'm just readin'," said Janie. She stood and held up her magazine, cover-out, to prove it.

"Hold still." Ernie was born with sad eyes. They drooped at the corners like he was going to cry. And his mouth wasn't happy either, not as a rule. Janie would smile and frown and cry and yell depending on how she felt, but Ernie only ever looked sad. Janie thought sometimes that Ernie's face muscles just didn't work.

"You upset, Ernie?" Janie couldn't read it from his face, but he was moving funny. His shoulders were bent, and his hands hung from them like hooks on the end of a couple of chains. He was looking right at her.

"Don't move," he said.

Then it came to her. Janie put her hand up to her mouth, made a fist and gasped. "You—you see a wasp, don't you?"

Ernie didn't answer—just kept coming.

Janie stood still. Jeez Louise, a wasp! Janie'd been stung last summer, out behind Ernie's shed, and oh! How it'd set her howling! There'd been a whole nest of them, and when she touched it wrong they'd stung her seven times, then spit poison into the sting-holes that made them hurt like the Devil, then stung her some more when she got mad and started whacking at the nest with her shovel. She'd learned her lesson about wasps that day—Ernie'd explained it to her: "Stand still when there's a wasp around. Stand still, an' if it gets near you, let it get a sniff and go on its way. It's more ascared of you than you are of it."

Janie didn't think that was possible. But she sure could stand still, scared as she was. She shut her eyes tight and clutched her story magazine to her chest. "Oh, Ernie, get it, get it, get it."

"I'm sorry, Janie," he said. "I shouldn't have eaten it. I was just so hungry, Janie, so hungry. Mr. Swayze said it'd be a good thing, but now it's in me."

What's all that got to do with wasps? she wondered for just a second, before she realized what was what.

He hit her in the stomach first, and she took that hit hard. Usually when Ernie hit her, she'd done something to deserve it, so she'd know it was coming and could prepare herself. But what'd she done? Read a story magazine? She hadn't broken nothing, hadn't swore or soiled herself or embarrassed Ernie in the grocery.

Janie bent forward, and as she did her hands came up. The story magazine ripped apart and the pages scattered around the porchroom. It felt like her innards had tore loose inside and she couldn't even breathe it hurt so bad. She fell on her knees and bit down on her lip.

Ernie cuffed her in the ear. She fell sideways, and her elbow hit the floor first, and that sent a juicy kind of pain up through her shoulder so strong she thought her heart would blow up from it. She put out her hand and managed to hold herself upright, but only barely and not for long.

Because next Ernie kicked that arm out from under her. He was wearing his big work boots, and they added weight enough to the kick that she fell completely.

She rolled onto her back. She was wearing boots too—not as big as Ernie's, but high and black and plenty hard in the heel—and though she knew better, she used them to kick up at her husband. She caught him in the knee, and it wasn't the right angle to knock him down, but it sure must've hurt. Because he yelled something fierce then—louder even than when he'd chopped near-through his pinkie finger with the wood-axe that time, mad enough to put a bit of fear in her.

He jumped back on one foot, and clutched at the other one with both hands and hopped around some. Janie finally sucked in some air, which was good because her eyes were starting to go all speckly for lack of it, and she started to get up.

She was up on one knee when Ernie let go of his knee and stopped hollering. His foot dropped to the floor with a thump, and his hands fell back to his sides again. Janie put her other foot beneath her and stood up. Hers and Ernie's eyes met, and Janie thought again about the wasp rule.

Should have done like I was told, she thought, fear still working at her middle like a little gnawing mouse. Should have kept still.

Let him get his sniff.

Because sad-eyed Ernie didn't look sad any more. His eyes had lost their droop, and his mouth had managed to turn itself up at the corners, opening a little more than usual in the middle. She'd seen him smile once or twice at least in their twenty years together, but Janie didn't remember her husband having so many teeth.

He jumped at her.

He came so fast she might as well have had her eyes closed. One second he was standing there grinning, showing off those teeth— the next, he was on top of her, and she was back on the floor. He punched and punched. Lying now on the floor with the sky turning black before her eyes, Janie remembered him hitting her in the stomach, in the ribs, a bad hit to her neck, and then, when she put her wrist up to block him, he *bit*—

And that was all.

"Ow," muttered Janie. She brought her hand up to her head, touched it to a crusted-over gash above her ear, and took it away again. She didn't remember getting that one. Must've happened after the neck punch and the bite; in that whole time Janie couldn't remember when the sky had gone from blue to black.

Janie put the hand underneath her, and pushed herself upright. She was scared that she wouldn't be able to stand up, and she was a bit dizzy at first. But she shut her eyes and counted to three, and when she opened them again she felt better. She got to her feet and looked around her.

The pages from the story magazine she'd ripped were still on the floor. Some of them had blood on them. There was a lot of blood on the floor where her head had been. The front door from the porch was closed. The floor lamp by the big window had fallen over. When Janie went to pick it up, she looked out and saw that the waves were so big they washed clear over the top of the dock. There was no boat at the dock. So Ernie was gone.

Janie looked at the floor where her head had been, and although she knew it would hurt, she touched the cut over her ear. The cut was shaped like a crescent, and had scabbed over it felt like. Janie knew better than to pick at it. She looked outside again.

Mr. Swayze's island wasn't very big—it didn't have room on it for more than his lodge, a shed for the gas generator and one dock for a motorboat. That was all Mr. Swayze needed, though. He liked to come out here to write his stories these days, and like he told them both when he gave them the keys last month, too much room is distracting.

Ernie was gone. He had given her a beating for no good reason and now he was gone. It didn't figure.

Somewhere outside, something fell over with a clang and a bong. It was probably a drum, one of the open ones that didn't seem to do nothing but collect rainwater by the side of the lodge. When she had met Mr. Swayze and they learned that he was a writer of scary stories, Ernie had said, "I guess you want a horror story, can't find nothing scarier than that acid rain. Kill a whole lake full of fish with just a drop. There's your horror story."

"That's pretty scary all right," Mr. Swayze had agreed. "I'll have to put it in my notebook."

Maybe the rainwater gave Mr. Swayze ideas for his acid rain story. Well, now it had fallen down and was spilt out everywhere and no good to nobody. Janie opened the front door and stepped outside.

The wind felt good on her—it was cold, colder than it had a right to be for early September, and it cooled her cuts and bruises like an ice pack. When she turned to face it, however, it took her breath away, so she moved with her back to the wind, down to the dock.

"Ernie!" She cupped her hands around her mouth, and called off across the waters. "Ernie! Come on back! I ain't dead! You got nothing to fear!"

For surely, thought Janie, that was what had happened. She had fallen down into her blood, and there had been so much of it, and she had been out like a light, and poor Ernie had thought the worst—that he'd killed her.

So he'd run. The OPP had already come by the house two times, on account of complaints from neighbours, and each time they asked Janie if he'd been doing anything to her. Like hitting or punching or kicking or biting, or even just pushing. Janie'd said no both times, and the second time—with Ernie in earshot—the one policeman had told her that she had to complain; they could only arrest him otherwise if he killed her and it was murder. "I don't want it to come to that," said the policeman, and Janie had replied, "Then me neither."

"Ernie!" She yelled so loud her voice cracked and turned to a scream. "Ernie! It ain't murder! It's okay! I won't complain!"

There was another gust of wind then, and it nearly blew Janie off the dock. It sent the water-drum rolling down the rock face, and it entered the bay with a splash that sprayed ice-cold water up the back of Janie's dress. Janie steadied herself, and opened her mouth for one more yell, then shut her mouth again.

It wouldn't do her no good. Ernie was long gone.

The drum clanked up against the dock, and Janie kicked at it as she passed it on the way back. The kick sent the lip of it underwater, and that was enough. The rain-drum started to sink.

There was a shelf in the lodge's living room that had every one of Mr. Swayze's books—although not one of them had his name on the cover. Mr. Swayze used what he called a pen name, so all the books were "by" Eric Hookerman even though Mr. Swayze wrote them.

There were a lot of books, and Mr. Swayze said that a lot of people bought them in their time. Janie thought that might be true. Sometimes, she would even see one at the drug store in Fenlan, and they only ever got in the best books. It was no wonder that Mr. Swayze could afford to own all that land outside Fenlan *and* this island here in Georgian Bay.

"I guess you can't call me a starving artist anymore," he joked one time.

"You're not starving," said Ernie. "You don't know what starving is, Mr. Swayze."

And then Mr. Swayze had laughed—a scary laugh, like those books of his must be. "I guess not," he said.

Janie had never read any of Mr. Swayze's books—she was just getting to reading stories now; anything bigger than ten pages made her feel sleepy, even if she picked it up in the morning. But she looked at the pictures on the covers, and she read the titles, and she had a pretty good idea what they were about. There was THE HAND, and it had a picture of an old dried-up hand with long fingernails and a drop of blood on the tip of each; THE BOTTOM OF THE WELL, with an old-fashioned hand-pump, and a snake poking its head down out of the spout looking all fierce and frightening; and ONE MILLION COPIES SOLD! THE DEAD BIRD, with a cover that was all black, but had raised parts that Janie could see as the shape of a bird with wings spread, if she held it just so in the light. That cover took some work to enjoy, you couldn't just look at it and see, but it was her favourite of them all.

When Janie stepped into the living room, she nearly tripped on ONE MILLION COPIES SOLD! THE DEAD BIRD. That book along with most of the rest were spread all over the floor.

"Oh, Ernie," she muttered, "look at the mess you made."

Janie flicked the light-switch on the wall, to get a better look at what had happened, but it stayed dark. Did the wind knock out the generator too? If it had, it'd be up to Ernie to fix it—Janie could lift and haul things, she'd always been a big girl that way, but machines and such were beyond her. She flicked the switch once more, to no avail, so bent down and in the grey light from the window she started to gather up the books. Fine thing that'd be, thought Janie. Mr. Swayze loans out his lodge to us, we ruin all the books he wrote. Never invite us to dinner again.

Sometimes, Janie wondered why Mr. Swayze bothered with Ernie and her at all. Mr. Swayze was smart, and he must know a lot of people, and he sure had a lot of money. Ernie and Janie didn't have much money—Ernie's work with his chainsaw and his contracting wasn't steady, and paid poor when it came; they sure didn't know many people; and smart? They did their best with what they had— but folks in town said Ernie and Janie were a good match for each other, and they didn't say so in a kindly way either.

Yet from the time he moved up to Fenlan, Mr. Swayze took them on. He bought the land back on Little Bear Lake in the 1980s some time, and after asking around hired Ernie to come lay foundations. Land was no good, and Ernie told him so—more than half of it was swamp, and most of the rest was bare, knobbly rock. Mr. Swayze said he knew that now, but he bought it because he liked the feel of it and hadn't been thinking practical. Was there nothing that Ernie could do? "Not for cheap," said Ernie.

"Then let's not do it cheap," said Mr. Swayze. "Tell me what it'll take."

It took a lot, but Ernie'd done pretty good for him by the time it was done. Found him a level spot on high ground to build his house, then brought in some fill and a digger and made a road across the firmer parts of swamp so Mr. Swayze could get in and out. Sunk a well through the rock, deep—so Mr. Swayze wouldn't have to be drinking swamp water—and strung a power line in so he wouldn't have to be using candles and oil lamps to see at night.

Janie'd spent more than a few workdays out at the site—in those days, she was as good a worker as any man and came twice as cheap, or so said Ernie. That was when they'd got to know Mr. Swayze and learned about what he did to make ends meet. And that was when he started inviting them for dinner—first at the farmhouse Mr. Sloan rented him about five miles up the concession road, then once his own house was done, in there.

Got so they'd dine with Mr. Swayze one time a month—whether at his place or theirs. And oh, those dinners would be fine! Mr. Swayze was a real good cook—a magic cook. He could take a chicken and make it taste like Thanksgiving turkey; make a cheap cut of steak into a restaurant-fine meal that'd dissolve on the tip of your tongue. He wasn't much on vegetables, but that was fine—neither was Ernie, and Janie didn't much care one way or the other.

Ernie figured that Mr. Swayze cottoned to them so well because there weren't many others who'd accept him in town. He lived alone, and Ernie said many in town felt that might be because he was whoo-whoo. When Ernie said whoo-whoo, that meant he was talking about a fellow that liked to lay with men and not women. But Janie didn't think that was true about Mr. Swayze on a couple of counts.

For one thing, the way Mr. Swayze was working, she didn't think he'd have time to lay with *anyone*, man or woman. The day he moved into his house at Fenlan, he started writing. From dawn to dusk, he wrote and wrote or so it seemed. When she was working in his yard, the typewriter was going clackity-clack all the day long. When they got together, there was always a new stack of paper by the typewriter and he would often go and just look at it, making a mark here and there. One time she asked him how he wrote so much, and Mr. Swayze said, "Because when I'm here, I feel like it. The place here inspires me. It's got a *soul* to it. I just look at the rocks, and there's a spirit in them. Sometimes I can find it written in their face. Do you understand what I'm saying?" "No," she'd said, which was the truth. So he winked at her. "Maybe you just inspire me, Janie."

Which was another reason she didn't think he liked to lie with men.

When she got up with a stack of books in her arms to look at the shelf, she saw what'd happened. The shelf was the kind that screwed into the walls, and right on this wall a couple of those screws had come loose. The shelf must have fallen off. Screw-holes must've been stripped, and it must've fallen off. Probably happened while she was outside just now.

Probably the wind shook it down.

Janie set the books down on the floor beneath it, and tried to reset the shelf. She found the screws on the floor okay, and the bracket for the shelf, and after feeling around on the wall found the holes they'd come out of. But when she lined up the bracket and tried to push the screw in with her thumb it wouldn't go. Even though it must've been stripped, the hole in the wood wasn't big enough. It'd take a screwdriver to put the bracket back on. Just like it hadn't been shook out at all—but unscrewed.

Janie punched the wall in front of her with her good arm, and even though she knew she'd likely be punished for it, she swore. What the hell was she worrying about the books for? Her Ernie'd gone off in his rented boat because he thought he killed her, and now there was a storm up on the Bay that'd swamp him in a second if he were out on it, and here she was stuck on an island with no phone or nothing. Mr. Swayze didn't even keep a radio here. He said he bought the place a long time before anyone had a radio on these islands, and he liked the privacy—like his place in Fenlan wasn't private enough. These days, Mr. Swayze had a radio in his boat, and he said another one here would just be a distraction.

"I'd welcome that distraction now," said Janie. "Goddamned right."

She giggled—let Ernie come and punish her *now* for *Goddamn* swearing—and felt bad about it almost right away. Then she took a breath, and felt her rib aching and her elbow starting to smart, and remembered the cut in her head, and thought about Ernie doing all those things for no better reason than because she was reading a story magazine . . . and she let herself laugh again.

"Let him," she said. "Let him come."

*

When she got to the kitchen, Janie wasn't laughing any more.

She went there figuring to empty out the fridge into the big cooler they'd brought with them, so that she'd at least have fresh food for a day or so longer. But the cooler was gone from where she'd put it by the stove, and when she opened the fridge, it was all empty—but for a little jar of French's Mustard and a quarter stick of butter that'd gone rancid yellow where the wrapping didn't cover it right.

The three steaks, the potato salad, the jar of pickles, the big jug of milk, two-dozen eggs and near a pound of bacon were all gone. She went and checked the cupboard next, and sure enough, the case of Campbell's Soup was gone too.

Lord, Ernie must've thought her dead for sure—in his big panic to get out, he'd left nothing behind to sustain her alive.

Nothing but the butter and the mustard that was here when they arrived. Janie thought about making a meal of that—she was starting to get hungry despite all her pains—but no matter how you made it, a dinner of butter and mustard just wouldn't taste right. Even Mr. Swayze, with all his kitchen smarts, wouldn't be able to make much of that.

"Butter and mustard go on food—they ain't food themselves," she said, and the little window by the stove rattled in its frame, like it agreed with her.

Outside, something cracked—like a tree-stem breaking when Ernie'd bend it back over his boot. Janie didn't look to see what it was, though. The wind would blow hard, and it would break things, and if you were fool enough to have a boat in open water, it would drive you to and fro and send waves as big as a house over your bow, and those waves would swamp you if your boat wasn't a big one too. There was no need to look outside again, because whatever it was that broke, it would just be another bad thing Janie could do nothing about.

And anyway, Janie was already started through the rest of the lodge. She was pretty hungry all right—it felt like she hadn't eaten in days—and she needed to do something for that.

But the lodge was picked clean of food—there wasn't even any liquor on hand, though she managed to find quite a few empties stashed in the wood-bin.

Janie searched the three bedrooms, looked under the mattresses and in all the wardrobes. She found her clothes—Ernie hadn't taken them with him, at least—and among them was her raincoat and boots. So after she'd satisfied herself there was nothing to eat inside, she pulled on her boots and did up her raincoat and went outside to see what was what on the rest of the island.

The wind was blowing worse by then. She had to lean against the door to make sure it'd open, and when she managed to get out it was a good thing she was wearing her yellow slicker and boots, because she would have been soaked to the skin if she weren't.

It wasn't raining. The water was coming up, not down, as it smashed against the high rocks on the edge of the little island and funnelled up through their cracks and bends in white fingers of spray. She squinted down to the dock, but she couldn't see it for all the flying water. Ernie's boat could be tied up there right now, and she'd never know it.

Janie didn't go down to check it out, though—she didn't think there was anything at that dock, and anyway . . .

She thought she'd figured something better. The lodge was on the lower of two rises on the island, built on the kind of bare rock that Ernie said made for bad land, and Janie thought she'd make for the higher one. At the top of that one, there were a few trees that'd managed to fight their way out between the boulders, and she knew that on some of these islands, you could find blueberry patches in such places.

And Janie did like her blueberries.

So although the rock was slippery most of the way and hard to see at times on account of the water, and although her arm was hurting and her rib still ached, Janie managed the climb. She was more than hungry now. She was *starving*, it felt like she hadn't eaten in days, and it was like she could taste those blueberries already.

Janie got her foot into a crack in the rock, and found another crack higher up with her fingers, and then it was just one more pull, and she was up—

And over.

"Ow!"

Janie fell on her behind, which didn't much hurt, but bumped her bad elbow on the way, which did. She could scarcely believe it, but the wind didn't seem to get up here.

She'd gone over a kind of lip of rock at the top, and as she looked around she saw she was surrounded by rocks about as high as her neck, with a half-dozen tree-trunks growing up right at the edge. It was like she was sheltered in the palm of some giant hand, the trees were its fingers, all pointing upward. "Wonder if there's blood drops on the fingertips," she said to herself, and giggled again.

Then she remembered what she'd come for: the blueberries.

Janie got up off her duff and started looking for them. The palm of this great big hand was covered in all kinds of greenery, so it would take some searching. She walked bent over for a little while, but her leg started to hurt so she got down on her hands and knees going through the low greenery. For awhile, she wasn't sure she was going to find anything—nothing but ferns and tiny little evergreens barely spawned from their daddies' seed—but finally, in a little corner of the palm where maybe the thumb would crick out, she found a patch of them.

"You-hee!" she howled when she sighted the familiar leaves. She didn't get up—just crawled over on hands and knees, like a baby hurrying across the lawn for his new toy. Saliva fed into her mouth and her still-sore stomach glowered and muttered impatient.

She grabbed at one of the blueberry plants, turned it over. Nothing there, so she grabbed at another one. And another after that. And one more—

And then she howled again.

Because it looked as though someone had been here before her too. Only they hadn't picked the blueberries.

They'd stomped them. Taken a pair of boots, and stomped over every square inch of this little blueberry patch. Janie's fingers were blue where she touched the leaves—but when she licked them, there wasn't even enough berry there for a sweet.

Jeez, but Ernie'd taken time to do a lot of things for his dead wife, before he ran away in his boat. Janie felt the hot coming on.

"*Baaa-sterd!*" she yowled, head turned up to the sky. "*Baaa-sterd!*"

She didn't care who heard it. She didn't care if she caused an embarrassment, or broke something valuable, or swore, or just did something stupid. She didn't care if Ernie was down at the dock now, listening to her—she didn't care if he came back up here right now to teach her another lesson. If there was a wasp's nest here, she'd probably find a shovel and hit it.

"Baaa-*sterd!*" she screamed, and as she did, she felt a gust of wind come down on her, pouncing like a tree-cat on a mouse. This high up from the waves, it was a drier wind, but it was cold all the same. She opened her mouth wide, and faced it this time, and when she yelled again the wind took it from her and she didn't mind.

"I'm *hung*-ry!" she hollered. And as the darkness came complete to the island, the wind hollered it too.

Janie would get spells some days. That's what Ernie'd call them, because that's how they must have seemed to him, like magic witchy spells that made folks strange. She called them her hots, because that's how they'd feel inside. She got hot, from her toe-tips up to her eyebrows, so hot she itched for things she couldn't say and did things she barely knew. One time, she went out and smashed all the windows in Ernie's pickup truck with his new axe-handle, then broke the axe-handle too somehow. Another time, she ran bare-naked out to the township road, and Ernie had to come after her with a rope and a stick to goad her back inside. Sometimes during her hots, she remembered seeing things. Folks dressed in black dancing jigs all across her roof so hard the ceiling started to wobble; or a lot of birds flying in a circle around her head and pecking at her sun hat so as to knock it off; or big old bugs crawling out of the cracks between the sidewalk stones outside the grocery carrying their grubs under their wings. Her momma used to think she saw into the spirit world, but Ernie called them dream-things and said for to pay them no attention. Like the wasps—let 'em have their sniff, and they'll leave soon enough.

When she woke up in the middle of the night, crooked up against a rock covered in dry white lichen, she thought she might have seen a dream-thing.

He came up over the same way she had—up over the rock from where the lodge sat—but he wasn't dressed for the cold wind. He wasn't dressed at all in fact. He was a funny man: bare-naked, not even shoes and socks on, and even his privates dangled out for all to see.

"Ain't you cold?" Janie asked, but the funny man didn't even look at her.

Maybe the cold didn't bother him. He had a lot of hair on him, looked like blue in the dark. It went all up his back and down his chest, and the hair on his head and chin was real long, and his beard came up near to his eyes. And it seemed like there was a fire in those eyes—Janie didn't get to look at them directly, but she could see that everywhere the funny man looked got covered in a flickery orange light, like it was sitting near the firelight of the funny man's eyeballs.

So fired on the inside, furred on the outside, maybe clothes'd just heat the funny man up too much for his own good. Sometimes Janie felt that way too, particularly when her hots came on.

The funny man was moving on feet and fingertips the whole time, and his face kept close to the rock, like he was snuffling it. He was saying something over and over—Janie thought it sounded like *Yum-tum, yum-tum, yum-tum*, which were no words that she knew. He crawled over the top of the rock, and face-first down the inside slope of it. It was a pretty good trick—Janie'd fallen on her behind when she tried to get over and then she'd had to stand on level ground and get her bearings. But the funny man didn't even need to do that. He just turned around and started moving along the sides of those rocks, like he was a spider or an inchworm or some sticky-footed fly. When he'd come to a tree, he'd squeeze behind it if he could fit, and if he couldn't just lift his arms over it and sort of jump-like with his long hairy legs, and keep on yum-tum-ing along the rocks like nothing had happened. Janie'd put her fist to her mouth and gasped at that—he was sure a good climber, the funny man was.

And he kept at it, until he'd gone half-the-way around the rock circle and come up beside Janie where she leaned against it. For a minute, she thought he was going to crawl over her like she was another tree, rub his dangly privates all along her middle and then go on along the rock like he hadn't rubbed nothing. But the funny man didn't. The rock glowed next to her shoulder where he looked at it, and then his fire-filled eyes moved up to her yellow-clad shoulder and made it glow, and underneath the sweat oozed out of her skin like pus from a dirty cut. And then he said yum-tum again, and she knew it wasn't words at all. It was the sound his tongue made when it licked against the rock, tongue-out-yum, tongue-in-tum, right next to her arm.

Janie pulled away from him a little—she sure didn't want that long, knobbly old tongue licking *her* next, any more than she wanted those privates on her middle—and quick as she did, the funny man yum-tum-licked the rock where she'd been leaning. A big strip of lichen came away when he did.

Janie put her hand to her mouth again, and let out a little squeal. Of course! That's what the funny man was doing—she followed the path he'd taken around the rocks, and the whole way she found a dotted strip as wide as a tongue, like the passing line on the highway.

"Hey!" she said, turning back to him. "That lichen any good to eat?"

But the funny man was already gone. Or so Janie recalled as she sat up in the middle of the night, and looked at the rock beside her.

The funny man must have been a dream-thing, because the lichen on the rock face hadn't been touched. He'd just given it a sniff, and made on his way.

Janie ran her fingers across it—it was rough and dry and flaked under her thumb, and it was blue like the funny man's hair. It didn't seem much better than mustard and butter, but then Janie didn't see any harm in giving it a try either. She leaned close to the rock—so close she could feel the match-flame heat of her breath bounce back at her.

"Yum-tum," she said, and swallowed.

Outside the rock circle, the wind had been roaring and splashing and rattling things all night. But by the time Janie was done eating, it stopped making all that racket and went quiet. The lichen meal didn't quiet Janie's stomach any, however. It was twisting and yelping up at her like a colicky baby. Her aches elsewhere weren't so bad, but her belly . . .

Her belly would need quieting.

Janie peeled off some more lichen—just a little, a strip not much bigger than a postage stamp—and put it on her tongue. It was dry and tasted like dirt, and seemed like even the wet in her mouth wouldn't go near it. She shut her mouth, and made herself swallow, but the dry lichen gritted up in her throat like she was swallowing sand. She didn't let herself cough, though. Just kept swallowing and swallowing until the last of it was down.

Then she got up, and looked over the rock.

The water was still now, and the sky was clear. There was a tiny bit of moon up there. It was just a little crescent, like the cut on her head, like a bite mark, and it didn't give off very much light. There were a lot of stars, though, and the dim moon let them shine all the brighter. Janie could see a long swath of them across the middle of the sky. Stars had names, each and every one—but Janie didn't know any of them.

She cast her eyes down, and looked instead at the rock-face she'd near licked clean. She was pretty stupid, she guessed—couldn't even find something good to eat when her belly needed it. Not but butter and mustard and dry old lichen from the side of a rock.

Stupid dumb hoo-er! hollered her stomach. If it were a bear it'd have bitchya!

"Quiet, stomach," said Janie. She leaned closer to the rock, squinted at it now instead of the sky.

There was something written on it where she'd cleared away the lichen. No, she thought as she looked closer. Not written.

Drawn.

It was a picture—of some kind of animal it looked like. But it was no animal she'd ever seen, not altogether. There was a snout, and a big twisty horn coming out the middle, like the horn had come out of the middle of the horse's head in the story magazine. But there were wings too—open wide like it was flying, or pinned, like on the cover from ONE MILLION COPIES SOLD! THE DEAD BIRD—and a snaky tail that turned around twice coming out its behind. There was someone reaching for that tail, but below the wrist was covered up in lichen still.

For just a second, Janie wondered what else she'd find, when she licked off the rest of the lichen.

But her belly wouldn't have any more lichen, it'd had more than its fill of that dry old awful stuff. And her mouth wasn't about to make no spit to soften it, neither. So she would just have to keep wondering.

Maybe, she thought then, that butter and mustard wouldn't be so bad to eat after all. Her stomach didn't complain much at the thought of it, so she got up from the rock and clambered up over the lip of the circle.

It took her hardly no time to get down this time. It must, she thought at the bottom, be the lack of a breeze.

Janie didn't go straight to the lodge, though. Because now that it was clear and the water was still, she got a good view of the dock.

And she could see a canoe there.

It was a pretty big canoe—near to three times as long as the ones she'd seen folks using in the lakes near Fenlan. Whoever'd brought it had hauled it up onto the rock rather than leave it in the water, and turned it over on its top—to keep any rainwater out of it, Janie guessed.

Janie tromped down the side of the rock to look at the canoe a little bit closer. It was bark—made out of birch-bark, like those little souvenir toy canoes you could get for ten dollars at the Indian Trading Post on the highway. But those canoes'd break like matchsticks and paper if you squeezed them too hard, and Janie didn't think that this one would give in that easily.

Lordy, breaking this canoe'd bring down a beating like she'd never felt before.

If Ernie were here to give it, that was.

Janie felt herself grinning.

Ernie ain't here. I'm on my own now. Just me and my hungry old belly.

Janie bent over and picked up the end of the canoe. It was pretty heavy, but Janie could lift cinderblocks all day and not complain. The wood at the other end complained some, as it scraped against the wet rock. Janie lifted it over her head, then stepped back and let go, and the canoe-end landed at her feet with a bang.

She walked around to the side of it. She kicked it, and it rocked back and forth. She kicked it again, harder, and it nearly rolled over upright before it fell back down in its old spot. It rolled, but it didn't break. That is some strong birch-bark, thought Janie.

Save it, said her belly.

"Who are you," said Janie, "to tell me what to do?"

She kicked the canoe again. This time, however, rather than kicking out, she raised up her foot and brought it down with her weight behind it. And that seemed to do the trick. The canoe didn't roll this time—it stayed put, and there was a great crack as one of the wooden ribs underneath the bark gave way. When she lifted her foot to look, there was a dandy-looking dent in the bark, although she hadn't holed it yet.

Don't break it, said her belly. I'm warning you, Janie . . .

And to make its point, Janie's stomach spewed a little acid, and some of the lichen that wasn't digested yet along with it, in a thin stream back up her throat.

"Yech!" Janie spat and swallowed and did it again and again until the taste was nearly gone. But her throat still burned when she stopped, and she felt all out of breath.

"Goddamn stomach," she said—daring it to try it again. Nothing happened, though; if Ernie didn't like swear-words, her belly didn't seem to mind.

Janie looked at the canoe and stepped back from it. Ernie'd always said she could use some self-discipline. She wondered if this was what he'd meant.

Janie turned away from the lake—she didn't feel as much like making mischief on the canoe anyhow. She went up the steps to the lodge, and as she went, she wondered just who it was who'd bring that canoe. Could have been the funny man, but he was a dream-thing, and that canoe was pretty real, so it probably wasn't the funny man.

Janie'd just started to wonder if maybe the owner of that canoe wasn't hiding up in the lodge waiting for her, thinking to do *her* some mischief, when she heard the shaking. It sounded like the wind had sounded outside when she woke up—like the bone rattle where it shook the eaves on the outside, with a crack! when it broke something and a bong! when it knocked down a drum.

But now, she was on the outside. And it sounded like the wind was on the inside. "Isn't that something?" she said, and hurried up the weather-worn steps to the front of the lodge.

She peered in through the big front window, and sure enough, that seemed to be what was happening. There was a fierce Georgian Bay blow whirling around the rooms of the lodge. As she watched, maybe three paperback novels bounced off the window as the wind drove them across the room. Some of the pages of the story magazine Janie'd been looking at were stuck to the window, and if they weren't all upside down she might have read them. Mr. Swayze had a little iron hanging light, and it was swaying back and forth in the breeze—occasionally swinging so high that the side of it hit the ceiling with a thunk! noise.

Janie pressed her ear to the glass. Oh, it was cold! Seemed like the wind had taken all the cold it'd brought with it outside, and moved it inside. As she listened, she could hear the yowl it'd brought with it too. And she could hear something else. It sounded like—

—a chopping.

Janie closed her eyes, and caught the rhythm. Thunk! Then a moment while the axe-head pulled out of whatever it was cutting. Then thunk! again. And the same all over. It was just like Ernie would get, when he was cutting wood for the stove.

"Yep," she said. "Someone's chopping."

Then there came a crack! and Janie jumped back and held her ear. She hadn't been looking, and it had taken her by surprise.

Something had hit the glass hard, hard enough to crack it. She glared at the glass, and the little spider-web of cracks in it. Something else hit the glass, in the same spot, and the cracks spread.

It was one of Mr. Swayze's books. BOTTOM OF THE WELL—the back cover, the part that contained a little summary of the story and what the *Philadelphia Enquirer* had said about THE HAND— "First-class chills! Hookerman writes like he's lived it!"—and what *Publisher's Weekly* had said about THE CLOUD—"Richly detailed and un-put-downable!"

Janie giggled. It was like the wind inside was showing it to her— like it'd hit the glass once to get her attention, then put this here for her to read it.

The glass shook a bit under the pressure, and Janie could hear it moan as the cracks spread further. Janie read the summary, out loud: "When . . . they dug for . . . water, they didn't expect . . . to find a more . . ." she struggled, turning her head as the book slid and shifted along the glass ". . . *an-ci-ent* . . . ancient!" She clapped her hands together and smiled. *Ancient.* That meant *old.* "Ancient hunger," she finished. "Now . . . it's . . ." She frowned. Lost? No. "Loose! An' . . . And . . . they'll . . . never be . . . the same!"

And that was as far as she got, because the book flipped over and she was looking in the eye of that snake-head coming out of the pump-spout. Then she wasn't looking at anything, because the wind-pressure finally got too great, and the glass exploded outward.

The wind must've knocked Janie off her feet, and knocked her out for awhile too. She woke up in the lodge's main bedroom, where she and Ernie had been sleeping—all warm and covered up in a big quilted blanket. She looked under the covers and saw that she didn't have clothes on underneath.

That wasn't the only thing that changed. She felt her rib, and her elbow, then the little crescent-cut over her ear. They all felt better; like they'd been mending a few days, not just a couple more hours. Her hair was tied back, like she liked it, and she smelled all clean and pretty, like she had a bath.

The only thing that didn't change was how hungry she was. It was like a wound in her middle, all the more nagging, because of the smell that was coming in through the doorway. It was the smell of cooking— the salty-greasy smell of frying meat, with some spices maybe.

Janie got up out of bed. She didn't see clothes, but that didn't matter—she just wanted some of that food. She threw the comforter over her shoulders and opened the door to the living room.

It was like nothing had happened. The books were all up on their shelf, and the pages of the story magazine were nowhere to be seen . . . And there was no blood on the floor either, although she didn't remember cleaning up any of it. She'd almost say that the whole thing was just one of her dream-things, but the room was still freezing cold, on account of the broken front window. Some of the glass from it was sitting in a little garbage can by the fireplace.

"Janie!"

She almost jumped out of her skin. Mr. Swayze was standing in the doorway to the kitchen. He was wearing a dirty apron, and held a spatula in one hand, and a screwdriver in the other. He was smiling, but he looked a bit worried too.

"H-hello, Mr. Swayze." Janie clutched the blanket around her shoulders.

"It's good to see you up and around," he said. "You look like you've been through a lot."

Janie looked down at her feet, which were thick and bare, and her toes were pointing together. She straightened them. "E-Ernie, he took—"

Mr. Swayze put up his hand, and his face went all serious. "I know about Ernie," he said. "Don't worry, Janie. I found him before he got far. Ernie's in hand. Everything's taken care of. See?" He held up the screwdriver. "I even fixed the shelf."

Janie felt drool ridging over her lips.

"Hungry," she said, and looked over Mr. Swayze's shoulder into the kitchen.

At that, Mr. Swayze grinned again—a big toothy grin—and he laughed. "I bet you are, Janie," he said, and laughed again.

"Lichen doesn't take you very far, does it?"

Janie's stomach twisted like a hand-wrung facecloth—oh, it wanted that food *bad*—but Janie stood her ground for a minute.

"Lichen," she said, frowning. "How'd you know about lichen?"

"Why Janie," he said, and his grin widened some more. "If it weren't for the lichen, you and I wouldn't be here, having this conversation now. That's how he gets in, Janie." And then Mr. Swayze shut his eyes, and opened his mouth real wide. "Yum-tum," he said, and his tongue flicked out and back, like it was a frog's or something. He opened his eyes again, and as he did Janie had to look away. They were too bright.

"You're a quick study, Janie—a lot quicker than Ernie, which I wouldn't have expected." Mr. Swayze stepped over to her, but she still wouldn't look at him. He put his hand under the blanket and rested it on the bare flesh of her shoulder. It was hot.

"I wouldn't have expected it," said Mr. Swayze, "but I have to say, I'm glad."

Janie took hold of Mr. Swayze's hand on her shoulder, tried to lift it away. "Don't go touching me," she said. But he wouldn't move.

Her stomach bent around behind itself, it felt like. *Hungry! Food!* And Mr. Swayze let out a breath of hot, stinking air. "The spirit's fed me," he said. His voice trembled, like from hunger. "It's the wind and the sky and the cold, but oh Janie, it's fed me. Done me well. Do you know what I'm talking about?"

"Let me go," she said.

"You know—you just can't say yet. It's the spirit of the land here. It's the wind-walker—and it's the spirit of you too, Janie. You were always close to it—but you've never been closer than today." He squeezed hard on her shoulder. "This is like the property at Fenlan—another special place, Janie. You saw the drawings on the rocks, didn't you?"

"Like your book covers," said Janie. She thought about the twisted horn, and the hand and the snake, and the wings of the DEAD BIRD, all there on the rock face where she'd licked the lichen away.

"Right," he said. "Very good. And all that, my Janie . . ." His tongue came out, and caressed the sharp tips of his front teeth. "All that's just a *yum-tum* lick and a bite away." His smile went broader, and his nose twitched, like it was catching the smell of the cooking in the other room.

"Food," said Janie. "You take the food from here and stomp on that blueberry patch, Mr. Swayze?"

"*Wendigo.*" He whispered it like a dirty word in church. "That's what they call me, Janie. And that old food was no good for you. It wasn't what you needed, any more than that butter and that mustard'd do the trick. And forget about blueberries! You're not a blueberry girl anymore, Janie. Now you come on with me to the kitchen—and eat some *meat.*" His eyes went all yellow with the heat in him.

"You may be *Wen-digo*, but you ain't Ernie," she said flatly. "I don't got to do nothing."

It was true, Janie thought. Because although the smell of cooked meat was all over her, although Mr. Swayze wouldn't let go even though she told him to, although she was so Goddamned hungry she could just about gnaw off her own arm for it and would have just loved to go into the kitchen for some meat now, none of those things could compel her. Ernie was the only one who ever really could, and he was gone.

Janie reached up and grabbed Mr. Swayze by the ear, which his big old grin had nearly reached. He stopped grinning when she twisted it and his face went like that wasp nest that time, all angry and twisted and ready to bite. She twisted it some more, and then there was some blood, and then Mr. Swayze's hand came away from her shoulder and took hold of her arm.

It didn't do him any good, though. Janie felt the heat in her arm before his hand got to it. She made a fist, and there was a tearing sound, and then Mr. Swayze howled, and the last bit of bloody gristle went snap! and his ear came clean off. Mr. Swayze stumbled backward, holding onto his head and squealing like a pig.

Without thinking, Janie pushed the ear into her mouth. It was crunchy, like a chicken knee, and it tasted a little bitter on account of the ear wax. She got it down in two gulps, and as she swallowed, her stomach stopped complaining.

The fire went out of Mr. Swayze's eye then, and he turned and tried to run from her, but she wasn't going to let him go. She kicked out, and caught him in the small of the back—and when he fell, she stood over him and kicked down, like she had on the canoe. She heard the crack of another couple of ribs breaking—these ones in Mr. Swayze's chest and not in the canoe. Her stomach didn't give her any trouble about breaking these ribs, though, or about breaking the skin on the next kick.

If anything, she thought it might be egging her on.

Janie kicked him once more in the head, and with that, Mr.

Swayze's neck cricked all funny and he stopped moving. For a moment, she thought about bending down and opening her mouth wide, and just finishing him that way.

Instead, she stepped back and sealed her lips.

Yum-tum, said her stomach as she moved over to the bookshelf. She pulled down the copy of ONE MILLION COPIES SOLD! THE DEAD BIRD.

Janie ran her finger along the book-cover's feather-bumps. They were pretty good feathers. She wondered for a minute whether they might have used a real feather to make it—some complicated thing where you pressed the paper on top of the feather with a steam iron, so the real thing would be there in the book. Maybe the book people had come out here, and rubbed it off the stone up the hill.

Janie opened up the book.

"*Pro-log-oo*," she said. "Oh. I get it. *Prologue.*"

Yum-tum. There were other smells too—more exquisite in their way, coming off of Mr. Swayze's cooling corpse by the kitchen door. Janie could imagine burying her face in that fresh meat, lapping up the blood like it was a fine liquor.

"The—the—" Janie concentrated on the next word. "Laughing," she finally said, and laughed herself. "The *laughing* man stood on the side of the dirt road and—and . . ."

. . . and watched the storm boil in from the west. It was going to be bad, he knew; twisters like claws from some ancient beast would scour the lands and lift the things of those lands high into the sky. The storm would ride this place—ride it, and devour it. Nothing would be left in its wake but ruin and sadness. The laughing man thought about that. It would leave the land exposed. And that would be bad for the ones who were left. Because they would be easy pickings, he knew.

Easy pickings for It.

Behind her, glass cracked as the wind outside grew, and flung something at the house—no doubt to get Janie's attention. She hunched over the book—let her mind go to the words inside it, the way the wind—the Wen-digo—wanted her mind to go to it.

Mr. Swayze's book didn't say it yet, but Janie had a pretty good idea what "It" was. In the book, it was more than likely that DEAD BIRD from the cover.

Janie closed ONE MILLION COPIES SOLD! THE DEAD BIRD and put it back on the shelf. There had been a photograph underneath the author biography at the back of the book, but it wasn't Mr. Swayze's. They'd taken a picture of a bearded man—hair down to his shoulders, up near to his eyes. Might have even been the funny man. Or maybe the Laughing Man? Laughing and funny: the words meant just about the same thing, as Janie thought about it.

"Yum-tum," she said.

The wind outside wasn't letting up—if anything, it was getting worse. Frothing the waters; scouring the land; exposing those that remained . . . Making them easy pickings.

Easy pickings for Janie.

That was just how it was going to be.

That wind was calling to her, it was time to move on, and somehow she knew she wouldn't be able to stay put anywhere for very long now. She ran her tongue along her sharpening teeth. Good thing she hadn't holed that canoe, else she'd be swimming.

Night of the Tar Baby

A nasty breeze caught the fumes off the still-bubbling tar pot and brought them along the shortest route it could find into Shelly's nostrils. It was the foulest thing that Shelly had ever smelled; tar fumes stank like distilled pain, a kick in the gut or a smack across the ear, and they made her cough when they reached down into her lungs. At the sound she made, her brother Blaine punched her hard in the side.

"Shut up!" he hissed. "We're gonna get caught!"

"You shut up!" said Shelly. It was a struggle to keep her voice from quavering—Blaine was thirteen, three years older than her, and he was starting to get his man-arm. He'd hit her harder than he knew, maybe, and her ribs ached from it.

"Quiet, both of you." Their dad crouched beside them, behind the highway sign that announced a new Petro-Canada service centre was coming here by October. His arms were crossed on the wash-basin he'd brought with them. The trowel dangling in his hand cut through the air to emphasize what he said. "This is just what I was talking about back at the house. This is why we're here tonight. Time to stop all the fighting."

"Whatever," said Blaine. "This won't land you back in jail, will it?"

"This," said Dad, "will keep all of us from jail, for the rest of our lives."

"Then why are you stealing tar, not paying for it down at the hardware?"

"Got to be filched," said Dad. "That's part of the magic."

"Whatever." Blaine rolled his eyes.

It was pretty clear that Blaine didn't buy any of this—and Shelly knew she should probably defer to her brother's judgement. After all, the last time their dad had been home for any length of time, Shelly was just five years old; Blaine, at eight, had known their father that much longer—lived through five more years of Dad's promises and schemes, aftermaths of his barroom fights and late-night visits from angry OPP patrolmen; Lord knew how many three-day benders with his former buddy Mark Hollins; and maybe one or two more solemn pledges to improve himself, and turn all their lives around.

Maybe Mom was right, and Dad was just full of shit.

Dad started down from the sign, and into the midst of the construction site. The workers had laid foundations for the garage in a huge cinderblock rectangle; there were more bricks stacked over by the trees, along with some lumber, and there was a yellow digging machine that Dad figured was to hollow out a place for the big tanks underneath the pumps.

But Dad didn't care about the digging machine, or where the tanks would go or anything else. He was after the tar pot, which had been left simmering through the night. Dad figured they had about half an hour from the time the work crew left, to the time the night watchman arrived—and that would be plenty of time to do what they needed to do.

Dad set the basin down beside the tar pot, making the bent-up twigs and wire rattle.

"Get the turpentine ready," he said. "Blaine, you listening?"

"I'm listening." Blaine reached into his pack, and pulled out the shoebox-sized tin of turpentine they'd brought along. "It's here," he said.

"All right." Dad set the trowel down a moment and rubbed his hands together. He reached into the breast pocket of his jean jacket, and pulled out a little brown plastic bottle Shelly recognized as one of Mom's old painkiller prescriptions. He pushed on the safety lid, twisted it open, and held it over the pot. After a couple of seconds, something thick and white like condensed milk dripped out, made a long, snotty line between bottle and pot. Dad held it there until the last was poured out, then threw the empty bottle behind him.

"Shelly," he said, "hand me the skeleton."

"Don't call it that," said Shelly quietly.

"That's what it is," said Dad, sounding puzzled. "But I won't call it that. Just give it to me careful."

Shelly reached down and lifted the thing from the basin. It wasn't more than two feet long—bigger than a newborn, to be sure; but not so big she should be scared of it. She shouldn't be scared; but when a still-green twig bent like an arm flopped against Shelly's knee as she lifted it, she nearly dropped the thing. Dad was right—this *was* a skeleton, and it was crazy to call it anything else. When she handed the skeleton off to Dad, she was trembling.

"I hate this," she said.

"I know." Dad smiled down at her with what seemed like real love—but it didn't make her feel better. He cradled the little wooden skeleton with nearly as much affection as he lowered it to the stinking tar.

"This is going to help us all," he said, as he dipped it head-first into the boiling tar. "Everything's better from now on."

"Dad?" said Shelly as they worked. "What do we need a tar baby for anyway?"

Dad was watching the tar. "You remember what I told you about Mr. Baldwin, don't you, honey?"

Shelly remembered the story, all right; Dad had told it his first night back, while everyone sat around the kitchen table not looking at each other and picking at their food.

Mr. Baldwin was Dad's prison buddy—his cell-mate for years. And Mr. Baldwin swore by his tar baby; a little man he kept under his bunk.

Mr. Baldwin's tar baby was made from a pot on the roof of the pen's south wing when it was under construction back in the 1970s and Mr. Baldwin had drawn work duty there. According to Dad, Mr. Baldwin was a puny fellow, more like a boy than a man in those days, and although Dad wouldn't say why, small size and smooth skin was always a problem in a jail house. "Particularly when you're like Mr. Baldwin, and won't stand for nothing," he said.

Mr. Baldwin had explained how he'd made the tar baby when he and Dad were cell-mates for a few months before Dad's release, and Dad had paid close attention. After all, Dad explained—Mr. Baldwin was still alive after all these years, and although he wasn't any bigger, and his skin wasn't smooth anymore, it wasn't scarred much either. Mr. Baldwin said he'd never been forced to do anything he didn't care for, and over time since that day on the roof when the tar baby got born, everyone got to calling him Mister.

"It was a good time, when I was in with Mr. Baldwin," Dad said, eyes focused far away and voice gone wistful. "No threats, no fights—nothing bad, nothing harmful. Men were respectful. The tar baby taught *everyone* a lesson."

"Sounds boring," said Blaine, watching the tar boil and bubble, the brambly skeleton now vanished beneath its surface.

"Hush," said Dad. "You don't know what you're talking about, boy." He leaned forward, peering through the thick fumes into the pot. "We need a tar baby, little girl, because your brother thinks peacefulness and respect are *boring*."

Shelly still didn't understand why Dad wanted a tar baby now that he was outside of jail, but she figured it was better not to press the point. Dad was concentrating.

"Is it done?" she asked instead.

"I think so. Lord, I wish Mr. Baldwin were here now. He'd know for sure."

"Maybe we should wait," said Shelly.

Dad thought about this, and shook his head. "No. It's time now. Blaine?" Without looking up, Dad held his hand out. Blaine rolled his eyes at Shelly, and hefted the can of turpentine. Dad took it, unscrewed the top and held it over the pot.

"Hold your nose," said Dad. He mumbled a verse about hair and salt and lizards, and began to pour. The turpentine in the hot tar made an awful dark vapour where it etched out the tar baby from the rest of it, and even though Shelly's nose was held tight, she could taste it on her tongue and feel it in her eyes as it rose up around them and blotted out the dim light of the evening. She shut her eyes against it, sealed her lips, but it was still around her; she felt it sticking to her like the tar it'd come from, and the substance of it stayed on her even when the smoke cleared and Dad, arms tar-black to the elbow and grinning like a little boy, pronounced them done for the night.

"Come on," said Blaine. "Get up off the ground, stupid, and let's go."

Shelly flinched back—expecting another punch maybe. But Blaine stood against the darkening sky with Dad, his hands tucked safely into his armpits.

"Before the cops come," said Blaine.

Mom was watching an old episode of *Frasier* on TV when they got back, and when Dad came through the door after Shelly and Blaine, she glared at him like he was trespassing. In a way, he was. This was, strictly speaking, Mom's house; she'd inherited it from her own mother, free and clear back before Shelly'd been born. The house was miles outside town, on an ugly flat scratch of land where the grass grew too high and you saw the neighbours by the smoke from their woodstoves in the winter. But it was theirs, free and clear.

Mom called it their haven; for without the security of a paid-off house in a jurisdiction where the taxes were low, who knew where their awful circumstances would take them? She couldn't work anymore, not since the accident at the restaurant three years back where she'd bunged her knee; a mortgage or even regular rent on a place like this would ruin them. She couldn't carry it on worker's comp alone.

"Keep that thing in the shed," she said, as Dad brought the basin inside. Mom probably wouldn't have sounded angry to anyone but Shelly, and maybe Blaine.

If Dad understood her tone, he didn't let on. "Won't do in the shed," he said. "Got to be here, or there wasn't any point."

Mom rolled her eyes. "*There wasn't any point.* You got that right." She picked up the remote from the side of the couch and pointed at the TV. Frasier's dad and the little dog vanished, and the room darkened a bit. With a grunt, Mom shifted her feet from the couch to the floor, and lifted herself on her cane. It was no mean feat; Mom had gotten *heavy* since she'd taken off work. "You going to catch a rabbit with that?" she asked.

Dad didn't get it, and Mom laughed unkindly.

"Mom's talking about Bre'r Rabbit," said Shelly, trying to help. "From *Song of the South*." She'd seen the movie over at her friend's house at Thanksgiving, and there was a tar baby in it. Bre'r Fox had used it to catch Bre'r Rabbit—and it'd nearly worked.

"Jail didn't teach you much, did it now?" she said.

Dad sucked in his breath, like he was about to say something— and he looked down at the basin in his arms.

"Oh no," he said. "We're not starting *this* again. Not now." He looked up, and his eyes had a calm about them.

"I'm putting this in the basement," he said. "You won't have to smell it, or even look at it if you don't want to. So it won't be any trouble for you—all right?"

"Whatever you say, *dear*," said Mom, then turned to address Shelly. "Lord, now, isn't it good to have a man around here? See, I wouldn't have any idea how to put a bucket of tar in the basement and *not* stink up my house with it. Stupid little me wouldn't know how to keep those fumes out of the vents, and before you know it, all the sheets'd start stinking like a blacktop highway in July!"

She was looking at Shelly, but she was moving towards Dad, stumping sideways on her cane like some kind of crab. Shelly tried not to glare at her: it seemed like Mom just couldn't give Dad a chance.

"And why, I'd *never* think to take my two children out to steal tar from a construction site! On a night just two days I'd been out of jail!"

Dad was grinning now. He held out the basin in front of him as Mom came nearer. The metal of it made a bonging sound as he lifted it an inch or so.

"Good thing," she said, raising her free hand and touching the rim of the basin, "my husband's come home to set things *right!*"

"Careful, Dornie," Dad said. "Don't want to get yourself into a state."

Mom still wasn't looking at Dad—she didn't stop looking at Shelly, and Shelly could see by her narrow eyes that Mom was working herself into quite a state indeed. If that state had been directed at Shelly, she would have been frightened for herself—but tonight, Shelly was just a channel, a way for five years and a day of bottled-up rage to get to Dad.

So Shelly just watched as events unfolded.

Mom's fist tightened around the edge of the basin, and she shifted her weight so she didn't need the cane under her and could lift it into the air so as to swing it. "I'll give you a *fuckin'* state," she said in a low and terrible voice, finally turning her angry eyes to focus right on Dad. The basin began to tip toward her under her weight. Dad smiled, and the metal bonged again.

There was a third bong, and it seemed as though Mom's already-unsteady footing slipped, and the basin overturned. Mom yelped, and tried to yank her hand away. Dad's grin opened up into a toothy smile, and he let the basin fall to the floor. Shelly shut her eyes as it hit—thinking about all the tar inside it, and how it'd be to clean up tar, how long it would take and what kinds of solvents she'd need to do the job to Mom's standards.

But when she opened her eyes again, she saw there'd be no need—the old shag carpet didn't have a drop of tar on it, because the tar baby was all over Mom.

It had taken hold of her hand first—two twig-boned fists grasped her fingers, and it must have used her fingers to swing on because all of a sudden its skinny tar-black legs were wrapped around her elbow. Mom was wearing a bright yellow tank-top, no sleeves, so it hadn't gotten on her clothes right at first. But as Mom reached over with her free hand to try and yank the tar baby off, she pushed the thing's back against her chest, and that did it. She was a mess.

Mom looked like a big bat as she lifted both arms away from her, strands of tar making a web between them and her chest—where the tar baby seemed to have fixed itself. *"Get it off!"* she hollered. *"Get this fuckin' thing off me!"*

Dad was laughing so you could hear it now. He bent over and slapped his blue-jeaned knee, and fell down to his knees and laughed some more, shaking his head.

"Look at that," he said. "Damn me if it's not suckling off you, Mama!" And he howled.

Sure enough, thought Shelly, it did look like the tar baby was suckling. Somehow, it had managed to get turned around and now its face—or at least the front of its head; the tar baby didn't really have a face—mashed into Mom's left breast, like it was taking milk.

With nothing there to hold it up, the tar baby started to peel away from Mom's tank-top; and for a second, as it turned first to face the ceiling and then forward, Shelly thought she could make out a little grinning face on the thing—mouth open, thin snot-strands of tar between upper and lower jaw, and tiny little button-eyes, staring up at Mom's tit. But the face went away as the tar baby turned, and it was just a mound of hardening tar again. Mom'd stopped hollering, and she'd started to sob. Dad picked up the basin from where it'd fallen on the floor, and held it under the tar baby. It fell into it with a bong.

Everyone stood silent. Mom was covered in tar—somehow, it'd gotten on her face and into her hair; it smeared down her shoulders and onto her hands like lines of thick, black finger-paint. Mom looked up at Blaine, and cleared her throat.

"Blaine honey," she said, voice calm and reasonable. "Fetch your Mom her cane."

Blaine did as he was told, but when it came time to hand the cane over, he didn't get too close to Mom. Shelly didn't blame him. Mom took the cane, propped it against the floor and pushed herself to her feet.

"I'll just put the baby in the basement then," said Dad, to no one in particular. He whistled as he carried the basin into the kitchen and down the stairs.

"You mean the *tar* baby," said Shelly, but Dad was beyond hearing.

Dad drank beer from a bottle at the kitchen table, and Shelly sat with him, sipping her Coke from the can. They didn't speak at all while the shower ran; Dad had just stared out the window into the dark yard, drank his beer, and occasionally reached over to pat Shelly on the hand.

For her part, Shelly just watched him. She hadn't seen Dad since she was just five—not properly anyway, not outside of a prison visitation—and he was for all practical purposes a complete mystery to her. He had last gone to jail for armed robbery—he'd used a hunting rifle to rob a grocery store in Huntsville with his buddy Mark Hollins, who'd gotten off as an accomplice and did hardly any time in jail at all. Shelly tried to imagine her father doing such a thing, and found again that she couldn't. When she'd gone to see him with Mom and Blaine, he was always laughing and gentle—even when Mom egged him on. It wasn't that there was any doubt he'd done the robbery; Dad had confessed to it and pleaded guilty when it came time to go to court. It was just that Shelly couldn't see how he'd done it, pulling out a gun and telling someone to hand over their money or they'd get it. Dad just seemed . . . too nice. Compared to the rest of the family, that was.

Finally, the shower shut off, and Dad squinted at the ceiling, like he was gauging something there.

"Out of hot water," he said.

"Maybe she's clean now," said Shelly.

Dad just shook his head. "Soap and water won't do a thing to tar. Your mother should know better."

Shelly nodded as though she understood, and swallowed the last of her Coke.

"She'll know better now," said Dad, staring back out the window.

They sat quiet again, as Mom stomped wet-footed on the floor upstairs and the vestiges of water drained from the bathtub through the old pipes under her feet, over their heads. Shelly squeezed her Coke can as if to crush it, but she didn't have the strength and the side just popped. Dad started at the sound, then smiled, and reached over to put his big hand over Shelly's. "Let's both squeeze," he said. Dad's thick fingers pushed on Shelly's, and for a minute she felt like he was crushing her against the can. But the metal crumpled easily under their combined grip, and Shelly laughed when Dad let go of her.

"Teamwork," said Dad. "That's what this family's going to be about, from now on, little girl."

"Teamwork?"

Dad nodded sagely. "Most families do it, you know—ours is just peculiar that way. Or it has been. We've been like a bad cell block in a bad jail; we're always fighting and squabbling and hurting each other. Won't be the case any more."

Shelly looked up at her father, who was staring back out the window. It was true what he said; they *were* like a bad cell block in a bad jail, or at least they were always hurting each other. Dad had a point.

"Mom's wrong about you," she whispered.

Dad blinked, and smiled down into the dregs of his beer. He gave Shelly a squeeze around the shoulders.

"You better go to bed, little girl," said Dad. "It's late."

The bathroom door opened upstairs, and Mom made her way noisily to her own bedroom. A minute later, the mist of her shower wafted down—carrying with it the combined scent of perfumed soaps, old angry sweat, and tar-fume.

It was, Shelly realized, the first time she'd smelled tar since Dad had shut the basement door and Mom had gotten in the shower. For whatever reason, the tar baby's smell had just stayed put. Shelly laughed to herself: Mom had been wrong on *that* score too.

Dad stood up, and patted Shelly on the back. "Come on, little girl," he said. "Daddy's going out for a walk—you get on up to bed."

Blaine was already in the top bunk when she came into the bedroom. He had his reading light on, and was propped up on an elbow over some kind of magazine—Shelly couldn't see what because of the angle, but she suspected it was one of his mountain biking magazines.

"I'm not turning out the light," said Blaine.

"Who said I want you to?"

"You always want to go to sleep early."

"I'm not the one in *bed* already."

Blaine glared at her, picked up his magazine, and rolled over so he was facing the wall. Paper rustled angrily as he positioned the magazine out of his own shadow.

"You're lucky," he muttered.

Shelly supposed he was right. Normally, after a little exchange like that one, Blaine would swing down from the bunk, grab Shelly in a headlock and take the last word in the argument by sheer might. Shelly would have to apologize—no, she would have to *beg*, and if she were lucky, that would be all it took.

Tonight, Shelly guessed she was really lucky.

She sat down on the bottom bunk and pulled off her T-shirt. The springs over her head creaked as Blaine shifted his weight.

"Lucky," he said again, his voice low and kind of scary. "I could come down and pound you right now. You know I'd do it."

Shelly unbuttoned her jeans, pulled them off and slid under the covers.

"You know that—don't you, shitty Shelly?"

"Stop it, Blaine."

"*Shitty Shelly*," said Blaine, and he started to sing it: "*Shitty Shelly shitty Shelly.*"

"Stop it," she repeated, but of course he wouldn't.

"Shitty Shelly shitty Shelly. What are you gonna do, shitty Shelly? Get mad like Mom did?"

"This is *stupid*," she said. "This is what Dad was talking about."

She rolled back on her haunches, and lifted her feet to the

mattress of the top bunk. Part of her screamed a warning: *Suicide! Don't even try it!* But the taunt was getting under her skin—Blaine knew how to get under her skin better than almost anyone—and she couldn't help herself. She bucked back on her shoulders, and pushed hard against the mattress with her feet—not too hard, just enough to send him a message.

She felt Blaine's weight roll to one side, and heard a crack! sound like snapping wood, and she felt the bed-frame tremble even as Blaine shouted. If she'd been even a little angry a second ago, it was all gone now; Shelly was just scared.

"You dumb bitch!" Blaine sounded an inch from tears. "You dumb goddamn bitch! That was my *head!*"

Before she could even answer, Blaine was half-way down the ladder from the top bunk. His head. She guessed she'd rolled him against one of the bed-posts, given him a good bang on the skull. Blaine was going to pound her all right. Shelly screwed her eyes shut and curled herself into a ball—waiting for the rain of fists that would follow, and hoping they'd just fall on her back and shoulders. She knew from bitter experience that if she let Blaine get to her stomach and face, there'd be no end to the pain . . .

But the punching didn't come.

Blaine made a strangling sound, and she heard the sound of his bare feet moving across the floor—and then she heard the door open and close.

"You're dead!" He yelled it from the hall, like he was chasing her, then repeated it from the bottom of the stairs:

"You're dead!"

Cautiously, Shelly opened her eyes.

"B-Blaine?" she whispered.

But of course he didn't answer: she was alone in the bedroom. Distantly, she heard the sound of a door downstairs opening and closing again. Shelly wasn't sure, but it might have been the basement door in the kitchen. She curled more tightly around herself, and shut her eyes again.

Shelly didn't sleep. Part of it was the Coke she'd had with Dad, but mostly she stayed awake thinking about the tar baby, and what it'd done to Mom. This, she guessed, was how it was when Mr. Baldwin got in trouble with the other men in prison back in the early days. She tried to imagine how it would have been—Mr. Baldwin's first night with the tar baby. Maybe the guy who had the top bunk there was looking for some trouble like Blaine had been, holding it and stoking it and building his meanness through the evening until it was something he could use, in the small hours of the night.

Behind her closed eyes, she could almost see the two of them, skinny little Mr. Baldwin lying still like a rabbit underneath his blanket, and the other prisoner—probably he was a lot bigger, and had been in a lot of fights, just like Blaine—him jumping down like he wants a piece, saying *"Shitty Baldwin, shitty Baldwin, shitty Baldwin"* over and over again. And because Mr. Baldwin wouldn't answer him, and wouldn't do what he said, and maybe earlier that day lipped off to him like Shelly had lipped off to Blaine, that other prisoner reached down to grab onto his shoulder, and give him a beating.

Only it wasn't Mr. Baldwin's shoulder he grabbed. He reached down to the bucket by his bunk, and that prisoner had his hand stuck deep in the tar baby's shoulder. Before he could think, he hit that tar baby again, and one more time, and that was it—he was stuck. Just like Bre'r Rabbit in the movie. Just like Mom tonight.

Shelly wondered if Mr. Baldwin laughed that first time, the way Dad had laughed when Mom had gotten herself tangled up in their tar baby.

Or, she thought with a shiver, *maybe Mr. Baldwin just lay in his bunk, all curled up trying to go to sleep, while his cell mate choked on tar on the floor beside him.*

Blaine had been downstairs a long time. And Dad was still out walking, and Mom hadn't budged from her bedroom.

And hadn't Dad said something about teamwork?

Shelly got out of bed and pulled on her T-shirt. "Mom!" she

shouted, pushing her feet through the legs of her jeans. "Hey, Mom!"

She walked barefoot across the floor of the bedroom and opened the door to the hallway. She took a breath to yell—

—and coughed.

The air in the hallway was sticky with the stink of tar, and she had a lungful of it. Shelly reeled back, covering her face with her hand, but of course her fingers were no filter and the damage had already been done. She coughed again, and gasped, and managed, finally, to yell—"Mom!"

Shelly stumbled forward, holding onto the banister around the stairwell as she did. The air seemed to get worse the further she went, and by the time she pushed Mom's bedroom door open, she was barely taking half-breaths. The door swung open, and Shelly ran past the bed—not even looking to see if Mom was there—and fell against the windowsill. Her lungs had hitched a final time, and now she couldn't breathe at all. With the last of her strength, she grabbed onto the base of the window and hefted it up.

Shelly pressed her face against the screen, coughed one more time, and sucked deep of the clean summer night air, looked at the empty driveway, the dark land around the house. In the distance, over the low treetops, she could see the lights from the highway.

"Mom," she said, not turning back, "we got to go downstairs and help out Blaine. I think he got messed up with the tar baby. He—he was picking on me, and he turned around and went downstairs, and I think he's in the basement . . ."

Shelly paused. In the distance, she could hear a car engine straining up a hill; crickets rubbed their legs together in the long grass of their front yard, and the thin breeze made the leaves of the birch-tree around the side rustle like paper. From inside the house, she heard a sound that must have been the refrigerator, a rattling whine as the compressors got going.

From Mom, she didn't hear a thing.

Shelly took another breath, turned around to face the bed and made her way slowly to the still, dark form laying atop the sheets. Shelly swallowed hard. The tar smell was pretty awful as she got closer, but she was expecting it now and she knew better than to breathe too deep.

Shelly stopped by her bedside, and looked down at her mother, Mom lay flat on her back, buck-naked, on top of the bedspread still wet with shower-water. Her feet were apart, and her hands were spread from her torso so no limb touched another. The tar had tinted her flesh from head to foot; it matted her hair, and gathered in globs around her shoulders and across her wide breasts, like tiny birth-marks. Mom's eyes were open, and they looked at Shelly steadily. Her chest swelled as she drew a breath to speak.

"Mom's not—" she paused, shut her eyes, and continued, her voice rough and deep, like she had a cold "—not feeling good now, honey. You go to bed."

Shelly shook her head. "No, Mom, I was telling you: Blaine's gone to the basement, I think." She stomped her foot, and heard her voice go whiny. "You got to *come!*"

"No good," said Mom. "Knee's acting up again."

"I think Blaine's in trouble, Mom. You got to come help him."

Mom licked her lips, then made a face like she'd bit a lemon.

"Tar's everywhere," she said. "Even on m' mouth."

"*Mom—*"

"Hey!" Mom's voice took some energy. "Don't you take that tone with me! This is *my* house, Missy!"

Mom lifted her hand up, as if to cuff Shelly, but she didn't get far: whether it took strength or will to pull away from her bed, Mom didn't seem to have enough of either.

"Your Daddy," she said, "is a very *bad* man."

Shelly opened her mouth to argue some more—to point out that Dad wasn't the one who wouldn't get out of bed to help his son; that Dad had paid for his crimes, if he'd even *done* them in the first place; that Mom wasn't always the nicest lady in town either. But she remembered why she was here: Blaine, she feared, had gotten himself into some pretty immediate trouble; and Mom was in some kind of trouble too. She didn't like to move around much as a rule since her knee had gotten hurt, but tonight, it seemed like she was *drained*. It was like when that tar baby had latched onto her breast, it had sucked something vital out of her.

"Don't know why I married him," said Mom, shutting her eyes.

"Maybe," said Shelly, "Dad would be better if you didn't keep being so mean."

Mom's brow crinkled.

"You don't know what you're saying, Shelly," she said.

"I know what I see." Shelly stepped away from the bed. "Dad trying to fix things, and you lying in that bed."

Mom's eyes opened now, and Shelly could see they were wet with tears. Now she did lift her hand, and brushed the air near Shelly's arm. Shelly flinched away—she didn't want those sticky-black fingers anywhere near her.

"You don't know him," said Mom, her voice nearly a whisper.

"He's my *Dad*," said Shelly. "Never mind about Blaine. I'll just help him myself."

Shelly stepped back into the hallway. A taste of salt came into her mouth as she closed the door on her Mom, but she swallowed it and made her way downstairs.

Dad had left the light on in the kitchen, and he'd left his empty beer out and Shelly's empty Coke-can out too. The smell was better down here, because he'd also left the kitchen door open, and a breeze washed through the screen door and through all the rooms on the first floor.

And of course the door to the basement was shut tight.

Shelly knocked on the door. "Blaine?" she called. "You all right?"

"Shelly!" Blaine sounded like he was muffled by something, talking through the hood of his snowsuit. "Shelly! I'm sorry I called you names!"

Shelly stepped back from the door. Now it was her turn to be speechless; in all her life, Blaine had never once apologized for anything.

"Shelly? You still there, Shelly?"

"I'm here," she said, cautiously.

"I'm sorry, Shelly!"

Shelly took a breath. "You're forgiven."

"Great," said Blaine, and his voice returned nearer to normal. "Give me a hand down here, will you? Bring down a towel, and—"

"—some turpentine?" Shelly finished for him.

Blaine laughed nervously.

"Yeah," he said.

Shelly laughed as well. It was like a weight had been lifted from her. All the way down the stairs, she was sure whatever happened with Mom had also happened with Blaine; the tar baby would suck the life out of him like it did from Mom. But he sounded okay, even improved by the experience.

Shelly went over to the counter, where Dad had put the can of turpentine, and lifted it down. She grabbed a tea-towel from the handle to the stove. "I'm—"

She was about to say *coming*, but she stopped, as a set of headlights appeared at the end of the driveway, and the sound of a truck engine broke the quiet. Bright headlights washed across the kitchen, shuffling shadows from one end of the room to another.

The truck rolled to a stop beside the kitchen—it was a big pickup truck, painted bright red, and Dad sat in the driver's seat. In the passenger seat, Shelly saw, was a long-haired, bearded man she hadn't seen in a couple of years: since when she was really small, and Dad hadn't been to prison for his second time.

It was Mark Hollins.

The man Dad had robbed the grocery store with—the one who'd gotten off with hardly any time in jail at all. He was laughing at something Dad was saying, and then he stopped and looked in through the window—straight at Shelly. He was still smiling, at least with his mouth—but his eyes had a different kind of look to them. If Shelly had been thinking of enlisting Dad's help in cleaning up her brother, pulling him out of whatever he'd tangled himself up in downstairs, the look in Mark Hollins' eyes dissuaded her.

"Shelly!" Blaine's voice was plaintive. "Come on!"

Shelly looked away from Hollins, and opened the basement door.

"I'm coming," she said. By the time Dad and Mark Hollins were out of the new truck, Shelly had closed the door behind her and was making her way down to where Blaine had gotten himself stuck.

The air had been okay on the first floor, but it was bad again in the basement. Shelly wasn't caught by surprise by it this time, though; even before she turned on the light, she expected the tar baby's stink would be the worst where it lived.

When she turned on the light, Shelly thought she might never breathe right again.

The basement was filled with tar.

It looked like two pages of a book, with a wad of black chewing gum squished between and stretched out as the book came open. Jump-rope-thick strands of tar stretched from wall to wall, ceiling to floor, casting shadows as black as itself. The strands twitched now and then, and before long, Shelly's eye was drawn to the likely cause of that twitching—two shapes suspended in the middle.

Her brother Blaine and the tar baby were locked together there, hanging about five feet off the cement floor, directly over the floor drain, and the now-empty washbasin the tar baby had come in.

The tar baby had come in the washbasin, but Shelly figured it would never leave in it. The tar baby had stretched and fattened to the point where it was almost as big as Blaine; bigger, she realized with a chill, than she was. Its legs were wrapped around Blaine's waist, and its arms, long and spindly, hugged Blaine around the chest. Its head—once the size of a softball, now about as big as the Nerf football Blaine kept on his desk upstairs—pressed against Blaine's cheek.

Blaine struggled to look up the stairs at her. His face was blackened with tar, and as he moved, one of the tar baby's hands slithered up his neck, to the back of his scalp. His eyes screwed shut and he sobbed, as the hand fell away again, pulling a small clump of tarry hair out with it.

"*Oh, Blaine.*"

Shelly whispered it—she was pretty sure Blaine couldn't hear her she was talking so quiet, but it seemed as though the tar baby could. Its head fell back from Blaine, like it had from Mom earlier in the night, and it cricked back on its skinny neck, so it was looking straight at Shelly. Last time she'd seen it, the tar baby seemed to open its mouth. Now, there was no doubt about it: the cut in the tar of its chin was fully formed, into a jagged grin like a jack-o-lantern.

"I'm sorry, Shelly. I'm sorry, Shelly. I'm sorry, Shelly." Blaine's eyes were still closed, and his voice was strangled with tears now as he repeated the apology again and again. It was like he was apologizing for every *shitty Shelly* he'd said upstairs. As Shelly thought about it, she started to feel the heat of anger come up in her again.

"Do you *mean* it?" she said, her voice low.

"I'm sorry, Shelly."

One of the tar baby's arms unfastened itself from Blaine, and the creature started to dangle. There was a sucking sound, as a strand of tar snapped away from Blaine's ankle, and he kicked his foot free of the other two still there.

"Do you *really* mean it? Or are you just saying nice to get in my good books? So I'll help you down?"

"Dad was right," said Blaine. The tears had stopped, and he was able to look at Shelly with a directness that made her want to cringe. There was a twang, and a couple of strands came loose of his shoulder, even as the tar baby's legs started to unwrap from around his waist. "We got to be better to each other."

Dad was right. Shelly felt her own anger melt away at that. Mom may not have understood, but at least Blaine did.

"Dad was right," she said. "That's right—teamwork."

"What?"

"Something Dad said," said Shelly.

Gingerly, avoiding the strings of tar along the way, Shelly made her way down the rest of the stairs to where Blaine still dangled. She held the tea-towel under her arm, and unscrewed the top of the turpentine, and soaked a corner of the towel with it. The tar baby's free arm dangled gnarly fingers near her cheek, but Shelly pulled away and the tar baby didn't follow. She handed the towel up to Blaine, making herself think kind thoughts.

"I hope you learned your lesson," she said, as Blaine touched the turpentine to the tar baby's other hand. Shelly stepped back as that arm came free. The tar baby was completely disentangled from Blaine, but it didn't fall to the ground—as it came free it swung up among the tar strands nearer the ceiling—like a big, sticky spider, in a web spun of its own substance.

Blaine fell to the floor as he came loose of that web—and it seemed as though he landed all right. But he winced as he stood, and his legs trembled under him.

"Dad was right," he said. "I wanted to hit you upstairs, and when I went to, I took a swing—and then I was down here! Hitting the tar baby, getting all stuck up like Mom."

Shelly nodded. "That's how it worked for Mr. Baldwin at prison, I bet," she said. "The tar baby smells the mad, and it doesn't matter who it's directed at; it draws the mad to itself."

"So why didn't you wind up down here? When you kicked the bed?"

Shelly thought about that. "I didn't mean to hurt you," she said. "I just wanted you to quit it—I didn't think you'd hit your head."

Blaine looked down. He really was a sad mess, Shelly thought—hair all black and sticky, and his pyjamas just as bad. And he looked weaker, too—the tar baby had taken it out of him, like it had from Mom. The only reason he was standing, Shelly thought, was because maybe Blaine had had more in him to begin with. "I guess it was because I wanted to hurt you then."

"I guess that's how it works," said Shelly.

"I'm sorry," he said.

"Stop apologizing."

"Okay." Blaine started scrubbing at himself, but it was clear even with the turpentine, it was going to be a harder job than he had the strength for right now.

"Come on," said Shelly—and she took his arm, sticky as it was. They started up the stairs together.

"What in fuck you get into, kid?"

Mark Hollins was sitting at the kitchen table, a bottle of bourbon open and half empty in front of him, when they came out of the door. The sleeves of his denim jacket were rolled up, and Shelly could see a dark green shape that had been tattooed underneath the thick black hair on his forearm. There was no telling what it represented. Dad sat across the table from Mark Hollins, and there was a paper bag on the table between them.

Dad didn't even look back.

"Don't curse in front of the children," said Dad.

"Ah, fuck you," said Mark Hollins. "Gonna learn it somewhere."

Now Dad did turn around, and he looked Blaine up and down. He nodded slowly.

"Learn your lesson, son?" Dad was smiling ever so slightly.

"Yes, sir," said Blaine.

"Good. Take that turpentine upstairs to the bathroom, and start washing yourself. I'll be up to help in a minute."

Mark Hollins finished a long pull from his bottle, and slammed it down again onto the tabletop. He spoke directly to Blaine.

"You take your time, son. Your daddy and me got some business."

As Mark Hollins spoke, Shelly saw Dad reach up and put his hand on the paper bag. Mark Hollins saw it too, because his eyes darted immediately to Dad's hands. They had that same discouraging look to them they had when he'd smiled at Shelly, and now even the smile was gone.

"Ah, shit, Scott—don't try this crap on me. We're splitting it like always."

"No," said Dad, his voice as level and calm as could be, "not like always. Not like when I did time for you. I'm keeping all the cash. And the truck. You *owe* me."

Shelly felt Blaine's hand on her shoulder—he was squeezing too tight, but she could tell he wasn't trying to hurt her. He was just scared—like she was starting to get. She was piecing things together, or maybe just admitting things to herself: like, where did that truck come from? Dad didn't even have a valid driver's license anymore, and the family hadn't owned a car for years. And cash? She wondered if the cash was in that bag on the table; and if so, just how they'd managed to get it.

"I owe you shit," said Mark Hollins.

"That's your opinion."

She and Blaine backed out of the kitchen and into the living room. Blaine's hand was trembling, and she could hear him sniffling as he pulled her further into the living room, around behind Mom's television chair. He crouched down, and Shelly crouched beside him, her arm over his filthy shoulders.

In the kitchen, the conversation escalated—at least on Mark Hollins' side. He slammed his bottle down on the table, not hard enough to shatter, but enough to send a gout of booze up through the neck and splash on his white-knuckled fist.

"Give me the Goddamn money!" Hollins stood up, and put his arms under the table. Dad lifted his beer and the bag, and swung back as the table fell over onto its side, empty beer bottles and Shelly's old pop can scattering across the linoleum floor. "I risked my *fuckin'* neck tonight!"

Dad got up from his chair and stood with his arms crossed—beer in one fist, bag in the other—and he chuckled, shaking his head.

Shelly pinched her nose as the smell of tar grew stronger—it seemed like she could actually see the fumes, coming out of the half-open door to the basement in a thin grey cloud. Blaine didn't cover his nose—he probably smelled enough tar his nose wouldn't even tell it—but his hands were up over his ears, and his eyes were shut.

In the kitchen, Hollins reached around to his hip pocket, and he pulled something out that flashed metal in the kitchen light. Dad stopped chuckling as Mark Hollins held it in front of him, and even Shelly could see what it was: an X-Acto knife.

"That's it, you fucker," said Mark Hollins. "You're right we're not splitting this money. You're going to give it all to me—isn't that right?"

Dad looked straight at his old buddy Mark Hollins, and shook his head. "Get out of here," he said, "if you know what's good for you."

And that set him off. Hollins shouted something Shelly couldn't hear properly, and he lunged with the X-Acto blade—

—straight at Dad, he must have thought—

—but in fact, straight through the door to the basement.

Mark Hollins made a painful-sounding clatter as he tumbled over the first few steps, but the falling-down sounds ended quickly. There was nothing afterwards but a series of shouts—first surprised, then angry and finally just frightened. Dad walked over to the doorway and leaned over, both arms outstretched against the door frame. He laughed like he laughed when Mom got it earlier on. "What were you saying, Mark?" Dad stopped to cough—the tar-fumes were pretty thick—and went on: "You want all the money? Truck too? You want this house, Mark?"

Mark shouted something back, and now Shelly was sure it wasn't just bad hearing on her part—he was making no sound anyone could understand.

"I'll leave you to figure your way out of that one," said Dad. "Then we can talk about how to divide things up, from now on."

He pushed himself off the door, and swung it shut, then looked to the living room.

"Blaine?" he said.

"Y-yes, sir?" Blaine stuck his head up from behind the chair.

"Get on upstairs like I told you to. I'll be along in a minute."

"Yes, sir," said Blaine. He got up and went to the stairs. Shelly followed, but Dad told her to wait behind a minute. He had some things, he said, to say to her.

Shelly went to her Dad. He picked up the table and set it right, and pulled the chairs back in place.

"You're in pretty good shape tonight, little girl," he said. "Didn't feel the need to hit the tar baby?"

"No," she said.

Dad nodded. "That's good. Not everyone needs to learn from their own mistakes. What did you learn tonight?"

Shelly opened her mouth, and closed it again. There was a noise from behind the basement door—like a big cushion hitting against the stairs. She had been about to say *team work*, but that sound stopped her.

"Little girl?"

"It's . . ." She looked down at her relatively clean hands. ". . . it's gotten bigger," she said. "There's tar *everywhere* now."

Dad nodded. "That's what Mr. Baldwin said might happen. His tar baby got pretty big in its time, although it didn't stay that way forever. Just while it soaked it up . . . all that anger . . . aggression . . ." Dad's face went sour ". . . *misplaced* authority."

"What does misplaced authority mean?" asked Shelly.

Dad patted her back. "Something you'll never have to find out about," he said. "Let's just say, the other prisoners aren't the only ones a fellow has to fear in jail. There's also the damn guards . . ."

The thumping from below stopped—but there was another sound now: distant sirens, wafting across the scrub from the direction of the highway. Shelly looked out the window at the red truck Dad had driven home from his walk, and at the brown paper bag Mark Hollins had wanted so badly he'd pulled out a knife and knocked over a table.

"Go upstairs now," Dad said. "Tell your brother I'll just be another minute."

Shelly did as she was told—but she stopped on the stairs, and peered over the banister to the kitchen.

Dad sat slouched back a bit in the chair, as peaceful and quiet as ever, as the sirens grew louder, and Shelly marvelled: she *still* couldn't imagine her Dad taking a gun and pointing it at a grocery store man, and saying he'd kill him if he didn't give over some cash. Any more than she could imagine him breaking the window of a shiny red pickup truck that belonged to someone else, and taking it for himself.

Mom was wrong, so wrong: Dad wasn't a bad man at all. In spite of what everyone thought about him. As Shelly continued up the stairs, she hoped the police who were running that siren could see the goodness in Dad too; she hoped they wouldn't be *too* mad about everything that had happened tonight.

The basement, after all, was only so big.

Other People's Kids

"The trouble with places like this," said my sister Lenore, "is other people's kids."

Nick, Lenore's third boyfriend ever and the coolest one yet, took a long sip of his coffee. "Other people's kids?" he said mildly. "As opposed to your own?"

"I don't have any kids right now, thank God." Lenore sat down at the picnic table next to Nick. "But I had the worst time in the line. There were two little boys—must have been twins—who were playing this game of SCREAM, which is exactly what it sounds like. Their mom didn't even notice." She set down her cinnamon pretzel and jammed a straw into the top of her diet root beer. "On my way back, I saw a kid running around with his poopy diaper. I know it was a 'he' because he was holding the diaper over his head and yelling, 'LOOKIT MY POOPY DIAPER!'"

"More SCREAM," I said.

"With poop." Nick smiled. He was *so* cool. "Kids are wacky," he said.

Lenore shook her head. "Terrible. Look around! Other people's kids are terrible!"

We looked around. The picnic common of Natch's Highway Grill and Fun-Park was full of kids, other people's kids, I guess, and yeah, they were all pretty terrible.

But why shouldn't they be? Natch's was located on the highway, exactly halfway between Carlingsburg and the Elbow Lakes tourist region, and today was exactly halfway through Labour Day Monday. So of course that meant that about a half of all the kids in Carlingsburg were on their way home from their family cottages. It was their last day of summer vacation, and each and every one of them knew that when they woke up in the morning they would be looking at just over three months before Christmas and their next scheduled good time. I myself had been facing this grim reality, along with the prospect of starting Grade Nine all but friendless in a high school whose main problem was too many cliques. So if these kids were a little hopped up on sugar and grouchy enough to fall down in the grass, kicking their legs in the air and screaming like the three-year-olds they were . . .

Hey, I could relate.

In fact, a couple of years ago I would have been one of those kids. We'd been stopping at Natch's every summer since Lenore was a little kid and I was a baby. Dad used to joke that Oliver Natch's old highway rest stop had grown up with me. When I was little, Natch's was just a burger joint on the northbound side of the highway, nestled in a semi-circle of low rocky hills, and surrounded by a dark forest of big pine and cedar trees. I was too young to remember it like that, but one of our family pictures is of the four of us standing in front of the little restaurant—Dad with a big suntanned arm over Mom's shoulder, Lenore holding me and giggling like an idiot while I grabbed her ear. I don't know who took the picture—maybe Mr. Natch himself did it, because he probably spent more time there in those days.

These days, my Dad figured that Mr. Natch was too busy counting his money to spend much time at the Grill and Fun-Park. Over the years, he'd put in about fifty picnic tables, slapped up two separate dining buildings with their own washrooms, set up a lame amusement park with a little carousel and the CARLINGSBURG RAIL MUSEUM in an old train car. Sometime in the last ten years, he'd built a completely enclosed footbridge across four lanes of highway to a parking lot on the west side—so people coming south back to the city could stop at Natch's too. Dad thought he must have bribed someone high up in the government to get permission to build the bridge across the highway like that. I didn't know if he did or not but he certainly could afford to. The place was packed. It was so packed there were actually security guards, wearing blue shirts and carrying walkie-talkies and strange black wands, making sure nothing bad happened to Mr. Natch's considerable investment.

"Okay," said Nick. "I see what you mean." He was looking at a table two over, where a four-year-old girl with pigtails had overturned her milkshake onto her brother's french fries. Her dad, a big-bellied bald man in a Carlingsburg Panthers T-shirt, sipped at his own milkshake without seeming to notice. "If that were my kid, maybe I would want to strangle her."

Lenore took a bite out of her pretzel. "*Our* kid," she said, "would never do that."

Lenore didn't notice how Nick winced, but I sure did. Nick had been wincing a lot over the past two weeks he'd been at our cottage. He winced when she talked about how after graduation next year, the two of them would apply to the same college. He winced when she talked about how before college, the two of them could audition for spots on the Up With People tour and spend the whole summer criss-crossing the United States spreading cheerful songs and right-thinking values to those "less fortunate" than Lenore. And he particularly winced when she would go on and on and on about all the things they'd do together after college. I wasn't surprised one bit when Nick offered to drive me back to the city along with Lenore, to give my parents some "alone time." "Alone time" was something he and Lenore had altogether too much of over the past two weeks.

"Hey!" The boy across from us got up, one soggy vanilla-flavoured french fry in his hands. His sister stuck her tongue out at him. "You little rat!" he shouted.

"Don't call your little sister names," said their father as he sipped at his milkshake and looked off into the distance, and the little girl smiled. "*Don't call your little sister names*," she said in a sing-song voice that was designed to be irritating. Then she crossed her eyes and turned over to look at us.

"Fezkul," she said.

I leaned forward, trying to figure out what she was trying to tell me. But she wasn't trying to tell me anything. Someone answered from behind me:

"Good girl, Blair. You are a rocking kid."

The voice sounded like a little boy—a little boy leaning right over my shoulder. I turned around, and for an instant, I saw him: a kid wearing low-slung jeans and a baseball cap, an oversized T-shirt and a big smile.

It was a smile with rows of saw-teeth. It made him look like a shark.

"Holy crap," I said. But then I blinked, and he was gone. Or I'd dreamed it. Or he was just gone. I shook my head.

The little girl giggled and clapped: "Fezkul!" she said. Her dad set his cup down on the table and looked at his watch.

"We should get back on the road," he said. "Your mother'll have my neck."

The girl stopped giggling and her face fell. "No!" she said. "Wanna go see Fezkul!"

She pointed across the picnic ground to the woods.

Her father made to protest, but she hollered back that "new daddy" would let her and just like that, he gave in.

"Weird kid," said Nick.

My sister shook her head. "She's not weird. She's manipulative. Her poor dad's probably just got them for the weekend, and she's probably been holding that 'new daddy' line over his head the whole time." She looked up into the clear blue sky overhead, as if asking God to back her up. "Divorce is so terrible. Let's never get divorced, Nicky."

"Um," said Nick.

"What's with Fezkul?" I said.

They both turned to look at me. "Who?" said Lenore, and Nick said, with a certain amount of relief in his voice: "*Fezkul.* That's what she said. I couldn't make it out. You got a good ear, bro."

"Fezkul," said Lenore. "It's probably some character off the Cartoon Network. Or out of one of your Dungeons and Dragons books." Lenore was forever dissing my Dungeons and Dragons books. "*Kids.*"

"Sure." I nodded like I agreed with her, but I didn't buy it for a second. I couldn't get the picture of that weird kid with the creepy smile out of my mind. That kid was no cartoon character.

"I got to go to the bathroom," I said.

"All right," said Lenore. "But don't take too long. Tomorrow's a school day."

"Do what you got to do, bro," said Nick as I got up and hurried off to the main building.

I didn't have to do anything, at least not in the bathroom. But I did have to go. There was something about that kid Fezkul; something about his voice, those teeth. I figured it must have been an optical illusion, those rows of shark teeth, but still . . .

I was having what my dad called a curiosity attack. Ever since I was two, these attacks would come on with varying intensity and they would cause me to do all sorts of things which, looking back, seemed pretty stupid: climbing telephone poles; sticking my head through metal grating; one time, eating a bug. Dad told me that this curiosity disease would—how did he put it?—"Doom you to a life of journalism" (which is what he did before he quit the newspaper and went into web design) "if it doesn't get you killed first."

What can I say? It's a sickness.

I started my search for Fezkul at the museum, and checked out the kids standing in line. There were only five of them, and twice as many parents. None of them looked like a Fezkul.

So I headed for one of the dining buildings. It was nice out, so there weren't very many people inside, just a couple of clusters of senior citizens who looked at me nervously while they munched on Natchie Burgers. A teenager in a bright orange Natch uniform was busy mopping up an immense puddle of something in the middle of the floor. There were some old video games—which struck me as the kinds of things that might attract a kid like Fezkul—but no. I nodded at one old woman, who nodded back and looked away, and stepped around the puddle, and so it was that I left the dining hall. Rather than try the other one, I figured I'd head for the heart of Natch's Highway Grill and Fun-Park—the place where it had all started:

The grill house.

"Hey, Fezkul," I said as I headed across the gravel to the old, glassed-in former donut shop where Mr. Natch worked his barbecue magic on squashed balls of ground beef and pepper. "Fezkul Fezkul Fezkul," I whispered. "Fezkul."

Now I remember some fairy tales where if you say the guy's name five times, he shows up like magic. Rumplestiltskin comes to mind. Or the dude in that old Clive Barker movie, *Candyman*.

That is not exactly what happened when I said 'Fezkul' five times.

I was just about to step up to the door and worm my way inside, when I felt the hot, sweaty hand of authority on my shoulder.

"Where's your parents, kid?"

I turned around and found myself looking into the glaring, stubble-covered face of—I glanced down at his nametag—Tom Wilkinson. His nametag was pinned on the left pocket of his blue security guard uniform. He did not look friendly, and he looked even less friendly when I answered: "I don't have any."

I know that's not entirely true. I have two perfectly good parents and I love them to bits. But you have to understand: my parents weren't here and I was with my sister and her boyfriend on the way back from the cottage to start school, and it was a lot easier to say I didn't have any parents because that was partway true right at the moment and . . . and . . .

I panicked, all right? And it was a bad time to panic. I admit it.

Tom Wilkinson struck me as that kind of security guard who'd gotten into the business after giving a really good try at being a policeman and somehow not measuring up. Maybe he didn't make the academy because he was too fat (which he was) or because he wasn't bright enough (which from the look in his tiny squinty eyes suggested he might not have been) or because he was just too evil for police work and had flunked the evil detector test.

As he turned me around and held up the weird little wand that they all carried close to my face, I was pretty sure that the evil detector test was what had got him.

"You," he said slowly, "are coming with me. Punk."

I had to walk fast to keep up with Officer Tom as we made our way through the line and around the back of the grill house. There was an old, broken dumpster out back—the lid didn't close properly, and the sides were kind of bent out. Beside it was a big metal door that said OFFICE on it, and I guessed correctly that that was where we were going. "Inside," he said as he swung the door open.

"Look," I said, "I was kidding about not having parents."

We were not in an office, but a little hallway. Ahead was a pair of swinging doors that led to the grill—I could smell the seared meat and deep fryer from here. But there was another door, also marked OFFICE. This one was actually the top of a metal stairway that went down two flights. "Down," said Officer Tom. I did as I was told, feeling terrible. At the bottom was another door, with OFFICE written on it. I was beginning to feel like the whole OFFICE thing was an elaborate joke. But this time, when we went through, there *was* an office. The room was walled in painted cinderblock, like a school hallway but without any lockers. In the middle was a lime green desk with a laptop computer plugged into a power bar big as a two-by-four. Seated behind it was a skinny man, who was sipping from a big bottle of water. He peered over it, first at me, then at Officer Tom.

"Yes?" he said.

"Mister Natch," said Officer Tom, "this kid knows Fezkul."

So this was Mister Oliver Natch. I thought back to when I was a kid—a real kid—to see if I remembered him. With his high forehead, curly blond hair and wide, expressionless eyes, you'd think I would have. But he didn't register. Mr. Natch nodded quickly and set his water down by the computer. And he knew about Fezkul.

"Does he?" he said, then turned his gaze on me. "You're one of Fezkul's? You seem old."

"I'm fourteen," I said.

"Hmm. That is old." He looked back at Officer Tom. "That *is* old,

Wilkinson. Why are you wasting my time?"

Officer Tom's mouth opened and closed, and he blinked. I thought that Natch might be doing something to Officer Tom's airway, like Darth Vader did in that old *Star Wars* movie. He looked like the sort of guy who would do that.

"He-he was saying his name," said Officer Tom. "A bunch of times. I thought—"

"Yes." Mr. Natch looked at him like he was stupid, which was a good way to look at Officer Tom. "You should be back on patrol," said Natch. "You know what day it is."

Officer Tom nodded. "You want me to find this kid's parents?"

"Back," said Natch, "on patrol. I'll talk with the boy a moment."

Officer Tom left, muttering under his breath: "Patrol. Like I ever see anything on patrol." Although I never would have thought it, I was sad to see him go. Mr. Natch tapped quickly on his computer keyboard, squinted at the screen, and looked at me, hard.

"*Fezkul,*" he said finally, then said it again, more slowly. "What's a boy like you, doing saying *Fezkul* on a fine Labour Day Monday like today?"

It was time to start telling the truth. "I heard a little girl say it," I said. "And then I saw another kid."

Natch nodded.

"Another kid. With sharp short teeth in his mouth and in his eye a mischievous glint? A glint that sometimes glows with inner hellfire?"

Something in Mr. Natch's own eye told me that my telling-the-truth idea was not a good one to stick to.

"I dunno," I said.

Mr. Natch looked very serious and he leaned forward. "I don't think that's true, now," he said. "Do you? What did you say your name was?"

I don't know why, but I thought then about movies and books where you told someone your name and it turned out they were a wizard and they had power over you. So I said "Stan," not Sam.

"Well, Stan," said Mr. Natch. "Are you enjoying your day here? At the fun park?"

"We're just stopped here for a bite," I said.

"Hungry work," agreed Mr. Natch, "driving south."

I shrugged—

"And you saw Fezkul."

—and shrugged.

Mr. Natch's eyes narrowed. He wasn't buying it, I could tell. But I wasn't ready to 'fess to anything either.

"Come around here, erm, *Stan*. I have something I want you to see."

I went around the desk and looked at the computer screen. There were pictures on it—pictures that looked like they were from security cameras, maybe during a big riot. Except the rioters weren't guys in bandannas; they were little kids. There was one where it looked like a dozen kids were crawling all over an SUV. One of them was bending its antenna at almost a right angle, and another one was standing on top of the cab, holding what looked like a torn-off side view mirror over her head like it was a bowling tournament trophy. There was another one where three kids were hefting one of the RAIL MUSEUM's signal posts between them while a bunch of others watched on. Another showed five kids at a dumpster behind the grill house, lifting what looked like a barbecue propane tank into it. One of the kids had a long barbecue lighter and was flicking it.

"Well?" said Mr. Natch. "Recognize anybody?"

I shook my head.

"Those pictures," said Mr. Natch, "are from one year ago today."

"Wow," I said.

"Yes. *Wow*." He put his hand on my shoulder. It felt like a tree branch. "And it's nothing, I fear, compared to what's in store this year. Now, Stan. Look more closely." And with that, he pushed me closer to the computer screen. "Recognize anybody?"

"I am not comfortable with you touching me, Mister Natch," I said. This is what I had been told to say if anyone touched me in a way I didn't like, and it had the effect I was looking for. Mr. Natch took his hand off my shoulder and apologized with a grunt.

But I barely heard him.

Because I did recognize somebody in the picture. Not any of the five kids—they could have been anybody. But standing just in the background was a boy, wearing oversized jeans and a baseball cap.

And he was moving.

I leaned closer. The kid was far enough back that he was just a collection of pixels—I couldn't make out his face or even what was written on his baseball cap. I certainly couldn't see his teeth. But I could see that he was sort of moving from side to side, like he was walking. He was also getting bigger.

"You do recognize someone," said Mr. Natch. "You can identify him."

The kid walked past the kid with the lighter, patted him on the shoulder, and came up right to the camera. He smiled—right at me—with those shark teeth in his mouth that looked just so cool on Mr. Natch's laptop screen—and he opened his mouth, and whispered, like it was right in my ear:

"*Dude. Use the water.*"

"Which one," said Mr. Natch. "Which one is Fezkul?"

"*On the power bar.*"

Those teeth . . . They were so cool.

"Him?" said Mr. Natch.

"*It will totally rock.*"

That was when things got kind of foggy. I remember grabbing the water bottle, which was about half full, and sort of pouring it—yeah, probably on the power bar that was right beside the laptop. There were some sparks, and some yelling, and the air smelled sharp. I remember being under the desk for a second, then opening a door, then running up stairs. I might have been in a kitchen for a second and I might not have. The next thing I knew for sure, I was leaning against the dumpster out back of the grill house. I was laughing and grinning and I don't think I'd ever felt better. It was like I was a little kid again, with the summer holidays and Christmas and Halloween—especially Halloween—all spread out before me.

"You rock, kid."

"I'm not a kid," I said and looked up.

The kid with the shark teeth was looking back at me. He was standing not two feet off, hands in his pocket and hat cocked high on his forehead. He was grinning.

"Fezkul?"

"Maybe not," he said. "Maybe sure. Whoever I am, one thing I know: you want to get out of here. Soon as old Natch finishes up with his fire extinguisher, he's going to be after you."

I pushed myself off the dumpster and it made a bong and a rattling sound.

"That dumpster hasn't been right for a good year," said Fezkul appreciatively. "A propane explosion can do a lot of damage." He clapped me on the shoulder. "C'mon, kid. I like your style."

And then he took off for the trees. Without even thinking about it, I followed him. Sure—part of me was worried about leaving my sister and her boyfriend without saying anything. About following this shark-toothed kid who'd talked to me from a JPEG on a computer screen. But you know what? That wasn't the part of me that was in the driver's seat. It was the part that was responsible for my curiosity attacks.

He was hard to keep up with. He scrambled up a tumble of bedrock like he was a mountain goat, then took off through some low ferns at just about a sprint. The woods got dark quickly beyond the Fun-Park, and the closeness of the trees made it very quiet. Soon we were running over bare earth, with just a couple of rocks here and there to trip me up. Fezkul finally stopped, in a little circle of trees. I pulled up, gasping for breath.

"I like your style," he said again, nodding as he spoke. "You're big... big for a *kid*."

That, I have to admit, got me going. He was starting to sound like my sister Lenore, who wouldn't tell me about *The Sopranos* or let me ride in the front seat. I glared at him. After all, Oliver Natch had just got finished strongly implying I was too old. "Don't call me a kid. I'm going to be in Grade Nine tomorrow."

Fezkul grinned, put his fists on his hips. "'I'm going to be in Grade Nine tomorrow,'" he mimicked, making his voice all high. "Maybe tomorrow you will. But today—" he smirked at me "—today you're here. You heard me, and you saw me. So live in the moment, Sammy: you're a kid. Yet—" and here, his grin got wider, "you're big. Big as I got, today."

He started walking around me, nodding and nodding, and I kept glaring at him until he got behind me and I couldn't see him. "Yeah," he said. "You're big."

"All right," I said. "so I'm a big kid. Who are you? What's with the teeth?"

I waited for him to come around in front of me. "What's with the teeth?" I looked over my shoulder. Fezkul wasn't there. I looked around in front of me again, in case he'd hurried there, then back again.

"Fezkul?" I hissed. "Kid? Whoever you are? Where are you?"

There was nobody. He'd taken off. Where, though? My curiosity was getting seriously cranked. The trees here were huge. I counted, and saw that five of them made a circle around this space that would have been a clearing if it weren't for the long branches of those five trees. They made kind of a dome in here.

"So the thing you got to wonder," said Fezkul, who suddenly appeared at my elbow, "is what can you do before you stop being a kid?"

"How did you do that?"

Fezkul wiggled his fingers in the air and said, "'What's with the teeth?'" in that high voice of his. Then he laughed. "So you're big— you're also bright enough to ask me questions. This I like. See most of these kids—you show them the way, they just get all giggly and stupid. Do what they're told. Cut loose."

"You tell those kids to cut loose. You take me to this place. What are you—" I looked around, putting it together "—some kind of a forest spirit?"

Fezkul snorted. "You watched *Lord of the Rings* one time too many, kid."

"Well—" I motioned at his freaky teeth, waved at the canopy "—come on! Look around you."

Fezkul put his hands in his pockets and sneered. "'Some kind of forest spirit.' How *imaginative*. Ummmm—no. Look. Let's cut to the chase. You're big. You're smart. You were good in there with the water and the power bar and you're pretty fast on the run. I repeat my question: what can you do before you stop being a kid?"

It's funny. The first time he asked me that, I just let it roll off me. The second time, though, got into me:

What *was* I going to do?

Tomorrow, I'd start Grade Nine, which was at the end, really, of my kid-ness. The teachers in Grade Eight at William Howard Taft Elementary School were forever reminding us of this: *You get to Grade Nine, boys and girls, it's a whole different world. You're going to be expected to start acting like young men and women. You're going to have more homework and you'll be studying for exams, and the things that you do will have consequences that will carry on for the rest of your lives.*

Consequences. The rest of your lives.

They didn't even get to the whole question of cliques, and already most of us were pissing ourselves with fear.

And for all that, they never asked us the basic question:

What will you do with the rest of your childhood?

And when you're done with it, what will you be left with? A world like Lenore's? All your days spent tense and fretful, thinking about getting married and having kids, believing Up With People is cool, finding the trouble with *everything*?

"Makes you dizzy, doesn't it?" said Fezkul. "It's like a—what would we call it? A tween-life crisis. But it's not like middle age. You can't exactly buy yourself a sports car and get yourself a mistress, can you?" I swore at him, and he said, "Oh, very adult, in an NC-17 way. That won't cut it, but this might."

"What might?"

Fezkul leaned forward, took a breath and opened his hands.

"Set fire to the grill." Fezkul grinned wider. "Don't let anyone escape." His eyes took a fire to them—that mischievous fire that Mr. Natch had seemed so interested in.

"Kill Natch," he said. "Kill him dead."

"What?" I took a step back. Those teeth were so *sharp*, and they seemed like they were getting sharper. "No way."

Fezkul shrugged and laughed. "Just kidding, kiddo."

But I could tell that he wasn't. And looking at me, I think he could tell I could tell that he wasn't kidding, because his smile went away and he got a strange, desperate look in his eye that put out the fire like a splash of cold water.

"Really, dude," he pleaded. "Big joke. No one's going to burn down—hey!"

I was already running. I'm curious, sure—but curiosity has its limits. One of those limits was meeting a strange kid with pointed teeth who tried to talk me into burning down a crowded restaurant and killing the man who built it.

So I ran. I took off through the trees in the direction I thought I'd come. At that point, I figured there was nothing better than for me to get back with my sister and Nick, get into Nick's car and get back home in time for school. I'd deal with the cliques and the consequences and the possible loss of my precious childhood—which I was getting pretty tired of anyway, truth be told.

I was also scared. This forest was pretty thick, and if Fezkul was some kind of forest spirit he could probably get me turned around so I'd be running in circles around the same tree until I fell down and died. But as I went further I could see that big highway overpass through the trees, and I realized: getting me lost wasn't Fezkul's game. Fezkul wasn't the kind of forest spirit that got you lost in the magic wood.

Fezkul was the kind of forest spirit that made you do bad. Sort of like a gangsta-rap Pied Piper. He'd almost gotten me—no, scratch that: he *had* gotten me, for a minute there when I spilled the water on Oliver Natch's power bar, then ran out of the door.

He'd gotten me, and I'd gotten away.

At least that's what I kept telling myself as I ran through the woods, towards what I hoped was the noise of Natch's Grill and Fun-Park, and not some evil forest trap for boys who didn't like Fezkul's tune.

It was some noise. There was a sound of shouting and screaming and laughing—a lot of laughing. It sounded like a lynch mob on a sugar high. There was a loud cracking sound, like timber snapping—then silence, and a big giggly cheer, followed by an even louder crash.

With that, I stopped running and started sneaking. The cheers following crash number two had a sound to them that I didn't like—they were high and hysterical and maybe just a little bit crazy. It was the kind of cheer that could take pleasure in anything—even burning down the grill house and murdering Oliver Natch.

I was coming up to the ferns through which I'd chased Fezkul then, and crouched down behind a big boulder all covered in lichen. There was more noise coming closer. I could hear cheering and shouting—most of it high-pitched—but one voice that was a little lower. It sounded like this:

"Help! Toddlers! Ravening horde! Gah!"

Like that.

And then, crashing through the ferns like a rogue elephant, came the person I was least hoping to see (next to Fezkul and Oliver Natch):

Officer Tom Wilkinson.

He was a bit of a mess now. His shirt, which had been a perfect black, was now slick with different kinds of stains and colours: ketchup, mustard, what looked like chocolate milkshake. It would have been funny looking at the mess on him, but that wasn't all of it. He was holding a cloth to the side of his head, and the cloth was soaking through red, and he was stumbling.

I stuck my head up. I could hear his pursuers, but I couldn't see them yet. I thought about it for just a second, before I waved at him and said: "Hey. Over here."

He stopped at that, then his eyes narrowed as he saw me and figured out who I was.

"You," he mumbled. "You are in a world of trou—"

He never got the "ble" out. Because having stopped, he got really unsteady on his feet. Then he fell over into the ferns.

Even if you're big for your age, like I am, let me tell you this: it's not easy pulling a 200-pound-plus security guard through ferns and in behind a set of boulders, particularly when there's a ravening horde of toddlers on his tail. You can do it. But easily? Ha. I laugh. We'd barely made it into the rock's shadow before the ferns started to shake and quiver and the horde came through.

From where we were crouched, you couldn't see more than the tops of their tyke-y heads, and the two-by-fours and golf clubs and baby canoe paddles that they were waving around like banners. With their little legs they were slow—which explained how Officer Tom had gotten away from them, injured as he was—and being pre-schoolers, they weren't particularly thorough. A couple of years older and another foot higher, and one of them might have spotted the trail of broken ferns I'd left dragging Officer Tom to the boulder. As it was, they made their way past us and into the deeper woods chortling and gurgling and swinging their sticks in the air.

When they were gone, I leaned over Officer Tom Wilkinson. He was blinking groggily, his hand back over the little cut in his cheek.

"You," he said.

"Me," I agreed.

"Mister Natch," he said, "told us to shoot you on sight."

"Shoot me?"

Even for Oliver Natch, that seemed extreme, and Officer Tom confirmed it: "Figure of speech. We don't get guns. Just these—" he slapped at his belt "—stun wands."

I looked at his belt. There, in the loop, was a gleaming black wand, about a foot long.

"It's got a battery," he explained, "and it gives you a little electric shock—well, a pretty big electric shock. Completely non-lethal, but it stops you dead. Well, not dead. But you know what I mean."

I looked at the wand and the wound on his head. "So why didn't you use it to protect yourself?"

Officer Tom gave me a pained look. "I know," he said. "But what was I going to do? They were little *kids!*"

I shook my head. *Pathetic*, I thought, and he nodded. "This was not my first career choice, you know."

"Didn't make it into the police academy?"

Officer Tom snorted. "You think that was it? Of course you do. Fat loser security guard working Labour Day at the Fun-Park. Must be a frustrated police academy wannabe because who else would be enough of a loser to get a job like this."

"No no," I started, but I must have sounded as insincere as I felt, because he said:

"It's okay. I get it a lot." He sat up and leaned against the rock.

"So what did you want to be?" I asked.

"You'll laugh," he said, and when I promised I wouldn't, he reached into his pocket and pulled out a business card. It had a picture of a dragon, and an email address, and the title: TOM WILKINSON: GAME CONSULTANT. I raised an eyebrow, and he nodded.

"A game designer."

"What—like Monopoly?"

"No." He looked at me solemnly. "You ever play Dungeons and Dragons?"

I grinned. The dragon on the business card made sense, and all of a sudden I liked Officer Tom a whole lot better. "I, ah, have some friends who do."

In fact, what few friends I had played Dungeons and Dragons and so did I. That year, I had a 10th-level paladin named Honorius Pyurhart who in June had single-handedly mopped the floor with the green dragon guarding the time portal at the bottom of the

Labyrinth of Flies. I hadn't played since my family had headed off to the cottage, and I despaired of ever running old Honorius again: the dungeon master, Neil Hinkley, was going into Grade Seven and so wouldn't be joining me at high school for another year. "Are you a gamer?"

Officer Tom nodded miserably. "Yeah," he said. "I was voted best dungeon master two years in a row at GenCon."

"Cool," I said. The weekend convention at GenCon was the Las Vegas for Dungeons and Dragons. One day, one day . . .

"I even got one of the game designers at Wizards of the Coast to look at my dungeon," he said. "But they said it was too—what was the word? *Avant garde*. That was it. *Avant garde*. Can you believe it?"

"Shocking," I said.

"So I work security. The only magic wand I got—" he slapped his belt "—is this one."

"That sucks," I said.

"And how."

We sat quietly for a moment, him pushing his handkerchief against his cheek, me leaning against the rock.

"What's going on out there?" I finally asked. "In the Fun-Park?"

"Pandemonium. That's what. The kids are everywhere. About a dozen of them managed to push over a swing set. They're shouting and swearing and knocking over garbage cans, and just like always, their parents don't do a thing. I tried to stop them, and they just formed into a posse." He lifted one foot and pointed at it. The boot, I saw, was undone, and one side of the lace had a broken bow on it. "Two of them tied my bootlaces together. I fell over and that's when I hit my head."

"And their parents didn't do a thing." I thought about little Blair, who poured a milkshake on her brother's fries and her father, who wouldn't do anything about it. I thought about the photographs that Mr. Natch had on his computer, of kids blowing up garbage cans and knocking over signs and vandalizing cars. There weren't any parents in those photographs.

"That," I said, figuring it out, "is the other part of Fezkul's powers. The kids—what they do—they're, like, invisible to parents."

"Maybe to their parents. But not to me," said Tom, fingering the wound in his head. "That's one of the reasons Mr. Natch keeps me on—I can sort of see when kids are getting ready to misbehave here. Most people can't. Even if they're not parents. Not on Labour Day."

"What's so special about Labour Day?"

Tom sighed. "It's the day that everything goes crazy here," he said. "For the past five years. Ever since Mr. Natch put up that walkway over the highway. I only came on last year, but I hear it's been getting worse every year. Last year, some kids blew up the garbage dumpster. And this guy—Fezkul—is behind it all. God knows what he's got planned this year."

I thought about my conversation with Fezkul just a few minutes earlier: Burn down the grill, he'd said. Kill Natch.

"Something pretty serious," I said. "Do you have any idea why he's doing it?"

"According to Natch," said Officer Tom, "he just hates people with the gumption to succeed. He just hates America."

"So, no idea."

Officer Tom smiled. "No idea."

"Why doesn't Natch just shut down? It's just for one day. He could open up again on Tuesday."

"You met him," said Officer Tom. "You think Oliver Natch is the kind of guy to back down? He just hires more security every year. It's like a holy war for him."

"That's just whacked."

"Tell me about it."

We sat there quiet again. Officer Tom peeled some lichen off the rock and sniffed it. "So you really don't have any parents, Stan?"

"Sam—that's my real name. Not Stan. And I do have parents. I'm just not here with them. I'm here with my sister and—"

I stopped.

I was here with my sister Lenore and her boyfriend Nick. They were waiting at the picnic table for me to come back from the washroom.

And they had been waiting a very long time, and I'd barely spared them a thought since I got hauled into Mr. Natch's basement office, and with everything that was going on at the Fun-Park, who knew what kind of trouble they were in.

"Crap!" I said. "I completely forgot about them!" I turned to Officer Tom, desperate. "Are they okay?"

He dabbed at his cheek. "Should have told me about them. Should have told me your real name. I could have saved you a whole lot of trouble."

"What do you mean?"

"Just after I left Mr. Natch's office, this girl stopped me. She was pretty, yay high, kind of light brown hair down to here, wearing low-slung jeans and an Up With People T-shirt. Sound familiar?"

"Yeah, that's Lenore. You nailed everything but pretty."

"Well," said Officer Tom, "she was looking for a kid called *Sam*. Not Stan. When I told her I'd picked up a kid called Stan she just threw up her hands and ran off."

I slumped against the rock, feeling like a first-class jerk. Who knew what kind of trouble she was in?

"We have to find her," I said. "And Nick. Come on."

Officer Tom held up his hands. "No way. I got an injury." He tapped his cheek. "And there's no way I'm going back *there*. We should stay here. Wait for things to settle down."

I looked at him. "You know," I said, "Sam and Stan sound alike. You could have figured out that a missing kid you thought was Stan could have been called Sam. Then you could have told my sister what happened, and I'd be safe with her."

He glared at me. "You saying that this is my fault?"

It was some glare Officer Tom could muster. But I wasn't about to back down.

"It sure is your fault," I said, "if you just sit here staunching your wound when there's trouble that you could have prevented." He didn't say anything, so I went on: "A real gamer wouldn't spend the whole adventure hiding behind a rock. That wound's not more than one hit point's worth if that—"

Officer Tom held up his hands one more time. "All right," he said. "Don't pull that Lawful Good guilt trip on me. I get. I get." He sighed, and cautiously stuck his head up over the edge of the boulder. "Okay, hero boy. Looks clear. Let's go."

It wasn't much farther to Natch's. But it seemed like we'd travelled to another country when we got there: the Sovereign Nation of Junior Kindergarten.

The place was a sea of little kids . . . if that sea were being kicked up by a monster big hurricane—the kind of hurricane that knocked over garbage cans and turned big picnic tables on their sides. The little kids ran this way and that, they screamed in high-pitched voices, and they tore at each other and property like wild beasts.

But inside that country, there was another nation that the hurricane didn't touch. A proud, oblivious nation: the Country of Parents. They sat around what tables hadn't been overturned, drinking their lattes and munching on their curly fries, talking to each other about the things that parents talked to each other about: getting back to work on Tuesday and the start of school and *do you remember last summer when there was too much rain* or *it was so hot* or *as bad as this one*, and hopefully winter wouldn't be too long this year so they could get going on another summer soon . . .

We were crouched low on the top of the rise, and had a pretty good view of it all. But it wasn't good enough to spot Nick or Lenore. It didn't seem as though they were in either country.

"They wouldn't leave, would they?"

"Your sister?" Officer Tom shook his head. "She seemed very responsible."

"*Responsible*." I huffed. "That's my sister all right."

"Don't give her a hard time," said Officer Tom.

"*You just think she's pre-tty.*"

"Shut up," he snapped.

I swallowed and looked around. "That," I said, "wasn't me."

Officer Tom looked at me, then drew a breath and put a hand on his stun wand. "Where?" he whispered.

"I don't know where," I said, "but I think I know who." That singsong, high-pitched taunt was unmistakable.

"Fezkul," I said. "Quit dicking around."

"Who's dicking around?" Some ferns rustled about a dozen feet away. "I'm just saying. Officer Tom there just thinks *she's pretty*. It's all pretty pervy, you ask me."

"Hey!" said Tom, aghast. "I didn't—"

"Don't worry about it," I said to him, still looking for Fezkul. "Where are you?"

"Where am I? Why, right in front of you, Poindexter." There was a chuckle at my ear. "Whatsamatter? Can't see me?"

I squinted. Nothing. I couldn't see him—no matter how much I wanted to, there was nothing.

Then he laughed. "Of course you can't see me. You're losing it—growing up. Becoming dull. Right before my eyes. Already, you can't see me any better than Officer Tom here. Soon as you give up Dungeons and Dragons for bridge or canasta or something, you won't be able to hear me either. Oh, I'm tearing up at the thought of it." Somewhere, Fezkul sniffed loudly. "You had such potential, kid. Such potential."

"Where—" I said, but he went on:

"Ah well. Maybe you can go on that Up With People tour with your loser sister. Know any good show tunes, Sammy?"

As he spoke, I thought I could see a shimmering, on top of a boulder that was shaped like a curled-over rabbit. I started toward it.

"Or should I say, Samuel. That sounds—so much more—adult. Samuel."

"I'm not Samuel," I said, and as I did, the shimmering started to resolve itself, and I felt another kind of shimmering in my belly. It was the feeling I got the first time I went to the end of the dock at the cottage, looked into the cold water that was deep over my head and thought: *There is* no way *I can jump into that*; younger, when my mom told me it was time to unplug the night light; and today, when I thought about the prospect of going into Grade Nine, friendless but for Neil and the rest of the William Howard Taft Elementary School Dungeons and Dragons gang who wouldn't be in high school for one more year . . .

"I'm Sammy."

And with the words, the shimmering came into focus: on the top of the rock, into the form of a kid: first, wearing something right out of a Dungeons and Dragons game—what looked like a doublet and hose, and for a second, with wings coming out of his back, and then in the baggy jeans, baseball cap and shark-teeth of Fezkul.

Fezkul clapped twice and grinned, teeth fanning out like a deck of cards.

It was not one of my proudest moments. I leaned over to Officer Tom and whispered: "I think I see him," and I put out my hand and whispered: "Give me the wand. I'll zap him," and Officer Tom fell for it. Why wouldn't he? After all, I'd just saved his life from the crew of psycho toddlers. And hadn't we just bonded over our mutual love of Dungeons and Dragons?

So he was completely surprised when I flipped the switch and jammed it into his thigh. With barely a qualm at having tricked poor old Officer Tom, I switched the wand off, stuffed it in my back pocket and said to Fezkul: "I am ready, oh master."

Or at least I think that's what I said. I felt like I'd just eaten a whole birthday cake: the kind that little kids get, with the white sugar icing that's about two inches thick and the soft sugary cake underneath. All my nerves were humming; the world seemed to be vibrating; I felt like I had to pee except that I didn't have to pee at all. So it is possible that what I said was "Glar worngo. Foo." However it came out, Fezkul seemed pleased. He held up his hands, shook them in the air and laughed like a midget mountain man.

Okay—it wasn't just "not one of my proudest moments." It was, up until that point in my life, the hands-down worst moment yet. I'd just betrayed my new friend Officer Tom's trust. I'd pocketed a weapon that was, if not illegal, then certainly restricted. And I'd thrown in with Fezkul, the demon-child who had told me to set fire to a restaurant and murder its owner.

And that wasn't the worst of it.

The worst of it was how good I felt about it all. Really good. The idea of arson and killing didn't strike me as anything more than a lot of fun. I tumbled down the slope to the Fun-Park, an overgrown maniacal toddler with mayhem on his mind.

The little kids gathered around me almost as soon as I'd stepped onto the grass. This, I remember thinking, must have been what Honorius felt like when he made his Leadership roll and convinced those elves to follow him into the troll cave—like one bad-ass paladin, that's what.

Oh, what to do? There were a few things that came to mind. If we could find more propane, we could just set it off in the grill's kitchen. Although I wasn't sure how to make it blow up without making me blow up too. We could fill a paper cup with root beer, put a lid on, then toss it into the deep fryer. The cold liquid in the hot oil would certainly be catastrophic—but would it go off, or just send hot oil everywhere? Dave Rigby had once tried to convince our dungeon master Neil that if you threw a sack of flour into a room, tossed in a torch after it and shut the door, everything would go up in a colossal flour explosion that could clear a whole dungeon level. Neil had said no way that would work, but who knew? It wasn't like we'd gone down to his condo's parking garage and tried it or anything . . .

"You're thinking too much," said the little pigtailed girl Blair. She pushed her way through the crowd and handed me a long barbecue lighter. "Fezkul said give it to you." Her brother, whose french fries she'd ruined just a little while ago, nodded encouragingly from behind her as I flicked the lighter and looked at the little flame that popped out of the end. It was a happy flame and it filled me with gratitude that she would bestow such a gift on me. Having nothing else to give in return, I handed Blair the stun wand. She flicked it on. Her brother lurched and fell, and she squealed appreciatively.

And we were off.

At first, we moved like a well-coordinated Marine unit—or a company of elvish archers led by one totally wicked champion of good, maybe—wending through the tables and the still-oblivious parents toward the prize of the Grill. A bunch of older kids broke off to go play video games, but when I told them to stick to the plan, they came back like I was a drill sergeant, or Honorius the Paladin. Soon, we had the Grill House surrounded.

We were met by four security guards, who waved their arms and threatened to call our parents, but like Officer Tom, they didn't have the stomach for a fight and they soon succumbed to Blair's stun wand. We tied their shoelaces together, and then headed inside. In my head, I could hear Fezkul's voice but I couldn't understand the words anymore. Just the encouraging tone.

So in we went.

We tore through the washrooms, stuffing the toilets with all the tissue we could find and turning over the garbage cans; we pulled down fire extinguishers and turned the no-slip rugs upside down; we tried to break the fluorescent lights up above but even I was too short for that. Finally, we came out in the front, where there was a counter and a soft-drink dispenser and some grills.

It was magnificent. I could, I think, have taken it all the way. I could have found a sack of flour, burst it open, tossed a Jumbo-Sized root beer into the deep fryer, set off a tank of propane with the barbecue lighter.

God knows the kids were waiting for me to do it; in the back of my head, Fezkul was telling me, in a language that I was beginning now to understand, to do just that: "Blow it up. Destroy the old wizard. Kill him. Kill his minions. Blow it up, boy! You are the champion! Get it! Blow it up!" Something like sugar was itching through my veins and I was ready for anything.

Anything but what I saw, coming around the cash register with Blair at my side.

"It's for the best," said Nick. He was sitting on one of the little plastic chairs next to the window. Lenore was sitting opposite him, her hands in her lap. Her eyes were blank.

"I can't believe it," she mumbled.

Nick looked down and then up at her again. "You can't say you didn't see this coming."

I moved closer. Lenore and Nick were as oblivious as any of the other adults—and as much a target. Blair raised the stun wand, aiming for Lenore's belt-line. I put a hand on her arm, and she frowned at me but held off. I looked at my sister. Her eyes were blank, but I could see her mouth twitching, as she tried to think of some answer.

"What are they doing?" said Blair beside me.

"They're breaking up," I said. "Oh man."

"I didn't see it coming," said Lenore. Her voice was low, a monotone. I'd never seen her like this. "Particularly not now—when we can't even find my brother."

Nick shrugged. "I know. It's not the best timing. But Lenore— we're just different people, you know? We want different things. And hey—your brother'll turn up. He's just goofing, I bet."

Lenore nodded, not looking at him. She crossed her arms, covering the Up With People logo on her shirt and hunching her back like an old woman's.

Nick leaned back and put his fingers in his front pockets and looked out the window. His head bobbed up and down, like he was listening to some tune inside his head. It was like Lenore wasn't even in the room. It struck me then: Nick may have been Lenore's coolest boyfriend yet, but that wasn't the same thing as saying he was cool. He was lame. Totally, completely lame.

And Lenore was alone. She may have been a real dork in a lot of ways, but she was my sister, and she was alone, and she didn't deserve that.

"I'm bored," said Blair and she sulked. "You said we could start a fire."

"No."

"I'm gonna," said Blair, and at that, I turned to her. She was such a little brat. She raised the wand at me, and I looked her in the eye.

"Stop!" I shouted it, and she stepped back, like I'd slapped her. At the same time, the rest of the kids looked at me.

"Stop," I said again. "Just stop."

I stepped over to Lenore and put my hand on her shoulder, and she jumped, then looked at me. She smiled, in a happy-sad way that broke my heart. "Sammy," she said. Her voice was broken. Nick blinked and looked over. "Whoa!" he said. "There you are. We been looking for you all over, bro."

"Don't call me that," I said flatly, and Nick held up his hands.

"Whatever," he said.

"You guys should get out of here," I said to Lenore.

She blinked. "Why?"

I was about to say: look around! But as I looked around, I saw that wouldn't do anything to motivate her. The place, as far as I could tell, was completely empty. There was just us, and a girl behind the counter in one of the orange uniforms who looked like she was swatting at bugs or something.

I didn't see the little kids; they weren't a part of this awful, adult world I'd stepped into. And I didn't want to see the kids; I didn't want to go back to that other world.

There were more important things here.

I gave Lenore a squeeze. "Let's just go," I said.

We met Oliver Natch in the middle of the bridge. He was leaning against the handrail, looking over the slowing traffic heading south to Carlingsburg. He didn't look as sad or as terrible as he might have before. He looked up as we came and gave me a little smile.

"Come again soon," he whispered as I passed near, and I said:

"Not likely," and he just shrugged.

"I can't blame you, Stanley," he said.

"Sam," I said and he nodded.

Lenore stopped beside me. Nick had kept walking, and stood at the far end of the bridge, waiting for us. Clearly, he wanted to get the rest of the drive over as soon as possible. You couldn't blame him—but of course we did.

Natch looked at Lenore. "Your sister?"

Lenore introduced herself.

"Lenore." Mr. Natch gave a little bow—a courtly bow, as if from another age. "Oliver Natch. I am charmed." And with that, he gave me a little wink. "Unlike your brother, I think."

Lenore gave a puzzled frown.

"What are you doing up here?" I asked.

"What? I am doing what I do every year this day and time when I fail to convince Fezkul's little *champion* to spill the beans. Waiting— waiting for the storm to pass." He reached into his pocket, and pulled out an old-fashioned pocket watch. "Which, I think, should be nearly finished." He craned his neck over my shoulder, and nodded. "Yes."

At the base of the stairs, the door to the Grill and Fun-Park opened, and conversation wafted up: "Come on, honey, up the stairs—" "—museum was cool!" "—how much longer to home?"

"So everything's okay?"

Mr. Natch shrugged. "Reasonably," he said. "There will be some cleaning to do. Perhaps a repair or two." Then he looked at me levelly. "It might have been worse, if little Stanley had chosen differently."

"Sam," I said, and he said: "Sam."

And at that moment, I felt a huge sadness, as I thought about everything I'd done—everything I'd taken part in. What I'd done to poor Tom Wilkinson.

"I didn't," I said. "He wanted me to ki—".

Mr. Natch put up his hand and stopped me.

"You chose," he said. "In the end, it is the choice that all the children make, when they sit at the cusp. They cannot go back—

only forward." And then, Mr. Natch smiled in a way that made me look away. "Oh! How it confounds him."

Lenore looked at him and looked at me, then grabbed my shoulder and leaned close. "Come on," she whispered. "This guy is creepy. And I just want to get home."

"Yes," said Natch, "you shouldn't tarry. Tomorrow, after all, is a school day."

We did tarry, just a bit. Lenore was in a whole lot less of a hurry for all of us to get in the car with Nick when we caught up so she put her hand on my shoulder and leaned close. "Wait outside a minute while I settle some things?" she asked and I said, "Sure."

I sat down on the rear bumper and watched the door to the bridge. It was flapping open and closed as kids and their parents came through it, heading back to their own cars and minivans and SUVs, escaping the broken spell of Fezkul, and as they went I wondered: *How long will that bridge stay up? How soon will it be before some kid takes Fezkul's advice all the way?*

And also:

How will I survive Grade Nine with all the cliques?

And then this lone guy came down the stairs from the bridge. I squinted to make sure it was who I thought it was. "Ha," I said, and I pushed myself up and headed over.

Tom Wilkinson blinked at me as he pushed the door open and limped out onto the gravel parking lot.

"You find your sister?" he asked. I nodded and he said, "Good." Then I extended my hand. He looked at it, shrugged, and took it in his own.

In the awful world of adults, some things are definitely harder. But some things are easier too, and this thing was one of those. So we just shook each other's hands like a couple of grown-up gentlemen and I said, "All right then?" and he said "All right then," and then I headed back to Nick's car to finish the trip home.

The Mayor Will Make a Brief Statement and Then Take Questions

"Good afternoon.

"The death of a child affects all of us deeply. We are a community of parents, of brothers and of sisters, of friends and neighbours. Any child lost is a loss for us all.

"We feel the loss of little Nicholas Fletcher especially keenly. Who among us does not recoil in horror, at the echoes of the squealing tires of the car that cut short Nicholas's brief, brilliant life? Who among us does not, in the early hours of these dark mornings, awaken clenched, bathed in sweat, eyes fixed unwillingly on Nicholas's unforgiving, uncomprehending stare?

"I have spoken with the Chief of Police, and he has assured me that his detectives have made the hunt for Nicholas's killer their highest priority. Make no mistake, it is a challenge, for homicide detectives are no different from any of us. They weep for Nicholas too; they feel his cool fingers on the napes of their necks, hear his soft, wordless whispering in their ears. The dreams he conjures wake them also. But with diligence and fortitude, I am confident they will apprehend the coward responsible for this travesty—and so, we pray, end this terrible chapter in our city's history.

"At this time I would like to thank the eyewitnesses who have come forward already, and urge others with any information that might help the investigation to do the same. And I would again like to speak to that motorist among us, who has so far remained silent.

"Come forward; admit to your crime. You will, in a very meaningful way, be saving your city, your community, your family.

"Yourself.

"As for the rest of us: what can we do to quiet our grief? We can recall that we are citizens of a fine, brave city—a great city, with brightly lit boulevards and fine restaurants and theatres, museums and stadiums; a kind city, with many strong and mutually supportive faith communities. Our city.

"Nicholas speaks to us from the dark corners, the cold spaces—but they are shadows amid light, a chill draft by a glowing hearth.

"It is from this place—the warm nest of our homes and communities, the cherished receptacle of our dreams . . . our sanity . . . that we must send a clear message:

"Nicholas—we grieve for you. We offer our comfort to your mother and your baby sister in their pain. We yearn to see the driver who killed you brought to justice.

"You truly do live on in our hearts, truly . . . truly . . . as no other boy, living or dead, ever has.

"Now please. Release those hearts. They are not yours to inhabit.

"As Mayor of this city, I beg you. Rest in peace, son. Please, Nicholas. Just stop."

The Pit-Heads

Paul Peletier and I drove up to Cobalt one last time, about seven years ago. It was my idea. Should have been Paul's—hell, almost two decades before that it *was* his idea, going to Cobalt to paint the pit-heads—but lately he hadn't been painting, hadn't been out of his house to so much as *look* in so long, he was convinced he didn't have any more ideas.

"Bullshit," I said to him, ignition keys jangling in my fingers, coaxing him outside. "You're more of an artist than that."

"No," he said. "And you're not either."

But Paul didn't have much will left to fight me, so he grumbled around the house looking for his old paint kit, the little green strongbox filled with the stuff he euphemistically called his Equipment. Then he climbed into the cab of my pickup, grunted, "Well come *on*, Picasso, let's do it," and we headed north.

Just to see.

There are other things to paint in Cobalt, after all: the black-and-umber tarpaper houses, built high on the rock with materials as likely stolen as they were bought; the roads wending dangerously through the lips of bedrock, like the untended streets of a medieval town; the grocery, built on top of an old mine shaft, a three-hundred-foot-deep root cellar where the owners dangle their overstock of meat and cheese against the improbable heat of high summer in northern Ontario.

We'd painted them all before, in every season and under every sky, and when the pit-heads were still up, they never got old.

So we turned off Highway 11, parked by the grocery and set up our easels. Paul dallied a bit in his strongbox—took out the old silver chain and put it around his neck, muttered a little prayer from his Catholic school days. And then, because there was nothing more but to get started, he reached into his kit and took out a blank pallet, squeezed out some acrylic from the little magazine of ancient paint-tubes he kept in a dark recess of the kit.

I even remember what we were painting. I've still got the panel at my studio—it's not very good, a not-very-confident study of one of those houses, rambling up a slope of rock and perched on a foundation of cinderblock. In a fit of whimsy, I included the figure of a man, bending down at the septic tank, tool box at his feet, an expression of grim determination painted on his tiny face. In fact, no one came out of the house the entire time we painted.

Or should I say, the entire time that *I* painted. Paul just sat there, lifting his brush, swirling it on his pallet. Setting it down again.

"Nothing here anymore, Graham," said Paul, fingering the chain at his neck, and squinting over the still rooftops of the town in the too-bright summer sun. "They're gone."

"They're buried, you mean."

Paul shook his head, and he smiled. "The mining companies'll say it's because of taxes. Hailiebury taxes dearly for a pit-head, next to nothing for a cement plug over a dark shaft."

Then he looked at me, the tiny pewter Jesus at the end of the chain caught in a vise-grip between his thumb and the hard stem of his brush.

"As long as the price of silver stays low, the pit-heads stay down. Holes stay covered, to keep the weather out of the shafts. That's the story, eh, Graham?"

"I guess those miners had the right idea, then," I said. "I guess it's time to go."

"I guess so," said Paul.

And so we packed up our brushes and pallets and paintings, and we followed the miners' example. Paul was inordinately cheerful on the way back, and so was I, I have to admit. There was an ineffable feeling of freedom leaving that town—finally admitting it was over for us there; we were strictly on our own, from that moment on. We made jokes, shared a few carefully chosen reminiscences, were just like old friends again on that four-hour drive south.

But much later, back at my own place in the cold dark of the early morning, I woke up with the once-familiar scream in my throat—

memories of the miner Tevalier's age-yellowed flesh, his cruel and hungry grip, renewed in my blood.

Trembling alone in my bed, I vowed to myself that I would not call Paul Peletier, and I would not go to Cobalt again.

Paul was the first one of our little group to visit Cobalt, and when he reported back on it, he didn't tell us the whole of the story. Not by far.

It was 1974, just a year after Paul's divorce, and he was making ends meet teaching landscape painting classes to art clubs in and around North Bay. In April, he drove up to Cobalt at the invitation of the Women's Art League of Hailiebury, and spent a weekend critiquing the septuagenarian League ladies' blurry watercolours out at the Royal Mine #3. He told us about it in July, when the four regulars in our own little Art League—me, Paul, Jim Osborne and Harry Fairbank—were camped on the south arm of Opeongo Lake, on what would turn out to be our last annual midsummer painting trip together.

"I wasn't up there to work, which is why it was such a damned shame. It was all I could do to keep my paints in their tubes," he said, leaning against the hull of his canoe as he spoke.

Jim took a swill from his thermos and grinned. Jim worked as a lawyer back in the city, and at the end of the year I figured he bought almost as many paintings as he produced. Privately, Paul told me that he thought Jim Osborne painted pictures the way that other men went fishing: he didn't want to catch anything, just get out of the rat race for a few days every summer and escape to the bush.

"*Keep your paints in the tubes.*" Jim rolled the words thoughtfully. "Or did you mean keep your tube in your pants? Those art club biddies can be pretty spry, I hear."

Paul laughed, but it was a distracted sound, barely an acknowledgement. He was never easy with vulgarity.

Paul continued: "The geography around this town is spectacular. It's all rock and scrub, a few stands of poplar and cedar here and there, and it's had the life mined out of it. But I don't think it's possible to make a bad painting there."

Jim was about to say something, but I shushed him.

"High recommendation," I said.

Paul grinned. "The pit-heads outside Cobalt are a Mecca for those ladies—they swear by them, and I can't argue based on the results."

"Practice makes perfect," deadpanned Jim.

Paul gave Jim a look, but I cut in before he could comment. "Just what kind of pit-heads are these?" I asked. I was only twenty-five then, and almost all of the out-of-town painting trips I'd been on had been with Paul and the rest—which pretty much limited me to Algonquin Park and one quick trip up to Lake Superior.

Paul pulled out his sketch pad and began roughing out an illustration: "Here's what they look like."

Harry put down the paint-smeared panel he'd been swearing over all afternoon and studied Paul's drawing in the failing light.

"Do you want to do a trip there?" Harry finally asked.

Paul swatted at a black fly on his neck, and examined the little bloody speck on his hand. "It'll be one hell of a drive—about eight hours from your place in good weather, and I want to go up in November when the snow will have started. It's a long way to go for a painting."

Harry took another look at the sketch, then at his own failed oil painting. "This—" he threw his arms up to include the entire Group-of-Seven, Tom-Thomson splendour of Algonquin Park on a clear summer evening "—is already a long way to come for a painting. And by the looks of things tonight, I don't even have a decent one to show for it. Give me a call when you've set a schedule; I'm in."

Paul smiled and set down the sketch on the flat of a rock for all of us to see. It was crude, but I think it may have been the most accomplished work we'd ever seen from Paul to that date. His carpenter pencil had roughed out the thick spruce beams that splayed out from the narrow, peaked tower head, which Paul had represented with a carelessly precise rectangle of shadow. The trestle emerged from the far side, a jumble of cross-beams and track that draped like a millipede over the spine of a treacherous spill of rock. The thin curves and jags suggesting hills and a treeline seemed like an afterthought—although Paul would scarcely have had time for one. He had completed the whole, perfect sketch in less than a minute.

"Any other takers?" Paul asked, in a tone that suggested there might have been a real question.

The forecast had called for frozen rain in the Hailiebury area, but by the time we pulled onto the mine road the air was just beginning to fill with fine, January-hard snowflakes. They caught in the crevasses and crannies of the low cliffs that rimmed the mine road, making thin white lines like capillaries of frozen quartz.

I watched Paul's taillights through the scratch of snow. He drove an old Ford panel van, and he had set up a small household in the back of it—a foam-rubber mattress near the back for sleeping, a little chemical toilet tucked in a jury-rigged bracket behind the driver's seat, a big cooler filled with enough groceries to feed him for several weeks if need be. And a 12-gauge shotgun with a box of ammunition, in a case beside the mattress, for painting trips during bear season. Paul made his living from his painting, but it wasn't enough of a living to spring for a week in a motel every time he went off on an overnight painting trip. The rest of us followed his lead.

It was scarcely four o'clock, but darkening towards night already, when we finally reached the pit-heads of the Royal Mine. We pulled up on the edge of a wide gravel turnaround maybe three hundred feet downslope from the nearest of the two pit-heads.

The turnaround was near the top of a great boulder of a hill, gouged by glaciers from the tiny slit of a lake that was barely visible through a stand of poplar to the north. The two ancient pit-heads rode that hill's peak, like signal-towers for some forgotten empire.

"We won't have enough light to get any work done tonight," said Paul as he emerged from his van. "But we should be able to go up and have a look inside before nightfall." He hefted a big, ten-battery flashlight on a shoulder-strap he'd tied together from old boot-laces.

Harry put his hands in the small of his back and stretched, making a noise like an old man. "Are those things safe?" he asked.

Paul tromped past him up the slope towards the nearest pit-head. "Not entirely," he said simply. "No, not entirely."

The pit-head was in disuse that year, so the main room underneath the tower was black and empty. Before anyone went in, Paul speared the flashlight beam inside and ran down a brief inventory of what would otherwise have filled the darkness: the great cable spool, driven by a diesel motor in the back of the hoist house, connected to a wheel that would perch in the very top of the tower, where the belfry would be if this were a church. The bare rock floor of the hoist-house was empty, though, the tower just a dark column of cold, lined by beams and tarpaper; according to Paul, the Royal company had moved their operation out of here three years ago, and had warehoused anything remotely portable in Hailiebury. He ran the flashlight beam across the floor in the middle of the chamber, where the cable would have attached to the lift platform. At first, I couldn't even see the mouth of the pit: Jim had to point it out.

"It's pretty small," said Jim, and he was right: the hole leading into the depths of the Royal Mine wasn't more than eight feet on a side.

"This was one of the first mines in the area," said Paul. "One of the ladies from Hailiebury told me it dates back to 1903, when the whole silver rush got its start. Story goes that a prospector found a vein of silver by accident, getting his boot out from where it stuck in a crack in the rock. This pit wouldn't be legal if it'd been dug today—the minimum width now is something like ten feet."

"You sound like a Goddamned tour guide," I said.

Paul chuckled. "Why don't you go in and take a look for yourself, Graham?"

Not taking my eyes off the pit, I stepped inside the structure. The top of the tower was partly open, and the north wind blew a steady beer-bottle C-sharp across it.

"How deep is it?" asked Harry.

"I didn't ask." Paul's flashlight beam followed me like a spotlight as he spoke.

As I got closer to the edge of the pit, it seemed as though the ground were actually sloping inward towards it, growing unsteady beneath my feet. A smell of machine oil and something like must wafted out of the hole. I stepped back.

"That's good, Graham," said Paul, motioning me back to the wall with the flashlight. "Don't get too close to the opening. I'd hate to have to tell your mother we left you at the bottom."

Both Jim and Harry sniggered at that, and I laughed as well, with deliberate good humour. I backed up a few more steps, until my shoulders were pressed against an old wooden ladder. The wood felt soft, ancient; like it would crumble under my weight.

"You find this place inspirational, do you, Paul?" I asked, fighting to keep the quaver out of my voice.

"The Art League ladies swear by it."

The ladder shifted minutely behind my back. From up high, a sprinkle of sand fell, catching like a miniature nebula in the flashlight beam. I tried to imagine how far that sand would fall into the earth before it found something to settle on.

"Well, we can't let Graham here soak up all the juice," said Harry. He stepped inside and peered up into the dark, nose wrinkling.

"Smells in here," he said finally. Jim stepped inside, sniffing.

Behind me, the ladder shifted again, and more dirt fell into the mine. The wind shifted up a half-tone in pitch and with it, the timbers high in the tower creaked. I let go of the ladder and inched further along the wall. I felt like a reluctant suicide on a high-rise window ledge.

"Paul, be a good man and swing that flashlight up there," said Harry, pointing to the top of the ladder. His voice was quiet, almost a monotone. Paul obeyed, and slashed the beam up through the cascade of sand, to the place where Harry pointed.

"Jesus H. Christ!"

I don't know which one of us yelled it; it might have been me, for all the attention I was paying. The only thing I know for sure is that it didn't come from the narrow platform at the top of the ladder, where the light-circle finally came to rest.

There was a man at the top of the ladder.

The light reflected back at us three times: dimly in each lens of the round safety goggles that he wore underneath his helmet, much brighter from the Cyclops-lens of his own helmet-mounted light. He wore a snowsuit, bright yellow underneath, but obscured by thick, hardening smears of mud. A shadow from a cross-beam fell on his chest and chin, enshrouding his features utterly. His arms dangled at his side, and in the mitten of his left hand, he clutched a crowbar.

Harry lifted his hands—as though the crowbar were a rifle, and the miner were a policeman placing the four of us under arrest.

"Hey, fellow," he said. "Just thought we'd take a look around before it got too dark up here. Hope we're not trespassing."

The stranger stood stock still, and didn't answer immediately. He was about fifteen feet above us, on a narrow platform that seemed to extend around the entire second storey of the minehead. The ends of the narrow-gauge tracks that the mine carts rode on extended out into space from the platform near his feet.

"*Bonjour, Monsieur Peletier.*" The voice was deep and gravelly, and the man up top didn't move as he spoke. It was almost as though the voice had come from somewhere else—the top of the pit-tower, maybe the depths of the mine itself. But Paul answered readily enough, and with an easy familiarity that sent a premonitory chill through me.

"*Bonjour, Monsieur Tevalier. Ils sont ici—oui, mon père, ils sont tous ici.*"

Paul's Northern Quebec French has always been a challenge for me, but even without the benefit of my Grade 10 French, the meaning of that simple sentence would have been unmistakable:

They are here—yes, my father, all of them.

No sooner had Paul spoken than the miner's left hand opened and the crowbar clattered to the floorboards over our heads. He stepped back, and for the briefest instant as the shadows passed from his face, we could see him—an absurdly weak chin framed by mutton-chop sideburns the colour of dirty snow; hard yellow flesh, drawn tight as a drum skin across high cheekbones; and of course, we could see his teeth. They were like nails, hammered down through the gums so far that they extended a full inch over the lips.

Paul turned the light away as the creature leaned forward. As it raised its arms to fall, I heard the flick of a flashlight switch and that light disappeared. Something moved in front of the door, and the darkness of the pit-head became absolute.

The creature took Harry first. He was the oldest among us, he'd been slowing down for years, and from that sheerly practical standpoint, I guess he made the easiest target. There were no screams; just a high whimper. The sound a beaten dog would make, if that dog were Harry Fairbanks.

"The rest of you, stand where you are," said Paul, his voice preposterously calm. "One wrong move, and you could find yourself dead at the bottom of the shaft."

"Oh, you bastard," said Jim, the words coming out in sobbing breaths. "Oh, you think you got us trapped in here, oh you Goddamned *bastard.*"

"Only for a moment," said Paul. "Only a moment. Stand still, and we'll all walk out of here together."

The whimper had devolved into a low moan, and it was quickly joined by another sound: dry clicks, the sound old men sometimes make with their throats, as they swallow their soup.

It was at that point, I think, that it occurred to me that Paul's warning to Jim didn't really apply to me: my back was still against the wall, and so long as I kept in contact with that wall, I'd be safe from making a wrong step into the pit. And the ladder to the second floor was only a step away.

Harry let loose a horrible, blood-wet cough, and with it, my decision was made: left hand still pressed against the rough tarpaper wall, I reached out and grabbed a rung of the ladder with my right. It was just as soft as I remembered it, but I didn't take the time to worry whether or not it would hold and in a single motion, swung myself around and started to climb.

The bottom rung snapped under my foot, but I was working on momentum at that point and managed to pull myself past it. The climb couldn't have taken more than a second or two, but it seemed like hours. I was torn between two dreads: of the moment the rungs snapped—beneath my feet, or my hands, or both—and I fell back into the mine; and of the instant that the creature below stopped swallowing, and reached up with whatever kind of claws it had hiding under those big miner's mitts, to grab my ankle and pull me back towards the pit.

But the clicking continued, and the ladder held, one rung and the next rung and the next, and finally when I reached for another rung, my hand fell instead on the rim of the second floor. As I scrambled to get up, my hand closed around the cold metal of the crowbar the creature had dropped, and when I got to my feet, I hefted it in front of me like a club. There was marginally more light up here, and I took a moment to get my bearings. What remained of the day filtered in through cracks in the far wall, and reflected dull steel gleam off the mine-cart tracks even as they converged toward that wall. I couldn't see clearly, but I knew there would have to be a door there—those tracks would lead out to the trestle, and the jagged heap of rocks that it traversed.

"Graham! For Christ's sake!" It was Paul, but I didn't take time to answer him. Something more important had suddenly occupied my attention:

The clicking had finally stopped.

And the ladder creaked under new weight.

I turned and ran towards the light. The floor was clear, but the boards had heaved over the years and I almost tripped twice before I finally fell against the huge door at the end of the tracks. It rattled on its runners as I righted myself. Behind me, I heard the sound of wood snapping, and something grunted—a sound a pig would make.

I found a metal handle about half-way up and lifted, but the door wouldn't budge. So I wedged the tip of the crowbar between the floor and the bottom of the door, and stepped on it. There were more splintering sounds; this time coming both from the door in front of me and the ladder behind me.

"Graham! Get back here!"

"Forget it, Paul!" I was surprised at how giddy my voice sounded, echoing back at me through the darkness.

"I'm doing you a Goddamned favour!"

Whatever was holding the door shut gave way then, and I nearly lost the crowbar as it shot up with the force of the released tension. In a fast motion, I scooped up the crowbar under one arm, and lifted the door up with the other. The pit-head was briefly filled with grey November daylight and I let the door rest on my shoulder.

The creature was at the top of the ladder. It had cast off its helmet and goggles, revealing patchy whips of hair on a mottled yellow scalp, eyes that seemed all pupil—they glittered blankly in the new light. Its chin and beard were slick with Harry's blood and its hands *were* claws. The gloves had been discarded on the way up, and they poked out of the snowsuit's sleeves, dead branches blackened by flame.

The thing held its arm up against the light for only an instant before it launched itself at me.

I swung my head under the door and, checking my footing on the trestle outside first, let go. The door clattered down, even as the creature fell against it.

I backed up a few steps and raised the crowbar again, this time holding it over my shoulder, like a baseball bat.

I don't know how long I stood there before it dawned on me that I could climb down any time I wanted; that it wasn't coming out.

Before it dawned on me just what kind of creature the thing inside the pit-head was.

I threw the crowbar ahead of me, and in careful fits and starts, made it to the ground.

Paul raised his hands and stepped away from the van. I held his 12-gauge cocked and ready at my shoulder, an open box of ammunition on the floor of the van beside the chemical toilet, which I was using as a stool. If the gun were to go off, it would do so with both barrels, and take Paul's head away in the process.

"Stay where I can see you," I told him, and he made no move to disobey. He was framed perfectly in the open panel. "But don't come any closer. No more tricks, all right?"

"I'm glad you weren't hurt," he said, and at that I swear I almost did shoot him.

"No thanks to you."

"No, Graham," said Paul, his voice very cool and reasonable considering his circumstances, "if you'd done what I told you to, stood still and waited for it, believe me—you'd thank me."

"Yeah, Paul. Just like Jim and Harry are thanking you now. I want you to hand over the keys to the van."

"So you can just drive away? Leave all this, leave your work behind?" Paul stood still, kept his eyes on mine as he spoke. "I'm disappointed."

I'd been in the back of Paul's van for about an hour before he'd shown up, and once I'd pried open his gun case and found where he'd kept the ammunition, I'd had little to do but think. Paul had set us up—set us up for something awful—that much was clear. Other things were clear too, but it was the wrong kind of clarity; I needed confirmation.

"That miner—that thing in the mine—it drinks blood, doesn't it?" I demanded. "We're talking about a vampire, aren't we?"

"It's not the only one," replied Paul. "There are maybe twenty or thirty of them, living down in the tunnels. When the mine's active, they feed on the miners."

"And when it's not active, they kill the tourists."

Paul actually smiled at that. "Don't be stupid. They don't kill anyone; how long do you think they'd be able to survive here in these mines if they did? They just—" he searched for the word "—just feed, they milk us if you like. And they always give something back. It's a transaction."

"So that thing in the pit-head—the vampire—didn't kill Harry?"

"He's sleeping in his car."

"Or Jim?"

"They're both fine."

I sat back and let that sink in for a moment. If Paul were telling the truth, my original plans—stealing Paul's van at gunpoint, hightailing it to the OPP station in Haileybury and reporting a brutal triple-killing-by-exsanguination at the Royal minehead north of Cobalt—would all bear some serious rethinking.

"What's the deal, Paul?" I finally asked. "Why'd you do this to us?"

"I didn't do it *to* you," he said, sounding a little exasperated. "I did it *for* you—particularly for *you*, Graham."

"So you keep saying."

"Look: When you joined our little group three years ago, you were just out of art college. And even though you're pointing my own shotgun at my head and it's probably not the wisest thing for me to do, I'll tell you: your work wasn't much to look at then, and three years later, it's still not much to look at. You might as well be doing paint-by-numbers. You've got technical skills that Jim and Harry would both probably kill for—hell, you went to art school for two years, you'd better have learned something—but artistically? You're all cast from the same mould."

When Paul was done, I lowered the shotgun. If I'd left it trained on his forehead, the temptation to pull the trigger would have been too great to resist.

"It may hurt to hear that," continued Paul, "but I think it's the case. It's the case for all of you, and more days than not, it's the case for me too. Which is why when this opportunity arose, I couldn't pass it up. And I couldn't have let any of you pass it up either."

"What opportunity?" My voice sounded like metal in my head.

Paul shook his head. "How do you think," he said slowly, "the Women's Art League of Hailiebury managed to produce such consistently good work here? You think they were born with talent? Or maybe that it was God-given? They made an arrangement, Graham—just like I did."

There was a rustling in the darkness behind Paul, and I raised the shotgun again. I could barely see Paul in the vanishing light; the shadows that emerged from the stand of spruce behind him seemed insubstantial.

"Let them inside," said Paul. "They'll change the way you see."

"Go to hell," I said.

The cold was fierce through the night, but I was glad for it; I managed to stay awake for all but a brief hour before dawn. Paul came by every so often, to check on me—he was waiting, I guess, for me to slip, for the miners to take me the way they'd taken the rest of them, so he could get inside and use his cot for the night. He would pound on the side of the van, shout—"Still corporeal, Graham?"—and tromp off laughing every time I told him to go screw himself.

For their parts, the miners weren't half as annoying. Their claws made a noise like branches as they caressed the side of the van, but they stayed clear of the windows after I made it clear that I was quite willing to shoot the next one that tried to smash its way through the glass of the front windscreen, or tried to jimmy the door locks with its long talons. They kept clear of me to the extent that when I finally did nod off, at about 6:30 in the morning, it was Paul and not the miners that woke me up.

"Rise and shine, young Graham!" he hollered. "The sun's almost up, and it's time to get to work!"

I snapped alert, hefting the shotgun from where it had slid down between my legs. I looked out the front window and confirmed it was safe. Dawn was a thin wash of rose watercolour on the flat grey sheet of November cloud.

"You're not still mad at me, are you?" Paul stepped into view outside the windscreen. "Come on, Graham, at least give me the Coleman and the cooler—the guys want some coffee."

I let go of the shotgun with my right hand, flexed my fingers; I could barely feel them. My feet were similarly numb. And the prospect of hot coffee was impossible to resist.

"I'm still mad at you," I said, and set the shotgun down on the floor. "Yes, you could say that."

I made the fingers of one hand into a claw around the handle of the side door; the thumb of the other hand pushed up the lock. The door slid open, and the fresh morning cold pushed the stale chill of my first night alone in the van into the vaults of memory.

I don't know why I stayed on the week. Harry, neck swathed in gauze and looking perversely healthy, better than he had in years, apologized for the troubles. He offered me a lift into town, even to pay for my bus ticket home if I wanted.

"The painter's life isn't for everybody," said Jim, still relishing his new artist's eye as he peered at the trees and hills through the "L" of his thumb and forefinger. "No shame in admitting that now rather than later."

Paul crouched against the wheel of Jim's Buick and stared at the pit-heads. They were black as coal in the scant morning light.

"No." I rubbed my hands together—feeling was beginning to return to my fingertips, and I figured that by my second cup of coffee I'd be able to hold a brush again. "I came up here to paint some pictures."

"Suit yourself," said Harry.

And so I fell into the ritual of genial artistry that the three of them had established a decade ago and I had joined three years past.

After an early breakfast, we all readied our paint kits, slung them on our shoulders and set out in different directions, to find our spots for the morning. Then it was work, about five hours straight, and back to the camp to compare notes and share some lunch.

In the afternoon, we'd go back to work—sometimes in the same spot as the morning, sometimes we'd swap. We tried to avoid one another while painting—there was no point in two of us working the same view—but we'd occasionally wander by between panels, just to see how the other fellow was doing.

As the week wore on, I found that I was doing most of the wandering. After finishing a half-dozen so-so studies of the pit-heads, the lake below them, the remains of a fallen spruce tree that lay smashed across the back of a boulder bigger than Paul's van, it seemed as though I'd exhausted the possibilities of the place.

So I wandered. And I watched, as Jim and Harry, even Paul, found their art in the skies and the soil of the Royal minehead, and turned out some of the most accomplished work of their lives.

Harry painted the pit-heads almost exclusively. At first, he chose the highest vantage-point, and worked in tight series' of sketches that took my breath away. He used primarily shadow in preference to line to define form, spotting nuances in the light that I, with my art-school trained eye, could only see in the land after studying one of Harry's panels.

Jim did a couple of studies of the pit-heads, then moved off downslope to the lake, where he watched the ice as it spread its crystals, submerging and cracking here and there as winter struggled to solidify its hold on the mine lands. His paintings were abstracts, eggshell whites and stipples of grey and blue—November ice was personified there. It was a complete departure for Jim that was no less shocking to him than it was to the rest of us.

Paul stayed with the pit-heads too. But unlike Harry, who circled them almost daily, Paul remained in a single position, and worked a single canvas, three feet on a side. In the past, Paul's work had always been characterized by a broad brushstroke, form suggested rather than stated. Colour had always been his medium.

With this canvas, Paul had discovered detail. And with his nightly visits to the pit-head with the other three, he had found the art with which to convey it. As I watched the intricate tapestry of his painting take form, the realization came to me:

Paul Peletier wouldn't need to teach art lessons in Cobalt any more. With work like this, he'd be able to write his own ticket.

None of the three were very good company when I visited them. Part of that no doubt was my fault; I'd been staying in Paul's van— alone, awake most of the night and with a shotgun on my lap. It was clear that I made them uncomfortable. And they, frankly, had better things to do than pass the time with me—they moved brush between pallet and panel with the hungry compulsion of newfound genius.

In my sleep-starved state, I compared badly against them. My outlines were tentative, frequently poorly drafted; my colours became muddy and indistinct as I tried again and again to correct them, make them match the land there, the sky.

On the fifth morning at the pit-heads, I knew I couldn't put it off any longer. When we finished breakfast and split up for the morning's work, instead of getting my paint-kit, I went back to Paul's van and picked up the shotgun, a box of shells, his flashlight, and a coil of yellow safety rope. As stealthily as I could, I made my way back up to the pit-head.

The cloud had broken that day, and the mineheads were bathed in clean sunlight for the first time since we'd arrived. But as I stepped inside, it was as ever, dark as midnight.

I tied the rope off against one of the larger beams supporting the tower. The shotgun had a strap, and I hung it over my shoulder while I wrapped the flashlight string around my forearm. It dangled aiming downward as I lowered myself into the pit.

By this time, I'd stopped being angry with Paul. I still wasn't about to come around to his way of thinking, but I realized that he hadn't been lying to me—he was only thinking of my best interests as an artist when he brought me here. He was doing me a favour, opening a door.

And he was, in large part at least, right. The destination beyond was a place that I very much wanted to be. It was just that Paul's door was not the route I wanted to take to get there.

I wrapped the rope twice around my waist, looped and tied the end, and, kicking the last vestiges of snow off my boots, lowered myself into the shaft.

I only lost my footing twice, both times near the end of my descent. The walls had become slippery with ice, and the first time I managed to recover my footing perfectly. The second time came just before the opening of the topmost tunnels, where rock had given way and crumbled around the tunnel's edge. I clutched the rope as it burned against my mittens, swinging free in the narrow shaft. Eventually I propelled myself inside.

The smell I'd first noticed at the top of the pit was stronger here: Heated metal and smouldering engine oil, an underlying *badness* that pervades old industrial sites—or, I guess, mineshafts that've gone dry.

I slung the flashlight in front of me, lowered the shotgun to my side, and peered ahead.

At the time, I don't think I knew precisely what it was that I was looking for. I certainly wasn't there to let the miners—the creatures, the *vampires*—feed on me; I didn't want to cement any transaction in that way. I still like to think that, had they been given a choice, Jim and Harry would have come to the same conclusion.

These miners had something, all right. But they weren't only doling out art lessons—those miners took something different away in return for their blood. And simply because they had so far only bestowed in exchange for blood was no reason to assume that blood was the only coin they understood—or that trade was the only way to draw the genius out of them. I hefted the shotgun to remind myself of that possibility.

The tunnel was wider than it was high at first, and I had to stoop under lips of shale and thick, tarred cross-beams as I moved along. After a time, the tunnel widened out to a space that must have been used as a lunch room when the mine was active. I played the light over the few artefacts that the miners had left: a metal-topped table, surrounded by four folding metal chairs; a stack of more chairs, leaning against an oblong wooden box—an oblong box!—which I pried open with shaking hands only to find it empty but for three badly corroded car batteries.

Sitting on the table was a fabulous anachronism—an ancient oil lamp, with a single crack snaking up from its base. Layers of soot made the glass nearly opaque. It would make a good still-life, I thought, and laughed quietly.

I should have brought my paint kit down.

Beyond the lunch room, the tracks ended and the tunnel took a steep downward slope. There were no steps, but long stems of cedar had been bolted to the rock wall on either side, making banisters. I descended the staircase, such as it was, and at the bottom found a room filled with buckets, made of wood slats and iron hoops and filled with a black liquid that was, after all, only water. The tunnel continued beyond that, and as I followed it I noticed that the long wires and wire-mesh lighting fixtures that had been stapled to the ceiling had been replaced by ornate lamp shelves, such as one might have found in a home around here, before the advent of electricity.

I had stopped for a moment, resting against the wall between two of these low sconces, when the miners found me.

Three of them stepped into the light, and stood frozen there as I hefted my shotgun. Unlike the first creature I'd seen in the pit-head, these wore nothing but a few rags over limbs that were taut with sinew. Their eyes were round and reflected back the flashlight beam like new pennies. The hair on their scalps and their chins was thin, and shockingly white.

"Don't come any closer," I said.

In response, the tunnel filled with a low chattering. I caught fragments of thick Quebecois French, mixed with other sounds: whistles, clicking; a pig-grunt; a wet, bronchial wheeze.

I don't think they understood me any better than I understood them. But they understood the shotgun all right. The trio watched me for a moment longer, then one of them turned and vanished into the dark. When the other two followed, I was after them.

We ran deeper into the mine. If the floor had been rough as the upper tunnels, I don't think I would have been able to keep up. But the rock down here was so smooth it seemed to have been carved, not dug.

The creatures finally escaped me in a wide room—so wide that its walls were beyond the reach of my flashlight. It had a low slate ceiling, supported with thick wooden posts at regular intervals. I stopped, scanned my flashlight across the shadows around me.

"*Bonjour, mon petit.*"

It was the same voice we'd heard in the pit-head. The one that had spoken to Paul, with such familiarity.

Paul had called it, what? *Monsieur Tevalier. Mon père.*

Father.

"Show yourself," I said.

Monsieur Tevalier's breath made a frosting on the hairs of the back of my neck.

I whirled, barely in time to face him. But I couldn't get the shotgun up as well. The flashlight fell to the ground and I felt his talons dig into my coat. I only caught the barest glimpse of his face as he lifted me into the dark. The mutton-chops had darkened, and the flesh on his cheeks had reddened, plumped out with the new blood.

"*Vous étudiez avec le maître,*" said the vampire—then, in thickly accented English: "*I show you the way.*"

How was it for Paul, the rest of them? How was it for the miners, for that matter—who made their own dark bargains here in the earth beneath Cobalt?

I can't say for sure, but it must have been different than the darkness was for me. The twin punctures of the vampire's teeth would have been an utter shock to them—until the moment it occurred, they would have had no reason to expect such a complete invasion as the vampire would have perpetrated.

I was prepared for the attack, though. Where five days earlier I might have looked away—forgotten the assault—as Monsieur Tevalier pierced the flesh of my throat in the rooms beneath Cobalt, I did not lose myself.

Tevalier spoke through my blood, and I was attentive.

He and his kind had been in the land here for as long as the mines had been in Cobalt, moving between the great rocks that remained when the world last thawed. As my blood pulsed down his throat in clicking gulps, he showed me: the earth pulsed too, and that essence that moved through it also flowed through Tevalier, through me. If Tevalier drained me, swallowed all my blood, then the earth's pulse would be all there was. The clarity would be absolute, because I and his land would be as one. In the early days of Cobalt I wondered at what the miners, the prospectors, would have made of that clarity.

Because that was the secret of Tevalier's gift. It dwelt in the razor-line between my heartbeat, absolute insularity—my life—and the earth's simpler rhythm, a final subsumation to the external—my death.

Should I ever stray too far, one way or the other, there would be Tevalier, waiting in the pit-head to nudge me back onto the artist's one true path. Did I understand the depth of my dependency? he asked me through my blood. I felt his tongue on my neck, rough like a cat's. Then, with the care of a physician removing a long hypodermic, he withdrew.

I thought again about the prospectors—thought about the strange town they had built on the earth above, the mining companies that had prospered in it, and the terrible bargain that had founded it.

Did I understand the depth of my dependency?

Before he could withdraw completely, I swung the barrels of the shotgun up, pressed them against the brittle flesh and bone that covered the vampire's heart.

"Je comprends," I whispered, and pulled both triggers.

The hardest part of getting out of the minehead was the climb up the rope, something I hadn't expected. But the run up along the tunnel had proven exhausting, and I was lightheaded already with the loss of my blood. When I fired off the last two shells back into the tunnel, the recoil nearly knocked me into the shaft. The buckshot did its job, though, sending the two vampires that followed me screaming back into the depths. I wanted to rest then, wanted the escape to be finished, but of course I could not, and it was not. I had to ascend the rope.

I lost the shotgun, and nearly lost the flashlight on the way up. Finally I did have to rest, so I tied myself off and dangled there in the shaft, the timber creaking above me and my limbs feeling like meat below; I had the feet of a hanged man.

From the depths, the vampires whispered a cacophony. I had removed their head with Tevalier, taken the one who had made them, shown them their own line—evidently, they had much to discuss. When I resumed my ascent, the whispers had grown quieter, and nearer.

It was near noon when I reached the top of the shaft, and that may have been what saved me. Cobalt is too far north for the sun to have shone straight down the open tower in November, but it made a bright yellow square among the upper rafters, and the light filtered down through the dust to make the pit-head brighter than I'd ever seen it. Clutching at the numbness in my throat, I stumbled to the door and out into the afternoon.

Only as the sun set, five hours later, was I able to calm Paul down and convince him that we had to leave Cobalt before dark. And then, I think it was only the screaming, hungry and subterranean as it echoed from the dark of the pit-heads, that convinced him:

Tevalier was gone; and with him went the razor-line that protected us, and gave us our art.

That summer, the Women's Art League of Hailiebury disbanded, after an early-June tragedy that made the national news reports and forced a six-week coroner's inquest. But throughout that inquest, not one witness stepped forward to charge that the deaths of Elsie LaFontaine and Betty-Ann Sale were the result of anything other than stepping too close to the edge of the mine-shaft.

In 1978, the shanty-town houses of North Cobalt were destroyed by a fire so huge it lit the sky for a hundred miles and kept them warm in Quebec. The Ontario Fire Marshall's office raised the possibility of arson a number of times in the course of its inquiries. But never was it remarked—at least not in public—how close some of the old mine tunnels came to the surface in that section of town. The news reports never dwelt upon the prevailing view in southern Cobalt— that North Cobalt wasn't so much burned, as it was cauterized.

Painting was good in that time. We took precautions, of course; when he got back to his studio, Paul went down to the library in town and came up with a whole list of them. Chains of garlic; Catholic-blessed Holy Water; crucifixes, one for each neck; and silver coins, to cover the eyes. He put them together in a green strongbox, and never came within a hundred miles of Cobalt without his Equipment. I preferred the simpler approach, and as my painting career allowed me to afford it, I expanded my arsenal to the very limits of the prevailing Canadian gun laws.

When the vampires came to our camp outside the pit-heads, we knew how to deal with them. We only allowed them enough blood to complete the transaction: attempts to get any more were met with garlic and holy water and buckshot. The razor's edge remained, even in Tevalier's absence.

It paid off for us all over the years. Jim went professional in the early 1980s and moved to New York in '86. Paul abandoned oils and embraced watercolour, and for five years made a fortune off royalties from art books and calendars featuring reproductions of his hyper-realistic landscapes and naturalist paintings.

We nearly lost Harry in 1981, when he got too close to the edge one night; after that he got spooked and stopped coming out. But he'd produced some damned fine panels in the meantime, and I know they'd pleased him.

And for myself, I did fine, I think; a lot of good work over those years. The rise of my career was far from meteoric—I have yet to see my work on postage stamps, the biggest interview I ever gave was to the North Bay Nugget, and I've still never been able to afford a new car. But groceries are never a question and I keep the furnace going all winter long.

The mining companies finally surrendered in 1985, and tore down every one of the pit-heads, capped the holes. In a way, I'm surprised it took them as long as it did; for Paul and Jim and Harry and me, adaptation was relatively easy—we were only up there two or three weeks out of the year, and when we were there, we knew how to behave. But the men who ran the companies in Cobalt didn't adapt so well; they didn't even have enough sense to put a guardrail around the edges of their shafts—let alone recast the bargains that had made them wealthy in the early years.

It was a scary time for us, in the years after the pit-heads came down. Paul stopped painting altogether, and has sat in an artistic paralysis ever since. Jim traded on his reputation and actually made the cover of *Esquire* after he hired a loyal coven of apprentices to do the actual painting, while he busied himself with what his publicist calls conceptualization, articulation. He's done quite well for himself, but I don't think he'll ever work again.

I, on the other hand, kept on painting. My work's gotten repetitive over the years, but I keep a couple of dealers in Toronto happy—if nothing else, my pictures are a good match for the style of sofa-beds and armchairs that well-heeled doctors and their wives favour as they furnish their cottages in Muskoka.

Art is in the narrow line between life and death—Tevalier was right on that score. I walked that line with Jim and Harry and Paul for more than a decade, against all my better judgement; and I'll admit, it does offer its intoxication.

Now, the pit-heads are down, the pictures there are done. Cobalt has been bled dry—of silver, of art, and of blood. The bargain, whatever coin it was that sealed it, is finished.

But here's the thing: in that bargain's wake, the town of Cobalt persists—a little quieter, maybe, hunched a bit around the scarred land and flesh that Tevalier and the prospectors and the mining companies that came after left behind. But the town accepts its strange shape, acknowledges its new limitations. Within them all, it persists.

I've been warped by Tevalier's knowledge too, and bent again by its absence. But when I wake up in the morning, after I've driven away the nightmares with my coffee and an egg and seen to the other mundane chores, I still pick up my brush and set to work. Because when art is finished, the land remains.

And whatever may have transpired in the past—whatever Tevalier's grave-cold shade accuses, in the small, quiet hours of the night—I don't need a bargain with anyone to paint that land.

Slide Trombone

We were cuing up tape for another run at "Black Mountain Side" when Steve set down his sticks, got up, answered the door-chime. Cool lake air wafted in through the empty doorway and blew the funk of weed and beer and slide lube from living room clear to kitchen. Steve couldn't see who was there. Then he knelt down, and not looking back, reported:

"It's a fish."

Lake trout. About six pounds. Scales the same colour as the clouds, which were just a shade lighter than the lake itself, which was near black. There would be rain soon. Steve cocked his head, nodded, and turned back to us.

"He wants us to keep it down."

Water roared a dull crescendo into the old claw-footed tub in the washroom, and that was the only sound until Vincent, the bass player, clicked a long barbecue lighter alive and held it trembling to the bowl of his bong.

"Fish don't care for Jimmy?"

That from Dave, his guitar propped up by the trombone stand: Jimmy being Page. Vincent coughed and squinted over his burbling bong; Dave got up and came over to the door.

"Not saying." Steve. The fish writhed on the little concrete stoop, gills grasping at the air. "But it's not unreasonable. We've been going all day."

Dave nodded. "Better put him back in the lake." He reached down nervously with thumb and forefinger, tried to snatch the flopping tail once, and again. From the washroom, the trombonist objected.

Vincent motioned to the cracked-open door. "Tub's almost full."

Steve pushed Dave's hand out of the way and grabbed the fish around the middle. It was lake-slick, hard to hold at first, but being off the stoop seemed to calm it and carrying got easier. We all followed Steve and the trout to the bath, watched as he lowered the fish to the surface of the water and let him slide in. Water splashed onto the linoleum floor. Dave turned the faucet off, which the trombonist had left to run.

"Fish will be okay." Steve shook the water off his hands and wiped them dry on his jeans. He went back to the drum kit, picked up his sticks, remembered what the fish said, put them back. "Better keep it down," he said to us, and we agreed.

We sat back. Passed the bong around. Sounds of the bowed guitar solo from "Dazed and Confused," transcribed for trombone, wafted in from the dock. Water splashed in the tub. Steve apologized, got up to shut the door on the music, the view: golden slide on a middle-finger tilt to the clouds' bulging black gut. Definitely rain.

"Have to talk about him." Vincent. Thumb cocked to the doorway. The dock.

The trombonist.

We all agreed that we did—opportunity not having arisen for two days now: from the time Steve pulled the van into the mall parking lot and we all waited as Dave found a spot in the trailer for the trombone case . . . from then to the beer and grocery run on arrival, the jam. Not a moment. So first order of business, now the fish was safe away and the trombone stand empty, was to put it to Steve:

"Where'd you meet him?"

"Back at the Rook?"

Steve shook his head. The Rook was a club downtown we played at, from time to time, back in the day. Steve sometimes still hung there. The Rook wasn't it. "Met him the same time you all did. When we pulled into the lot."

"How'd you know to go there, then?"

"You seemed pretty sure of where you were going. You know he was going to be there?"

That one left Steve short. Steve guessed he did know he was going to be there, standing under the floodlit entrance at the south end of mall, the hockey bag with his stuff propped next to the long black trombone case, which stood upright on the bell. Question suggested

Steve had got a phone call or a note to set time and place, and Steve couldn't say that he had.

Finally: "Neither of you seemed surprised when the time came. Dave, you helped him load up. Looked like you two were catching up on old times."

"Point, there. What'd you talk about, Dave?"

"It's a mystery."

"Quit fucking around. We don't have a lot of time here."

Dave hadn't been fucking around. Mystery is what it was. "Talked about a lot of things. Can't say exactly." Wasn't good enough, and Dave knew it. He frowned and thought a moment. "Asked him if he was still using the valve trombone, or'd gone slide." Which we all knew was a strange thing to ask, given Dave had met him the same time we did and had no idea what type horn he used to play. "Slide, he said. Same as always. He asked me . . ." Bong went to Dave. "Mmm. Asked me if I wanted it."

"The trombone?"

"No. Something else. Didn't say what. But something else."

Bong went to Vincent, then Steve. Thunder came and went. Dave got up, came back with beer. Took the bong. We thought about that question: Did Dave want it? From that: Did we want it? Was it worth having? Rain started up.

"So who is he?" Vincent. "We never had a trombone back in the day. I remember *that* much."

"Our music doesn't lend itself to trombone."

"You wouldn't think."

"And yet."

We grew thoughtful. On the one hand, we remembered how it was: band class and bands didn't mix. Dave had made that clear from Day One, as we hunched in the dull October light, greying our grey cafeteria lunches further. Dave wouldn't even tolerate a lead singer—and if one of us pointed out Robert Plant by way of argument, well we could just fuck off. Steve and his axe, Steve and the microphone. Same thing. And for band class?

"Point of this is not formal training. Point is, you got to feel the music—that's how Jimmy does it. That's how we do it." Plenty of trombonists in band class. And who needed them?

On the other hand . . .

"I helped him load his trombone into the trailer." Dave, perplexed. "I know."

"What do you want?"

"What?"

"Far as what the trombonist asked if you wanted it. What, exactly?"

Vincent.

Always got the Friday fish and chips. Wispy moustache over baby-smooth chin. That and the belly fat and the greasy black hair not quite straight inoculated him against the attention of the big-haired girls—Sue, Maryann, Sue's friend . . . who? . . . the big-haired girls who followed us set to set, tried to keep up, talk about the way the music moved, finally reduced to regurgitating tag-lines from Creem critiques and just nodding, kneeling on the floor while Dave told them how truly full of shit they were, showed them what he meant on air guitar.

"I don't know what I want."

Dave, who'd stopped being such an asshole long back.

Steve cracked a beer. "Sure you do. You want the music. Always have."

Dave thought he should tell the rest of us how full of shit *we* were on that count. But we looked at him that way we did. He nodded.

Rain like applause on the roof. Water splashed in the washroom. We all sat quiet, not wanting to upset the fish any more than it was. Figuring the storm would send *him* back inside soon anyhow, rainwater dribbling a line from spit valve back to the kitchen chair he'd occupied all day, before the door chimed.

"Speaking of the fish."

"Trout."

"Trout. You're sure he thinks we're too loud?"

"Asked us to keep it down."

"Asked *you* to keep it down. Not like *we* heard anything."

"You saying I made it up, Vince?"

"Not saying that at all. But I got to wonder: that fish tell you to keep it down the same way you knew to stop at the mall before we left town?"

"You see what he's saying?"

"What we're getting at?"

What we were getting at was this: perhaps Steve had heard directions from Vincent's house to the south entrance of the mall as a faint whisper in his ear, in a language that he had not heard since the womb, or even prior that.

"I see." Steve stepped into the washroom. Shut the door. Set his beer down on the sink. Looked down at the trout, which hung near the drain, still as death.

Steve, alone in the washroom. Sucked a deep breath. Looked at his hands, thicker now than then, white little lines along the creases . . . Thought about how they once held one of the big-hair girls—Sue's friend, the one with the red hair and the freckles on her shoulders. Her name wouldn't come to him. But her face—wide mouth, cheekbones sharp . . . eyes that looked at him, seemed to *see* him . . .

Not the one he'd married.

That one now: she never saw us—playing, we mean. Steve could barely summon her face; when he did, it was obliterated by hot lights, the smell of old beer and cigarettes. Steve took a long breath. Blinked. Thought:

I used to be . . .

Steve regarded the trout, lowered his finger to touch the surface of the water. Trout twitched its tail, swung suddenly around to back of tub. And she came to him.

Her.

A day ago, standing in the driveway, left foot jittering in its flip-flop, arms crossed, as Steve hitched the trailer to the back of the van.

Hot summer wind blew piss-yellow air from the highway, coloured by the afternoon rush. Her brow creased; not angry, not exactly.

"We have to get on the road."

Might have said more; but too much had been said already. And he knew it. She thought he smoked too much; thought this was a bad time to go off.

Night before: she boiled it down for him as they lay together.

"You're disappearing."

"Stare into the abyss," he said softly, staring that night at the square of silver the street lamp made on the ceiling. Staring.

Listening.

Humming along.

"Don't go," she said. Fingers fluttered at his chest.

That day: She shook her head, threw up her hands. Went back inside.

This day: Trout splashed. Agitated, in clean bathwater.

Dying.

Rain hit on the roof. Wind blew across the open window like it was the top of a beer bottle. That was it: we kept ourselves quiet. "Dazed and Confused" was long done. Steve took a breath. Swallowed his beer in two big gulps.

There was a wide plastic bucket under the sink. Steve took the bucket, lowered it into the tub so it filled with water. Trout swam into it. Steve lifted it out with both arms.

"Trout didn't mean be quiet." Steve, on his way to the front door. "Meant what it said."

Vincent: "Keep it down?"

"Keep what down?" Dave.

"Same thing trombonist asked *you* about. Not the music, either. More." Steve, outside now. "But it's too fuckin' late."

The rain soaked us fast under storm-black sky. Squinting, hand sheltering eyes, it was hard to see where the lake started.

We made for the dock, empty now. Walked out to the end of it.

Dave had been right: should have taken fish back to the lake right away. Claw-footed bathtub was no place for a six-pound lake trout. Dave helped Steve lower the bucket to the water, dip it below the surface. Splashed. Trout jumped out, scales breaking surface in a broad arch. Lightning flashed, dazzlingly close. Trout corkscrewed deep into the black.

"Be free!" Vincent, arms up in the air. Steve, lowering himself to sit on the soaking dock. Dave, standing, half-finished beer in his right hand, held shoulder height; left hand, absently noodling the strings of his invisible axe; head bobbing to the rhythm of an inaudible drummer.

The rain was cold and hard but not unpleasant. Not on any of us. Vincent reminded us of the St. Patrick's Day set, back at the Rook, that year. Dave wrapped tight in blue spandex culled from the ladies' section of the Goodwill. Wailing out "Misty Mountain Hop" like we owned it. Steve smiled, blinked away the water running down his forehead, pasting thinning hair into his eyes. Looked out at the water, black stipple frosted with misted rain. He flipped over the bucket, started tapping. Vincent, pointing back at the house. Door wide open. Light spilling out. Three gentle strums across the worn strings on Dave's acoustic, warming up for a run on "Black Mountain Side."

"The tape?"

Dave shook his head. "Missed that bridge last time. Off my game. Listen."

A shadow moved across the door. "Black Mountain Side" took shape. "He's in there." Vincent. Started back.

Not just him. Another lightning flash. Close—thunder right away. There was Dave, hunched over the guitar. Fingers in their intricate dance. Head bobbing. Behind him: Steve. Tap-tapping on the wood block. Head bobbing in time with Dave. Vincent was there too. But hard to see him through the door. Didn't matter: the noodling acoustic of "Black Mountain Side" doesn't have much to do for a bass player. Less still for a trombonist.

He stepped outside. Just a step. Onto the stoop. Palm cupped outward to catch some rain, horn resting on his shoulder so the slide caught even more, making little round jewels on the golden finish, running tributaries 'round the bell, feeding the torrent running off the bottom to the trombonist's toe.

"I was wrong," said Steve, and Vincent frowned and thought and said, "Yeah," in slow drawl, and Dave asked Steve, "What?"

And he shrugged horn from shoulder, set mouthpiece to lip, and he blew that long, sad note, and Dave saw what we were talking about:

Black plywood stage underfoot, lights hot as noon, air humid with beer-fume and lung-smoke. Us.

"You were wrong about the Rook."

"Yeah."

And we looked at each other through the thick air of the Rook on that night, and Dave turned to the microphone, and swung fingers over string, barely touching, and that note—that same long note—it rose up behind him, behind everything, and Steve thought: *Stare into the abyss. The abyss stares back.*

Sing to it. It might just join in.

Rain came harder again. No end to the lake now. No start, either. And trombone fell from lips. But the song remained.

And so we slipped through it, a flash of scale in the deepening dark, while Steve and Dave and even Vincent finished the Side, and the deep and incongruous moan of the trombone carried us back.

The Inevitability of Earth

When Michael was just a kid, Uncle Evan made a movie of Grandfather. He used an old eight-millimetre camera that wound up with a key and had three narrow lenses that rotated on a plate. Michael remembered holding the camera. It was supposedly lightweight for its time, but in his six-year-old hands, it seemed like it weighed a tonne. Uncle Evan had told him to be careful with it; the camera was a precision instrument, and it needed to be in good working order if the movie was going to be of any scientific value.

The movie was of Grandfather doing his flying thing—flapping his arms with a slow grace as he shut his eyes and turned his long, beakish nose to the sky. Most of the movie was only that: a thin, middle-aged man, flapping his arms, shutting his eyes, craning his neck. Grandfather's apparent foolishness was compounded by the face of young Michael flashing in front of the lens; blocking the scene, and waving like an idiot himself. Then the camera moved, and Michael was gone—

And so was Grandfather.

The view shook and jostled for an instant, and the family garden became a chaos of flowers and greenery. Finally, Uncle Evan settled on the pale blue equanimity of the early-autumn sky. A black dot careered across the screen, from the left to the right and top to the bottom. Then there was a momentary black, as Uncle Evan turned the lenses from wide-angle to telephoto. The screen filled with the briefest glimpse—for the film was about to run out—of grandfather's slender figure, his white shirt-tails flapping behind him, all of him held high above the ground by nothing more substantial than the slow beating of his arms; the formidable strength of his will against the Earth.

Michael groaned and lifted his hand from the cool plastic covering of the armchair. He reached over and flipped the switch on the old projector. The end of the film slapped against the projector frame and the light in the box dimmed. The slapping stopped and the screen went black, and the ember at the tip of his grandmother's cigarette was the only light source in the basement rec room.

"I remember that day." Michael's voice sounded choked and emotional, near to tears, and it surprised him. He wasn't an emotional man as a rule, and he hadn't cried since . . . since who knew when? Maybe the day that film was made. It also dismayed him—sentiment was a bond, and he couldn't afford more bonds. Not if he wanted to follow Grandfather.

"Do you?" said Grandmother. Her voice was deepened by smoke, surprisingly mannish in the dark. "You were very young."

"It was a formative moment," he said. "It's not every day one sees one's grandfather fly," he said, and cleared his throat. "I should think no one would forget such an event."

In the dark, Grandmother coughed, and coughed again. It took Michael a moment to realize she wasn't coughing at all; she was laughing. "What is it?" he said irritably.

"Your formality," she said, and paused. The end of her cigarette glowed furiously as she inhaled. "I'm sorry, dear—I don't mean to laugh at you. You come to visit me here, and I'd hate you to think I'm not grateful for your company, after all these years without so much as a phone call. But I can see how you'd like to find him."

"Can you?"

Michael felt a cloud of smoke envelop him and he choked again—this time, he thought, with more legitimacy. Grandmother was a rancid old creature, stale and fouled with her age; he'd be glad, finally, to be rid of her along with everyone else when he finally took to the sky.

"Yes," she said. "The two of you are of a kind—you look alike, you walk alike, you speak alike. You, though, are a better man." There was a creaking in her chair, and Michael flinched as her hand fell on his thigh, and gave him a vigorous pinch. "A better husband, yes?"

Michael flinched—he hadn't told her about the separation yet, about the necessity of untying himself from the web that was

Suzanne, and the things Suzanne had said to him on the doorstep; he hadn't told anyone in the family in point of fact, because they were part of the web as much as Suzanne was. He patted Grandmother's hand.

"Where's Grandfather now?" he asked.

Grandmother sighed. "You must know, hmm, dear? No one else has his address?"

Michael didn't answer. She knew no one else had his address; how many places, how many other family members he'd checked with, before coming here. It was Uncle Evan who'd finally sent him, told him the only one to talk to about Grandfather was Grandmother.

Your Grandmother has all the facts, said Evan, as they sat in the sunroom at his lakefront condominium. *Gave her the notebook, the film, oh, years ago. She's the family keeper, you know. She's the one to talk to.*

"All right," she finally said. "Turn on the light and help me up— I'll fetch the address while you wind the film."

"If you tell me where it is—"

"I'll get it dear." Her tone left no room for argument.

Michael leaned over to the floor lamp, groped up its narrow brass stem and pulled the chain. The room filled with a light yellowed by the dusty lampshade, and that light struck Michael's Grandmother in profile. It did not flatter her.

When she was younger, Grandmother was reputed to have been something of a beauty, but from the time Michael could remember she had fattened to an ugly obesity. Some of that weight had fallen off over the past ten years, but it had not improved her. Gravity had left Grandmother a drying fruit, flesh hanging loose over the absent girth. It had also left her with diabetes and high blood pressure, dizzy spells and swelling feet. But for all that, she still wouldn't let her grandson climb the stairs to the kitchen for her. Michael allowed himself a smile—he obviously wasn't the only one "of a kind" with Grandfather in this family.

Of course, no one else would view it that way. Grandmother was the family's legendary victim. Everyone had heard the story of how Grandfather had seduced her when she was young and beautiful, then cast her off with the birth of Michael's father and uncle. The years spent raising them had taken that youth and beauty. He had done more, in fact: disowned the family, disappeared from view. But never mind that—the family's umbrage was entirely directed to Grandfather's shabby treatment of Grandmother.

Listening to the family stories, one would think Grandmother had been left in some gutter with nothing but the clothes on her back and a bent walking stick, not in a comfortable Etobicoke bungalow, with the mortgage paid and two grown sons to dote on her every need.

No, Grandmother had a power to her, a gravity, just as much as Grandfather had the will to defy that gravity. Eventually, the will was not enough—Grandfather would have been ground-bound, as he liked to say, after a few more years with Grandmother.

He's understood that intimately, from the first night he decided to leave Suzanne. They had been married for just three years—and as marriages went, he supposed theirs was a good one. But as he lay in bed with her, feeling the Earth impaling him on bedsprings sharp as nails, he knew it could never last. Not, he thought, if he ever meant to fly like Grandfather.

Flight, Michael was beginning to realize, was essential to his survival. When his Grandfather had refused to take him in the air that afternoon at Uncle Evan's old place, he had merely been hurt; but as the years accreted on his back—along with more hurts and disappointments, slights and insults and injuries—he began to realize his desire to fly was more than a desire. It was a need, bone-deep and compelling, like nothing else he'd ever felt. Once he'd defeated gravity, Michael was sure, nothing else could weigh him down.

"Michael!" Grandmother called from upstairs. "I found it!"

"I'm coming, Grandmother! For Heaven's sake, don't strain yourself!" he called, and started up the stairs. He was puffing when he reached the top.

Grandmother was sitting at the kitchen table, an array of envelopes and letters spread in front of her, cigarette smouldering in a brown-stained glass ashtray, a sky the colour of an old bruise framed in the window behind her. She held a small brown envelope close to her breast. She was wearing thick reading glasses, and her magnified eyes looked almost comically worried, or perhaps surprised.

Michael pulled out a chair and sat across from Grandmother, smiled at her. He extended a hand across the table, and Grandmother smiled back, her dentures white and perfect in the midst of her age-sagged face. Still holding the envelope close to her, she took his hand in hers and gave it an affectionate squeeze. Gritting his teeth, Michael squeezed back.

"I haven't seen or spoken with your grandfather in years, you know," she said.

"I know," said Michael.

"It was . . ." she squeezed harder, and enormous tears appeared behind the lenses of her glasses. ". . . it was very painful between us. You cannot know, dearest Michael. The things one must do. Your Suzanne is such a lovely girl, and you . . . you are such a *good* boy. You are both so terribly lucky."

"Yes," he said. Grandmother's hand was thick and dry, and its grip was formidable. If it had been around his throat, Michael thought crazily, that would have been the end of it . . .

"Lucky," he said. "The address, Grandmother?"

Grandmother's eyes blinked enormously behind the glass. "Is something wrong, dear? You don't look well." She let go of his hand, and it flopped to the tabletop.

"I'm sorry," said Michael. He flexed his fingers. Although they appeared normal, they felt swollen, massive. "I'm just a little anxious, I guess."

"To see your Grandfather," said Grandmother. "Of course you are. Well I can certainly help you with that."

They sat silent for a moment, regarding each other—warily,

waiting for the other to move first. Michael felt himself beginning to squirm.

"May I—?" he finally said, and extended his hand again, eyes on the letter.

Grandmother didn't move. "There is a condition," she said.

"Yes?"

The envelope crinkled as her hand tightened around it. The flesh of her neck trembled like a rooster's and her eyes widened to fill the lenses of her glasses. A weight shifted badly in Michael's belly as she opened her mouth to speak.

"You must go to visit him immediately," she said, "and you must bring me with you."

Although Grandmother's tone seemed to preclude argument, Michael attempted it anyway. He told her a meeting now would be painful—after all, the two of them hadn't parted on the friendliest of terms, had they? He pointed out that he, Michael, hadn't seen Grandfather for many years—and he was uncertain enough as to how the meeting would go in any event. Couldn't he visit Grandfather once on his own, and then perhaps broker a meeting between Grandmother and her ex-husband for a second visit? Or perhaps he could convey a message?

"Michael," Grandmother said quietly, "I'm afraid I don't have time to wait for a second visit. Also, I'm afraid I don't care to risk, if you don't mind my saying, your good will on this matter. My condition must stand. I would like to make this trip as early as possible. Immediately."

Michael almost laughed at that—the world was crushing him, and he had planned on setting out the following morning. Now, with the added weight of Grandmother's condition on his shoulders, the pull of the Earth was so unbearable, he'd probably leave as soon as he got the address.

"Are you well enough to travel?" he finally asked.

"Wipe that smirk off your face." Grandmother's eyes narrowed and her mouth became an angry line. Michael felt his face flush—he hadn't realized he *had* been smirking. "Of course I'm well enough," she said. "I'll get my coat."

She stood easily, pushed the chair back underneath the kitchen table, and hurried off to the closet.

Some days, Michael felt the Earth knew of his plans to escape it, and reached up with an extra hand to hold him ever more firmly. It had been bad the day he left Suzanne—ironic, because that was the very act he suspected might liberate him utterly, not yank him closer to the ground he had begun to despise. Now that he was so close—to Grandfather, to his secret—it felt as though the Earth was actually pushing him down, driving him into itself like he was a stake.

God, he just needed some time alone with the old man! Simplification, isolation, was not enough—there was something else the old man knew, and Michael needed to know it too.

He remembered the day Uncle Evan shot his movie, the day he saw the miracle of his Grandfather's flight. His father, genial sadist that he was, had built him up for it, on their way over to Evan's: *Grandfather's a miracle worker, Mikey—just like* Jesus. *Maybe if you ask him nicely, he'll work a miracle for you!* He remembered his mother trying to shush his father. *That's not why we're going; don't get Mikey's hopes up*, she said, and to Michael: *Grandfather's not like Jesus.*

As it turned out, Grandfather showed up almost four hours late, and Michael was the only child there—so of course the waiting had made him crazy. It had in fact made everyone crazy. Michael's father drank too much, and wound up spending what seemed like an hour sick in the bathroom, and his mother paced, feigning interest in Uncle Evan's movie camera, which he loaded film into, in a black cloth bag; or the notebook. It was filled with crabbed handwriting, mathematical equations, and an array of charts and diagrams Evan had assembled, to try and explain the phenomenon of Grandfather's seemingly miraculous flights. She flipped through the book with Aunt Nancy, then called Michael over and made him go through it too, and finally shut it and put her fingers to her eye-sockets and shooed Michael away.

We'll work it out, said Aunt Nancy, resting her hand on his mother's shoulder. *Once we've got it on film, we'll work out what's happening . . . Make it right.* From the bathroom, Michael heard a retching sound and the toilet flushing, and his father's drunken cursing that everyone in the living room strove to ignore. Michael had finally asked to be excused, and went outside to watch for Grandfather's car, from the sweet quiet of his uncle's garden.

The car finally arrived, and Michael watched as his parents and aunt and uncle hurried outside to meet him. Uncle Evan opened the driver's door—which was opposite Michael—and at first Michael thought he was helping Grandfather out. But he wasn't; an enormous, round arm reached out and grabbed his arm, and that was followed by thick, hunched shoulders topped by a head plastered with black, sweaty hair. There was some fumbling below the roof of the car that Michael couldn't see, and finally the immense woman started toward the house, borne by two canes and dwarfing even Michael's father, who Michael thought was the biggest man in the world. The woman, Michael realized, was his Grandmother—whom he had not seen since he was very small.

Grandfather emerged next. He was wearing a neatly pressed suit, and he straightened it as he stood next to the car. He glanced briefly to the house, where the family were all occupied herding Grandmother through the side door, glanced at the sky, and skipped—actually *skipped*—over to the garden, where Michael sat. He thrust his hands into his trouser pockets, and looked again at the sky.

Michael waved at him. *Hello, Grandfather*, he said. He waved again. *Grandfather, it's me!* Finally, when the old man still didn't respond, Michael reached out and grabbed the fabric of his pant-leg, and pulled.

There was a crunch, and Michael jumped back as Grandfather's feet came back into contact with the ground. It was true! Grandfather could fly—he was flying just then, even if it was only an inch above the ground! Michael looked up at the old man with awe. He *was* like Jesus!

At the tug, Grandfather did look down, and his eyes, furious points of black, met with Michael's. His lips pulled back from his teeth, in a snarl. *How dare you!* he snapped, and raised his hand, as if to cuff his grandson.

The hand lowered again, however, as Uncle Evan shouted hello, and strode over, camera in hand, to begin.

We're ready to go, said Uncle Evan, and Grandfather straightened, pulled his suit flat. *I don't know why I agreed to this*, he grumbled. *You're not going to send this to the television, are you?*

Don't worry, Dad—this is just for the family, Uncle Evan said.

Grandfather nodded, grudgingly satisfied. *Where shall I stand?* he asked, and glared at Michael again.

Michael trembled, and felt as though he was going to cry.

Later, Michael did cry. Michael's mother held him, glaring at Grandfather's back as he skipped back to the car, his flight finished and his corpulent wife re-installed in the driver's seat, to bear him home.

You're ground-bound, boy, Grandfather had said when he landed, and Michael had asked him if he could fly too.

Oh yes, Michael had cried that day. *Ground-bound*, Grandfather had called him, and he had been right—about him, Grandmother, about the whole pathetic family. They were all bound to the Earth; gravity hooked their flesh and winched it, inch by inch, year by year into the ground.

All of them, that was, but Grandfather.

Grandfather knew how to remove the hooks, free himself from the tyranny of Earth. He wouldn't tell Mikey the boy. But he would sure as hell tell Michael the man.

"We must take the Highway 400," said Grandmother as Michael started the car. She wouldn't give him the address—she insisted, rather, on giving directions from the passenger seat, so Michael might better concentrate on the road. Michael backed the car out of the driveway.

"Will you tell me where we are going?" he asked. "At least

generally? It helps me to know."

Grandmother put a fresh cigarette in her mouth and fumbled with her lighter.

"Generally?" She chortled. "Generally, we're going to see your Grandfather."

The car filled with Grandmother's rancid lung-smoke. Michael tightened his hands on the steering wheel, and thought, not for the first time, about putting them around Grandmother's throat.

It seemed as though the drive took a day, the traffic was so heavy and the conversation so sparse. In fact, it was just barely over an hour before they reached the appropriate exit and Grandmother told him to leave the highway here.

"You know your way," said Michael as they waited at the stoplight. It was snowing now—vector lines of white crossed the beams of his headlights, and little eddies swirled close to the asphalt. Now that they were stopped, Michael cracked open his window and savoured the fresh, clean air. "You must have been out here before," he said.

"I used to drive here quite frequently, as a matter of fact." Grandmother regarded him, cigarette pinched between two fingers. Her skin was yellow in the dull instrument lights. "You will turn left," she said. "Then I must concentrate on the landmarks—the next turn is difficult to find."

"I don't know what landmarks there are around here," said Michael. Ahead of them was nothing but November-bare fields, and town lights making a sickly aurora on a flat horizon.

"The light's green," she said. "Turn left."

Michael made a wide left, and tapped the gas pedal, to push the car up the slight rise over the highway.

"It's good you left Suzanne," said Grandmother as they accelerated along the dark stretch of road.

"What?" Michael felt the blood drain from his face. "What did you say, Grandmother?" he managed.

Grandmother stared out the front windshield, smoke falling

from her lips like water from a cataract. "Watch the road, Michael."

Michael turned back to the road. As they drove, the darkness had completed itself—even the lights from the town to the north seemed impeded here, although Michael didn't see the trees that might have blocked it at the edge of the roadway.

"What did you say?" he repeated. "About Suzanne?"

"Only that it is good," she said, "that you left. I often wish your Grandfather had taken that route himself."

Michael was about to argue—Grandfather *had* taken that route, hadn't he? He'd left Grandmother, presumably to take to the skies and never look back. He opened his mouth to say so. But he couldn't force the air out; the jealous Earth pulled it to the base of his lungs.

"Why are you slowing down?" Grandmother asked. "We aren't there yet."

"S-sorry," he whispered. He glanced at the speedometer—they were down to 30 kilometres an hour. The road was posted at 80.

The car's engine strained as he stomped the gas pedal, and he held the steering wheel as though clinging to a ledge. Grandmother laughed.

"I'm sorry, dear," she said. "It's just that I never thought I'd be urging my grandson to *speed up*. But never mind—go as slow as you like. We're coming to the turn-off soon."

They turned onto a narrow road of cracked pavement and stone and deep wheel-ruts. The sky was dark, but there was nowhere really dark on this land; there were no shadows, no trees to cast them. Nothing grew higher than a few inches here—so the town light reflecting from the clouds painted the landscape a dim, silvery green.

Michael was breathing better now, and he could speak easily again. But he still felt the Earth pulling at his arms, his feet. A filling in his molar ached mightily, and the pain of it leaked across the inside of his skull like a bloodstain.

At length, he broached the subject of Suzanne again with Grandmother. Had Suzanne called before he'd arrived? Or had she spoken with someone else in the family, who'd reported the separation to Grandmother? How had Grandmother learned of the situation with Suzanne? Michael was certain he hadn't told anyone . . .

"I'll tell you a story," said Grandmother instead of answering the questions directly. "I met your Grandfather when he was in university. It was the Depression—1933, and no one had any money, certainly not my parents. But his family was one of means, even in those times. So Grandfather was able to go to school. He was lifted by the toil of his father. Do you understand, Michael?"

"Grandmother." Michael spoke in a low voice that sounded too much like a threat. He tried again, this time achieving at least a plaintive tone. "Grandmother, I understand. But—Suzanne?"

Grandmother motioned ahead. "Eye on the road, Michael. It's difficult along here."

Michael massaged the steering wheel, and looked ahead. The glow of his headlights illuminated cones of a complicated and undeniably damaged landscape. Keep his eye on the road? It was hard to tell where the road was in this jumbled plain of rock and asphalt. He let the car slow again while he peered into the dark, trying to make out a roadway.

"I met your Grandfather along the boardwalk by the lake, near the Sunnyside Amusement Park," she said. "There was a dancehall there—it was called the Palais Royale, and the price of entry was too dear for any of us, my friends and I. Even should we have scraped together the fifty cents they demanded, none of us owned a dress fine enough for the gentlemen who would frequent such a place. None of us owned a gentleman who would make a suitable escort . . . But we coveted it, all the same—we stood upon the boardwalk, the lake at our backs, listening to the fine songs and the gay laughter. Wanting the thing we could never have."

"Imagine that." Michael muttered it, barely a whisper, but Grandmother heard anyway. She raised her eyebrows and the car ground to a halt. Michael felt his fingers slip from around the steering wheel. His hands pounded down onto his thighs, and he winced in pain. He bit his lip against the urge to cry out, though. The quicker Grandmother finished her story, the quicker they'd find Grandfather—and God, he needed to find Grandfather.

"Please—" he shut his eyes and pulled his hands from his thighs "—go on."

"Your Grandfather also stood outside the dancehall sometimes," she said. "Only nearer the lake; we would sometimes see him, a strange and mysterious man, staring out at the waters. On the night we met, in the midst of June, I remember my friends were late. It was still dusk when I arrived, and the music had not yet started— although the motorcars were already pulling up to the front door, the beautiful ladies already stepping from the cabs with their dashing escorts. And there he was, your Grandfather, standing in his place by the beach. Seeing me alone, he called to me. 'Please, madam, I seem to require some assistance,' he said. 'Why, me?' I asked. 'Yes,' he said, 'please come down now.'

"Were I with my friends, I should never have done so—imagine, an unescorted young lady, going to the side of a perfect stranger!— but I was alone for the moment, and curious; there was something odd about him.

"As I drew nearer, I saw he was near the waterline, his trousers rolled up and his feet buried up to his ankles in the sand. He wore a white dinner jacket, I remember, and held his shoes and socks in one hand." Grandmother put her hand on Michael's arm. "'Thank you,' he said. 'I'm afraid I've gotten stuck.'"

"Help me," said Michael, who was feeling increasingly stuck himself.

"Yes," she said distractedly.

Grandmother's fingers squeezed on Michael's arm again, and as they did, he felt a great rush of fresh, cool air swimming into his lungs. Grandmother's eyes locked with Michael's. "I felt myself sinking a little in the soft sand," she said. "As though I'd just been loaded down with a parcel. My back bent, and my belly sagged. Then, easy as that, your Grandfather stepped out of the mud."

Michael lifted his hand, flexed the fingers and drew a deep breath. He looked at Grandmother wonderingly.

"I must finish the story," she said. "Grandfather stepped out of the mud, and onto the water."

"You mean—" *into*, Michael was going to say, but stopped himself. He could tell by her eyes that Grandmother had meant what she said: Grandfather stepped *onto* the water. Grandmother nodded.

"He walked out a dozen yards, and danced a little jig. I remember how his toes splashed the water so delicately. 'Just like Jesus!' he shouted, grinning like a fool. 'And I couldn't do it without you!'

"Of course, I was enthralled. As was he—for that evening was when he learned to fly," she said. "Suzanne, bless her, has been spared the suffering—for you haven't yet thought it through, and you've left her. Intact."

"What are you talking about?" Michael's voice conveyed threat again, but this time he didn't bother to correct it. "Grandmother, this is a dreadful game you're playing. Now answer my question, please— how did you find out about my, ah, situation with Suzanne?"

Grandmother's smile was thin and cool.

"Why, Michael," she said, "we have known about your situation since you were a small boy."

"You can't have known—Suzanne and I only just separated a month ago. Why didn't you let on earlier? In your house?"

"Don't take that tone with me." Grandmother glared at him through wide lenses. Now something in her tone had become as threatening as Michael's had earlier. "Suzanne is incidental. Your true situation is that you were a selfish, stupid boy then, and now you have grown into a selfish and stupid man. We decided you bore watching since the day we made this place."

"You—made this place?"

"I suppose I shouldn't be surprised you don't recognize it," she said. "It has changed since that afternoon."

"This is enough," he snarled, and opened the car door. Whatever spell had ensnared him a moment ago was gone now—he could walk as well as anyone, air came and went in his chest with ease, and his arms were strong and mobile again. He slammed his door, and strode around the front of the car, to the passenger side. Anger grew tumourously in his belly. Hadn't he waited long enough? Grandmother had been playing games with him all evening—*just one condition*, she said; *bring me with you; I'll tell you a* Goddamned *story*. And . . .

And now, she insulted him. Called him selfish, stupid. Then and now.

"Get out!" he shouted, pulling the door open and grabbing Grandmother by the arm, squeezing deliberately too hard. "You said you'd take me to see Grandfather, and now by hell you will do so! Is he even here?"

She came out of the car easily—almost too easily, for a woman of her size. Lifting Grandmother was like lifting a heavy coat, nothing more, and Michael stumbled back with wasted momentum when her feet landed on the ground. He regained his balance, and made a fist at her.

"I have to see Grandfather!" he shouted. "You'd better take me to him!"

She coughed again. Her eyes seemed enormous in the flat cloud-light. Infuriatingly, they didn't seem particularly frightened. She regarded him levelly as she reached into her coat pocket and pulled out a package of cigarettes.

Michael managed to hold his rage in his fist while she dug out her lighter, lit the cigarette, while she puffed the cigarette to life, up until the point where the smoke came cascading from her lips—and then it was no good. The anger leaked away, and left only a crumbling kind of shame behind. Michael grimaced at it. He'd threatened his Grandmother—manhandled her! What could be worse, more base, than that? His hand dropped, open and empty, at his side. When he finally spoke, he did so quietly.

"Please, Grandmother," he said, "I need to fly."

At that, Grandmother let loose another coughing laugh. "Evan told me this would be difficult," she said. "Come on," she said. "I'll take you to your Grandfather. He's in the garden."

"The garden?"

"You remember, dear—from the movie."

At once, it came together for Michael. He looked around the landscape—now nothing but a flattened plain, mottled with stone and debris, but fundamentally equalized by the force of the Earth. In his memory, he drew up the past—the house, with its wide glass doors, and the trees and the garden, the chaos of greenery there. The memory of it floated over the ruined ground like ghost towers.

Grandmother walked through them easily—she wasn't even using a cane—and Michael followed. After a time, the ground beneath his feet altered, and Michael realized he was no longer walking on gravel. The ground was brick now, smashed brick and masonry, mixed with the occasional splintered piece of wood.

"This place," said Grandmother, "was an unfortunate side effect. But it was early, and we didn't quite understand the forces involved. And we did have to act quickly—so I suppose we really can't blame ourselves."

"Why did you have to act quickly?" Michael thought he might know the answer already—as he looked around, as far as he could see there was nothing standing above ankle height. There was nowhere for Grandfather to hide. Not above ground.

Grandmother stopped then, and turned around—turning, Michael saw, as though she were standing on a Lazy Susan. Or floating above the ground, just an inch. She fished into her purse, and pulled out a coil of what looked like rope. She tossed it in the air, and it unravelled slowly, drifting to him as though floating in water. Michael reached out and caught it easily. As he held it, he saw it wasn't rope at all—it was a length of plastic hose, ribbed with wire.

"If we hadn't done something soon," said Grandmother, "then your Grandfather would have driven us all into the Earth, with his foolish indulgence."

"Where is Grandfather?" said Michael. "I have to talk to him."

Grandmother smiled in a way that was not very Grandmotherly at all.

"Look down," said Grandmother.

Michael looked down—and immediately realized his mistake. Gravity seized him with two strong hands around his skull, and he fell hard to his knees. He dropped the hose and put his hands out to break his fall—

And they sank into the ground.

Michael yanked back with his shoulders, but his hands wouldn't come out. It was as though they were set in cement. He tried to lift his knees, but they were embedded in the ground as well.

"Help me." The words came out as a whisper, but Grandmother heard them.

"Of course, dear," she said, and then he saw her feet beside him. She bent down and lifted an end of the tube she'd tossed him. "I'm sorry—I should have explained. It goes in your mouth—that's very important." Michael felt a hand on the back of his head, and Grandmother's other hand set the tube firmly between his teeth. "Clamp down," she instructed.

Michael sank further—his groin was pressed against the ground, and as far as he could tell his thighs were almost completely submerged. In the distance, he heard the sound of a car engine.

Grandmother let go of the hose and his head, and moved further back. Her cold, strong hands pushed down on his behind. There was a crunching sound, as his pelvis slid through stone and wood and dirt. "You'll thank me for this later," she said. "It's better to go down feet first."

The car engine grew louder. Out of the corner of his eye, Michael could see the glimmer of headlights. Finally, they grew very bright, illuminating the ground beneath him like a moonscape, and the engine stopped.

Michael heard a strangled moan then—dimly, he realized it was his own, carried through the tube that began in his mouth and ended a few feet away.

There was another tube, he saw—sticking out of the ground, just a few feet in front of him. If he listened, he was sure he could hear the faint noise of breathing coming from it.

The car doors opened and closed, and Michael heard voices:

"Mother," said one—sounding very much like Uncle Evan. "Are we too late?"

"You *are* late," said Grandmother, grunting as she continued to work at Michael's back, "but I am managing."

"Well now you can take a rest," said a woman—Aunt Nancy? "We can take over from here."

"Very well." Grandmother let go of Michael, and he tried to struggle. But he was at an odd angle—bent forward about forty-five degrees. He could thrash his shoulders, wave his head around, but that was as much as he could hope for.

Soon, he felt more hands on him. Together, they pushed down harder than Grandmother could—so very soon he was nearly upright, waist-deep in the ground. His breath whistled through the tubing, cut by sobs.

He could see the other car now. It was a big American sedan, a Lincoln maybe, and as he watched the back door opened, and a third person got out.

It was Suzanne.

He tried to spit out the tube, so he could speak with her, *plead* with her—but as quick as he did, Uncle Evan pushed the tube back in.

Suzanne's feet crunched on the debris as she walked over to him. He couldn't see her face well—as she approached, she became not much more than a slender silhouette in the Lincoln's headlights.

"Do I have to do this?" Her voice was quavering as she bent to her knees, put her hands on Michael's shoulders. Michael thought he could see the glint of moisture on her cheeks—and was absurdly touched by it.

"It is the only way, dear," said Grandmother. "Don't worry—he'll be fine. The Earth looks after its own."

"I'm sorry," she whispered. "I thought we could work it out."

Suzanne pushed down on Michael's shoulders, and he felt himself sinking further—the Earth tickled his collarbone, enveloped his throat and touched his chin. Suzanne had moved her hands to the crown of his skull, and now she pushed down on that. Desperate, Michael spat out the tube.

"Suzanne! Wait! Maybe we can work it out!" he gasped, as the ground came over the cleft in his chin, pressed against his lower lip. "Help me up!"

Suzanne took her hands from his head at that.

"No," she said—although her voice was uncertain. She reached down, picked up the tube, and jammed it into his mouth. "Your Grandmother explained what happens when I help you up." And then her tone changed, and it sounded very certain indeed. "I can't let you use me like that."

Then she pushed once more, and Michael was into the ground past his nose. He sucked cold, stale air through the tube. All he could see now was Suzanne's boots, her blue-jeaned knees, and the inch or so of space between them and the flattened ground.

"That's enough, dear," said Grandmother, her voice sounding far away. "The Earth can do the rest."

Suzanne's hands lifted from Michael's head, and he watched as her feet, her knees lifted further from the ground. He heard laughter from above—liberated, unbound from the Earth—and then that same Earth came up to fill his ears. The only sound was the beating of his heart.

The beating of his own heart, and faintly, the beating of one other.

"Grandfather," he said, but the words were mangled through his tube and must have sounded like a bleat to anyone who lingered above. His tears made little pools on the ground in front of him. Although it was cold and hard that night, tightly packed in its own formidable grip, the Earth swallowed them greedily.

Swamp Witch and the Tea-Drinking Man

Swamp witch rode her dragonfly into town Saturday night, meaning to see old Albert Farmer one more time. Albert ran the local smoke and book, drove a gleaming red sports car from Italy, and smiled a smile to run an iceberg wet. Many suspected he might be the Devil's kin and swamp witch allowed as that may have been so; yet whether he be Devil or Saint, swamp witch knew Albert Farmer to be the kindest man in the whole of Okehole County. Hadn't he let her beat him at checkers that time? Didn't he smile just right? Oh yes, swamp witch figured she'd like to keep old Albert Farmer awhile and see him this night.

That in the end she would succeed at one and fail at the other was a matter of no small upset to swamp witch; for among the burdens they carry, swamp witches are cursed with foresight, and this one could see endings clearer than anything else. Not that it ever did her much good; swamp witch could no more look long at an ending than she'd spare the blazing sun more than a glance.

As for the end of this night, she glanced on it not even an instant. For romance was nothing but scut work if you knew already the beginning, the end and all the points between. The smile on her lips was genuine as she steered past the bullfrogs, through the rushes and high over the swamp road toward the glow of the town.

By the time she was on the town's outskirts, walking on her own two feet with the tiny reins of her dragonfly pinched between thumb and forefinger, the swamp witch had a harder time keeping her mood high. Her feet were on the ground, her senses chained and she could not ignore the wailing of a woman beset.

It came from the house which sat nearest the swamp—the Farley house—and the wailing was the work of Linda Farley, the eldest daughter who swamp witch knew was having man trouble of her own.

She had mixed feelings about Linda Farley, but for all those feelings, swamp witch could not just walk by and she knew it. There was that thing she had done with her checkers winnings. It had made things right and made things wrong, and in the end made swamp witch responsible.

"One night in a week," swamp witch grumbled as she stepped around the swing-set and onto the back stoop. "Just Saturday. That's all I asked for."

Linda Farley was a girl of twenty-one. Thick-armed and -legged, but still beautiful by the standards of the town, she had been ill-treated by no less than three of its sons: lanky Jack Irving; foul-mouthed Harry Oates; Tommy Balchy, the beautiful Reverend's son, who wrangled corner snakes for his Papa and bragged to everyone that he'd seen Jesus in a rattler's spittle. Swamp witch was sure it would be one of those three causing the commotion. But when she came in, touched poor Linda's shoulder where it slumped on the kitchen table, and followed her pointing finger to the sitting room, she saw it was none of those fellows.

Sitting on her Papa's easy chair was a man swamp witch had never seen before. Wearing a lemon-coloured suit with a vest black as night rain, he was skinny as sticks and looked just past the middle of his life. He held a teacup and saucer in his hands, and looked up at swamp witch with the sadness of the ages in his eye.

"Stay put," said swamp witch to her dragonfly, letting go of its reins. The dragonfly flew up and perched on an arm of the Farleys' flea-market chandelier. "Who is this one?"

The man licked thin lips.

"He came this afternoon," said Linda, sitting up and sniffling. "Came from outside. He says awful things." She held her head in her hands. "Oh woe!"

"*Awful* things." Swamp witch stepped over to the tea-drinking man. "Outside. What's his name?"

The tea-drinking man raised his cup to his mouth. He shook his head.

"He-he won't say."

Swamp witch nodded slowly. "You won't say," she said to the tea-drinking man and he shrugged. Swamp witch scowled. People who knew enough to keep their names secret were trouble in swamp witch's experience.

The tea-drinking man set his beverage down on the arm of the chair and began to speak.

"What if you'd left 'em?" he said. "Left 'em to themselves?"

Swamp witch glared. The tea-drinker paid her no mind, just continued:

"Why, think what they'd have done! Made up with the Russians! The Chinese! Built rockets and climbed with them to the top of the sky, and sat there a moment in spinning wheels with sandwiches floating in front of their noses and their dreams all filled up. Sat there and thought, about what they'd done, what they might do, and looked far away. Then got off their duffs and built bigger rockets, and flew 'em to the moon, and to Mars. Where'd they be?"

The tea-drinking man was breathing hard now. He looked at her like a crazy man, eyes wet. "What if they'd been left on their own?"

And then he went silent and watched.

The swamp witch took a breath, felt it hitch in her chest. Then she let it out again, in a low cough.

"You're infectious," she said.

"What?" said Linda from behind him.

"Infectious. The dream sickness," she said. "You look at the past and start to think maybe that could be better than now. You can't move, it's so bad—can't even think."

The tea-drinking man shrugged. "I been around, madame."

"*Around*," said swamp witch. "Surely not around here. This place is mine. There's no sickness, no dreaming sadness. These folks are happy as they are. So I'll say it: you're quarantined from this town." She glanced back at Linda, who looked back at her miserably, awash in inconsolable regret.

"That's how it is."

Swamp witch glared once more at the tea-drinking man.

The tea-drinking man smiled sadly.

"I am—"

"—sorry," finished swamp witch. "I know."

And then swamp witch raised up her arms, cast a wink up to her dragonfly, and set a hex upon the tea-drinking man. "*Begone*," she said.

He stood up. Set his saucer and cup down. Looked a little sadder, if that were possible.

"I was just leaving."

And with that, he stepped out the door, through the yard, over the road and into the mist of the swampland.

"Stay away from my hutch, mind you," swamp witch hollered after his diminishing shade. "I mean it!" And she thought she saw him shrug a bit before the wisps of mist engulfed him and took him, poor dream-sick man that he was, away from the town that swamp witch loved so.

Swamp witch left shortly after that, and she didn't feel bad about it neither. If she'd been a better person, maybe she'd have sat with the girl until she'd calmed down. Maybe cast another little hex to help her through it. But swamp witch couldn't help thinking that one of the things poor old Linda was regretting was her own complicity in the bunch that'd driven swamp witch from her home those years ago and into the mud of the Okehole Wetlands for good.

Let her stew a bit, an unkind part of swamp witch thought as she left the girl alone in her kitchen.

And even if swamp witch wasn't feeling mean, she felt she had an excuse: after having spent a moment with the tea-drinking man, swamp witch couldn't be sure what regret was real and what was just symptomatic. So she called down dragonfly to her shoulder and headed off to town. That's what Saturday was for, after all.

It was very bad, worse than she'd thought. This tea-drinking man hadn't, as swamp witch first assumed, just started his visit to town setting in Linda's Poppa's easy chair. That was probably his last stop on the way through, spreading his dreaming sickness all over the town. Wandering here or there, giving a little sneeze or a cough as he passed by a fellow fixing his garage door or another loading groceries into his truck, or worst of all, a woman by herself, smoking a cigarette and staring at a cloud overhead wondering where the years had gone. He would leave behind him a wake of furrowed brows and teary eyes and fresh fault lines in healed-up hearts.

And those were the ones he'd passed. The others—the ones he spent a moment with, said hello to or spoke of this or that—

—there would only be one word for those:

Inconsolable.

Swamp witch was set to figuring now that the tea-drinking man wasn't just a carrier of the bug, like she'd first thought. He was guilty as sin. He was a caster.

And swamp witch was starting to think that he might not be alone. He might not, he might not . . .

She closed her eyes and took a breath.

When she opened her eyes, swamp witch headed across the downtown with more care. Her dragonfly hid in the curl of her hair and she kept underneath awnings and away from street lamps, and as she did, dragonfly asked her questions with the buzz of its wings.

—What does tomorrow bring? he asked.

Swamp witch opened her mouth to speak it: *sorrow.*

But she did not. She simply stopped.

—And the day after? wondered dragonfly.

—Who knows? whispered swamp witch. But she did know, and she stopped, in the crook of two sidewalk cracks. All she could see was her boy, whose name would be Horace, lying with the gossamer yellow of new beard on his face and his eyes glazed and silvered in the sheen of death. Her girl Ellen, old and bent, rattling in a hospital bed. These were not tomorrow—nor the day after either. But they were bad days ahead—days she'd rather not have happen.

—Dream sickness gotcha, said dragonfly. Only you regret what comes, not what's been.

—You are wise, said swamp witch, her voice shaking. She tried to think of a hex to drive it off, but the ones she knew were all for others.

—Think backwards then, dragonfly suggested. Think of the time you were born.

Swamp witch tried but it was like trying to turn a boat in a fast-moving river. Always she was bent back to forward.

"Need help?"

Swamp witch looked up. There, standing in the middle of the road, his hands behind his back, was the yellow-jacketed tea-drinking man. He had a half-way grin on him that salesmen got when they wondered if maybe you were going to buy that car today all on your own, or maybe needed a little help. He unfolded his hands and started strolling up the way to see her.

"You were banished," said swamp witch. "I said *begone!*"

"I went," said the tea-drinking man. "Oh yes. I *begoned* all right. Right through the swamp. Steered clear of your home there too. Like you demanded."

"Then why—?"

"Why'm I here?" He stepped up onto the curb. He shook his head. "Let me ask *you* a question."

Swamp witch tried to move—to do something about this. She didn't want him to ask her a question particularly: didn't think it would go anywhere good.

"Just hypothetical," he said.

Shut up, thought swamp witch, but her lips wouldn't move, plastered shut as they were by contemporaneous regret.

"Oh what," he said, "if the town were left on its own?"

"You asked me that earlier."

"Well think about it then. What if you'd just left it. Left it to have a name and a place in the world. Left the folks to see the consequences of their activities. Vulnerable you say and maybe so. But better that than this amber bauble of a home you've crafted, hidden away from the world of witches and kept for yourself. Selfish, wicked swamp witch."

"What—"

The tea-drinking man leaned close. He breathed a fog of lament her way.

"I didn't care for it," he said. "Tossin' me out like that."

Swamp witch swallowed hard. "I don't," she said, "feel bad about any of that."

He smiled. "No?"

Swamp witch stood. "No." She stepped over the crack. Away from the tea-drinking man. "No regrets."

As she walked away, she heard him snicker, a sound like the shuffling of a dirty old poker deck.

"None," she said.

Swamp witch lied, though. To hide it, she meandered across the parking lot of the five and dime, tears streaming down from her eyes, feeling like her middle'd been removed with the awful regret of it all but hiding it in the hunch of her shoulders.

It was low cowardice. For what business had it been of hers, to take the town and curl it in the protection of her arms like she was its Goddamned mother and not its shunned daughter?

She took a few more steps, over to the little berm at the parking lot's edge. Then she walked no more—falling into the sweet grass and sucking its green, fresh smell.

"You lie," said tea-drinking man.

She looked up. He was standing over her now, his grin wider than ever she'd thought it could be, on one so stoked with regret.

"You are beset with it," he said.

And then he spread his fingers, which crept wider than swamp witch thought they could—and down they came around her, like a cage of twig and sapling.

"Begone," she said, but the tea-drinking man shook his head. He didn't have to say: *Only works if you mean it, that hex. And then, it only works the once.*

And with that, he had her. Swamp witch fell into a pit inside her—one with holes in the side of it, that looked ahead and back with the same misery. She shut her eyes and did what the sad do best: fell into a deep and honeyed sleep, where past and future mixed.

She awoke a time later, in a bad way for a couple of reasons.

First, she was in church: Reverend Balchy's church, which was not a good place for her or anyone.

And second, dragonfly was gone.

In the church this was a bad thing. For swamp witch knew that Reverend Balchy had against her advice gone in with the snake dancers' way, turning many in his Baptist congregation from their religion, and welcoming in their place whole families of the Okehole corner rattlers that the Reverend used. Sitting up on the pew, swamp witch feared for dragonfly, for there was nothing that a corner rattler liked better than the crunch of a dragonfly's wing.

Swamp witch called out softly, looking up to the water-stained drop-ceiling with its flickery fluorescent tubes, the dried, cut rushes at the blacked-out windows, the twist of serpent-spine that was nailed up on along the One Cross's middle piece.

She poked her toe at the floor, and snatched it back again as the arrow-tip head of a corner rattler slashed out from the pew's shadow. Swamp witch wouldn't give it a second chance. She gathered her feet beneath her and stood on the seat-bench, so she could better see.

"*Dragonfly!*" she hissed.

There was no answer, but for the soft *chuk-a-chuk* samba of snake tail.

That, and an irregular thump-thump—like a hammer on plywood—coming from the hallway behind the dais.

Swamp witch squinted.

"Annabel?" she called.

"Yes'm."

From around the top corner of the doorframe, Annabel Balchy's little face peered at her.

"You come on out," said swamp witch.

Annabel frowned. "You ain't going to transform me into nothing Satanic, are you?"

"When have I ever done that?"

"Papa says—"

"Papas say a lot of things," said swamp witch. "Now come on out."

Annabel's face disappeared for a moment, there were a couple more thump-thumps, and the girl teetered into the worship hall, atop a pair of hazelwood stilts that swamp witch thought she recognized.

"Those your brother's?"

Annabel thrust her chin out. "I grew into them."

"You're growing into more than those stilts," said swamp witch. Like the rest of the Balchies, Annabel was a blonde-haired specimen of loveliness whose green eyes held a sheen of wisdom. Looking at her, swamp witch thought her brother Tommy would no longer hold title as the family's number-one heartbreaker. Not in another year or two.

"We got your dragonfly," said Annabel, teetering over a little slithering pond of shadow. "He brung you here, in case you didn't know."

"I didn't know," said swamp witch. "I'm not surprised, though. He's a good dragonfly. Is he all right?"

"Uh huh. We got him at the house. Figured you could take care of yourself, big old swamp witch that you are. But we didn't think he'd be safe among the Blessed Serpents of Eden."

"They're just plain corner rattlers, hon, and I'm no safer than anyone else when one decides to bite. But thank you for protecting dragonfly. Did he say why he brung—brought me here?"

"Figured it'd be the one place where the angel couldn't come."

"The angel."

"In the yellow suit," said Annabel. "With a vest underneath black as all damnation."

"Him. *Huh.* He's no angel."

"That's what you say. He's huntin' you, and you're a swamp witch—"

"—so it follows he's got to be an angel." Swamp witch sighed. "I see."

"Papa said you'd probably be wondering why we didn't give you up to that angel."

"Your papa's a bright man," said swamp witch. "The thought did cross my mind."

"Papa said to tell you he don't like the competition," said Annabel.

Swamp witch laughed out loud at that one. "I believe it," she said. "Oh, yes."

Laughing felt good. It may not be the antidote to regret, but it sure helped the symptoms fine. All the same, she took a breath and put it away.

"He sent you to see if I was dead, didn't he?"

Annabel looked down and shook off a rattler that was spiralling up toward her heel. "Yes, ma'am," she said, a little ashamedly. "But he said you might not be. If, I mean, you was righteous."

"So I'm righteous then?"

Annabel crooked her head like she was thinking about it.

"I expect," she said. "Yeah, good chance you are."

"All right," said swamp witch. "But if you don't mind, I'll take no more chances. You still got that spare set of bamboo stilts I know

Reverend used to use in back?" Annabel said she did, so swamp witch held out her hand. "Think you could toss 'em my way? I'd like to go see my dragonfly and maybe your Papa too."

A moment later, the church hall was filled with a racket like summer's rain on a metal shed. Swamp witch was making her escape, and that pleased the corner rattlers not at all.

Swamp witch dropped the two stilts by the Reverend's porch and went in for her meeting. The porch was screened in and the Reverend was there, sitting on an old ratty recliner covered in plastic. Dragonfly was sitting quiet on the table beside him, in a big pickle jar with a lid someone had jammed nails through, just twice. Reverend looked as smug as he could manage, his face stiffened like it was with all the rattler venom.

Swamp witch understood there were days he'd been different: all stoked with holy-roller fire, straight-backed with a level gaze that could melt swamp witch where she stood. That was before he'd found the serpent spittle, before swamp witch had found her own calling.

Did *he* have any regrets? she wondered. Maybe taking the snake tooth into his arm, letting it course through him 'til he couldn't even sit up on his own? Raising his young by nought but telepathy and bad example?

Did he regret any of it? She thought that he didn't.

"Papa says you look like hell," said Annabel.

"Thank you, Reverend. You are as ever a font of manly righteousness."

Reverend lifted his hand an inch off the armrest, and his lips struggled to make an "o."

"Papa's cross with you," said Annabel. "He called you a temptress."

"Well make up your mind," said swamp witch, laughing. Then

she made serious. "We got problems here, Reverend."

The Reverend agreed, making a farting noise with his mouth.

"This tea-drinking angel," said swamp witch. "You reckon you know what he's here for?"

"You," said Annabel.

"You answered too fast," said swamp witch. "What's your Papa got to say?"

The Reverend's hand settled back onto the arm of his chair, and he sighed like a balloon deflating. Dragonfly's wings slapped against the glass of the jar.

"Angel wants Okehole." Annabel put her head down. "All of it." She looked up between strands of perfect blonde hair. "Its souls."

Swamp witch rolled her eyes. Everything was about souls to the Reverend. Flesh to him was an inconvenience—a conveyance at best and lately, a broken down Oldsmobile. The tea-drinking man wasn't an angel and he didn't want souls. But she nodded for the Reverend to keep going.

"He's aiming for you," said Annabel, "because *you* got all the souls."

Which was another thing that Reverend believed. This time swamp witch would not keep quiet. "I do not have all the souls, Reverend. You know what I done here and it's not soul stealing."

"Ain't it?" said Annabel. "Puttin' us all in a jar here—just like your bug! Comin' to visit each Saturday and otherwise just keepin' us here? Ain't that soul stealin'?"

Swamp witch sighed. "Tell me what you know about your soul-stealin' angel."

The Reverend sighed and coughed and his head twitched up to look at her.

"He came by here this afternoon," said Annabel. "Annabel—that's me—brought him some iced tea made like he asked. He talked about the Garden—about the day that Eve bit that apple and brung it to Adam. He asked me, 'What if Adam had said to Eve: *I don't want your awful food; I am faithful to Jehovah, for He has said to me: "Eat not that fruit."* What if Adam had turned his face upward to Jehovah, and said: *I am content in this garden with Your love, and want not this woman's lies of knowledge and truth. She has betrayed you, O Lord, not I. Not I. If that happened, would you sustain on serpent venom? Would she be the keeper of your town's souls?"* Annabel nodded and looked right at swamp witch. "By 'she' I took him to mean you. That's what Papa says."

"So what did you say to that, I wonder?" said swamp witch.

The Reverend's lips twitched, and Annabel hollered:

"Begone!" The Reverend's eyes lit up then as his little girl spoke his word. "I am not some shallow *parishioner*, some *Sunday-school dropout*, some holiday churchgoer—oh no, the venom as you call it is holy, the blood of the prickly one and I am His vessel! Begone! Git now!"

"Your faith saved you," said swamp witch drily.

"Papa ain't finished," scolded Annabel. "He says the tea-drinking man got all huffy then. He was calm up 'til then and suddenly his face got all red. The rims of his eyes got darker red, like they was bleedin', and the lines of his gums got the same colour as that. And his teeth seemed to go all long and snaggly with broke ends. And he said to my Papa:

"*'You don't tell me what to do. You don't tell me nothin'. This town will weep for me, like it wept for her.'*"

"Her being me," said swamp witch.

"Ex-actly," said Annabel.

"So how'd you best him?" asked swamp witch.

"Didn't," said Annabel. And the Reverend grinned then. "Just agreed to keep you occupied. 'Til the tea-drinkin' angel were ready to finish you off."

The Reverend's hand rose up then, and fell upon the jar. His fingers covered the two air-holes in the lid. Dragonfly fluttered at that, then calmed down—no sense in wasting oxygen.

Swamp witch reached for the jar. But the Reverend found the rattler's quickness in his elbow and snatched it away so fast dragonfly banged his head on the side and fell unconscious.

"Why, you lyin' deceitful parson!" hollered swamp witch. With her other hand she reached for her pebbles, intending to enunciate peroxide or some other disinfectant canticle. But the pebbles were gone—of course. Annabel and perhaps her brother Tommy had leaned down from the top of stilts and pulled them from her pocket while she slept in the Reverend's church. "You're in league with him!"

Annabel leaned forward now, and when she spoke her Papa's lips moved with hers: "You ought never have been, swamp witch. You ought never have come here and shut the world from this place. You say you are protecting people but you are keeping them as your human toys, like a she-devil in a corner of Hell. The angel will drive you from here, madame! Drive you clear away."

"Take your fingers off'n my dragonfly's air holes," she said. She was most worried right now about her dragonfly. For blinking and recollecting conclusions, she saw that she would not be spending long now in the Reverend's company. But her dragonfly wasn't with her either, and that caused her to suspect that the poor creature would soon suffocate if she didn't do something.

The Reverend, to her mild surprise, moved his finger up. Or perhaps it slid. No, she thought, looking up, he meant to. His face twitched and his lips opened.

"You should never have come," he said. In his own voice—which swamp witch had not heard in many years now. And behind her, the breeze died and slivers of moonlight dissolved in the shadow of the tea-drinking man.

The Reverend stood up then, and Annabel cried: "A miracle!" and the Reverend took a step toward the edge of the porch, where the yellow-suited tea-drinking man stood, smile as large as his eyes were sad.

"O Angel," Reverend said, his eyes a-jittering with upset snake venom, "I have delivered her!"

"You fool," said swamp witch. And she stepped behind the Reverend, took hold of the jar that held her dragonfly, and said to him: "Carry me to Albert."

That was when the tea-drinking man bellowed. At first, she thought he was angry that she was getting away—trying to sneak behind the Reverend, climb upon her still-groggy dragonfly and sneak out through a hole in the porch screen. If that were the case—well, she'd be in for it and she braced herself, holding tight on dragonfly's back-hair.

But as she swirled up to the rafters of the porch, she saw this was not the case. The tea-drinking man was distracted not by her, but by Reverend Balchy's sharp, venomous incisors, that had planted themselves in his yellow-wrapped forearm.

Reverend Balchy stopped hollering then, on account of his mouth being full, and Annabel took it up.

"Gotchya, you lyin' sinner. Think you can use me? Think it? When swamp witch come to town she took away most of me—you'll just take away the rest! Well fuck yuh! Fuck yuh!"

Dragonfly swung down, close past tea-drinking man's nose, and swamp witch could see the anger and pain of the Reverend's ugly mix of rattler venom and mouth bacteria slipping into his veins. There'd be twitching and screaming in a minute—at least there would be if tea-drinking man had normal blood.

Tea-drinking man didn't seem to, though. He opened his own mouth and looked straight at Annabel:

"What," he said, "if you spoke up for yourself? What if you walked the world your own girl, flipped—" he grimaced "—*flipped* your old Papa the bird, and just made your way on your own-some."

Annabel looked at him. Then she looked up at swamp witch, who was heading for a rip in the screen where last summer there'd been a fist-sized wasp nest.

"I'd never be on my own-some," Annabel said. "Not so long as *she* protects me."

And then swamp witch was gone from there, escaped into the keening night and thanking her stars for the Reverend's poison-mad inconstancy. The tea-drinking man bellowed once more, and then he was a distant smear of yellow and the stars spun in swamp witch's eye.

Was it cowardice that drove swamp witch across the rooftops of her town, then up so high she touched the very limits of her realm? Was she just scared of that tea-drinking man? What kind of protector was she for little Annabel, the Reverend, all the rest of them? Maybe when the Reverend was faking out the tea-drinking man, when he said "you should never have come," he was right. For when she'd come hadn't she stolen away the Reverend's faith and the comfort of self-determination from her people and hadn't she just kept them like she wanted them? Had she ever thought through what it would be if it come to this?

—Why'd you take me there? she said. Were you in league with the Reverend?

Dragonfly didn't answer.

—Did you know about the Reverend's double cross?

They flew low through a cloud of gnats, who all clamoured—yes! yes!

—Can I trust no one? swamp witch despaired.

—Hush, said dragonfly. It swung back through the gnats, and swamp witch could see the mists of her home, the Okehole Wetlands, rising from amid the stumps and rushes. Now let's go home.

Swamp witch thought about how comfortable that would be. And with that, she realized she wasn't scared of the tea-drinking man. She was scared of something else entirely.

Swamp witch dug her knees into dragonfly's thorax and yanked at dragonfly's hair to make a turn.

—Uh uh, she said. After all that, I'm not lettin' you make any decisions. You know where we got to go.

Dragonfly hummed resentfully, and together they flew down—down toward the business section at the east end of town. There, the smoke and book waited for her, orange flickery light from its sign illuminating a patch in front like a hearth fire.

She reached to the ground by the road, and picked up two pebbles that seemed right, and stuffed them in her jeans, then in she went.

Albert Farmer sat in the front of the store, which was the nice section, all scrubbed and varnished and smelling of fresh pipe tobacco. The not-so-nice section, with the girly magazines and French ticklers and the cigars from Cuba—that was in the back, and this part was nothing but nice. Just some cigarettes and old-fashioned pipes in a display case, and a magazine rack that held nothing to trouble anyone—*Time*s and *People*s and *Archie* comic books, *Reader's Digest*s and a lot of magazines about guns and cars and fixing up houses. Albert sat behind the counter, smoking a hand-rolled cigarette and sipping at a glass of dark wine he made for himself.

"Sweetness." He smiled in his way as swamp witch slipped through the mail slot and sat at the counter. "I thought you mightn't come."

"The town is under attack," said swamp witch balefully.

"I know," said Albert. He pinched off the end of the cigarette, and stepped around the counter. "Come here."

He looked guilty as hell. But swamp witch stepped over across the floor anyhow. Dragonfly, traitorous insect that it was, flew in back to sniff cigar-leaf and browse pornography.

Swamp witch said: "You know anything more about that?"

Albert smiled. He had an easy smile—teeth too white to have smoked as much as he seemed to, half a dimple on one cheek only. It broke swamp witch's heart every time she saw it. So when he just stepped up close to her and held the palm of his right hand forward, so it hovered over her left breast, she just let her broken old heart bask in his heat. Her arms fell upon his shoulders, and then crept down his arms, over the shortened sleeves of his summer shirt. O Lord, she thought as he pressed hard against her middle, wasn't this what a Saturday night was for? Couldn't it just be forever?

Swamp witch knew it couldn't. One day a week was part of the bargain.

She pulled back and looked at Albert levelly.

"Why did you bring tea-drinking man here? Why did you let him in?"

Albert frowned. He started to deny it, but looked into swamp witch's eye and knew he couldn't.

"How'd you know it was me?"

"I remember the future," she said. "I remember the ends of things."

"There's no joy in that," said Albert Farmer.

"I know." Swamp witch stepped away and shook the lust from her head. "It's not like the beginnings. Those are the real joys."

Albert nodded. He leaned back against the counter; appeared to think, but it was hard to say because the lights were low.

"Are they?" he finally said. "Beginnings, I mean. Are they the real joys? You ever think much about ours?" Swamp witch looked at him. "You don't of course. Or else you'd never say that about beginnings. Maybe you'd have killed me by now."

It was true that swamp witch didn't think about beginnings but it wasn't that she couldn't.

"I loved you," she said.

"You still do."

"I still do. But we're busting up. I know it."

Albert's smile faded and he nodded. "That's how the night ends," he said. "Will you have a glass of wine with me?"

Swamp witch shrugged, like a sullen teenager she thought, and mumbled, *"Mayuswell,"* and leaned her butt against the countertop so she wouldn't be looking at him. She heard the wine gurgling from bottle to stemware, and Albert came around the front of her and gave her the glass. She looked into it, swirled it a bit.

"You knew it had to come," he said. "From the day we made this place, you know this had to come."

Swamp witch sighed. She did know—she did remember. But what pleasure was there, in recalling a game of skill against this—this roadside mephistopheles, during the worst afternoon of her life? That was well hidden away, that memory.

At least it was until this moment—this moment, when she once more recalled the crossroads, just to the south of town near the sycamore grove where she sat, bruised and angry and waiting for a bus or some conveyance to take her away. When she said:

I'd just like to send you to Hell.

And when not a bus but a shiny little two-seater from Naples rolled up, and he stepped out and set down the checker board and said, "Would you now sweet mama?" and she said, "Maybe not exactly," and he said, "Well, care to play me?" and she said, "What for?" and he said, "What do you want?"

"I wanted my town back," said swamp witch, bringing the wine glass from her lips, "just my town. And just Saturdays. Just Saturdays. And I won it."

"Fair and square," said Albert.

Swamp witch set down the glass. "I cared for it here," she said. "It was mine and I cared for it."

"Yes," said Albert. "It was yours. And you cared for it, all right. But not forever. You knew that."

"Not forever?" she said.

"Only," he said, "so long as I could keep winning."

"What do you mean?"

"Oh, swamp witch. I was wandering, as I sometimes do, the other day—and I came upon a crossroads as I often do—and there who should I see but a sad old sack of a man. And I said to him as I must:

Want to play a game?" Albert took a long pull from his wine glass. "And he said to me as he was wont to: I'd love a game this afternoon. And so we set down and played."

"Checkers?" said swamp witch unkindly.

"A word game—a remembering game. And oh, he was good, and at the end of it—"

"You," said swamp witch, "are a sorry excuse for your kind. You never lose a game you don't want to. And now . . . You lost my town, didn't you?"

"There are those who've been hankering for it for some time now."

"Yes—but *you*." She set her glass down. "You ought to know better."

Oh, he ought to. But swamp witch saw in Albert Farmer's eyes, the back of them where the embers sometimes smouldered, that he didn't. Couldn't help himself truly. He was a kind man and kind men helped others with the things they wanted. Fine if swamp witch were the other. But nothing but hurt or betrayal, if it be someone else.

Now, swamp witch knew with regretful certainty that she would not only lose Albert this night—but possibly the town as well.

"Others fight him, you know," she said, thinking of the Reverend and his poisonous bite. "Others love me better."

"Oh, Ma—oh, swamp witch," said Albert, correcting himself, "you think I don't love you well enough? That is a stinger, my dear. I've as much love for you as is in me. Now come—" he draped his arm over her shoulder "—there's little time."

"Is there?"

"Look," he said and pointed between the gossamer window covers to the street. There, sure enough, was the tea-drinking man—his suit was a bit mussed and the skin around his eyes was dark with snake spit, which was also why he was moving so funny, swamp witch supposed. He stood a moment in the middle of the road, tried to smooth his hair with his hand and stomped his foot like it was a hoof. Then he looked over to the smoke and book.

Was there a sense in fighting it?

Swamp witch knew better. She leaned over to Albert, and smothered the little space left between them with a kiss. He tasted of salt and wine and egg gone bad, but swamp witch didn't mind. She let herself to it and lived in the instant—the instant prior to the end, and when she pulled away, the tea-drinking man was there at the big window, looking in with socketed eyes and a terrible, blood-rimmed grin.

"Why'd you let him win?" she said.

Tea-drinking man's ankles cracked as he stepped away and pushed open the door, jangling the little bell at the top. The sickness was coming off him like a fever now. Swamp witch held onto Albert harder and slid her hands into her pocket.

"I ain' feeli' well," said the tea-drinking man.

"You ain't lookin' well," said swamp witch. "That venom'll kill you."

Tea-drinking man shook his head. "Nuh," he said. "Nuh me."

He reached around them, arm seeming to bend in two spots to do it, and lifted swamp witch's wine glass. Unkindly, he hawked a big purple loogie the size of a river slug, let it ooze into the glass and down the side. It fizzed poisonously.

"This is who you gave me up for," said swamp witch. Albert's shoulders slumped.

"'Twas only a matter of time before they saw what happened here," said Albert.

Swamp witch sighed. She snaked her hand underneath Albert's arm. They stood there at the end now—seconds before it would occur, she could see it clear as headlights, clear as anything. She brought her lips to his, and said: "Goodbye," then added, fondly: "Go to Hell."

And with that, Albert stepped away and smiled his sweet smile, and in a whiff of volcanic flatulence, did as he was told and stepped to the back of the store.

And it was just her and the tea-drinking man.

"Why di'—*did* you ever want this place?" asked the tea-drinking man. "I's a rat hole."

"A snake pit," agreed swamp witch. "I agree with your sentiment some days. I wanted it because it was rightfully mine. Why'd *you* play Albert for it?"

"Symmetry," said the tea-drinking man.

"That explains not a thing," said swamp witch.

"All right." The tea-drinking man took a ragged breath. "You took this place off—" he looked into the air for the word and found it in the old dangling light fixture over the cash register "—off the grid. The world ran its course, my dear—ran to dark and to light and good and evil. Why, those of us on the outside took the time we had and made things. There are towers, dear swamp witch—towers that extend to heaven and back. Great wide highways, so far across you can only see the oncoming autos as star-flecks in the mist. We've built rockets. Rockets! We've gone higher than God. And yet this place? Stayed put. All those years. Why?" He gave a drooling little sneer. "Because it's rightfully yours?"

"That's right," said swamp witch. "And whatever you say, it's better for it."

Tea-drinking man shrugged. And although he never seemed too inflated, he seemed to deflate then. He slumped a little, in fact.

"What did you think you would accomplish?"

Swamp witch shrugged now. What did it need to accomplish? She wondered. What was the point of this accomplishment anyhow— of taking your powers and making the world into a place of your dreams? Why look ahead—when all that was there were endings and misery? Why not make a pleasant place now?

"And you fester in your swamp," said tea-drinking man, "wallowing in the muck with your insects and rodents and frogs. I'd drain that swamp, I was you."

Swamp witch looked at him, and as she did, she saw another ending: one in which all of Okehole County was nothing but an embodiment of tea-drinking man's hopes and dreams—victim of his regrets.

It was an end, all right—a point too long before she buried her own children and faced her own end. Swamp witch did not like to look upon ends long, but she couldn't look away from this one: it filled up the horizon like a great big sunset.

"You have got the sickness," she said. "The dreaming sick. You won't now give it to me. And you won't give it to our town. You won't give it to this county."

"I already done that," he said simply, sadly almost.

—No he hasn't, said dragonfly, buzzing up from the back of the shop. Hop on.

The tea-drinking man tried to grab her, but he was sore and half-paralyzed now from the Reverend's bite, and he just knocked over a box of chewing tobacco and mumbled swearwords. Swamp witch felt her middle contract and the smoke and book get big and she flung her leg over the back of dragonfly. Tea-drinking man called after her: "You shouldn't have!" but swamp witch already had, and she wouldn't let the itchy virus of regret get at her now.

Swamp witch soared. She climbed again to the very top of her domain—the place where the dome of stars turned solid and fruit-drunk swallows'd stun themselves dead. Dragonfly set up there, buzzing beneath the sallow light of Sirius, and swamp witch leaned over to him and asked him what he'd meant by that.

And dragonfly whispered his answer with his wings, buzzing against the hard shell of the world so they echoed down to earth. Swamp witch peered down there—at her town, her people, who from this place seemed even tinier than she was now. She smiled and squinted: could almost make them out. There was little Linda Farley, her eyes dried up and a big old garden hoe in her hands; Jack Irving, with a red plastic gas can, riding shotgun in Harry Oates' pickup; Bess Overland with a flensing knife and Tommy Balchy, beautiful young Tommy, with a big old two-by-four that'd had a nail driven through it. He was leading the senior class from the Okehole County High School, and a bunch of straggling ninth-graders, down Brevener Street, toward the front of old Albert Farmer's smoke and book.

Swamp witch smiled a little, with sudden nostalgia. The last time she'd seen her folk like that had been before she'd met Albert—just before, when she'd been invited to leave her home town—on pain of death pretty well. She saw that so clearly, she knew, because it was so similar to her recollection of what was about to happen.

Tea-drinking man was going to pick up the telephone in Albert Farmer's shop, dial a long-distance operator who hadn't heard from Okehole County in Lord knew how long, and tell the others that he'd done it. "Symme'ry," he'd say, then repeat slowly, "*sym-met-tree*. Is restored. We got it."

And at the other end, a voice that ululated like wind chimes would laugh and thank him and tell him that his cheque was in the mail, the board of directors was pleased, there was a new office with a window waiting for him, see you later and stop by the club when you get back. And tea-drinking man would with shaking hand hang up the phone, and step outside to survey his new town.

And then—like before, when swamp witch had come out of the pharmacy, the glamour fresh upon her, two smooth pebbles in her pocket and the knowledge that she could do anything—*anything!*—then, the town would set upon him.

Swamp witch had been faster than tea-drinking man would be. Swamp witch had also known the town, known it like her own soul practically, and she'd cut down the alleyway between Bill's and the Household Hardware and muttered "glycol," and vanished from their sight, leaving them all hopped up and pissed off with nothing they could do.

Slow, sick old tea-drinking man, who'd swapped his dreaming sickness for snake sick, wouldn't have the same advantage.

They'd do to him what they couldn't ever do to her.

And that would be the end.

—Think, she asked dragonfly, once they got that out of their system, tearin' themselves up a witch, actually beatin' one—think it'd cure them of all the regret that fellow'd stoked 'em with?

Dragonfly pondered the question and finally said:

—You don't ask a question like that unless you know the answer.

—You are a wise bug, said swamp witch.

—Not wise enough to know where you want to go next.

—Hmm.

Last time this had happened, swamp witch had figured she'd head straight for the wetlands and wait it out. Then, she'd been sidetracked by a game of checkers and the promise of certainty. This time, as she directed dragonfly down toward the mist of the wetland and past that to her tiny hutch, swamp witch vowed that she would not pause on her way there. She would spend the next six days in the swamp, thinking about what she'd do on the seventh. It would take a lot of careful thinking leading up to Saturday, because for the first time in her life, she'd be free that night.

The Delilah Party

Mitchell Owens spent much of his seventeen years a quiet boy, sitting very still in the darkest part of a very dark room. Most people could not figure him out, and as far as Mitchell was concerned, the feeling was mutual.

But his older friend Stefan wasn't most people. He picked up on Mitchell's vibe right away, as Mitchell was still squeezing into the back of Stef and Trudy's Explorer in the parking lot of the Becker's convenience store where they had met three times now. Stefan looked over his shoulder, looked again with his eyes a little narrower, then turned around so his knees were on the seat and his skinny chest was pressed against the headrest.

"Looks like you ate a bug, Mitch," he said.

"Didn't eat a bug," said Mitchell.

"Just an expression," said Trudy, eyeing him herself in the rearview mirror. She was haloed in the light of the Becker's sign so from behind her blonde hair looked like the discharge off a Van de Graaff generator—black as midnight in the middle of her skull, leaping bolts of yellow on the rim. The rearview mirror told a different story: her eyes were in full illumination, a blazing rectangle of light.

Mitchell stammered when he spoke up:

"Th-they took away my laptop."

"I see you don't have it with you," said Stefan. "By *they* I assume you mean the police."

"Yuh."

"Bummer," said Stefan.

"You'll get it back," said Trudy.

"Did they follow you?" asked Stefan.

"No."

"Why would they follow Mitch?" Trudy put the Explorer into gear, and tapped the gas so that Stefan lurched against the seat. "Fuck, woman!" he said, and Trudy said, "I've got a name. Sit forward. It's more comfortable."

"Fuck," said Stefan again, and he winked at Mitchell. "Do up your seatbelt, Mitch. Woman—Trudy's—in a mood."

"Fuck you," said Trudy as they pulled out of the parking lot, and at that, Mitchell felt himself smile. He would get the laptop back. Of course he would.

The Explorer pulled right onto Starling with only a little room to spare before it joined the early evening traffic and subsumed itself to its pattern: drive a bit and stop awhile. Watch the light from red to green, red to flashing green, red to red while the other side got flashing green. Wait and go. Go and wait. Mitchell was feeling better and better. The laptop would be his again. It was part of the pattern.

"So they treat you okay?" said Trudy.

"Why wouldn't they?" said Stefan.

"Cops are fucking fascists. They get a kid like Mitch here and they'll just be pricks to him."

"They got your laptop," said Stefan. "You have anything on the hard drive?"

Mitchell didn't know what he meant and said so. Stefan and Trudy shared a glance, and Trudy pulled into the left lane so she could turn onto Bern Street when her turn came.

"We've got some friends coming over," said Stefan conversationally. "From the news group. I think you've met some of them. Remember Mrs. Woolfe?"

Mitchell thought about that. He put the name to a tall woman with glasses and a dark tattoo that crept over the edge of her turtleneck sweater like foliage. "Was she the one who was always sad?"

"Lesley?" said Trudy. "She wasn't sad."

"She just wasn't smiling," said Stefan. "But that doesn't mean she was sad."

Mitchell nodded. Those were two expressions that Mitchell was always mixing up. "Not sad. Just concentrating."

"Right."

The Explorer swung vertiginously through the intersection about a second after the light switched to amber. Mitchell glanced back sceptically. Sure enough, it was red before they'd cleared it. He was sure someone was going to honk.

"So what did they ask you?"

Stefan was half turned around in his seat, so only one eye looked back at Mitchell. The skin of his forehead was puckered up over his raised eyebrow. He was either being worried or casual.

Mitchell said: "They asked me how well I knew Delilah. They wanted to know if I ever emailed her or knew her in this chat room that I guess she went to."

"Our chat room?"

Mitchell shook his head. "Another one. Not like the one we have. Hers was for wrestling. They asked if I had any pictures of her on my computer or anything."

"Which you don't."

"Pardon?"

"You don't have any pictures of her on your computer," said Trudy. "Right?"

"Oh. Right. I don't."

"And you didn't bookmark the chatroom."

"I use the computer at the library for that."

"Then you have nothing to worry about."

"Why would I be worried?"

"No reason," said Trudy, and Stefan said, "You might have something to worry about if you did something. I mean—"

"No reason," said Trudy again.

"Okay."

Mitchell leaned back in the Explorer's seat so that Trudy's eyes were gone from the rear view mirror and all he could see was the dark roof of the Explorer. He unzipped his jacket because the heat of the car was getting to him. The Explorer turned right at Sparroway Circle, and then turned right again at the entrance to Number Five Sparroway Circle's parking garage. Mitchell did a little cha-cha thing on his left thigh with the first two fingers of his right hand as the Explorer made its way through Level One of the garage, which included most of the guest parking, then his fingers made their way to the lock switch as they prowled across the slightly better-lit Level Two. He locked and unlocked the door three times then made himself stop when they pulled into Space 152. Trudy and Stefan pretended not to notice—just locked up the car for good using a button on Trudy's keychain, took him to the elevator which they opened using a card on Stefan's keychain, and got on board. The door closed on them and the elevator started going up.

"School was bad today," said Mitchell.

Stefan pushed his hands into the pockets of his dark leather coat. Trudy bent her head forward like she was looking at her feet, then suddenly turned her eyes to the side so they were looking at Mitchell.

"What are we," she said, "your parents?"

"No." Mitchell's parents were another story. "You're my friends."

When the elevator got to the very top of the building it opened up on a wide hallway. There were only two apartments on this floor— one at either end of the hallway. Stefan and Trudy's apartment was on the right. The other one belonged to a guy named Giorgio Piccininni, but it was basically vacant because Giorgio was in Italy doing real estate or something. There were voices coming from Stefan and Trudy's place and Mitchell thought he heard the sound of their Media Centre. He recognized the voice on the home theatre from the news channel and he thought he recognized the voices talking but it was hard to tell.

"I'll wait out here," he said.

Trudy took his arm. "Come on, scaredy-cat," she said. "We went to a lot of trouble to make sure this place was safe for you." Then she pushed the door open the rest of the way and gave him a little push. "Inside."

Mitchell stumbled through the double doors. The main room was high, with a big sleek chandelier hanging down from a ceiling that was two entire floors up. At one end was a kitchen that opened up on a dining room. At the other end was a sitting area, which faced a television set that was almost as big as the Explorer. Five people were sitting around it, watching the 24-hour news channel. Mitchell couldn't remember who all the people were, although he had met them all before—three times in person, and many, many times online in the chat room. Three of them were men and two were women. He didn't think either of the women was Mrs. Lesley Woolfe. The news anchor on television was Gloria Stahl. She was talking about Delilah Franken and her high school sports record.

"Just make yourselves at home," said Trudy.

One of the men turned to the door and waved. He was completely bald and his eyes were jiggly.

"Hey, Mitch," he said. "Hey, guys. Everything going okay out there?"

Stefan smiled. "You know as much as we do." He walked over and sat down on the arm of the sofa. "More, maybe. What's she going on about?"

The woman nearest Stefan rested her hand on his knee and smiled up at him. "The Police Chief's had another press conference," she said. "He just did the usual: asked that anyone with information about poor Delilah's disappearance should call CrimeStoppers. Didn't have anything new to say."

"Well of course he didn't," said Trudy. She put *her* hand on Mitchell's shoulder. Her thumb touched the back of his neck and he took a sharp breath.

"Can I go on the computer?" asked Mitchell.

The woman by Stefan shook her head, but she smiled or seemed to. "Mitchell Owens," she said, "you *are* a prize."

Trudy's hand slid off Mitchell's shoulder and she took him by the hand. "Come on," she said. "I'll boot it up for you."

"I know how," said Mitchell. But he let her lead him to the sunroom anyway. He stood there for a moment, looking down over the flickering lights—the patterns of brake lights and headlights and signs and window lamps. Mitchell looked back when the computer chimed up to its logon screen.

"You are a prize," said Trudy, typing the password which was BLENDER. "Shelly was right about that."

"Ah," said Mitchell. "Shelly." That was her name.

Trudy's eyes flashed again. "Do you like her?"

"What do you mean?"

"Could she—" Trudy gestured in the air with her hands and looked at the ceiling. "You *know.*"

Mitchell blinked. "What do you mean?"

Now Trudy's eyes widened and she looked down at him with a tight little slit of a mouth. When she spoke, she whispered like she was shouting.

"*You* know *what I mean!*"

Mitchell looked over at the computer screen. The wallpaper was new—a scan of Delilah Franken, the one from the police website. Her hair was darker than it should be. She was wearing her graduation gown and she didn't look comfortable in it. He moused over to the START menu and fired up Photoshop.

Trudy seemed to calm down. She put her hand on Mitchell's shoulder and leaned close to his ear. "What are you up to there, Mitchy?"

"Make her happy."

"Oh." Trudy chuckled. "Well go to it, sport."

Mitchell found the JPEG and opened it up. It was a big file and when he zoomed into 100 per cent all he could see was her mouth, a bit of her chin and the bottom of her nose. That was good. It looked like there was a blemish on her chin, maybe some acne because she was so stressed out about graduating, so he cloned some skin from her cheek onto it, then he opened up the **Liquify** filter and went to work on her mouth. Delilah was one of those girls who smiled like she was sad, with the mouth turned down at the edges. Mitchell fixed that, edging the pixels at the corners up and up and up. Once he was satisfied Delilah was happy enough, he applied the changes and went to work on her hair, which in the picture was a dingy brown. He magnetic-lassoed it with a one-pixel feather then went into **Image>Adjustments>Curves**, and he lightened it up and improved the contrast so it looked like she had blonde streaks which is how she wore it these days. He liked the idea, but not so much the effect: the feather made the background glow too much around her hair, like a halo. But he didn't know how to fix it either. So Mitchell left it the way it was and saved it under another file name. He closed it, then he went into **File>Open recent** and opened it again. He did it again, four times.

"Wow. She sure is happy."

Mitchell took a sharp breath.

"Really happy."

He took his hand away from the mouse.

"Fucking overjoyed." Laughter followed. Mitchell turned around.

The whole party, all seven of them, were there. Shelly was dangling a mostly empty wine glass beside her as she pressed against a skinny grey-haired man, who was leaning against the doorframe beside Stefan, who was bent forward over the back of an office chair, his hands on the arm-rests straddling the bare arms of another woman with short dark hair and light-coloured jeans who was sitting there legs crossed, one bare foot with manicured toenails brushing the shoulder of the bald man, who sat on the floor almost cross-legged. Behind them, a blond-haired fellow wearing a black T-shirt stood on his toes to look at the computer screen. Trudy was crouched down beside Mitchell, her hands on the desktop and her chin resting on her knuckles. She looked up at Mitchell.

"Happy now?" she said. Stefan laughed, Shelly giggled, and that set everyone else off.

Mitchell looked back at the picture. Delilah smiled back out at him, and he thought he could see why they were laughing. She was smiling wide: too wide, as wide as the Joker did in *Batman*. As he looked at it now, he saw the problem with that. It was unnatural. Delilah had never smiled that way. Not even in grade school. If she did, why she'd rip her cheeks right off her cheekbones and then there'd be nothing but blood and tears. Mitchell guessed it was pretty funny, seeing Delilah Franken smiling like that.

He let his breath out.

"I'm done on the computer," he said. "Can I have something to eat?"

Trudy's knees made a cracking noise as she got up. "Sure thing. Let's go to the kitchen."

The others spread to make a pathway for Trudy and Mitchell out of the sunroom. Looking over his shoulder, he saw that they all gathered around the computer, to get a closer look at the picture he made. Mitchell felt an unfamiliar sense of pride. They were looking at his picture—his work. Even if he hadn't gotten the hair right, that was something.

Trudy opened the refrigerator and pulled out a tray covered in Saran wrap. She stood quickly, balancing the tray on the fingertips of one hand while she cocked her hip and planted the other hand there. "Canapes?" she said.

"Canapés," said Mitchell. Trudy had pronounced it like Can Apes.

"You got it," said Trudy. She set the tray down on the countertop and peeled back the plastic. Mitchell took a little roll of prosciutto and melon and bit into it. It was salty and sweet, watery and oily. A nice-enough mix that he took two others.

"So how was school?" Trudy leaned against the stove and crossed one ankle over the other. "You said it was a bad day."

Mitchell took a breath. He didn't think they wanted to hear about anything like that because they weren't his parents. But maybe that was just when Stefan was in the room. Mitchell chewed and swallowed another canapé.

"It was a bad day. They made us go to an assembly. This . . . this guy from the school board talked to us for about an hour. Some girls were crying. Even though she'd already graduated. They were crying. Can you believe that? Right there in the assembly with everybody looking."

"What did he talk to you about?"

"After that was History of Europe. I hate History of Europe and it sucked. And phys-ed. I don't see why I have to take that when what I want to do is—"

Trudy cut in: "You don't want to talk about that assembly, do you?"

Mitchell put the third canapé in his mouth and sucked on it, pulling the cool sweet melon out from the prosciutto sheaf. More laughter came from the sunroom. Trudy pushed herself off from the stove and came closer to Mitchell. She leaned over and whispered into his ear: "So what do you think of Shelly? Think she's pretty?"

"I think you're pretty."

Trudy seemed to freeze for an instant. Then she pulled back a bit, turned to her side and leaned on the island beside Mitchell. "She's pretty, all right," said Trudy. "Stef sure thinks so."

Mitchell took another couple of canapés but he didn't eat them yet.

"She's a year or two older," said Trudy. "Than me. And Stef. That should make a difference."

Mitchell thought about that. "O-older girls can be pretty," he said and Trudy smirked. She put her hand on Mitchell's shoulder, and sidled her hip closer to his. "Yeah," she said, as her hand slid from the shoulder nearest her to the one farthest. "You *would* think that."

Mitchell swallowed. Trudy leaned her head to one side so it rested on Mitchell's shoulder. He felt stray hairs tickling his face, like little electric sparks. Trudy's hip was touching his own. "Oh, Mitch," she said. "You are *so* fucked up."

"And that's what she likes about you," said Stefan.

Trudy lifted her head to look around, but she didn't move her hand or shift away. "Mitch and I were just talking about you."

Stefan came around the island. He was holding a glass of red wine and smiling maybe. "Me?" He set the wine glass on the counter beside Mitchell, and looked hard into Trudy's eyes. "I'm flattered."

"You're an asshole," she said.

"*Why, I oughta,*" he said, making a limp fist that opened like a flower when he let it drop to his side. Then he laughed. "How you doing, Mitch?"

"Good."

"Really? Good." He reached over and took Trudy's hand off Mitchell's shoulder. "You should save your energy, man." Trudy raised her eyebrows at Stefan. "She on her way?" she said and Stefan nodded. "Just coming off the highway," he said. "Like, two minutes ago."

"I'm going to go to the bathroom," said Mitchell. Trudy and Stefan stopped and looked him up and down, then Stefan laughed. "I can see that," said Trudy, smirking. "Go on," said Stefan. "Use the one upstairs. It's quieter."

Mitchell left them in the kitchen. He passed the dining room table where there were more canapés laid out and he took a cracker with some brie cheese on it. In the living room, the Media Centre was off the news. Now the screen was filled with a security camera picture from the basement garage, looking at the elevator they'd come up in. The bald man and the woman with paint on her toenails were sitting on the couch. Her feet were in his lap, and he was giving one of them a massage while she twisted the other this way and that at the ankle, like she was stretching it. They watched Mitchell pass by and climb up the spiral staircase to the second level, and didn't take their eyes off him until he went into the main bath.

Mitchell closed the door behind him as the lights flickered on. He lifted the toilet seat and unzipped his fly. He stood there for awhile like that, then zipped up and washed his hands. He caught himself in the mirror, leaning forward, his hands held together under the thin stream of warm water. His eyes were open wide, his mouth small and slack and round, like he was always saying "oh." His dark hair was too long and fell over his forehead, which was still pimply. There were the beginnings of a beard growing on the chin, but you could still see the big pimple underneath the left side of his lower lip. Mitchell looked at his face and thought: what would I see if I saw me on the street? At school? He thought about that, and thought again: *a sad boy.* He made a smile, and looked, and thought: *a happy boy.* He brushed the hair aside from his forehead, and stood up straight, and kept smiling and he thought about that, but finally thought:

Who knows?

Mitchell found a hand towel and dried off, then went out. He heard the sound of another door closing downstairs. He stepped to the railing and looked down, as the rectangle of hall light narrowed and vanished on the first-floor tiling. The couple on the couch sat up, and from the kitchen, Stefan said: "Lesley!" and Trudy said: "How'd it go?"

"Fucking nightmare."

Mitch looked down and saw the top of Lesley Woolfe's head and her shoulders, as she made her way to the couch. She twisted her head on her neck so that Mitch could see her throat, wisps of dark hair mingling with body art that was emerging from the collar of a simple white blouse. With one arm, she flung an overcoat onto the chaise lounge by the downstairs powder room. "Fuck," she said again, drawing the syllable out this time, "me."

She sounded sad, but what did Mitchell know?

"Nothing went wrong, did it?" said Trudy.

"Traffic," said Lesley, "was the shits. Wouldn't move faster than a slow walk south of Tenth Line. I was afraid it would wear off and she'd wake up at a red light."

"But it didn't," said Trudy. "She didn't."

"Would I be here if it did?"

Stefan came out of the kitchen with a tall glass of wine. Lesley took it and sipped at it. "The cameras?" she said.

"All taken care of," said Stefan.

"And—?"

"Upstairs," said Stefan. "Right above you."

Lesley started like something bit her, and looked around and then up. Her eyes were wide, then narrow. They weren't smiling. "Hello," she said after a few seconds. She held up her wine glass and tinkled it back and forth. "Want a sip?"

"He doesn't drink," said Trudy.

"I didn't ask you," said Lesley, not taking her eyes off Mitch. "Well, Mitch? How about it?"

Mitchell moved to the spiral staircase and climbed down. He stood face-to-face with Lesley Woolfe. She stood five inches taller than he did and she still did not smile. But she offered him the wine glass, and he took it by the stem. He swirled the red liquid, looked at it, sniffed it like he'd seen rich men do on television. It smelled a bit rotten, but Mitchell sipped at it anyway. It tasted sharper than it smelled, but it wasn't so bad. He took another sip, bigger this time.

"Now," she said, her eyes widening and her nostrils flaring, "we both die." She paused for a heartbeat. "Poison," she said. "Very painful."

Mitchell dropped the wine glass. It hit the side of a table then clinked on the tile floor, and somehow it didn't break. Mitchell stepped back, staring at the wine spill spreading along the skinny grout lines, holding onto his chest, drawing a breath.

Lesley finally smiled. Smiling, she threw her head back, so the dark geometries etched on her throat were in full view, and laughed, then twisted her head to the side and she smiled even more, and looked back at Mitchell, and said:

"Mmmm, look at him. So scared of dying."

"Why wouldn't he be?" said Trudy. She looked at Mitchell. "She was kidding."

Mitchell had worked that out. About the same time that he worked out that he hated Lesley Woolfe. He bent down and picked up the wine glass, and looked around. The faces looking back at him might as well have been smooth skin, no eyes or mouths or noses, staring in blank, blind disapproval. Like mannequins.

One of the mannequins came over with a roll of paper towels and bent to his feet, spreading them over the spill so the wine stain blossomed in fractal majesty over the bumps and divots. The mannequin turned its head and presented its blank face to Mitchell. Then it swiped up the paper towel and crumpled in its hand, and replaced it with a fresh one.

"What's going on with him?" said a mannequin from the living room.

"I think," said the voice of Stefan, "that he's having an episode. Good fucking going, Les."

Another voice: "Is this, like—dangerous?"

"Of course it's dangerous," said Lesley fucking Woolfe's voice. "That's why we chose him. Delectable Delilah. For Dangerous Mitchell. That's the point."

Someone giggled. Someone else said, "Shut the fuck up," and someone else said, in a whisper, "Will you fucking *look* at him?" and then the mannequins fell quiet.

Mitchell took a breath and closed his eyes. This had happened before: often enough that he'd been to doctors for it. They had tried drugs and other therapies but mostly drugs, until Mitchell started gaining weight and breaking out and doctors started worrying about his penis maybe not developing properly. His mom finally went to a woman who taught transcendental meditation out of her basement, and Mitchell had learned a mantra, and at bad times he found that helped. So he started to say his mantra, which was a secret, and he said it again and again with his eyes closed until he thought he could open his eyes.

Stefan looked back at him from a dining room chair that he'd pulled over. The rest of the mannequins—the people—were gone. But Stefan was there, arms folded over his skinny chest, hard to say whether he was smiling or not.

"Where did everybody go?" asked Mitchell.

"Lesley took them across the hall."

"Mr. Piccininni's apartment." Mitchell didn't know Stefan had a key. "What for?"

"A little show and tell," said Stefan, "before the show. You doing okay now?"

"What are they looking at?" said Mitchell.

Stefan motioned over his shoulder to the Media Centre. Mitchell looked. It was a view from another security camera. But this one wasn't in the lobby—it looked to be mounted on the ceiling of a bedroom filled with nice dark furniture and with the painting of a waterfall on one wall. There was a big double bed on the far side of the room, covered in a thick comforter. Something was moving under it, just a little bit. Mitchell stepped closer to get a look, but the picture was fuzzy and then someone stepped in front of it and he couldn't see the bed. Then other people stepped around the bed: Shelly, the bald guy . . . Lesley Woolfe, her arms crossed and chin pressed down against her collarbone so it wrinkled and puckered . . . Trudy.

Trudy stepped around between Lesley Woolfe and what looked like a dresser, then leaned over the bed. She looked at Lesley and said something, and Lesley shrugged, and Trudy reached over to the comforter, and lifted the edge of it, and with her other hand covered her mouth and her eyes went wide. But she smiled so whatever she saw must have been okay.

"You're welcome," said Stefan.

"Pardon?"

Stefan leaned over to him. "Look at that grin. You know what's coming, don't you, pal?"

Mitchell looked at Stefan, who was grinning broadly. "It was supposed to be a surprise. That's what Lesley wanted to do. Just bring you in there, and *voila!* Leave you to your devices. But I know you, Mitch. You don't like surprises. They make you squirrelly."

"Squirrelly."

Stefan wiggled his fingers by his ears. "You know. Buggy. Nutzoid."

"Oh."

"I'd have told you sooner," he said. "But I figured it was better to wait until at least the police had talked to you. You know, just in case. You know the saying: 'what you don't know—'"

"'—can't hurt you.'"

Stefan pointed at Mitchell with his index finger, twisting at the wrist, and he winked. "Just lookin' out for you, bro."

Mitchell pointed back at Stefan. "Back at you," he said, and Stefan laughed.

Stefan reached over the back of the sofa and picked up a remote, and turned the Media Centre off.

"Just try to act surprised," he said.

"Okay." Mitchell stepped around the sofa and sat down beside Stefan, who inched away but kept smiling.

"You're doing better now," he said, "without the big group."

"Yeah."

"That's part of it with you, isn't it? Big groups." Stefan shook his head. "Man, high school must just be hell for you."

"Yeah." Mitchell looked into the empty wine glass, which he was still holding onto. "Just hell."

"That where you first met her?"

"Her?"

"Her. Delilah."

"Oh. No. Not high school."

"Grade school?"

"Yeah. Grade Three. She was pretty and strong. She stuck up for me when these guys tried to beat me up."

Stefan let out a long, low whistle. "Grade Three. That's pretty serious."

Mitchell shrugged, starting to feel impatient. He'd told Stefan about all this stuff weeks ago, in the chat room. "Where'd you meet?" he asked.

"Me?"

"You. You and Trudy. You meet in Grade Three?"

Stefan grinned and slunk down on the sofa. "Oh no. Not Grade Three. Not my Trudy. We met through the news group. Started posting on the same topics, you know? Started IMing each other, built up, you know, a rapport. We actually saw each other face-to-face the first time Lesley called a meeting. After fucking AOL shut us down."

Mitchell held the wine glass up to his eye. The distortion at the base of the glass made the very narrow stem seem huge, a concentric storm of glassy circles. The middle, though, was perfectly clear. He could see the fabric of his jeans through it, made tiny by the four-inch lens the stem made. "She's beautiful," he said.

Stefan nodded. "Trudy's a hottie," he said, staring at the blank Media Centre screen. "She's also real compatible, you get what I mean. Not every woman knows what to do with a guy like me . . . But she can be a fucking cunt sometimes. Not like your Delilah."

"My Delilah." Mitchell turned the wine glass onto its side. He examined the stem, looked through it. Everything was squashed down and stretched out: it made the living room unrecognizable.

"My Dee-Lie-La," said Stefan. "She's sweet. So fuckin' pure. Can't fault your taste. Man, she was a sweetie. I can't tell you how it was to hold her, to put my arms over her shoulder . . . the feel of that sweet butt, the way she went limp when I put the cloth over her face . . . Knowing, man, knowing she was for you."

"For me."

"I was sorry to let Lesley take her, but that was the deal, and she wasn't for me. But you. In a few minutes—man, you'll be able to live your every dream."

Mitchell held the glass in two hands, brought the stem closer to his eyes, so he could see the whole world. It looked like nothing he'd ever even dreamed. "She's not a cunt," he said softly.

"What?" Stefan leaned forward. "What are you doing? You are so fucked up, Mitch. It's what we like about you. I can't tell you how long it took us to find a fucked-up kid like you."

Mitchell bent the stem. Except that it didn't bend because it was glass; it snapped, right at the base. He turned to Stefan, who was right beside him, and lifted what was left of the glass and jammed the stem into the inner tear duct of his right eye, past there against something that was probably bone. Stefan shouted "Fuck!" and grabbed at him, but Stefan was a fair bit weaker than Mitchell Owens.

A moment later, Mitchell wiped his hands on his jeans and pulled the TV remote out from underneath Stefan's twitching thigh. He turned on the Media Centre.

The bedroom was different now. The comforter had been pulled aside, and it was all twisted to the right of the bed. The bald man was sprawled across the under sheet. He was clutching his face and there looked to be blood coming out. He was rolling slowly back and forth. The bedside lamp had been knocked over—or maybe thrown—and beside it, Shelly was slumped, her neck at a funny angle. The blond fellow was on the other side of the bed, in the corner, his shoulders hunched and his head down. He was trembling. Mitchell looked at the remote, and pressed a couple of buttons, and he was looking at the parking garage elevator door, which was opening. Mrs. Lesley Woolfe was in there. Her eyes were wide and she looked like she was concentrating. When the door finished opening, she stuck her head out, looking to the left and the right, and then hurried off camera. He clicked again and again, but nowhere could he find any sign of Trudy.

Mitchell looked up. Somebody was pounding on the door to the apartment: pounding and pounding and pounding. Pushing Stefan's head aside, so he was lying on the sofa rather than sort of sitting up, Mitchell went to the door and looked through the peep-hole. "Oh," he said. "You."

He opened the door, and Delilah Franken pushed through. "Oh thank God! Oh thank God!" she said and fell into the apartment, and Mitchell put his arms over her shoulders. She smelled awful, like she'd peed herself, and her streaky-blonde hair was matted, and he could see that there was blood on her shirt. "Call the police!" she said. "Call the police!"

Mitchell helped her into the apartment. He steered her away from the sofa, but sat her down in the dining room and stepped away. She looked at him with wide eyes and a frown, like she was mad but not exactly.

"Y-you," she said. "Mitchell . . . Mitchell Owens? Your mom and my mom were friends. You remember me—right?"

Mitchell nodded. "Delilah Franken," he said.

She leaned forward, wiped a greasy strand of hair from her eyes, and with shaking voice spoke slowly. "Mitchell, I don't know what you're doing in a place like this, but I am *so* glad that you're here."

Mitchell didn't know about that: she didn't look particularly happy. She looked like she was . . .

Concentrating.

"Now you have to listen carefully," said Delilah. "The people in the next apartment kidnapped me. They're some fucking internet sex cult. I think they planned the fucking thing, for a long time . . .

222

I don't know, but that's what I think. But whatever—they grabbed me from behind and knocked me out, and took me to a farmhouse somewhere north of here, and they kept me there for three days. Then they injected me with something and brought me here. I got away—I hit a lady with a lamp, and scratched this guy's eyes, and a bunch of them just yelled and took off. One of the women locked herself in the bathroom and she didn't seem to be coming out. But I'm afraid she might come . . ." She looked up suddenly. "Shit. Is the door locked?"

Mitchell went over to the door. "I got to call the police," said Delilah, and Mitchell shouted, "Okay," as he looked through the peephole again. The hallway was empty, but the door on the opposite side stood ajar. "Where's the phone?" said Delilah.

Mitchell didn't answer. He watched for a moment longer, then opened the door and stepped to the other side.

"Oh. Never mind. I see one by the sofa," she said.

Mitchell shut the door behind him and crossed the hall between the two apartments. He ignored the shout of surprise that came from behind him. It was not a shout that interested him. It was, in spite of what Stefan and Mrs. Lesley Woolfe and the rest of them thought about him and his infatuation, a shout that had interested him less and less over the past few weeks.

He stepped into the vestibule of Giorgio Piccininni's apartment. There was a mirror hanging there. He smiled into it and he smiled back out of it. Mitchell Owens thought he could tell exactly what was inside him, just by looking.

So Mitchell looked away from there and into the dark room in front of him. He started toward the darkest part, and as he went he whispered:

"Trudy."

Fly in Your Eye

It drifts through your vision, a detached retina on patrol. You blink, you rub your temples, you think about seeing the eye doctor real soon. But you look again, and you realize, no, you were wrong. There's nothing remotely retinal about this thing. Six stickly legs, disco-ball eyes, a big hairy ass, brown-tinted wings stretched akimbo. Just looking through 'em makes you want to scratch.

Crawled inside through your tear-duct while you slept. Happens one time in a hundred when a tourist goes down to that place, stays one night too many in a room where the fumigation hasn't took. The locals have a name for those flies—translates either to Sneaky Devil Bat, or Mean Little Eye Mite, depending on which edition of the Fodor's you got.

Maybe given time, it'll decompose. Surely it couldn't be alive in there—you don't know much about flies, but one thing you're pretty sure about is that flies do not have the right gills for extracting oxygen from eyeball juice. The fact that it's always in a different position when it drifts past your iris doesn't prove anything. What you're seeing's an optical illusion—fly tilts this way or that, wings seem to have moved, proboscis extends a little further, sucks a bit back. Truth is, that fly's drowned. And drowned means dead, and before long dead has got to mean decomposition. It's only a matter of time.

You decide to wait it out. Don't much feel like leaving the house, so you order in some groceries. The phone's getting awful jangly, and you pull it out of the wall. And who needs cable television when you got yourself a fly to watch?

So garbage day comes around and you take the TV and the telephone and your hi-fi stereo set while you're at it, and lay them all out neat as you please on the curb. They're gone before the truck arrives, but you don't see who took them.

You start to wonder how big that fly in there really is. Some days, it fills your whole vision—everywhere you look, there's the fly, looking right back. Other times, it's a teeny little speck. If you weren't looking, you wouldn't even notice it was there.

Mail comes every morning, mostly bills. But you stopped reading it, after the fly switched eyes.

You woke up that morning, and it took you the longest time to figure out what was so unusual.

First you thought, maybe someone rearranged the furniture, but as you looked that didn't seem to be the case. Then you were thinking, if not that, then maybe somebody painted the walls. But no, they were the same dirty beige as they were when you moved in here. And finally, it hit you.

It was the fly.

Floating there in your other eyeball—the clean eye, the empty eye, the eye that had no fly or so you'd thought—brown-tinted wings pressed back all sleek and smug against the bristly little curve of its rump. Fly moved, and that's all it took: overnight, it changed *everything*.

So you closed your eyes and thought to yourself: the mail can *wait*. And you kept 'em closed, covered 'em up, because that way you don't have to look at that Goddamn fly anymore as it jumps from one eye to the other, alive and well against all reason.

Awhile goes by. You don't have many friends, but the few you do have come calling, wondering if you're okay. You pretend you aren't home, and it seems to work: they leave.

Why don't you go to a doctor? Somehow, you just can't get your head around the idea that this fly's a simple medical condition. Maybe the Fodor's had it right—the first edition, not the new one—and this fly's a Sneaky Devil Bat, come straight up from Hell to steal your soul. What's a doctor going to do for that?

You're just about ready to go to a priest this morning when you figure it out. You jump out of bed laughing, pull the bandage off your eyes. The fly's gone—you can tell it without even looking! It *was* only a matter of time.

You fling open the curtains and watch the light stream in. Beautiful morning, isn't it? Middle of summer, sunshiny day, birds flying through the trees. It's a shame you can't hear their singing, over the buzzing in your ear.

Polyphemus' Cave

The horror in the sawmill wasn't far from his mind the night he saw the giant. He'd thought about it briefly in Los Angeles, after he saw the telegram announcing his father's death. He considered the slow swing of barn-board doors across the mill's great black belly, each of the three times he'd had to stop to change flat tires on his brand new Ford Coupe. He thought about it again, stopped in the afternoon sun at the top of a steep slope just west of the Idaho line, to deal with his boiled-over radiator. The water steaming from under the hood made him think about how the rainwater dripped from the tackle and chains in the sawmill's rafters as he lay facedown in damp sawdust. He retched yellow bile into the roadside dirt and started, maybe, to cry. The horror of that night was clearer in his mind then than it had been for years.

But a hundred miles ahead when the sun had at last set, the spruce trees at the side of the road spread apart like drawing curtains and the nude giant stepped into his path. The sight of it drove The North Brothers Lumber Company and its terrible sawmill from James Thorne's thoughts like a spurned beau.

The giant clutched a splintered rail tie in front of him like it was a baseball bat. He glared into the Ford's headlamps with a single eye—a great green orb flecked with yellow around a pupil wide and deep as the Idaho sky. It hovered in the middle of his skull, beneath a great curling mass of black hair. James slammed his foot on the brake pedal and the Ford's tires bit into the road, sending stones rat-a-tating into the depths of the wheel well.

My God, thought James. *He's big as trees.*

He leaned forward in the seat to get a better look. The giant crouched down too and leaned towards the car. A leathery lid crossed his eye as he peered in. They studied each other in that instant. James felt as though that eye was looking through him: drawing the rest of his terror from him like sweet liquor at the bottom of a dark glass.

Then the giant made a noise like a dog's barking, his lips pulled back from teeth that seemed filed to points. With a swing of the rail tie, he splintered the tops of two trees on the far side of the road and disappeared again into the wood. Crickets chirped and tree limbs cracked, and James Thorne's heart thundered in his chest.

"He's big as the trees." He said it aloud, with a bit of a laugh. He wanted to say it to his pal Stephen Fletcher, a lean young black-haired colt of a boy who dressed sets back on *The Devil Pirates*. For the past month he'd spent many of his after-hours undressing James. Stephen was smooth and young and eager to please—and James wished Stephen were here now. But he couldn't take his lover home. Not any more than he could admit to having him in Los Angeles.

James set his mouth and engaged the clutch. The Ford Coupe crunched across the gravel with a noise like breaking glass. He rounded a bend, and came out in the great bowl of valley in the Coeur d' Alene mountains. The road was still high enough that he could see the dim etchings of the familiar peaks against the night sky that surrounded Chamblay. In the valley's middle, miles distant, James could make out a glow among the trees.

This was new for him. When he'd left home, the Grand Coulee Dam wasn't even half built, and the only light in Chamblay came from candle, kerosene and the sun. James smiled bitterly.

After dark on a moonless night, Chamblay could hide in itself.

The road carried James down a sharp slope and drew alongside the Northern Pacific line that served the town. The tracks gleamed silvery in his headlamps for an instant before he turned back parallel to the line.

That was the line that, according to his mother's cryptic telegram, had something significant to do with his father's sudden and untimely death.

"Mmm." He smiled a little, and thought about the giant in the road again—not just the eye, but his immense, sculpted thighs, the dark beard that tumbled halfway down the broad chest . . .

"What a thing," he said. "What a marvellous thing. Put that in a picture, no one would believe it."

The giant, of course, would be the perfect thing for the pictures. Particularly pictures like *The Devil Pirates*. In the person of the brave and over-energetic Captain Kip Blackwell, James had battled a giant octopus, not one but two carnivorous gorillas, a host of man-eating midgets from Blood Island, and of course, several of the fearsome Devil Pirates themselves. For all that battling, Republic still wanted another batch of a dozen episodes before the serial ran its course. The giant man in the road, with the peculiar eye in the middle of his forehead, naked as the day he was born—he'd fill out four of those episodes, maybe more, all by himself.

James thought about that—about unsheathing his rapier against a giant more than twice as tall as he—leaping across the otherwise unconvincing deck of the *Crimson Monkey*, dodging the blows of the giant's papier-mâché club, slashing out theatrically with his sword to bring a dozen yards of sailcloth onto the monster's roaring head. Perhaps, to be true to the plotline, they'd be battling over the honour of the lovely Princess Rebecca, who had disguised herself as a cabin boy back in episode three to join Kip and his crew on their frenetically eventful voyage.

"Wouldn't do to lose that fight," said James, thinking for a moment of what would become of his co-star, tiny Alice Shaw, in the amorous clutches of the giant. He slowed down as he drew through the closed-down business section of Chamblay, past the Episcopalian church his parents frequented, the schoolhouse where he'd learned to read—and finally outside the old clapboard house where he'd spent the first seventeen years of his life. James smiled and shook his head: the preposterous picture of a twenty-foot-tall man mounting a five-foot-two-inch woman provided a comic, if grotesque, distraction to the matter at hand.

He was still thinking about it—or about the giant, the magnificent giant that he might have seen or might, the more he thought of it, simply have dreamed—as he pulled his suitcase from the Ford's trunk, let out a long sigh, and made his way up the path to his mother's front door. The telegram that had brought him here sat folded in his jacket pocket and he made himself think of it. It was a reminder of what he ought to be feeling.

DEAREST JIMMY STOP I HAVE TERRIBLE NEWS TO DELIVER STOP YOUR FATHER HAS BEEN KILLED IN ACCIDENT ON TRACKS STOP PLEASE COME HOME STOP ALL IS FORGIVEN I LOVE YOU STOP YOU ARE THE MAN OF THE HOUSE NOW STOP PLEASE COME STOP LOVE ALWAYS YOUR MOTHER STOP

"Oh."

That was what James had said when the script girl had handed him the slip of onionskin paper from Pacific Telephone and Telegraph. He'd set his glass of water down. Read the words from the telegram once, and then again. Endured the girl's hand on his arm, the sympathetic cooing noise she made. He gave her a smile that was meant to look strained—the smile of a grieving son, bravely facing the death of his beloved old dad.

"Well," he said. He unbuckled the leather belt and scabbard. He draped it over the canvas back of his chair. He walked back behind the false adobe wall of the Castillo de Diablo set. He found a spot where no one could see him. Crossed his arms. Put his hand on his forehead, and waved away a carpenter who'd stuck his head back there to see what was wrong. Then laughed, silently but deeply, until tears streamed convincingly in little brown rivers down the layers of orange pancake encrusted on his cheeks.

His dad was dead. Some terrible accident on the tracks. Well, wasn't that rich. The town would probably be having a parade for Nick Thorne, his strapping, iron-jawed Paul Bunyan of a father . . . And now—

—now, *he* was the man of the house.

There was only one word for it.

Rich.

Three days after the telegram, in the middle of the night, James trod up the front steps to the family house. He didn't know much more now than he did then: he'd just sent off one telegram before packing up his car and heading off. He found that he didn't *want* to know more than his mother chose to reveal in that fifty-word telegram. So he just composed one of his own:

DEAREST MOM STOP I WILL BE HOME IN THREE DAYS STOP DO NOT WORRY ABOUT THE COST OF BURIAL I WILL PAY STOP YOUR SON JAMES STOP

There was light inside the house. He was not surprised to see that it was not electric. His father hadn't worked a decent job since the last time the North Brothers had run their mill, and that was years ago.

But the kerosene flame gave James an odd sort of comfort. The yellow, flickering light was proper and right for a town like Chamblay. Electricity was for New York and Los Angeles. This little place wasn't ready for it.

He paused to look inside. There was his mother, sitting in one of the hard, high-backed chairs. She held the black covers of the family Bible in front of her face like a fan. She heard him coming—he knew her well enough to tell that—but she pretended not to. As he watched through the window, she licked a forefinger and turned a page.

James leaned over and rapped twice on the windowpane. His mother looked up. Widened her eyes in unconvincing delight, as though he were the last person she'd expect to see at the window on an August night some four days after the death of her husband. "Jimmy!" Her voice had a far-away sound to it through the windowpane. She shut the Bible on its marker, set it down and hurried to the front door, which she flung open with a clatter.

"Oh, Jimmy!"

James patted his mother's back. "Hello, Mother," he said, as she buried her face in the crook of his shoulder and moistened his shirt with tears. "Hello."

"Now tell me what happened," he said, as they sat across from one another in the dining room. "What happened to Dad?"

His mother smoothed out her print dress and looked down. "I'm sorry, hon—I guess I didn't put too much in that telegram. Thought you might have read the newspapers. About the derailment and such."

James shook his head. "I don't have much time for that, what with my schedule."

His mother smiled and patted his hand. "Well, you've got time to come home when I need you most. That's a blessing."

"They gave me ten days," said James. His mother's smile faltered, so he added: "I'm sure I can arrange a little more."

"Oh." The smile returned. "Well, good."

"Now. Was it the derailment? That—"

"That killed your father?" James's mother folded her hands in front of her and fixed her eye on the Bible. "Not directly. I can't believe you hadn't heard of it. There was a newspaper man who came all the way from Seattle to interview me and take pictures. He said it'd play in all the Hearst papers, what with the circus angle. Biggest one since 1918, he said. I'd have written more if I'd known."

James frowned. "The *circus* angle?"

"It was a circus train," she said, sighing. "Twillicker and Baines Circus. Come down from Canada. Old steam engine, six rickety old freight cars and a couple of Pullmans. Wasn't even supposed to stop here . . ."

"Ah." James nodded. He *did* remember the story now—the Twillicker and Baines wreck had come up a couple of times while he was in makeup. The circus train had derailed somewhere "up north."

There'd been a kerosene fire. Some animals had gotten loose. A lot of people had been killed. There was a number, but he couldn't remember what it was. He shut his eyes—as much in shame as in grief. Maybe someone had said the word Chamblay in connection with the wreck. If they had, James just hadn't made the connection between the wreck and his home. Even when his mother told him of his father's death.

What did that say about him?

"There there, dear." His mother patted his hand. "It's been a long day's drive for you. I see that pretty car of yours outside. You don't want to hear about your father right now. Why don't you get some sleep? Lots of time to talk in the morning."

"I'll sleep in a moment." James opened his eyes and took his mother's hand in his and looked her in the eye. It had been years since he'd fled Chamblay, and every one of those years showed in her face. Now grief was added to the mix. She looked very old. "Tell me about Dad now."

His mother nodded. "The train wreck happened in the middle of the night. They're still trying to figure exactly how, because there wasn't any other train involved. It made a terrible noise, though. Sounded like the ground was being torn. Your Dad—well, he went out to see what was what. You know how he could get."

James didn't answer. He *did* know how his Dad could get. Old Nick Thorne had a reputation to uphold in the town: he was the strongest and most capable man there was, after all. A terrible explosion sounds off in the middle of the night? He'd be out there in a flash.

"He joined the fire crew. The wreck was just a mile south of the station house, so he hopped on the back of the truck as it passed. Last time I saw him alive."

"Was he caught in the fire?"

James's mother shook his head. Tears were thick in the corners of her eyes. They gleamed in the kerosene light, as her mouth turned down and her brow crinkled angrily.

"Trampled," she spat. "Crushed underfoot. By that damned *elephant.*"

James's bed was as he remembered it: an iron-framed monstrosity, barely wide enough for one with a mattress that sagged deep in the middle. If two people got on that bed, its rusted springs would scream to wake the dead. Otherwise, there were few possessions left in the room. He stopped his mother from apologizing.

"I've been away a long time," he said. "It's fine. Now go to bed."

The room had a small window in it that overlooked the town. Light poured in from below, painting squares on the ceiling and walls. It reflected back from a small tin mirror nailed onto the opposite wall. His mother absently straightened it. James took her gently by the shoulder and led her to the door.

"Bed," he said firmly.

When she was gone, he undressed himself, hanging his trousers and shirt on a hook by the closet. He sat on the bed for a moment— listened to it squeak as he bounced a little. The briefest flash of nostalgia overcame him, then—of another night, when he felt the bristles of his friend Elmer Wolfe's neck against his shoulder . . . When the springs screamed, loud enough . . .

. . . loud enough . . .

"A Cyclops!" James snapped his fingers. That's what you called a giant with an eye in the middle of his forehead. He'd seen drawings years ago, in the old Bullfinch's Mythology they had at the schoolhouse. A huge, one-eyed man who lived in a cave and was ultimately blinded by a gang of Greek sailors.

James went to the mirror. The light from the window was enough to see himself by. But the mirror made him into a funhouse image—his chin was cartoonishly long; the thin moustache he'd cultivated for his Captain Kip role looked as though it'd been drawn by a drunkard. He leaned closer and it was better: the nearer you get to a bad mirror, the less the distortion.

Finally, he found he was literally looking himself in the eye. Just inches from the mirror, his own eye seemed huge. The light was wrong to make out the colour—but it took little imagination to paint his iris yellow and green. To imagine the iris—big and black as an Idaho sky. He could lose himself in that eye. No, scratch that: he *wanted* to lose himself in that eye.

"Mmm," said James. His hand crept down to his crotch—took hold. He smiled. Shut his eyes. How would it be, he wondered, to lick that thing—that massive thing, while hands as wide as his back squeezed his shoulders; a thumb as wide as a post gently, maybe even painfully, spread his cheeks.

Eyes still closed, he backed across the room to the freshly sheeted bed and fell into it—lost already in a fevered and vivid dream.

James and his mother spent the next morning at the Simmons Brothers Funeral Parlour in town. His mother had made pretty much all the arrangements before he'd arrived in town. It was going to be a good burial, in the Chamblay Hill Cemetery, with a nice oak casket and a polished headstone made of granite. It was far more than his mother could afford on her own. James made out three large cheques, while Mr. Simmons prattled on about the tragedy of the train wreck and the evil of circus folk and the better place that Nick Thorne had gone to. When they were finished, James took Mr. Simmons aside.

"Tell me," he said quietly, "what really happened to my father. It was no elephant—was it?"

Mr. Simmons crossed his arms and lowered his head.

"An elephant," he said carefully, "was involved. But no."

"Not an elephant," said James. "But it was a big thing." He took a leap. "A—Cylcops, I heard."

Mr. Simmons fixed him with a glare. "Circus folk," he said sharply. "Circus folk have all manner of queerness to them. Giants and midgets and clowns and trapeze artists. Big enough man can call himself a Cyclops if he wants. I should stay well clear of them, if I were you, son."

"Where are they?"

"By the creek—camped like wicked hoboes in the North Brothers' common. But they won't be there for long."

James suppressed a smile. *Wicked hoboes.* "I see."

Mr. Simmons' glare faded. "I'm sorry," he said. "I've buried nine good men who lost their lives trying to put out the fire on that train wreck. Your father far from the least of them. Contrary to what some might say—a busy day's no pleasure for an undertaker."

"I'm sure it's not," said James.

"But son—" Mr. Simmons put a pale hand on James's arm "—circus folk aren't nothing but gypsies, you know. They'll cut your throat and steal your wallet, give them half a chance. They'll overrun a town, steal its children. Don't go out there looking for vengeance."

"Vengeance?" James was honestly puzzled, and that was betrayed in his expression. "Why would I—"

"For the death of your father," he said, then added quickly: "Although I can see such thoughts are far from your mind. That is good, young sir. I apologize for thinking you a hothead. Other sons and daughters have been angrier about the goings-on with the circus folk. If I may say—your mother has raised a fine and temperate man. I am told that you do quite well for the family. In the moving picture business. I've a nephew in Spokane who's a great fan of the pictures. I shall tell him we've met."

"Give him my regards," said James. "And now—one more thing—if I could . . ."

Mr. Simmons smiled sadly. "See your father? I'd advise waiting 'til tomorrow. There's some work to be done. To make him as he lived. Do you no good to see 'im now, son."

James hadn't been about to ask to see his father's corpse. God, that was the last thing he wanted to see. He'd wanted to know more about the circus folk. About the Cyclops. But Mr. Simmons wouldn't talk more about that. He'd just think that James was fixing for vengeance, and try and stop him. So James just returned the sad smile and nodded. "Tomorrow, then," he said.

"You're far away," said his mother outside the house.

"Yes." James ran his hands over the knobby wood of the steering wheel. Stared into space, at the far western ridges that were partly obscured in low cloud right then. "Sorry."

"That's all right, dear." She sat in the car, looking at him.

He smiled at his mother. "Listen. If it's all right with you, I'd like to take a little drive by myself."

His mother took a breath, patted his arm. "Of course, dear. You haven't been back here for almost ten years. And now you're back, it's to bury your—" She stopped, lifted her handkerchief to daub her eyes.

"Yes."

James let his mother go inside, and put the car into gear. He wheeled back through Chamblay's downtown. It was looking livelier during the day. Livelier, in fact, than it had in some time. He counted maybe a dozen trucks, covered with black tarpaulins. Big, dangerous-looking men in dark suit jackets leaned against their fenders, leering at passing townswomen. From behind the wheel of the Coupe, James leered at them. *Turnabout's fair play*, he thought, imagining himself in their midst—a giant in their midst—plucking first one, then the other, screaming into the air . . . Ramming them face-down into the sawdust—into the dirt . . .

God, James, he thought as the little fantasy took form in his mind, *you are a* depraved *one*.

Back in Los Angeles, Stephen had taken to chiding him about that very thing. "They'll let you go, you know, if the press gets wind of your shenanigans," Stephen said to him, curled against his stomach in the heat of a Sunday afternoon not long ago. "They'll cut you loose."

"No fooling." James had reached around front of Stephen, took hold of him lightly and ran a fingertip in the warm space between his thigh and his scrotum. He gave Stephen's nuts a sharp little squeeze. Stephen sucked in a breath—James could feel the cheeks of Stephen's arse tightening around him. "I guess we should stop, then. Maybe I should find religion. Or—" he pulled his hand away "—take little Alice up on one of her many offers. Knock her up. That'd settle it once and for all."

"Oh, go to hell," said Stephen. "You wouldn't know what to do."

"Wouldn't matter," James had replied. "She'd know what to do. And she *wants* to fuck me."

"Everybody wants to fuck you," said Stephen. "You're Captain Kip Blackwell, for Christ's sake. But I have to tell you, *Kip*—that unenthusiastic flirtation you play at with her in the canteen isn't fooling *anybody*."

"It fools Alice," James had said.

"You think?"

James set his jaw. Put his foot on the gas pedal. He took the road to the mill—then, following the wood smoke and tire ruts, made his way to the creek-bank where, according to Mr. Simmons, the circus was encamped.

There was no Big Top; not shooting galleries nor cotton candy stands nor halls of mirrors. The remains of the Twillicker and Baines Circus was mostly people, and those people had spread in a makeshift shantytown along the grassy east bank of the Chamblay Creek. Little tents pitched here and there, charred swaths of orange and green and blue fabric. Some of the folk had dug out fire pits in the needle-covered dirt. They were surrounded by trees, spruce and pine so high that from the camp's far side, they obscured much of the snowy mountain peaks to the west.

James stopped his car and got out. The place smelled of wood smoke and burned fat. He tromped down the slope to the first of the tents—where a young woman sat beside an older man, broad-chested with a long, drooping moustache. He wore a battered felt bowler hat, and his arm was in a sling. She wore a pale blue cotton sun dress, mismatched with the torn fishnet stockings of a dancing girl.

"Hello," said James.

"Good sir," said the man, tipping his hat. "Clayton O'Connor, at your service." The woman smiled wanly. "And this is Clarissa."

James stood there awkwardly for a moment. They didn't appear to recognize him—which as he thought of it wasn't unusual: circus folk had a show of their own to perform Saturday afternoons. There'd be precious little time for the pictures, what with all the fire-eating and clowning and lion-taming to fill up the day.

"Good afternoon," James said. "James Thorne. I'm looking—that is—"

"The eye," said Clarissa, nodding. She got a funny look in her eye.

"Do not mind her and her riddles, friend," said Clayton O'Connor. "She's new at the Sight."

James smiled. "*The Sight*. She's a fortune teller?"

Clayton nodded, and removed his bowler cap to reveal a balding crown covered in intricate tattoos. "An oracle," he said.

"Ah. Of course. Oracles speak in riddles, don't they?"

Clayton shrugged, held his hat in front of him. "It is a mixed blessing, good sir." He extended the hat a little further, like a bowl. "Prophecy is good, but it's nothing," he said, "without sound interpretation."

"I see." James laughed. "Prophecies are free, but interpretation costs a penny."

"Five pennies."

James's first impulse was to walk away—leave the tattooed

man and his abstruse young oracle to prey on the next townie that happened by. But he dug into his pocket, and came up with a nickel he thought he might spare. The oracle was a good shtick, and these people had just survived a train wreck; he couldn't begrudge them their little grift. He tossed the coin into the hat. "Interpret away," he said, and knelt down beside them. "Tell me . . ." He paused, looked across the creek to the dark evergreen wood. Some of the circus folk between himself and the river were taking note of him—of his new automobile. A dwarf limped up to it and gave the rear tires a malicious little kick. ". . . tell me about the Cyclops."

Clayton looked into his cap—with his damaged fingers, he pulled the nickel out, turned it over and examined both sides.

Clayton paused a moment, then looked James in the eye. "You've seen it, have you, sir?"

"The Cyclops? I have." James took a breath. "Yes."

He shook his head. "And you're here anyway."

"I have to find him. It."

"Father," said the oracle, throwing her head back theatrically and gasping at the sky. "Here for his father."

"Hmm." James wasn't sure how good Clarissa was at oracling. But as an actress—well, she made wooden little Alice Shaw look positively Shakespearean.

"That has nothing to do with this. My father's dead."

James looked at Clayton, then at Clarissa. Her eyes fluttered shyly to her hands, a sly smile playing across her lips. Clayton raised his eyebrows in a questioning way.

Clayton nodded. "A lot of men are dead by that monstrosity's hand," he said. "That's why we're here."

"That's why *you're* here," said Clarissa, looking across the creek but pointing straight at James.

James ignored her. "All right, Clayton," he said. "Tell me about this thing."

Clayton looked at him levelly. "That's more than interpretation," he said, rubbing two coinless fingers together as he spoke. "That's a tale."

Sighing, James dug into his pocket for a couple more pennies. When he'd added them to the nickel, Clarissa feigned a swoon across the log where she sat, and Clayton started talking.

"The Cyclops," said Clayton, "was with us for less than a season. Sam Twillicker found the beast in a deep cellar at a ranch in eastern Texas, where he'd been guesting over the Christmas break. Baines and Twillicker had had a bad run of luck with the Hall of Nature's Abominations the past season. The mermaid had come unstitched and spewed straw and cotton all over her case in the middle of our St. Louis show in May. In the early morning hours of July 8, our prized geek Skinny Larouche ran off into a Kansas cornfield with a pair of chickens and the previous day's nut. Later that month, Alfie Fowler took ill with something in his intestine. In August, the bug moved to the gut of brother Mitch, and by Labour Day we'd lost our genuine Siamese twins. Perhaps, said Charlie Baine, the days of sideshows were winding down and they ought just fold up the rest of Nature's Abominations and concentrate on the Rings. But Twillicker didn't buy that; to him, a freak tent was as much a part of the show as clowns and lion-tamers and the high wire. So when his host in Texas mentioned the thing he was keeping in the cellar, and intimated that he had intended the thing's stay should be temporary—'I'll have to kill it or be rid of it, and I'm not sure I can kill it,' he said—Sam Twillicker was intrigued.

"Of course, intrigued's not the same as fooled. Twillicker took care not to let his interest show.

"'We have an excellent strong man,' he said cagily. 'You've got a fat Greek with an eye out? I might put a patch on my Wotun the Magnificent, change his name to Polyphemus and call him the one-eyed giant—and not have spent a penny more.'

"'It would not be the same,' said the host. 'For mine—he has seen the Trojan women and sung duets with Sirens and walked the sea bottom at the heel of Poseidon. How can you compare?'"

"'You ought have been a barker, my friend,' said Twillicker. 'For you could make the rubes see all those things and more in even my poor Wotun, with pretty words like that.'

"'Not the same as seeing it for real, though.'

"Late in the evening, Twillicker walked outside the ranch house, to do just that: see it with his own eyes. They climbed down a tunnel past a padlocked door in the Texas scrub, and stepped out onto a ledge in a room like the bottom of a giant well. The thing—the Cyclops—was below them, lolling against the wall amid a carpet of whitened bones. Flies buzzed and flitted in the lantern beam that Twillicker's host shone down, and the creature looked up into it with its single great eye, so wide that Twillicker could see the pair of them reflected in it.

"'How big is he?' said Twillicker.

"'Twenty and five,' said his host. 'From toe to skull top, twenty and five feet.'

"'And that eye,' said Twillicker. 'Sitting unnaturally in the middle of the forehead like that. It's real?'

"'It better be,' said the host, 'for the beast has none but that one to see by.'

"'My God,' said Twillicker.

"The bones rattled and crunched below as the Cyclops stirred. Both men stopped their conversation, as the thing drew himself to his feet. Standing, the Cyclops was nearly eye level to him. His breath came at him like a hot Mediterranean wind. His eye blinked. A hand, big as a door, came up over the lip of the ledge—Twillicker barely had the wit to step back into the tunnel before it could grasp him. The Cyclops opened his great mouth, and rumbled something that sounded like Greek. Hot, unbreathable air followed them up the tunnel as they backed away from the grabbing hand.

"'That,' sputtered Twillicker, as they climbed the stairs to the Texas night, 'that thing was going to eat me!'

"'Not likely,' said his host. 'The Cyclops likes lamb better than man. But still—better he didn't get hold of either of us. Because that eye—that eye of his is a hungry eye.'

"'What do you mean by that?'

"'What I say. It's a big eye—a God's eye—and it hungers for the sight of a man's soul. It'll drink that sight right out of you, if you let it.'

"Twillicker spent another three days at the ranch—thinking mostly about what that meant. He didn't know about getting his soul drunk up—but he surely wanted to see that Cyclops again. He wanted to see him something fierce; it took all his will not to steal down that hole again, and look at the beast once more. How many times, he wondered, could he haul a rube back and back again to see this beast, if it had such a draw on a seasoned ringmaster as Twillicker?

"He came back a month later with the right cash and equipment for moving the creature. By March, he had a rail car rigged up and fresh signs made. By the middle of April, the circus was on the move again, and Nature's Abominations was back in business.

"There were practical problems. For one thing, the Cyclops was not a professional. It was more like keeping an animal than an employee—as they discovered when our roustabouts tried to use the Cyclops's strength to haul up the big top outside Denver and three of them wound up in bandages and splints, raving for days from their trials at the Cyclops's hands. The creature's unruliness kept him out of the Big Top as well. He couldn't be trusted around townies without thick bars between he and them, because unlike our old geek Larouche, depravity was no act for the Cyclops. He leered—at everyone, in a measure, but he paid particular attention to the aerialists. One time—" here Clayton paused, and patted Clarissa on the shoulder "—one time he got hold of this girl here. Didn't he darling?"

Clarissa's eyes rolled into her head and she trembled for an instant. Then she blinked and nodded.

"Took five of us to get her back," he said. "Clarissa tore a ligament, and that was it for her on the trapeze. Looked at her for a little long—maybe drunk a bit much of her poor wee soul, hey, girl? And she hasn't been the same since.

"But for that, no one could deny that with the addition of the Cyclops to our roster, the Twillicker and Baine Circus had turned a corner. Every town we stopped opened its purse to us and our monster. Rubes loved Hall of Nature's Abominations now that the Cyclops sat in its middle. They forgave the two-headed ewe that floated nearly invisible in a milky brine. They didn't mind that the geek cage was still empty, or that the two Italians who played the Siamese twins didn't even look like relations. They hurried past Gerta the Doll Woman and Lois the Chicken Lady. Didn't heed the resentful glare that our own Wotun the Magnificent gave them, as they sat through his Nine Feats of Strength that raised sweat-beads big as dimes on shoulders and a brow that had one time seemed immense. They each paid their nickels, and gathered in five-dollar crowds in the Hall's middle for the headline of our show—and listened, as Twillicker himself rolled the spiel outside the curtained-off cage of Polyphemus, Son of Poseidon.

"'He has seen the Trojan women and sung duets with Sirens and walked the sea bottom at the heel of Poseidon,' Twillicker would bellow. 'He has fought Ulysses, battled Odysseus, and shook a fist at great Jove himself! Ladies and gentlemen—I give you—'

"And their breath would suck in, as the bright red curtains drew from the front of a tall, steel-barred cage.

"'—I give you Polyphemus! Son of the Sea God Poseidon!'

"And the curtain would open, and the men would gasp, and the children scream—and the women, some of them, would faint dead away at the sight of the naked giant Polyphemus. His lips would pull back from a shark's-row of teeth, and his great arms would rise to rattle the bars of his bolted-together cage—and he'd take a taste of them with that eye of his.

"And then, as fast as it'd risen, the red curtain would fall back in place, and the next crowd would come through. By the time the circus was ready to pull up, all the crowds were filled with familiar faces. They all felt the same draw Twillicker had felt that first night. By the time the circus left a town, the coffers were filled to overflowing with fresh torrents of silver.

"The Cyclops became a part of the circus like he'd always been there. The cat wranglers and elephant handlers and the roustabouts had all worked out a drill for moving him, from his cage to the railcar and back again—figured out how to feed him without getting too close to those giant hands, those lethal jaws—and devised a way to wrap the ropes and chains around his wrists and ankles and middle, so he couldn't squirm much. Charlie Baine looked at his books, and understood that for all the food he was buying for his Cyclops, profits were still higher than they'd ever been. As for the freaks, now relegated to second-class oddities in the shadow of Polyphemus? They rattled the change in their pockets and shrugged. Even Wotun couldn't complain much, about being upstaged by the Greek giant. It was as good as pitching the tent next to the Grand Canyon. Folks'd pay to watch your show, just because it was on their way to the view.

"And the view," said Clayton, "doesn't ask for a cut of the nut."

"But the Cyclops wasn't just a view," said James. "The Cyclops felt differently."

Clayton winked at him. "No fooling you, sir. 'Tis true. The Cyclops felt *differently*. And why wouldn't he? For we kept him like an animal, although he was a thinking beast. He stood in his cage, listening to Twillicker holler his spiel, enduring the stares of the glassy-eyed rubes. Submitted to the will of his wranglers. And always he watched. With that great eye he has. He watched and he paid attention. Listened to what Twillicker said, and made out the words. Listened to the rubes muttering amongst themselves. Heard the wranglers and the freaks and the clowns chatter on. Two weeks and a day before the tragedy here—" he gestured behind him to the camp "—he spoke."

Clarissa the Oracle stood, her eyelids trembling in a sideshow trance. "*I am Polyphemus,*" she said in a deepened voice. "*Son of the Sea God Poseidon.*"

"Dear Clarissa started talking then, too. She'd given up the trapeze, and been fooling with tea leaves and Tarot cards instead. We thought she might open a fortune-telling booth. When the words started to come—the poetry—it dawned on us all that little Clarissa should start calling herself the Oracle."

"From the Greek stories," said Clarissa.

"It was a theme," said Clayton. "The Cyclops didn't speak much. But the words he did speak commanded respect. He seemed to speak the things in a man's soul. The things that did not wish speaking. Perhaps—perhaps he did what Twillicker's Texan host said he did: drank in the souls of men and women through his great eye, and spat up truth. For is it not true that the Cyclops were the sons of Gods?"

"The sea god Poseidon," said James dryly.

"You mock," said Clayton. "But you shouldn't, because you've seen him."

James couldn't argue with that.

"The talk continued off and on," said Clayton. "Sometimes it would be just a few words a day. Words we could understand. Words in strange tongues. All mixed up. It was a kind of parroting. After a time, the talk became incessant. He talked as the wranglers tore down his cage, roped his wrists and led him to his rail car. It went on even after he was chained in, we all boarded, and the train was underway. Talked and talked and talked through the night, louder even than the engine whistle sometimes—softer than a whisper in your ear at others. Far into the next night, and into the mountains— the giant's voice lived in our skulls. That can be the only thing that drove Twillicker to do what he finally did."

James shivered as the wind shifted over the circus shanty town. In the distance, he heard a rumbling sound of car engines. "And what," he said, goose flesh rising on his arms, "did Mister Twillicker finally do?"

"Unbound him," said Clayton. "They found Twillicker's body near to the Cyclops's car after the wreck. The giant killed him, we can only think—after Twillicker clicked the locks with the key we found on 'im. Perhaps the Cyclops told him something he could not ignore. Or perhaps—"

"—perhaps the temptation to take a look was too strong to resist," said James quietly.

"Split up the middle was he, into Twillickers two," said Clarissa helpfully. "One good, one wicked—and—"

She stopped. Rubbed her arms. Looked back to the road.

"What's wrong, deary?" said Clayton.

"Wicked," she said, very quietly, as the first black-draped truck crested the hill and stopped, to let its load of bat-bearing men out to the circus's hobo town.

"We should run."

"You are all trespassing. By the authority of the Chamblay Sheriff's Office and the owners of the North Brothers Lumber Company—on whose property you are squatting—I'm placing all of you under arrest."

The speaker was a thick-set man with short bristly white hair and thick brown sideburns who stood on the hood of the second truck in. He wore a suit jacket and black wool pants, tucked into rubber boots that came up near his knee. He held a long double-barrelled shotgun propped against his hip. Maybe two dozen men carrying baseball bats and wearing dark suit jackets surrounded him.

"Don't make trouble for yourselves." The man lowered the megaphone and motioned down the slope with the barrel of his shotgun. His men started to move.

James was already ankle deep in the river. Clayton and Clarissa, and a crowd of others with the circus were with him.

"Who the hell is that?"

"Pinkertons," said Clayton, huffing as he sloshed. "That one was here day before yesterday. There was trouble with a couple of the roustabouts."

Pinkertons. James shuddered. This wasn't the first time he'd heard of the detective agency; when he was a boy, a gang of Pinkerton men ran herd on the men who worked the lumber mill. His father's most prominent scar, a puckered pink thing that extended along his forehead up past his hairline, dated back to the first time Pinkertons came to Chamblay.

Dating to a night . . .

When the bedsprings screamed, and . . .

. . . Jimmy tasted the sawdust in his mouth . . .

There was no doubt about it. James's feelings about Pinkertons were . . . complicated.

The Pinkerton men moved through the camp like armed locusts. They knocked down tents and sent pots of hot water flying and splashing into cook-fires. Three of them descended on a dark-chinned roustabout and pummelled him to the ground. Two were studying James's coupe, parked a dozen yards up-slope. Another two chased down a pair of dwarfs straggling behind the exodus to the creek, while five more waded into the waters after the fleeing mass of circus folk. At the top of the slope, their captain stuck a cigarette in his mouth as he watched it all unfold.

"Get away from my car!" shouted James.

"Christ," said Clayton, a dozen steps ahead by now. "Hurry, boy. He'll crack your skull! Run!"

James was about to turn and do just that, when the shadow passed briefly over their head.

The Pinkerton captain looked up. He dropped his cigarette, still unlit. The boulder crashed down in the middle of his truck—sending glass and metal flying through the air. The Pinkerton men who were following them turned and gaped at the sight.

Clarissa screamed then.

"Oh, Lord!" shouted Clayton, pointing at the opposite bank. James looked, and froze, creek water lapping icily at his ankles.

The Cyclops stood there, a bronzed giant in the sunlight. He raised an arm to shield himself against the flames, then waded into the creek and bent down and reached into the water.

James stood transfixed as the Cyclops's muscles strained to yank a huge, river-rounded rock from the creek bed. Lids the size of window covers crinkled over his single eye and his sharp teeth bared in the sunlight as he hefted the rock to shoulder height. James swallowed and gasped as the beast straightened, the muscles rippled down his abdomen.

"What're you staring at? Come on, boy!" Clayton yanked James's arm and hauled him stumbling downstream. Behind them, there was a gout of water high as a geyser as the rock crashed in the path of the five detectives who'd followed them. James ran, as best he could, through the fast-moving shallows of the Chamblay Creek. He didn't look back when the terrifying roar sounded out across the valley; kept moving when he heard the two gunshots, and the screaming. He finally stopped with the rest of them, when they reached a small rapids in the creek.

Clayton helped Clarissa onto a low, spray-soaked shelf of rock that split the creek. James hauled himself up, and for the first time looked back.

The circus camp was blocked now by a low rise of trees. A black plume of smoke rose above them and into the sky. There was another scream—distant and strangled—and then Clarissa pointed and cried out: "Look!"

A man was flying—his legs and arms wheeling as if for purchase on the air. He must have been a hundred feet up, before he started falling again. There came another roar. Clarissa covered her ears.

Clayton shut his eyes against the tears. The others who were lucky enough to make it to the creek cowered in terror.

And as for James—

James Thorne found his hand creeping to the belt of his trousers. He pulled it away, and ran it through his hair.

"My God," he said unconvincingly. "The horror."

The camp was ruined when they returned, and the Cyclops was gone. But he'd left his mark. People were down everywhere: strong men and acrobats and clowns and roustabouts, and the hard men from the Pinkertons. Some must have been dead, because it smelled like barbecue. The beast had marked his exit with a gateway of smashed and broken trees. Clayton bent down onto his knees and clenched his good fist. Clarissa knelt beside him. The two of them wept softly.

James stepped back from them: surveyed the place. It was a terrifying mess. Was this what the undertaker Simmons had meant when he said the circus folk wouldn't be here for long? Had he heard tell that the North Brothers had gone and hired Pinkertons to clear out the town? James felt a little sick: if he'd been more on the ball, he might have been able to muster a warning, rather than waste these people's time telling him tales of the Cyclops.

The lame dwarf who'd kicked his car tire hobbled past, and pausing, glared up at him.

"Ain't you the movie pirate?" he said.

"Captain Kip Blackwell," said James. "That's right."

"Well why don't you get your fat piratey arse moving and take care of that beast? Make 'im walk the fuckin' plank! 'Bout time someone did."

"I'm not a real pirate." James held up his hands. "Look," he said. "Not even a sword."

The dwarf bent down over one of the fallen detectives. "Well, fuck my arse, if this ain't your lucky day." He stood up, holding a baseball bat nearly as long as he was tall. He handed it to James. "Now you've got a choice—you can use this one—" the dwarf pointed to the bat "—or this one!" and James yelled as the dwarf swatted his groin.

"Ha! Unless you want to save it for the Oracle bitch, who—hey!" The dwarf yelled, as Clayton grabbed him with his good arm and lifted him off his feet.

"That's enough," said Clayton.

"Wotun! C'mon! Fuck you! Put me down!" The dwarf's feet pinwheeled in the air. James raised his eyebrows.

"Wotun?"

In one motion, Clayton set the dwarf on the ground and shrugged at James. "Not much of a strongman now, I'm afraid. We're all put in our place. By that thing."

James hefted the baseball bat. He looked to the crack in the woods the Cyclops had left behind him. Back at Clayton O'Connor, the former Wotun the Magnificent.

Clayton took off his bowler.

"You want company?" he said.

James shook his head. "No."

"I can tell what you mean to do," he said. "Are you certain you dare to?"

James felt himself smile a little. "You have no idea what I mean to do," he said, and set off toward the edge of the trees—where the Cyclops had marked his path.

As he tromped through the woods, James thought about his last day on the set. The last scene he'd shot before they let him go. Two of the Devil Pirates had tossed him into the Sarcophagus of Serpents— where Captain Kip would spend the next episode, while Princess Rebecca and the rest of the *Monkey*'s crew contrived his rescue and James Thorne contrived to bury his old Dad.

"Jimmy!" Alice Shaw hurried to catch up to him, as he stalked away from the plywood Sarcophagus left over from last year's *King of the Mummies* serial. He sighed and stopped.

"Alice," he said.

She stopped in front of him, set her fists on the velvet britches that were Princess Rebecca's single nod to disguise. "I just wanted—to offer my *condolences*."

"Thank you."

"Because we can all see how *torn up* you are. About your father's death."

James frowned. "Well, it's been a long time—"

Alice stepped closer to him, took his hands in hers as though they were sharing an intimacy. In a way, they were. "You know, Jimmy," she said, "you should really learn how to act."

"Alice?"

"You'd fool more people." Alice stepped back. "Why are you even bothering to go?"

James crossed his arms. "To bury him," he said.

"Something you wish you'd done long ago?"

He sighed. "If you like, Alice."

She wagged a finger at him. "I know what you are, Jimmy Thorne," she said. "The only question is: what did your horrible old father do to you to make you this way?"

James wondered if he'd ever feel the proper things about his father's death. He felt as though he were circling those things as he walked—getting closer to the feelings of grief and loss and everything else that went with facing a father's death.

But the fact was, he wasn't thinking about that. He was thinking about the Cyclops. And he wasn't thinking about how he'd kill him, either.

The path led him to the bank of the creek where it twisted around a cropping of rock and tree. With a trembling, he knew where he was:

The North Brothers Lumber Company's sawmill.

The last time he'd seen it, the mill was up and running. The whine of the saw blade would cut across the valley as teams of horses hauled giant logs up the round-stoned creek-bank to the mill's black and hungry mouth. Inside, men would unhitch the logs and haul them further along with complicated block and tackle. Nick Thorne would be first among them, the muscles in his thick forearms dark as mahogany, straining at the weight of the spruce and pine logs cut down from the mountain slopes all around them.

Now the place was still as a tomb, its wooden walls and roof grey as stone.

James swallowed. His hand was shaking as he set the baseball bat down in the pine-needles beside him, and set out across the creek shallows. The mill's great black doors were open. Inside was dark as the mouth of a cave.

The last time James had been inside the mill, the scent of pinesap was overpowering. Pinesap and machine oil and a bit of fear sweat.

Now, it smelled like a slaughterhouse.

At first, James was afraid the Cyclops had brought humans here—some of those folk Mr. Simmons had said had gone missing. But as his eyes adjusted to the dark, he saw that wasn't so. The smell was from something else. Animal carcasses hung from chains wrapped around the rafters. He first passed a couple of shapes like big cats, their skins torn off as they hung maw-down to the sawdust-covered ground; something that might have been a boy, but James gathered to be a monkey carcass, hanging by a single, hand-shaped foot; and, what was left of the elephant. The bloody trunk brushed James's shoulder as he passed underneath and a cathedral of ribs hung over his head. A cloud of flies that had been feeding there followed James for just a few steps then abandoned him as he left the Cyclops's larder, and moved into the next chamber of the mill.

James stepped around a thick post. Looked down, where the floor of the sawmill sloped from wood down to dirt. Light leaked in through the warping barn-board of the mill's wall—reflected off a pool of oily water that had collected at its base. The Cyclops crouched by that pool—poking with an extended finger at a dark shape in the water.

The Cyclops rumbled something indecipherable, in a deep and lazy voice. Mottled sunlight from the pond flickered across the giant's flesh.

The Cyclops stood high enough to brush rafters, while at his feet, the shape rolled and sank beneath the water.

The Cyclops's nostrils flared and he made a bellows-like huffing sound as he sniffed. He turned to face James.

In two great steps, the Cyclops had closed the distance between them. He leaned down, so that his eye—big as James's head—was just a few feet off.

James gasped. This close, the Cyclops's eye was fantastical. Colours shifted across the broad surface of its iris like oil across a sunlit pool. As for the dark in its middle, that grew and shrank as the creature focussed on James—

—the darkness was hungry.

The Cyclops reached around with both hands, and tucked them under James's arms. He lifted him like he was a small child. The Cyclops muttered ancient words as he turned James from side to side—studying him like he was a doll.

James kicked his feet back and forth in the air beneath him. He looked down: his toes were at least a dozen feet from the floor. He could barely breathe, the creature was holding him so tightly. He stared into the Cyclops's great eye, and the Cyclops stared back.

Memory drew from him like pus from a swollen wound.

He felt a sob wrack across his body. The Cyclops ran a great thumb down his chest. When it settled, James gasped. The Cyclops grinned.

James squirmed in a terrified ecstasy. The giant's thumb was thick as a man's thigh, but far more nimble. The feeling was primordial—it was as though it yanked him back to the night when his old friend Elmer Wolfe slept over—and had found his way into James's bed—pressed close to him—and then the springs . . .

. . . the bedsprings . . .

They screamed.

The mill was dark when Nick Thorne and Jimmy arrived there. It was in the hours before dawn—long before the morning shift would arrive. Nick pushed the boy around the side of the building, and through the great, blackened doors. It was dark inside.

"You want to lie with men, boy?" Nick cuffed his son hard enough to send him to the ground. "You like that, do you?"

Jimmy heard himself whimper—and hated himself for making so weak a noise. He was covered in sawdust. Face-down on the ground. His father smelled of liquor and sweat. "I'll show you what it's like . . ."

Jimmy tried to press himself into the ground—as though he could escape that way, by enveloping himself in wood shavings. But there was no escape. His father's hand, thick and callused from working a lifetime in the sawmill, pushed hard between his legs, pushed his nuts up hard into his abdomen. He gave a cry that sounded to him like a squeak.

"That's what it's like, queerboy." His father grunted, took back his hand, and undid his trousers.

"That's what it's like, queerboy." The Cyclops brought James close to his face. He opened his great mouth, and a tongue came out, thick as a marlin and rough like a towel—touched James's middle, taking a taste of him. The Cyclops huffed, and smiled and lowered James to his own middle. Now James was staring straight into another, smaller eye. James felt his feet touch the ground, and the giant's hand pushed him, guided him forward.

James rubbed his face against the shaft of the giant's penis. It was wide as a drum, and the leathery flesh trembled as he caressed it. The Cyclops moaned. The hand stroked James's back. It wasn't squeezing him anymore. But James knew it held him there as surely as were it a fist clenched around him. Shaking with fear and lust, and tears streaming down his cheek, he raised his own arms and embraced the immense shaft.

The memory kept coming. The vivid, awful memory of his father, the heroic Nick Thorne, buggering him for what seemed to be an hour on the floor of this place. To teach him a lesson, he'd said. The old man had rolled him over before he was done. Demanded . . .

. . . demanded . . .

There had been a sharp *crack!* sound before he could do anything else, and his father had fallen down, clutching his skull. A man with a baseball bat was standing behind him. First ordering him off the property—telling him he was trespassing. Saying something about being an "agent of the mill." Showing a little eye-shaped Pinkertons badge on his chest. Then, seeing Jimmy half-naked in the sawdust, shutting his mouth. The baseball bat came up again, and down again. That was when Jimmy had said it:

"Stop killing him! He's my Dad!"

"Sweet Jesus," said the man from Pinkertons.

"*Sweet Jesus,*" said the Cyclops.

James looked up. The Cyclops moved his hand from his shoulder, let him step back.

"Shit and hell." Not a dozen feet off, the grey-haired man from Pinkertons stood, blood in his beard and his shotgun raised, along with a fresh troop of detectives. "It's a monster, boys. Kill it."

The Cyclops let James go, and turned his great eye to face his attackers. James sat down in the wet sawdust and finally felt the tears—hot and salty and honest—streaming down his cheeks. They weren't the tears of mourning. Those, James realized, would never, ever come. The roar and light of gunfire and screams filled the cavernous mill. James was nearly deaf from it, weeping in the dark, when the Cyclops turned his gaze back to him.

Now why, wondered James as he gazed up into the Cyclops's

encompassing eye, would anyone stick a spear into that?

James dropped two polished nickels on his father's waxy eyelids. Gunshots echoed through the valley, as another wave of detectives assaulted the sawmill, and James thought about old Nick Thorne's death: fighting his way through the flames—looking everywhere but up—before he was plucked into the sky and flung down again, amid the screams of his fellows.

James stepped back and put his arms over his mother's shoulders. He tried to ignore the stares of the other mourners. He was a mess. He'd come directly here to the Chamblay Cemetery from the sawmill. His shirt and trousers were stained and torn from the night spent in the crook of the Cyclops's arms, amid the heaps of dead men left over from the first Pinkertons assault. His chin was dark with morning beard. It was quite scandalous—showing up such a dishevelled mess at his father's burial. He supposed he would have to get used to that when he went back to Hollywood. There would be quite a lot of scandal then. Republic would more than likely, as Stephen had put it, cut him loose once it all came out.

It may as well come out. Because he couldn't go back to the cage of lies he'd made for himself in Hollywood—to being Captain Kip Blackwell of the Seven Seas—any more than Clarissa the Oracle could go back to the trapeze now that the horror of her own tiny soul was drunk dry, or than Clayton O'Connor could trick the rubes into thinking he were a true strongman, or than Sam Twillicker could live another day once the Cyclops had sucked his soul right from him.

But he would have to take this one step at a time. His mother looked at him with wet, uncomprehending eyes. "*What happened to you?*" she whispered.

"Quite a lot," said James as Mr. Simmons' shaking hands closed the lid of his father's casket, and his sons prepared to lower the old man into the space they'd carved for him in the earth. James felt himself shaking too, around the great, empty space in him where the sawmill had crouched all these years.

"I'll tell you all of it this afternoon," he said.

The Webley

Wallace Gleason walked alone that day.

Some days past, he and Rupert Storey had fought a hot, angry storm of a battle that ended in tears and blood. Wallace had come out on top; for at the end, it was he standing, fists clenched at his side, eye-whites standing out like flecks of ivory against his tanned, dusty flesh. His best friend Rupert was on the ground, red ribbons of snot strung down his chin and into the dirt. Rupert bled; Rupert cried. Wallace did neither.

The dog hunkered low in the grass. And it took note of Wallace walking past the quiet, broken-down shacks that every so often emerged from the woods along this stretch of road.

It was a stretch that one time might have had some life to it. When the Evers Brothers sawmill was up and running, the little houses were full of men and their wives and their children, come to Fenlan to make a good wage. A dog would take note of no one boy more than any other. But this was 1933. The passages of boys were few and far between these days.

Wallace thought he took the road slow and victorious, more man now than ever before. But the dog thought differently. It had not seen Wallace's prowess in the sand pit, what a beating he had been able to inflict upon his foe. The dog only saw the boy, unsmiling, head down, shuffling along the route that he had taken many times in the company of his best friend Rupert.

The dog launched itself.

It was a big boy of a dog, a German shepherd. Maybe some wolf in it. Wallace was not much bigger. When the dog bounded across the overgrown lawn of its house, snarling, barking—Wallace screamed.

The dog reared up on its hind legs, its front paws on Wallace's shoulders. Their eyes locked. Wallace dropped his grammar textbook. He stepped back and fell, and scrambled up before the dog could set upon him.

The dog gave only a short chase. It bounded after Wallace as he bolted along the dirt road to the crossing where it met the main road into town. There he stopped, barking twice more, as Wallace ran off to his school, alone, his grammar text left fanned open in the road by the dog's house.

It was only when the boy was out of sight that the dog turned back.

Rupert Storey walked alone too, and had each morning since his ignoble defeat at the hands of his best friend Wallace.

On his own, the trip to school went quicker. Having some brothers meant fewer chores. No longer waiting around at Wallace's house each morning this past week meant Rupert had arrived at school fully a quarter hour earlier.

Wallace found him, leaned against the tall maple tree at the back of the schoolyard. Rupert was keeping an eye on the Waite sisters, themselves engrossed in a game of hopscotch with some others in the Grade Four section of their class . . . none half as beautiful as those two: Joan Waite, at twelve, a year older than Rupert—dark hair falling in curls to her shoulders, framing her wide Waite face, cheekbones that came up in the shape of a heart. Nancy, a year Rupert's junior, somehow born with straw-blonde hair, grown to the middle of her back and braided into a long plait. She had the same upturned nose, though, the same heart-face, the same golden freckles, as her sister.

They all played on, not one noting Rupert's steady gaze.

Rupert turned that gaze on Wallace.

"What?" he said.

"You can come to dinner tonight," said Wallace.

"Who says I even want to?" said Rupert.

But of course he did want to. Mrs. Gleason put on a fine spread for Wallace, his father the Captain and sister Helen—each night, not just Sundays. Rupert could sit by Helen, he reasoned, and not even talk to Wallace if Wallace didn't apologize with more than a dinner invitation. So when Wallace asked him if he *did* want to, Rupert said, "Sure, I guess." And at the end of day, he waited around until Wallace got out of detention for leaving his grammar text, and the two of them headed back together, on a longer route than usual, to the Gleason farm.

Wallace did say he was sorry but took his sweet time, finally mumbling it as they started up the long drive to the farmhouse. The scope of the apology didn't exactly cover the sins involved.

"Sorry your lip got cut. I don't know my own strength sometimes."

But Rupert figured it for as good as he'd get. "All right," he said. "It wasn't bad as that."

Wallace half-grinned then and almost undid it. "You cried like a little baby," he said.

But when Rupert pushed him, starting something all over again, Wallace put his hands up. "No fighting today, brother. Today, we got to stick together."

"All right." Rupert let his hands dangle at his sides. They trudged up the drive to the house and climbed up on the porch. The Captain was there, sitting on an old cane chair, sipping well-water from a tin ladle. One suspender dangled off his shoulder; his white shirt was stained with sweat, which beaded on his sunburned forehead. Seeing Rupert, he lifted the ladle to him as if in a toast.

"Good afternoon, Captain Gleason," said Rupert.

"Afternoon, Lieutenant Storey. Corporal Gleason." The Captain winked and finished the ladle of water. He dipped it into the bucket beside his chair and offered it to the boys. It had been a hot walk; Wallace took it and gulped down half of it, and Rupert grabbed it away and finished it.

"Can Rupert stay for supper?" asked Wallace when they handed the ladle back.

"Can Rupert stay for supper? I don't know. Depends on whether our Helen's up to fending off the attentions of her young suitor tonight."

Wallace glared, Rupert blushed, and the Captain laughed. "You're always welcome at our table, Rupert." He sniffed the air and said to Wallace: "Your mother's roasting pork tonight. With apple. Ought to be plenty." Then back to Rupert: "Go on inside. Say hello to Mrs. Gleason. Keep your hands to yourself with my daughter. Think you can say Grace?"

"Yes, sir."

"I think so too. Now scoot."

They went inside and through the sitting room. Rupert always liked spending time here. Captain Gleason had become a captain serving with the Perth County Fusiliers in the Great War. It was a rare ascent, so said the Captain, to go from enlisted man to officer in the course of a war. For the Gleason farm, it brought prizes: a decommissioned German Maxim gun, mounted in the corner; and a helmet from a Hun, a bullet hole in it right at the crown, hung on the wall beside family photographs. By the west-facing window perched a small metal sculpture of an angel, polished black, which Rupert and Wallace understood had been lifted from the bombed-out ruins of a French church, brought back as hidden booty in a soldier's duffel.

Rupert went through there to the kitchen, where he found Mrs. Gleason and Helen, tending supper on the woodstove. Helen was a woman of fifteen—black hair cut to her shoulders—a small mouth with full red lips—brown eyes that laughed . . .

Skin like silk, like gold.

She and the Waite sisters . . . they were in the same league, as far as beauty went. Rupert put his hands in his pockets and said hello.

There was some fussing. Rupert was unsure about whether the Captain and Mrs. Gleason knew about the battle between him and their son last week in any particulars. But Mrs. Gleason at least must have intuited that something had been wrong, she being so relieved now that things seemed right. Helen, smile plastered on her face, asked Rupert some questions—mostly about how his brothers were keeping, and he answered as best he could. He would have kept talking 'til dinner was served, but Wallace motioned him back to the sitting room so he excused himself and left the women to their work.

"I got something to show you," said Wallace. He beckoned Rupert over to a dark cherry-wood cabinet, on top of which was a case with medals and decorations that Captain Gleason had earned, all arranged on a bed of red velvet. He pulled open the top drawer, which was as high as their chests. He looked around apprehensively, then lifted it out.

It was a holster of dark, oiled leather, with straps wrapped tight around it. Wallace held it in both hands like it was treasure, which, Rupert supposed, was exactly what it was.

"It's Father's Webley revolver," said Wallace. He held it out. "You can hold it."

Rupert touched it, but pulled back before Wallace could put the weight of it in his hands. The revolver was for officers; Rupert didn't feel right about holding it, not unless an officer said he could, and even then . . . Wallace shrugged and took it back in his own arms. He cradled it like it was a baby.

"There's no bullets in it," he said. "I know where they are, though."

"Put it back," said Rupert. "Come on."

Wallace shook his head. "Remember how I said we have to stick together, brother?"

Rupert swallowed, and nodded.

Carefully, Wallace unwrapped the straps from the holster, and with one hand pulled the revolver out. It was huge in his hand, butt curved like the blade of a scythe. The barrel was short, but wide.

"Good," he said, holding the gun so it pointed out the window, toward town. He closed one eye and sighted down the barrel. But the gun was heavy enough he couldn't hold it that way for long. "'Cause tomorrow, we're going to have to."

"Put it back," said Rupert again.

"Yeah." Wallace slipped it back into the holster and set it back in the drawer. "Don't worry, brother. We'll be safe."

"Safe from what?"

Wallace slid the drawer shut, and walked over to the Maxim.

"There's—" Wallace hesitated. *A dog,* is how he should have finished, but the word *dog* wasn't the word he was looking for to describe the dog that had assailed him that morning. "There's a beast," he said. "We can't let it be."

"What do you mean to do? And what do you mean 'we'?"

Wallace took hold of the grip of the Maxim. He sighted down it.

"I mean *we,*" he said. "And you know what happens if *we're* not?"

Rupert didn't have to say. He knew. "Tell me about this beast," he said instead, and listened, as Wallace described the thing, and what he meant them to do about it.

Rupert said the Grace at supper. Mrs. Gleason said he did fine, but Rupert knew he hadn't; he'd mumbled and stuttered through the whole blessing, and when he sat down he was sweating. Helen poured him a tall glass of water at the end of it. She even said, "You're very welcome, Rupert," and smiled at him after he thanked her.

Meantime, Wallace brooded. He had wanted to get his father to tell the story of the Webley again, but Rupert had said that wouldn't be a good idea, given everything he had in mind. Wallace didn't see what the problem was. His father told the story often enough, whether to the family, or to pals over draft beer at the tavern. He had been in transit, promoted to lieutenant after his lieutenant had taken a bullet, on his way back to the war.

Well, you must understand, an army officer doesn't come from places like Fenlan, where we work with our hands and our backs. Officers are fancy fellows. Gentry. They ought to have a sidearm. They bloody well ought to provide it themselves.

And for officers commissioned on the home front, that's an easy thing. For those of us who send our pay home . . . something else again. So. (And he rubbed his hands together, and got a wicked look to his eyes.) *There I am, on a troop transport crossing the channel. Back to action. And there are a band of officers, young fellows. From the Imperial army. They stick together—even sleeping together, lying like spokes of a wagon wheel, heads at the rim, feet in the middle. And in the middle of that: they stack their pistols.*

And so I wait . . . I wait until the last of them starts snoring. And ever-so-quiet, I step between them, and snatch one of their pistols—a Webley revolver, short-barrelled like they carry in the Royal Navy. And creep back to where I'm billeted with the Canadians—tuck the gun away with my kit—and under the bright stars of Heaven, sleep the sleep of the just.

And the next day, sure enough, we're sitting at breakfast, and isn't one of those fellows complaining at me: how blimey an' dash it, you can't trust an enlisted man. "They'll steal your sidearm, fast as look at you!"

"What," I say back, "is the world coming to?"

And Father would chuckle. The same chuckle, every time he told the tale, at the same time in it. The chuckle was part of the story. And it was a *great* story.

But Rupert had been clear. "You want to do this thing, don't go letting anyone think you're thinking about it. Not that I think you *should* do it."

So Wallace sat and ate his supper and Rupert held himself in check, and at the end of it, Wallace saw Rupert to the end of the driveway and bade him good night.

Wallace Gleason rose early. It was easy, he told Rupert when they met at the foot of the Gleason driveway. He had not truly gone to sleep.

"I didn't want to let anything happen to the gun," he said, yawning, stretching. The butt of the Webley appeared as his shirt stretched past it. The casual gesture made Rupert nervous, and he looked around quickly. But they were alone on the road.

"Is it loaded?" he asked, and Wallace nodded.

"But there's no bullet in the chamber," explained Wallace. "So we're safe."

"Just stop stretching," said Rupert, and they headed into town, to school.

Rupert had not slept much either, and when he did sleep, his rest was troubled by dreams: of a huge, black-pelted wolf lurking atop the hay bales of Rupert's barn . . . watching his brothers as they flung open the doors, as they came into the great, dark space, unwitting . . . the flash of its red eyes, the only hint that it was there, hunting.

He knew, in the light of morning, that this nightmare hound was not Wallace's beast. The same as he knew that taking the Captain's revolver to the dog that had troubled Wallace so was a dangerous game.

It was a game, however, that he couldn't quit. There was more at stake than friendship.

They started to school—along the route that Wallace and Rupert always took. First, a mile along the concession road. They passed three other farms before getting to the road between the farms, and the town. Another mile or perhaps a bit more, on this road. The dog's road.

Along here, the properties were smaller, and farther from one another. Anyone farming what soil there was, would be doing it to feed themselves rather than for market. Most of the houses along here were not even managing that. Roofs needed shingling; fences, a coat of paint. There were no lawns, few gardens. Neither Rupert nor Wallace knew anyone who lived here. As far as they knew, no one did.

They slowed past one. Rupert peered up the driveway—a short

ribbon of dirt and gravel, dressed in low flowering weed. The house at the end of it was one floor, with a small porch on the front. The wood had been painted a pale green. The shingles were green with moss. An apple tree bent close to the south side. Looking close, Rupert could see the bruised red curves of fruit that had fallen into the high grass.

Wallace stood on the balls of his feet, craning his neck as though there were a fence to look over. The house was quiet.

"This is the place," Wallace said gravely. He worked the Webley's grip where it protruded over his belt, kept peering at the house. Rupert stood there with him, and looked.

This wasn't how the plan was supposed to go. Wallace had gone over it just minutes before.

Okay, so this dog (he'd started to call it a dog by that morning) *... it comes down the driveway. Fast. So fast you have to run. It's like you don't have a choice. The dog knows this. And it gets on you. On your tail. And then you're done for. Except this time, when the dog comes . . . we'll trick it. It'll start coming at us, and then I'll take the Webley. And I'll sight down the barrel* (he checked around, then pulled the gun out, and sighted down the barrel). *And then: I'll let fly* (and he made a quiet sound like a pistol report through his teeth). *And that'll be the end of that damn dog.*

"Maybe it only sees you when you're moving," said Wallace. "We should go back, and walk by the driveway again."

"We should just go to school," said Rupert. "Maybe on the way home . . ."

But Wallace was already doubling back, beckoning him to follow. Rupert sighed and walked back one house, and then they both turned around and crossed the driveway again.

It was the same this time as the last: nothing.

Wallace stood as he had before, staring at the house. A pickup truck rolled past them on the road into town. It kicked up a small cloud of dirt around them; the morning sun through the leaves gave it a glow like magic dust.

Wallace's mouth turned down at the corner, and he glared through it at the house. He swore under his breath, and then at volume: "Goddamn." Rupert, liking the look of the dust in the light, kicked up more dust with his feet. And looking down, he spied Wallace's grammar text. He picked it up.

"Hey," he said. "You drop this?"

"Goddamn!" Wallace's face went red, and his shirt went up, and the Webley drew across his white belly, and it was pointing right at Rupert.

The gun barrel wavered in Rupert's face, and as the dust settled around them, Rupert thought about their battle a week ago in the dust, the sickening feeling of Wallace's fist in his face, the taste of dirt, and wondered: *Should I have apologized?*

The book fell from his hands. And after a long moment, Wallace lowered the gun.

"I won't shoot you," he said flatly. "We got to stick together."

"Don't point that at me again," said Rupert.

"I already said I won't shoot you." Wallace bent down and picked up the book. Tucked it into his bag one-handed, while the Webley dangled from the other.

"The dog—" Rupert was about to say that it wasn't coming. But as he spoke, he glanced at the house. The screen door rattled, and through the slats in the porch railing, he could see the flank of an animal. Wallace saw it too.

"Goddamn," he said, and crouched down.

Rupert looked some more, and finished the thought. "The dog isn't coming."

The dog had settled on the porch, at the end near the apple tree. Squinting, they could make out his eyes—unblinking, peering through the slats and the high grass at them.

"Should we walk past again?" asked Rupert. Wallace hushed him.

"I'm gonna see if I can hit him."

"Not from here you can't."

"I bet I could."

Rupert shook his head. "Best luck, you'll just wound him. Then he'll be angry, like a bear."

Wallace considered this—and, Rupert hoped, considered the wisdom of retreat—just putting the Webley away, dumping the bullets first, and going on to school, grammar text retrieved and calling the game even. But Wallace was considering something else. His lips set thin against his teeth, and he nodded briskly. "You're right," he said, and pulled off his book bag, and set it down in the slope of the ditch. Then, keeping low, Webley held in both hands, he made his way up the driveway.

Rupert didn't follow. It felt like the dream, him watching his brothers file into the barn—the wolf, hiding in wait. He couldn't do anything then. He couldn't—wouldn't—*couldn't* do anything that morning. Not anything but watch, as Wallace walked down the driveway, gun held in front of him.

The dog shifted, and Rupert could no longer see its eyes. Wallace could, and he lifted the gun. "Here, doggy," he said. His voice sounded higher. The gun wavered in front of him, as Wallace tried to sight down the barrel.

A low growl came from the porch. Even as far as the end of the driveway, it raised hackles on Rupert's neck. Wallace moved his finger behind the trigger guard—touched the curve of the trigger. Peered through the grass and the slats, looking for the eyes.

And then, as he watched—the dog vanished. There was nothing but the peeling green paint on the porch; the screen door, half-ajar.

Wallace didn't see the dog leap. Rupert did. It was the first time he saw the dog in full, in morning light. It *was* a beast.

It came up over the railing of the porch fast—touching it with front paw, then pushing off a second time with its hindquarters. The old wood of the railing protested at the launch, and the animal flew, a twisting, dark missile. It came down hard amid the high grass. Then it came up. And down again, lost in a swirl of weed. Up once more, lunging high and throwing off barks like punches—as Wallace raised the gun.

Rupert shut his eyes, expecting thunder from the Webley's short barrel, and the barking to turn into a short yelp, and a thump! Then maybe another shot, to finish the kill. He shut his eyes and then held his breath.

There was no shot. Rupert opened his eyes. He looked out at the empty yard. Held in perfect silence, for a perfect instant—long enough, just, to let him think: *Wallace is gone.*

Then the dog's back, curved and shaking, emerged over the grass. And the scream came. It was a bleat—a baby scream. It was, a deep part of Rupert knew, how *he'd* sounded, pressed into the dirt, crying out under the flurry of Wallace's fists.

The grass rustled and the dog's head came up, eyes turning to show thin crescents of white. It dropped again and another cry came, and Rupert, a shameful grin seeding his face, thought:

Wallace is gone.

He couldn't even pull a trigger, thought Rupert. *He couldn't even manage that.*

Rupert bent down, and reached into the scrub. His hand closed around a rock. And he stood straight, and without aiming, he pitched it. The rock went too far, clattering onto the porch and falling just short of a window. He picked up two rocks next time, one in each hand, and he threw them fast, one after another.

The second rock hit home and the next fell short. The dog yelped and its muzzle flashed up as the third rock thumped into the ground. Rupert and the dog met eyes an instant. Its eyes were not red but black, as unreadable as a bug's. Its teeth flashed. It growled.

Rupert reached down again. His hand closed around sand and pebbles, and by reflex, he flung them, not even standing up to do so. They made a rushing sound as they cascaded off the leaves of a shrub.

The dog snapped its jaw. It barked twice. Rupert reached down again. This time his hand found a bigger rock, rounded at the edges but flattened, like the wing of an aeroplane. It was wedged in hard-packed dirt. Sand tore at the flesh on Rupert's knuckles as he wedged his fingers underneath to pry it up. The dog barked again. It started toward him.

Rupert strained. The rock came up. It was the size of a lunch plate, and heavy. Half of it was dark with soil. A centipede fell from it as Rupert drew back. The dog came up again, and he could see its tongue, lolling behind fangs that were long and yellow, sharp as a snake's.

Wallace appeared over the grass—rising up on one knee. His face was filthy, and one arm was red with his blood. His eyes were wide and wet. He didn't have the gun. He wouldn't look at Rupert.

Rupert threw the rock overhand. So hard his shoulder wrenched. He would not be able to throw again with that shoulder, it hurt so badly. The rock spun through the air. It hit the dog in the head with a *crack!*, glanced off it and thumped to the ground. The dog yelped and turned.

Wallace ran, parallel to the road, across the yard. He stumbled in the grass before sobbing, and righting himself, and for a moment, Rupert thought the dog was going to take off after Wallace. Rupert didn't care. He turned too, running as fast as he could, heading to town, the school.

They met up half a mile on, out front of the Baptist church. Even then, the two didn't speak until they neared the school. Wallace had rolled his shirtsleeve around so the blood didn't show, at least not much. Rupert jammed his scraped hand into the pocket of his trousers. Both kept their faces still, eyes on the road ahead—and that was all it took for two battered boys to make their way through town unremarked.

As they sighted the school's red brick walls at the end of Grissom

Road, peeking through the dying leaves of the oak in back, Wallace finally spoke.

"The Webley," he said, and Rupert said, "I know. You left it."

They walked more slowly now. It was only half-past eight, and they wouldn't be missed at their desks until five minutes before nine.

"I left your book bag too," said Rupert, and Wallace said, "Fool."

It was early, but the school yard was nearly full. A group of younger boys were tossing sticks in the air, watching them whirl and spin. Leaping out of the way as they fell.

"There was a smell there," said Wallace. "Did you smell it?"

Rupert shrugged; he didn't know if he had or not.

"Smelled like a slaughter," said Wallace. "Like the trenches in France."

"Maybe I did smell that," said Rupert. The smell was all the Captain would talk about, when pressed on how it was to fight the Hun in the trenches. *It smelled of slaughter,* he'd said. *It is a stink you never forget.*

"Did you get a look?" said Wallace.

"What do you mean?"

Wallace was quiet a moment.

"We have to go back," said Wallace.

Had they come any nearer to the school, it would have been too late; the teacher on yard duty would have seen them, and attendance would have been unavoidable. As it was, Wallace and Rupert didn't entirely escape notice as they veered away from the schoolyard, and without another word made for a ditch behind the White Rose filling station, beneath a stretch of pine trees. It was a place where they had hid before and thought to be safe now.

"Where's Wallace Gleason going?" said Nancy Waite, as she started the two ends of her jump-ropes twirling and she and her big sister Joan began to skip. "I think I know," said Joan.

*

The lot in back of the filling station smelled of oil and gasoline and privy: this last, because the station's toilet was an outdoor model, hiding in a cloud of bushes and flies that also hid the ditch from easy view. It was here in the ditch that Wallace and Rupert settled in, to rest up and devise their plan.

"Dog's hurt," said Wallace. "From the rock. That's going to make him worse. Like a bear."

"I just wanted to scare it," said Rupert.

"We came to *kill* it," said Wallace, glaring as he clutched his arm. As though his injury were Rupert's fault and not his own.

Rupert just nodded. He didn't ask why Wallace hadn't pulled the trigger after he'd gone to the trouble of bringing a gun—why he hadn't killed the dog, which he'd planned to do. But Wallace knew the question was in the air; something in Rupert's nod made that clear. Wallace tried to explain it.

The first time was just to Rupert. And he didn't get to the nub of the matter.

"It wasn't just the smell," said Wallace. "That was bad. But the dog. It was like hypnosis. Like when an owl spots a mouse. Under its nest. Where it's got bones of other mice piled up."

Rupert didn't think that made any sense, and Wallace was inclined to agree as soon as he said the words. He had the *gun*. All he had to do was pull the trigger. The two sat quietly for a span.

"How's your arm?" Rupert asked finally, and when Wallace said, "Hurts."

Rupert said, "We should see a doctor."

Wallace shut his eyes, and clutched his wounded arm jealously.

"We should go back, anyway," said Rupert. "Soon. Someone might find it if we just leave it there. The Webley."

Wallace's eyes cracked open, and he looked at Rupert, and he said, "I can't yet." Rupert thought Wallace might be ready to cry. But—to his disappointment—Wallace just looked away.

"I think that dog's a killer," he said. "It's a *devil*."

The second time Wallace had cause to explain himself came middle morning. Wallace insisted that they keep resting. He had shut his eyes and was dozing—not dangerously, not like he might die—when Rupert shook his friend's shoulder, Wallace mumbled that he just needed to rest up and ordered Rupert to keep a watch. This Rupert did. He lay on his belly so his eyes peered over the edge of the ditch, through the bramble—like barbed wire along a trench in the War, except that Rupert was watching the brick wall at the back of the White Rose station and not no-man's land. When the gravel bit into his knees, he shifted to his side. Twice, when he judged things quiet enough, he got up and walked in small circles at the bottom of the ditch to stretch the cramps out of his legs, pinwheeling the soreness from his arm while his thoughts about Wallace and the Webley and the dog circled each other.

Rupert was back on his belly when Nancy Waite appeared around the side of the station. The sight of her stopped his breath.

Nancy was wearing a pale yellow dress. Her hair was combed back from her forehead, held there close to her scalp with a white ribbon. The rest fell golden and, today, unbraided down her back. She clutched a brown paper bag in front of her. She moved with great, guilty care, checking over her shoulder, peering through bushes. Rupert willed himself still, until she finally turned around and vanished around the corner of the garage.

Rupert let his breath out. He looked back and Wallace looked up at him. His friend's eyes were pasty, and dull, and it was clear: Wallace had no idea what Rupert had seen. Rupert himself wasn't sure—what he'd seen, who he'd seen, if he'd seen anything at all.

"Hey! What're you doing in there?"

"Wallace?"

"Are you in there?"

Rupert turned back. It wasn't just Nancy; Joan Waite was beside her, standing right behind the garage, in full view. Nancy giggled as she and Joan peered through the brush. Wallace rolled onto his knees and, grunting, stood up. Joan was wearing her pink sweater and the pale blue dress. Her hair was tied back. Rupert swallowed, his mouth dry as sand.

"Shhh!" said Wallace. He planted himself beside Rupert, and motioned with his good hand for the two to come over.

They bent down around the shrubbery and lowered themselves into the ditch—beside Wallace, Rupert noted.

"We saw you heading off from school," Joan explained as she flattened out her skirts in front of her, and added: "I remembered this place." Rupert looked at his hands, which had drawn closed into fists.

Nancy looked at his sleeve, which was now brown with old blood.

"Holy cow!" she said. "What'd you do?"

"Were you fighting again?" Joan, for the first time, looked at Rupert—a little accusingly, he thought.

"No," said Wallace. "We—"

And Wallace paused, and thought about it for a few seconds, and he explained himself to the Waite sisters.

First, he described the dog, in such a way that Nancy made fists herself, and held them to her mouth, and even elder sister Joan gasped and looked away. He related the encounter of the day before so that Joan declared his survival a miracle. Then he got to the battle.

"Me and the dog sized each other up. It wasn't like before, where the dog figured it could just take me. It knew I came ready. So it kept back—in behind the railings of the porch, where I couldn't get a clear shot."

"Did you shoot it?" asked Nancy, aghast. She seemed to relax when he shook his head.

"I couldn't get a shot. I just kept looking at it, sitting there in front of the door. And then I saw it."

"What'd you see?" asked Joan.

Wallace had developed dark rings around his eyes. The effect was chilling when he opened them wide. "There was a dead man," he said, and added—before Rupert could say anything— "I was trying to figure it out. That was the smell. *Death*."

The Waite sisters sat rapt, staring at Wallace. Joan's lips parted and she clutched at her skirts in her lap. Nancy held her sister's shoulder.

"I didn't see a dead man," said Rupert quietly. Nancy spared him a glance; Wallace and Joan ignored him, and Wallace continued:

"You could see his legs through the door. They were skinny. Like a skeleton's. He was lying on the floor of the living room, where he *died*."

"Do you think the dog killed him?"

Joan asked it softly. Wallace shrugged, and winced.

"You should get a bandage," said Nancy. "And go see a doctor. Maybe you got rabies."

"We can't do that," said Rupert, his voice louder than he intended. "Wallace lost the Webley when he got scared and dropped it without even shooting."

"I was bit!" said Wallace, and Rupert said, ". . . after you dropped the gun," and Joan said, "That's enough," and they all sat quiet a moment.

"We have to get the gun back," said Rupert finally. "Wallace'll get a beating if we don't. So we're resting up."

"When are you going to go?" asked Nancy.

Rupert started to say, *When Wallace is good and ready*, but Wallace cut him off. "Right now," he said. "Wanna come?"

"We've only got ten minutes until recess is finished," said Joan. But she sounded uncertain.

"Someone might pick up the gun if we wait," said Wallace. Silently, Rupert admitted that he was right.

Nancy opened up the bag she was clutching, reached in, and

handed Wallace a sandwich wrapped in waxed paper. She gave Rupert another one. The smell of peanut butter was thick.

"We thought you must be hungry," explained Nancy, and Joan said, "That's why we came."

"We can eat on the way," said Wallace. Taking the sandwich in his bad hand, he used his good arm to push himself up, and stumbling barely at all, he headed along the ditch, in the direction of home, of the dog's house.

The Waite girls looked at one another; Rupert looked at both of them.

"We have to get the gun," said Rupert.

Nancy nodded; Joan shrugged. "Might as well," she said, and Rupert felt his heart race.

They walked in a line down the ditch: Wallace first, the Waite sisters following, first Joan and then Nancy, hanging close. At the back, Rupert. The ditch was excellent for their purpose, running deeper as it left the town, so that by the time they were past the business section and behind houses it was almost a gully. They bent low as they passed a lady hanging sheets in her back garden. But they needn't have; she hummed around a mouthful of clothes-pegs as though she were alone in the world. When they were past, Nancy Waite giggled, and Wallace shot a glare back over his shoulder.

"Sorry, Wallace," said Joan, drawing out his name like it was "Mother," and laughing. Rupert laughed too, but he made a point of keeping it down.

There came a point where the walls were nearly cliffs, huge round rocks covered in slick moss; long pools of green-slicked water spread still in the shade of bent willow trees that towered at the edge, dangled roots in the air above their heads. Somewhere in the shadows, something splashed.

Had the Waite girls ever been down here? Rupert thought not; they both stayed quiet as they walked along this section. Because

Rupert had been here before, he knew where they were: just a dozen yards from the main road to town, maybe a quarter mile from the concession road that would take him and Wallace home. Where the dog and its house were.

But the Waites lived in town—on Ruggles Street, in a red brick house that climbed up two storeys with awnings painted white— on the other side of town. They were going into strange territory. Rupert's territory. Wallace's. They didn't become talkative until the trees spread, and they came back into the hot light of morning.

Nancy slowed, so she and Rupert walked side by side.

"There's not a dead body there, is there?" She asked the question as they climbed up a slide of sharp gravel, around a steel culvert and onto the concession road. Rupert's breath was hot and dry in his throat; he had a hard time getting out what should have been a simple answer.

"I—I didn't see one," he said, then—afraid if he said *no, Wallace made that up,* she and Joan would just leave them and go back to school—added: "But there could have been."

"Wallace wouldn't lie."

She reached the top just before him, and skipped off to join her sister, who was walking beside Wallace now. A scent, of soap and sweat and something else, lingered in his nostrils. Rupert crested the top and ran to catch up with the three of them.

"It's not far now," said Wallace, and that at least was true.

But they dawdled, so it took longer than it should have to reach the house where the dog lived. By the time they got to the top of the driveway, there was no getting around it: they were all four truant now.

Joan peered at the house. It was still, and very bright now that the sun was high. The front door was a rectangle of perfect black.

"It looks like nobody lives there," she said. "It looks abandoned."

"We should just get the gun," said Rupert. "You remember where you dropped it?"

Wallace pointed in a general way to the left of the house. "Over there."

"Where was the body?" asked Nancy.

"Inside."

Rupert studied the yard. A breeze came up, carrying a sweet smell of fresh hay from somewhere beyond this place. It tickled the high grass. "I saw it fall," said Rupert finally. He headed up the driveway a few steps and pointed to a spot. "Maybe here."

"What about the dog?"

The question barely registered; Rupert couldn't even say who asked it. As he moved closer to the house, it seemed as though he were moving in his own quiet world—as though he were following a thread of raw instinct, some part of his mind that didn't think in words or even pictures, but just compelled. He almost could have closed his eyes as he stepped off the driveway into the grass, and kept on his course. Eyes open, eyes closed: the memory of the gun tumbling through the air just here, just so—landing in this place, not that or that—was just as vivid one way or the other.

Just as true—true as any other memory, *like the silk touch of golden skin in the early, cool hours of a late-August Sunday . . .*

. . . the hard impact of fist in gut . . .

. . . the hot memory of accusation . . .

. . . the trajectory of a gun, set loose from sweat-slicked hand—through sky—

—to dirt.

The gun lay nested in the grass at his feet. Rupert let his breath out and bent down—behind him, someone said: "You found it?"—and wrapped his fingers around the barrel. He lifted it first, like a hammer or an axe, then took the handle in his other hand—wonderingly put his finger through the trigger guard—and turned around.

The three of them stood close together—Wallace next to Joan, who held his arm. Nancy, clutching Joan's skirt hem. The gun was heavy, and big for his hands—but finally, words returned to him, and he thought:

I could almost hit him. Miss the sisters. But hit him. Almost.

"I've got it," said Rupert, and lifted the gun above his head. Wallace nodded, and held out his hand: "Give it here."

Rupert took a breath, and looked at Wallace. "Not yet," he said.

Wallace looked back at Rupert. "What do you mean? Come on."

Rupert shook his head. "You said there was a body in there," he said. "I want to see." He beckoned with the gun and turned away from them, to face the house.

"What about the dog?" said a Waite sister—which one, Rupert could not say. He took hold of the gun by its stock, holding it in both hands and climbed the steps to the porch.

The house consumed Rupert.

That was how it looked to Wallace, watching from the property's edge with the Waite sisters at his side. The brilliant morning sunlight shone off the roof of the house, making dark shade under the eaves of the porch. Rupert stepped beneath them, and he faded in shadow. One step further, and he vanished into the black.

"What about the dog?" said Joan Waite.

"It's got to be there," said Wallace, and Nancy said, "I don't hear anything."

The house was indeed silent. Wallace thought this strange. There should be barking and shouting—a gunshot, maybe, as Rupert tried to shoot the thing coming at him in the dark sitting room, up from the cellar . . .

What was Rupert getting up to in there? Wallace held his hurt arm close to him. He thought about the other door . . . across the hall from his room at the house . . .

Rupert had stepped through that one too, just as sure of himself.

"That house looks haunted," said Nancy, finally.

"Is there really a body?" asked Joan.

"Wallace saw it," said Nancy.

"I saw it," said Wallace, but he didn't look at either of them as he spoke. Wallace had not seen a body when he looked through the door of that house—not then, not the day before either. He thought he might have seen something. But as he thought about it, the thing he saw twisted and bent into all sorts of things.

"Rupert's really brave," said Nancy, "to go in there by himself."

"Not that brave," said Wallace.

"He fought you," said Joan. "Even though you're stronger."

Wallace looked at both of them now—first Joan, then Nancy—and he tried to make a fist using his hurt arm, but the fingers wouldn't close. Joan had a little smile; Nancy was shading her eyes with her hands as she peered at the quiet house.

"He touches girls when they're sleeping," Wallace said. "How brave is that?"

Nancy's hand came down and she looked at Wallace. Joan's smile broadened and she laughed, and her voice went high. "He *what*?" she asked.

"That's why we fought."

"Who—"

"My sister."

"Helen?"

"She's really pretty."

"Helen."

"When?"

"Last Saturday of the summer," said Wallace. "I let him sleep over at my house. We talked about stuff and went to sleep. And in the middle of the night—when he thinks I'm asleep—he gets up from the floor and sneaks out the door into the hall. So I followed him. He went across the hall to my sister's room. And that's where I found him."

"Touching her?" Joan's voice stayed high, but her smile turned into a grimace, and Nancy said: "Ewww!"

"Yeah," said Wallace. "She was sleeping. He put his hands all over her leg. All up and down. While she *slept*." Wallace paused, and looked at each Waite girl in turn.

"He likes you two, you know. Can't decide which one he likes best."

"Eww!" said Joan, and Nancy's eyes went wide.

"Rupert Storey ain't brave." Wallace winced, and pushed, and his swollen fingers closed into a fist.

"He's just a degenerate. He had it coming."

Rupert pinched his nose, but it didn't do much good. The stench in here was foul enough to taste: of piss and shit, and something sweet, and of smoke.

It was dark. The windows in the front room had blinds drawn down, and they glowed a sick yellow with the sunlight. There were three things that could have been the dog—a body—but as Rupert's eyes adjusted, he fathomed that none of them were, that he was pointing the Webley at a rocking chair on its side . . . a barrel . . . a stuffed sitting chair, now bleeding its straw onto the floor.

And there was a sound. Of breathing.

Rupert uncovered his nose and lifted the Webley with both hands. The breathing was slow and wheezing. There was no rhythm to it; each breath was its own task. As Rupert moved further into the house, it seemed to grow louder, as if the house itself were a great lung drawing those unsteady breaths. Like Rupert was a bone, caught in its throat.

There were two rooms at the back of the house—a door on either side of a woodstove. The first was filled with rags and a broken bed frame. A pane of its window was broken, but the glass wasn't cleared. A cloud of flies tickled against Rupert's face, and drove him back. He let them. The breathing was quieter in this room. The cause of it was in the second room if anywhere.

If the dog was anywhere in here, that's where he would be.

And as for Wallace's dead body—

The door was half-open. Rupert stepped around the woodstove, and pushed it the rest of the way. This room was darker still. There was a bed underneath the window. Someone was in it.

Rupert stumbled—the floor here was wet with something—and he gagged. The smell here was terrible—it was like stepping inside a shallow privy.

The breathing stopped, and there came a hard wet cough.

"Let me stay!"

The voice was reedy and high, straining as though shouting but not much louder than a whisper. Something in it made Rupert decide it was a man's. As he stepped further into the room, his eyes confirmed it—a long beard like nettles trembled against the pale light of the blind, as the fellow tried to sit up.

"I won't be here long," the man continued. "I ain't well."

Rupert kept the gun up, all the same. There were other things in this room. At the foot of the bed was what looked like a long duffel bag. On the floor, scattered here and there, were empty cans; along the windowsill, the silhouette of three more cans.

It was dark on the floor beside the bed. The man looked down there, and the darkness moved.

"My dog," said the man. "Jack. Named him after my brother. Jack's been on the road with me five year now." A cough. "He ain't doing well either. Came in hurt today." The man shifted onto his side. "That a gun you have?"

Rupert squinted. The dog began to resolve itself from the shadow. It was lying on its side. It was breathing fast and shallow—as he looked, Rupert could make out the twitching of its rib cage. Its head was down, and there was a little shine from its eyes—and a bloody glistening, on the raw side of its head. Where, Rupert was sure, the rock he'd thrown had hit it this morning.

"You come here to drive me out, boy?"

Rupert looked up at the man, and shook his head.

The man covered his mouth with a shaking hand and coughed. Now that he was closer, Rupert could see more of him. His hair and beard were dark, but he looked very old.

"But you got a gun."

"A Webley," said Rupert, and the old man nodded.

"That's a kind of gun," he said. "You know how to use it?" When Rupert didn't answer, the old man said, "Thought not."

Rupert bent to get a better look at the dog. The floor was covered with a fair bit of blood. The dog's fur around its head was matted with more blood. Its tongue lolled. It looked back at Rupert, and a soft whimper came out, a sound like a leak in a tire.

"If you ain't here to drive me out," said the man, "could you do me a favour?"

"What?"

"Shoot my dog." The man in the bed coughed, and made a sound like a whimper himself. "Jack don't deserve to suffer, watchin' over me like he has."

Rupert looked at the gun in his hands. It was heavy, and slippery with sweat. He thought about the noise it would make if it went off. A noise like that would draw the neighbours, the police. Even if it didn't . . . the Captain would see a bullet had been fired.

"Give it to me, if you won't. It won't . . ." he coughed ". . . it won't take a moment. And I'll give it right back."

Rupert looked at the dog. Back at the old man. "The gun doesn't belong to me," he said. "I can't."

"Please, kid."

Rupert stood straight, lowering the gun to his side, and stepped out of the room.

"I can't," he said.

The Waite sisters and Wallace had made it as far as the porch. When

Rupert came out, Nancy commented on the smell and Joan said, "Well?"

"There's no body," said Rupert.

"I knew it!" said Nancy. Wallace looked at his feet.

"But there's a fellow in there," said Rupert. "That's maybe what Wallace saw."

"Someone lives in *there*?" said Joan.

"He's not well," said Rupert. "He told me to get off his property."

"What about the dog?" said Wallace.

"Here's the gun," said Rupert, and handed the Webley over, butt first. "Take it back home. I won't tell the Captain you took it."

Wallace snatched the gun back and held it close to his chest. He looked over Rupert's shoulder, and back at Rupert. "What about the dog?" he said again.

Rupert just shook his head. Wallace took a step toward the house and stopped and turned around.

Joan Waite put her arm over Nancy's shoulder and held her close. "I can hear it," said Joan, and Nancy said she could too: "It's everywhere." But Rupert couldn't hear anything—and neither could Wallace, although he strained to.

On 24th September, 1939, the town had a dance for Wallace Gleason and some others, at the Fenlan Rotary Hall. That summer, Wallace had signed up in the 1st Canadian Infantry Brigade. He was to ship out to Belleville for his training—and from there, perhaps a boat down the St. Lawrence and all the way to England.

Rupert attended reluctantly. He had not yet made up his mind to enlist and had been seeing less of Wallace and the Gleasons the past few years in any event. But his brothers were going—Paul, the second-eldest, had shipped out in the summer, and the whole family had gone to his party—so Rupert relented. He put on a jacket and tied his tie, slicked down his hair and perched on the wheel-well in the back of the Ford.

It was a warm night for September, and they threw the doors to the hall open, so the fiddle music wafted through the twilit streets almost to the edge of town. Autos were parked two deep along the sidewalk, and everything was bathed in the orange glow of electric lanterns strung along the sides of the hall, and over the main entry hung a banner: "IN THE ARMY NOW."

"Paul should have waited," said Leonard as they passed beneath it and into the dance. "What a send-off!"

The Storey boys split up after that: Leonard, to lift a glass of beer with some fellows he knew from the reopened sawmill; Philip, to get a closer look at the fiddler. Rupert spotted the Captain, a widower two years now, so sitting by himself, watching as his son Wallace and a town girl raised dust on the dance floor.

"Why, Rupert Storey!" said the Captain. "It's been some time! How've you been keeping?"

Rupert sat down and brought the Captain up to date. He had been accepted at the University of Western Ontario, and expected to be starting classes in a week, and hoped to gain admittance to the medical school there eventually. He allowed as he might also enlist, as Wallace had, but wanted to see how higher learning suited him first. The Captain stopped him before he could be accused of babbling.

"One way or another, you're leaving town," he said. "Good, though we'll miss you. But you'll find your way. That's what young men do."

The conversation cut short when Helen and her husband arrived. She being six months with child, Rupert offered her his chair immediately. She smiled hello and patted his hand and told him he was a gentleman. Rupert thanked her and excused himself.

It seemed as though the whole town was crowding into the Rotary Hall. Rupert wasn't fond of crowds, and kept to the periphery. He was too young for beer and not much of a dancer, so he set up near the punch bowl. Wallace greeted him briefly there between dances—clapped him hard on the shoulder and produced a steel hip flask of rum. Rupert took a dutiful swig and Wallace took one too. Then he nodded, hit Rupert's shoulder once more and headed back to the dance floor where his girl was waiting.

It wasn't long after that that Rupert spotted Nancy Waite approaching the punch bowl. She was wearing a long green frock, and her blonde hair was pushed back with a white ribbon, holding an unlit cigarette high as she danced and shimmied through the crowd. Rupert found a box of matches in his pocket, and by the time she arrived he had one lit and ready to offer her. She blinked and laughed and leaned into the flame.

"I was coming for the punch," she said, and Rupert poured her one of those too. They clinked glasses and sipped their punch and Rupert told Nancy about his university plans. "I'm going to school too," she said, "in Kingston. With Joan. In a year. I hope." She set down her glass and crossed her fingers.

"Are you going to ask me to dance?" she asked.

He smiled and dipped his head. "I'm not very good at dancing," he said.

But she didn't give up, and finally he did ask her.

They didn't dance for very long, just barely a song, before Nancy admitted defeat. "I'll never doubt you again," she said. And as they left the dance floor, Rupert thought: *That's it*. But Nancy surprised him.

"It's hot in here," she said and she was right.

Ducking through the thinning edge of the crowd, they made their way through one of the side doors and into the parking lot that backed onto a stand of trees. The music grew quieter—quiet enough that Rupert could make out the chirping of crickets. He pulled the matchbox from his pocket, but Nancy shook her head and took his hand instead.

"Do you remember," she said, turning to face him, her eyes themselves seeming to dance, "what we did that day?"

Rupert felt a small twist in his gut, and his nostrils flared at a half-remembered smell, and he started to look away.

But with her free hand, Nancy touched the nape of Rupert's neck—and she stood on her toes—and she drew his mouth close to hers—and Rupert just said, "Yes."

When he kissed her, she tasted of everything.

Acknowledgements

Nobody writes a decent story by themselves.

These stories, decent and otherwise, wouldn't exist without the wisdom of the members present and past of the Cecil Street Irregulars workshop and the Gibraltar Point sf workshop; without the guidance of ChiZine's editors/publishers Brett Alexander Savory and Sandra Kasturi most recently, and editors Don Hutchison, Michael Rowe and Robert Morrish earlier in the game. And they'd be no good without family. My parents Lawrence and Olga offered nothing but love and support in a long sequence of thumbs-up to these stories; if they wondered about the content, they—mostly—kept it to themselves. My brother Peter read, and reads, them dutifully. My long-lost cousin Joe tracked me down just last year, and unwittingly spurred me on to write "The Webley."

It is true. Nobody writes a decent story by themselves.

Copyrights

About the Author

David Nickle

David Nickle lives and works in Toronto, Ontario in the company of his partner Karen Fernandez, and not far from an old filling station where his grandfather John Nickle briefly pumped gasoline in the 1930s. David was born somewhat later, in 1964.

Since then, he has authored numerous short stories and one published novel, *The Claus Effect*, with Karl Schroeder—all while cultivating an unfortunate singing voice and a tragic affection for the music of Tom Waits.

He is not finished yet.